Born and bred in New Zealand, Craig Marriner has spent much of his adult life wandering the globe, and has lived in Australia and Europe. He is currently based in London. His first novel, *Stonedogs*, won Best First Book and the Deutz Medal for Fiction at the 2002 Montana New Zealand Book Awards. A feature film of *Stonedogs* is currently in production.

craig@marriner.info

craig marriner

southern style

V

VINTAGE

Many thanks to Creative New Zealand
and the Buddle Findlay Frank Sargeson Trust.

National Library of New Zealand Cataloguing-in-Publication Data
Marriner, Craig, 1974-
Southern style / by Craig Marriner.
ISBN-13: 978-1-86941-710-9
ISBN-10: 1-86941-710-0
I. Title.
NZ823.3—dc 22

A VINTAGE BOOK
published by
Random House New Zealand
18 Poland Road, Glenfield, Auckland, New Zealand
www.randomhouse.co.nz

First published 2006

ISBN-10: 1 86941 710 0
ISBN-13: 978 1 86941 710 9

Text design: Elin Bruhn Termannsen
Cover design: Katy Yiakmis
Cover photographs: Getty Images
Printed in Australia by Griffin Press

To Shereen: I know you'll find another dream and make this one come true as well.

To Farah and Rathwan, the sister and brother I lost.

To Dad, a better bloke than he realises.

To Nana, who can read a bit further this time.

And to everyone I ever shared a pint with in Olde London Town.

HERE'S TO YA!

1

RYAN

I blame all this on that Scottish prick. 'Jock', he called himself. Yeah, I know: real creative. Didn't stop him doing a number on me, though. Smoother than a peeled onion, our 'Jock'.

He wouldn't get near me these days, tell ya that for fuck all. Four years is a fair while in a town like this. Still, it had to happen: every London virgin eventually gets fucked, and there are worse breakings in than the one I copped. Seen that first hand. And my school fees were paid up in less than a day too.

Can't count the first three days; barely left the flat during those. First long-haul flight and it kicked the fuck out me. Touched down at 6 a.m. Crimbo morning. Gatwick Express to Victoria Station, a dirty excuse for daylight giving me my first taste of urban sprawl British style. Kinda dampened the spirits a little, that did. A young Kiwi I met on the plane — drank piss with, rated stewardesses with, watched India by night with — I remember how his face grew sicker and sicker as each casual monstrosity unfolded, until we hit Croydon and the bloke had seen enough:

London had broken him without a word. He vowed to jump on the first train to Edinburgh where some mates were living.

Mine were in Battersea. At least their flat was in Battersea: they'd both headed to Belgium for Crimbo/NewYear. Lived off pot noodles the few hours I wasn't entwined with a radiator heater, and finally got the body-clock sorted on a sparkling Wednesday morning, one of those clear winter days where the sun's so welcome even the cold can go fuck itself.

Broke out the map and a Red Army greatcoat I'd bought a week before in a Perth army surplus. (Forty-degree heat haze over Barrack Street; here's Ryan with half a woolly mammoth on his arm.) Buses and tubes weren't my go yet — Jock showed me the ropes there, Samaritan that he was — but I was happy walking. So busy gawking at the sights I didn't even spit the dummy when a fuck-up took me on a five-click detour, Vauxhall Bridge instead of Chelsea.

Buckingham Palace. What drew me there — how many times I've asked myself that — to the scene of my deflowering? Never been the monarchist type. Lisa would say it was serendipity or providence, karma perhaps, or that a Jock would've been lurking even if I'd hit St Paul's instead. Maybe it was nothing more than recognising a name on the map with an easy route to it.

What interests me more, though, is what it was that made Jock pick me. You don't exactly grow up gullible in WA mining towns, and I'd come away unscathed from three years living fast in Melbourne and Brissie too, so how could a simple twenty-four-hour plane flight paint a big neon cock on a forehead that thought it'd been around the block a time or two? I mean, there were at least fifty of us on the bandstand, with our maps and our daypacks and our accents, when big Jock sidled up.

I had my coat off by then, toasty enough in jumper, thermals and exercise. He told me I must be from Canada to laugh at the cold so.

Lesson 1: Flatter.

I grinned and told him I was Aussie in that ringing tone I used to use. I was happy to have someone to talk to.

Lesson 2: Select a straggler.

Then he started shooting small talk, real casual, a bored man killing time.

Lesson 3: Stress the encounter's frivolity.

He'd left his wallet at a friend's house and was here to collect it from the guy, who served in the Guards — a unit Jock himself had recently retired from after twenty years' distinguished service — and was due off duty in a while.

Lesson 4: Establish your credentials.

Jock was married to an Australian and had been out there once or twice.

Lesson 5: Patronise.

Maybe he had too, or else he preyed on Aussies so often he'd made an effort to absorb all they said to him. Perhaps he'd even read up on the place, 'cause the dialogue was fucking smooth, mate. Not that I had an urge to cross-examine the cunt, but that was down to him too. I was just a lonely kid ten thousand miles from Down Under, yarning with a man who liked it there.

Lesson 6: Match mark to homework.

A wind picked up and I was suddenly having all sorts of dramas folding my map. Big Jock, veteran of 'a hundred manoeuvres on Dartmoor', stepped in and closed it like a book.

Lesson 7: Demonstrate consideration and capability. And yeah, *Lesson 8: Open your favours account a.s.a.p.*

As for the rest, anyone who can't identify at least another eight of these themselves had best be buying a chastity belt with their plane ticket.

I told him I was on my way to Baker Street to book a place on a tour bus heading up to Hogmanay in Scotland. By this time he was getting impatient with his mate not showing up, and he half suspected the bloke might've forgotten their rendezvous and nicked off to his local boozer — located, as chance would have it, near Baker Street.

Chose his rope well, eh? I fancied a drinking buddy and a pub session as much as any Ocker in a foreign city who hasn't been laid yet, and within another minute I'd appointed Jock my London and beer guide.

Couldn't believe my luck really. Here was a tour you won't find in the *Lonely Planet*: the site where the IRA bombed the Household Cavalry and put two of them in the ground; Wellington's Arch which was actually made of smelted-down French cannon captured at Waterloo. A guided tutorial on tubing, though with mortified Jock not having his wallet on him I practically had to buy his ticket for him at gunpoint.

I should still've escaped, though, woken up and stormed from the bedroom with me grundies halfway on, because that afternoon, as I was buying my Hogmanay ticket, a Saffa dude behind the counter clocked Jock lurking outside and was going to call security. Something about the big Scottish fuck clearly jarred the bloke's eye. But he didn't know Jock like me, and I defended my pal's dignity with a sharp, 'No need for that, mate. He's with me.'

Yeah, well, the rest was plain sailing for Glasgow's finest. The pints I bought oiled his routine no doubt, and made my limbs more pliant. Seventies smack-pushers run off estates by Jock and his vigilante pals; pranks pulled by young Guardsmen on cranky sergeant-majors; invisible snipers on Belfast rooftops; a bloke drinking in the pub who owed Jock forty quid from four years past, the decision to let it slide rather than embarrass him in front of his lady.

And then the *coup de grâce*, the low sigh, the old fear revisited as Thatcher plucked Jock from the nightmare of Ulster and dropped him in one worse. Goose Green. The scar where the Argie bullet took him in the belly, the one reserved for the viewing pleasure of sons and doxies, me wrongly assuming myself an honorary member of the former group, shaking his hand for it.

Soon after that he was asking me how good his credit was, that bloody friend still not appearing and Jock with a bloody dinner to get to and no time to get home and back with his cheque-book. I didn't even need to think about it, honoured to pull out a fifty for this working-class paragon. Only Jock needed a little more — didn't explain what for, just a man-to-man gaze to make a mockery of words — and soon three more of my fifties had been swallowed by that big hairy fist.

Jock couldn't dally long after that; the first course was at eight and he'd had a thing for mussel chowder since his Cyprus days. We were to meet in a Chelsea pub later on, and even if pestilence or falling masonry *did* keep him from the engagement, I had his address and number.

But as I waved at him through the pub window, old Jock just sorta sneered a little and flicked his fingers. Contempt was plain, maybe some loathing too, and as I rewind and slo-mo the shot it sometimes gives me comfort to imagine that the loathing was all for himself.

Though I seriously doubt it.

Needless to say, he never showed at The Chelsea Potter, nor had they heard of him, and next morning 'his' number gave me nothing but the chick on the BT recording. *The number you rang is no longer in service. Please check that you have dialled it correctly or that it was not concocted by a con-man.*

So I rocked round to 'Jock's gaff' in Lavender Hill, a sickness seeping through the dumb trust. He'd bragged of the 'high-rise' apartment block he owned a flat in, and it looked the part from a distance too, as if Ross and Chandler could be at one of the windows, blowing each other for Ugly Naked Guy. Far from confirming his story, though, this turned out to be the final insult, Jock's cheeky flourish.

Oh yeah, funny cunt too. Because they don't call them 'high-rises' over here; they're called 'tower blocks', and if you're broke — and at the head of a five-odd-year waiting list — the government will rent you one at about seventy quid a week.

I learned that day that the slums in these parts are twelve storeys high. The *Lonely Planet* won't tell you that either. Jock didn't just send me to a bogus address, he sent me to a vertical ghetto. Denial was strong, though, still audible above the deeper voice now hollering its ring off, and at the housing estate I found myself waylaying the migrant/dero/homeboy types, asking after Jock from 265, like it was Ramsay Street and everyone surely knew everyone from barbies and driveway cricket. They barely bothered shaking their heads, and when this rangy black guy with tats up his neck stood over me and said, 'I fink yous in the wrong place, bruv,' I knew he was talking about more than the address.

Good shots, those Argie riflemen. Hit Jock right where his appendix used to be.

———

That was my first taste of a London housing estate. It wasn't to be my last, though.

As I thread through the after-work crowd of suits and tradesmen, put my pint on a table and take out my phone, I'm hoping for the chance to visit another one. And soon. I'm running out of time here. Though there's no way in the fucking world I'm going to show up there on a Friday night without my visa in order and an escort waiting.

Call-catcher text. Two missed, one each from Matty and Lisa.

They can wait. But one from Katrina, who hasn't called me in weeks. Just seeing her name again feels like a swig of bad eggs.

Mega pain in the arse, mobiles. Everyone's like 'Oh, how did we get by without them?', but ya know what? We fucking well did. And the amount of *shit* a mobile can suddenly drop you in just seems to multiply. I've had mobiles unmask me more damningly than a fucking trial lawyer could have. Rock-solid stories incinerated in seconds.

But I guess they come in pretty handy if you're a sad twat with bugger-all mates, like me in about thirty-six hours.

I try Kevin's mobile again: voice-mail. No choice but to try him at home.

Fabien answers: 'Wassup?'

'Kevin around?'

'Who wants to know?'

'. . . Ryan.'

'Na, he aint. Whatchu want then?'

'Any idea when he'll be back?'

'Bout 'alf ten.'

That's not what I wanted to hear, you little try-hard prick. 'No worries, mate, that's cool. Might try him then.'

'Oi, ow did you get on wiv that Angelika bird then, that dancer you met roun 'ere? You end up ringing her?'

And I'm so not gonna go there. 'Na, she gave me a wrong number, mate, sold me a dummy. Tell Kev to call me if you see him . . . What's that, you're breaking up on me, bad sig—'

END CALL.

Sit back and sip, gazing through the window at Hammersmith, Central London. Five o'clock; the sun's long gone but it's bright out there. Solid traffic, solid people. Solid money. Enough to make you sick at times: a square metre out there is worth more than the property my old man slogged decades of his life for. Fortunes everywhere, distilled and frozen and stacked.

Not helped by me not having enough readies right now to pick up the farewell present I promised I'd buy for Matty. Melyvn's offered me credit on it, but the terms are a little iffy.

Half an hour later and still no word from Kev. 'Just do it' time. Fortune fucking favours.

Finish my second pint and pack my shit in with the brand new Playstation games cramming my bag. Still don't wanna stand up though.

A bird walking by on the street returns my stare for too long, so I smile at her and get one back. That's the signal, and I'm swinging my bag on, scrolling for Melvyn's number in my phone.

———

ALEX

Look, man, just cross the road and walk in. What's the worst that could happen?

The lights go red; four lanes of black cabs and double-decker buses pulling up, pedestrians pouring on to the crossing. The worst that could happen? Let's see now, I could get in there, see nobody I know in the crowd, order a drink and get stranded all alone. Alex out for a quiet, lone beer after work . . . on a Friday . . . in a pub thronging with friendship and merriment. What would I do then? Pull out the *Financial Times*?

Or worse: I could enter, see plenty I know (technically), order a drink, approach a circle . . . and get stuck for a fitting greeting.

All chat stops; six, seven, eight pairs of eyes ask: 'What are *you* doing here?' Then semaphore: 'Who invited the new boy?'

Well, no one as such. But I could hardly miss all the talk around me this week, could I? 'The Happy Angler, Friday night, Matty's leaving do. *Not* to be missed.'

Because I may, in principle, have met a lot of them in the fortnight since I started, but the welcome hasn't exactly been tropical. Nobody sitting near me in the canteen; nobody giving me the lowdown, the who's who; no invitations to join the mob off for a pint 'down the club' at lunchtimes. Jesus, I have a hard enough time getting people to tell me what my bloody *duties* are or assign me work; and in a workplace that size, with so many different departments and shifts, it doesn't take much for a bloke left alone to start floundering.

I catch myself rubbing my eyes under my glasses. Some kind of allergy to the traffic fumes, I think.

Sure could've done with getting some Dutch courage on board before arriving here. But I couldn't risk any of them seeing me on the train like that: all alone, sipping guiltily on a can. Not a good look. And quite aside from the initial embarrassment, word of it might have filtered up to Julian. And that, folks, would not have been a handsome addition to the old CV.

Ahhh, to hell with it — and with them. Just cross the road and walk in, whatever happens happens . . . Na, traffic's got a green light again. I'll go next time, promise.

Have to, too. This needs sorting urgently. Each day's getting harder to face than the last, and each day gives me more lost ground to make up. It'll be too late soon; I'll be tarred so hard with the curiosity brush I'll never wash clean. Wouldn't be the first time a work crew's done that to me.

Good amount of Southerners among them too. Expected a bit of fellowship really. That Lisa chick seemed cool, took the time to chat with me, but I haven't seen her around much this week.

As for that Aussie wanker . . . So much of this is his fault. Doug puts me under his care on day one, asks him to show me the ropes, and within five minutes Ryan's fobbed me on to Luca, who's new himself. Hasn't said a word to me since, old Ryan. Too busy holding court and posing.

This would've been a lot easier if Luca hadn't chickened out at the last minute. We could've walked in together, a mutual safety-net. But Luca wasn't specifically invited either, couldn't bring himself to crash it, gutless Italian wonder.

But I need this job like you wouldn't believe.

So go!

The light's beeping as the crossing gets a green . . . What's the rush anyway? Think I'll kill a bit of time in that pub I passed earlier. It looked quiet enough. Get a pint or two down.

'Oh, sorry.' Span away so quick I almost knocked a girl over, but she just gives a curt nod and looks away. Hottie, too. Love those big slits up the calves of her trousers. Love th—

She looks back again and catches me perving, but I'm five steps clear before the blush settles in. I can hear her laughing about me with her friends. I get around the corner and slow down a bit. That second pub's out of the question now, so long as I have to pass by those girls again.

And that's almost enough to have me packing up and heading home . . . though I use the term loosely. A lumpy bunk — one of seven — in a cobwebbed corner of a musty hostel dorm. The endless snores, farts and rows of Nigerian migrants, Slavic kitchen hands, Palestinian refugees. Three on night shifts, sleeping all day, so no let-up from that sickly bodies-in-bed smell, so much worse when the body's a strange male avoiding the bacteria riot in the cold showers. Six bad-breathed mouths snapping should I dare to crack a window open — about the only time they speak to me. Sink invisible beneath a pile of dirty dishes so ancient they've fused together. A stove-top green from accumulated spillage. Mildewed curtains overhanging the sparking wires of disembowelled power-points. Patches of floorboard giving springily beneath me . . . on the sixth floor. Mice scampering for cover whenever a light comes on, growing bolder as movement dies down, leaving their shit everywhere. And yesterday the discovery on my pack of some *larger* droppings . . .

Back home, in NZ, there's a slang phrase we sometimes use for 'bad'; we say 'rat shit'. I'd used it a lot and never really stopped to ponder its origins. Why not dog shit? Pig shit? But I know better now. It's simple: coming across rat shit means there are rats nearby. Living around you. *Amongst* you. And that's bad. That's very bad.

Gotta get out of that hovel! How it's escaped condemnation up till now is beyond me. How did I last one night there, let alone a month?

Still, it's pure economics, isn't it. You get what you pay for, and if you don't like it you should dig deeper or work harder.

It's great around here, though, love these modern 'high streets', the buzz of it still fresh. I'll get a couple of cans from some-where and just walk. The bright lights, the brand names, the billboards, the window displays, the happy shoppers — the sheer energy of it all seems to radiate a warmth the winter night can't touch. A celebration of how far we've come. Nourished by enormous streams of invisible capital, consumers wanting for nothing and business with a free rein to provide it. Eight million people living life to the full, a city bursting with jobs and opportu-nity. Sell us something and enter. Take a bite. The power is yours.

There's a mirror in a Marks & Spencer display. No one seems to be looking at me, so I stop and check it out. Not that happy with the haircut: she left it too long around the ears, can't have under-stood the accent when I told her what I wanted. Sick of this sandy blond nothing colour too; pissed me right off when the fashions changed and it was no longer cool for guys to bleach. Glad someone told me. Could do with some new rims for the glasses. Can't fault the threads though, bro. The successful project success, and that's what this overcoat and shirt do. Maybe a bit much for the work Julian's started me on, but that'll only be until I've learned the job from ground level, bonded a bit—

Gotta get into that bloody pub! 7.45 now. I'll be in by 8.30, no later, and that's a solemn oath.

Need a wholesalers badly, or whatever it is they call them here . . . *off-licence*, that's the one. Maybe I should ask someone . . .

And suddenly there's one of *them* before me, outside a Starbucks, sprawled on the ground, leaning against a full bin-liner with an army-green sleeping bag across his legs. He's begging for money, a few coins glinting in an upturned beret: 'Spare change, please. Spare any change, sir?' His beard and hair are matted with gunk; newspapers sprout from tears in his boots.

He clashes with the setting like a hyena at Crufts.

His eyes meet mine, the whites a dirty yellow, burst capillaries a riot in his cheeks. I put his age somewhere between fifty and five hundred.

The shock of these sights is starting to wear down, but I don't think the disgust ever will. It really is an absolute disgrace. Jesus, this city is one of the most advanced and prosperous in the world, oozing wealth and abundance, a cornerstone of the developed world, champion of opportunity and hope . . .

'Spare any change, sir? It's awful cold out and I aint eaten nufin in three days.'

The stench of him hits me as I stop and look down. 'No doubt because you were too busy drinking, eh?'

A city which thousands of the Third World's impoverished are daily risking life and limb to enter, and *these* types, with the natural-born right to apply for any job that's going, that UK citizenship others part with thousands for — these types can't even manage staying sober long enough to feed and house themselves.

His face shifts guiltily. 'You'd be drinkin n all if you was in my position, lad.'

I told my mum about them on the phone the other day. She felt sorry for them.

Shaking my head: 'If I was in your position I'd have a shave and a shower and go and get a job. It's pretty simple really.'

I like the look in his eye less by the second. I've heard these types will lash out for ten pence or for the hell of it, let alone at someone offering them a little hard truth. I take a step backwards as he raises his voice. 'Oh, is that so, guv'na? You knows it all, does ya? You've worked it all out in your seven'een, eigh'een years?'

'Twenty-two actually.'

'Same thing, init. Tell me then, Mr Philosophy . . .'

His voice gets louder, drawing attention, so I just turn and walk away.

When an idea occurs.

Turning back to him, fishing in my pockets for a 20p coin: 'I'll give you this if you tell me where the nearest off-licence is.'

————

LISA

Riding the Tube, Southern Style by Lisa Tailor. Still undecided on the title, but that one's got to be the forerunner right now. Nicely middle-of-the-road. To the point, but non-inflammatory. Because it could just as easily be called *Reclaiming What These Lying Bastards Owe You*.

Of course if London Underground were ever to get wind of it, they'd brand it something like, *Illegal Handbook On Criminal Defraudment*. Because that's what they call it. Defraudment. I'm serious! As if you're bouncing million-quid cheques round the gaff instead of just trying to save an extra pound or two before plain living in this Hive has sucked up your wages again.

Not that I'd ever be stupid enough to commit any of this to paper while I'm here on the trains (haven't committed *any* of it to paper yet, but I'll be ready to start in a week or so). You see, when one's as skilled as I am at this form of asset redistribution, even getting caught once in a while is no big deal, especially if your apprehender is a heterosexual male; but when you're standing there lamenting to the piglet the 'fact' that you have no ID on you, you really need to be able to let him search your bag when he asks, as they tend to. And it won't do your case a lot of good if he finds a notebook in which you've written something like:

Chapter Five: On-board Inspections
a) The Classic Switcheroonie
You'll soon find out the hard way if you travel a route where on-board inspections are common (see Chapter Four: Minimising the Impact of Apprehension). From then on you'll have to suffer your journeys in relative discomfort: take the central-most carriage and stay standing, somewhere allowing you to look down both sides of the train, through the windows of the interconnecting doors. Remain alert for the tell-tale hats of inspectors. On days when you see one approaching, keep your cool, wait for the next stop, then alight from the train. Jog down the platform and enter those carriages through which the inspector has already passed.

*You should be safe now, but if your journey is a long one you may
need to repeat the manoeuvre. Keep the distance between you and
the piglet as wide as possible. Use the connecting carriage doors
only as a last resort, as such travel is rare, noisy and noteworthy.*

*There will come times when bypassing the inspector is impos-
sible, usually when the ubiquitous 'signal failures' or other breeds
of budget skimping and incompetence cause your train to stop
mid-station. Don't despair. Look closely at your fellow passengers
until you see one who, like you, is intensely aware of the closing
inspector. In other words, pinpoint another fare-evader through
body language, and relocate until their position lies between you
and the piglet. Dealing with them will occupy the inspector for a
minimum of three minutes — time enough, with luck, for your
train to stutter its way to the next station and safety.*

It's a good vibe on the trains tonight, though. Always is on a
Friday. I can sit down for once and chill, a far cry from travelling in
the morning. Everyone loose, relaxed, their lives returned to them
for a couple of days. Like weary Danny over there: landscape
gardener, I'm guessing. Been working like a kaffir in a Park Lane
garden which simply *must* be ready for the tea-party season. A half
hour in the bath, then a six-pack in front of the West Ham match.
Or Tim and Sally near the doors, smart jackets and trundler bags.
Eurostar to Paris, or EagleAir to Dublin, fleeing the Hive for a day
or three. Lucky bastards.

Not that I'm complaining. I wouldn't miss tonight for return
tickets to Rio. It's the end of an era, no doubt about that, and it *must*
be marked in style. And with what I've got in my underwear, this
one's going to have more style than Milan through fashion week.
Thank god for Kevin. He doesn't make house calls for anyone, or
let anyone tick up the amounts he just sorted me for. Sure, he's
getting some pretty spectacular perks out of the arrangement

himself, but that's all over now, like I just told him. I'll mark the pills up by two quid and the grams by a little more, just to cover my time and shit. They're mostly presold anyway, so I'll have no trouble shifting them. It's not like I'm dealing or anything, just hooking up friends.

The train jerks to a stop at Covent Garden and a trio of guys in kilts jumps on. Gee, I wonder where *you're* all from. They're juiced already, giving that 'classic' line to some poor Latino girl, threatening to prove how Scottish they truly are, hahaha. I feel like stealing Ryan's gibe from the other week, telling them how national alcoholism must have blasted holes in the collective Scottish memory because the worst crime the English ever committed up there was decreeing that all Scots must wear skirts so that the occupying English would have something to laugh about.

The house's sure going to be glum for a while. You think we'd be used to it by now. Kimberly, Rouen and Amy all lost to us since Christmas, and now Matty's on his way. He's not happy about leaving either. Nor is Ryan. Matty was Ryan's right hand through all that social civil-war bullshit with Trent, and the Ryan faction's copped a few desertions and defections in recent weeks. The loss of Matty could be the death knell.

Not so sure that Ryan gives much of a fuck any more, though. He's always had other shit going on, and he's just started some mystery moonlighting gig. He clams up when asked about it. I've been through his drawers once and his phone twice and didn't learn a thing either.

What I *do* know is that Matty's room is still up for grabs. It was my job to find someone decent to fill it. Haven't really had the time to look, though. Not an ideal state of affairs, because the extra rent will be spread out around the rest of us.

Oh shit, that's right, the new Kiwi guy at work was looking for a place! Forgot all about that; been off sick most of the week. What was his name? Alan? Albert? Said he was living way up Finsbury, was looking to move nearer the warehouse. Not sure the others'd thank me for bringing him in. They've got him pegged as a bit of a snob. But he was fine with me. Wonder if he'll be along tonight? Fat chance. He'll have his own shit going on.

A guy boards the train, and though there are plenty of free seats he chooses to sit right beside me. Not bad-looking but he's got 'sleazeball' written over him in capitals. He starts talking to me straight away, just asks me how I am and what I'm up to as if we've already met before. I keep the answers brief and cold, but obviously not brief or cold enough for this chancer because he's soon asking if I'm South African. I mutter a yes and turn away, but he starts on about some brother of his who was recently in South Africa on a course, and how violent things are getting down there.

Me: 'Africa's always been a violent place.' I'm so not getting into this with this tosser.

'Yeah, but it's gotten a lot worse since the blacks took ove—'

'Not really, it's just that more whites are getting hurt these days and white deaths are bigger news than coloured deaths.'

A dubious smirk: 'That's the whole point to you, though, right? That's why you're all abandoning the place.'

'First of all, it's far from fucking *all* of us. Second, who's to say things won't get better? Europe's fine now, yet just a few decades ago you guys were still doing shit that makes South Africa look like the Garden of Eden.'

The train pulls into my stop, and I farewell the wanker with an 'As you were.'

Then I'm off, bustling with the flow, through passageways plastered in advertising, the capitalist saturation that is London. A promotion for every occasion, a city of a million square metres of billboard and poster, of boardroom chicanery hollering into your face, brawling for that tiny cubic millimetre somewhere in your skull. Even all the way down here. Thirty-odd metres of clay and sewerage, a million tonnes of concrete and metal, Roman bones and sacked castles will not be allowed to come between you and the spin in the City of Lies.

By the time the escalator spills me on to the echoing station concourse my purse is wedged in the waist of my jeans, under the jacket, and my daypack contains little more than make-up, a newspaper and tampons. It's a big station this one, and at this time on a Friday the place is heaving. Ryan taught me to carry an empty beer can in my bag for when traversing crowded areas in London: wave the can around, stagger a bit, look a little surly, and the Herds in this Hive will part like you're Moses. More effective if you're a guy of course, but you'd be surprised. But I had to give that up when I stopped buying tickets.

The press of bodies intensifies, the Herd sweeping me along on its migration for the exit gates.

Once more into the breach, dear friends.

Chapter Three: Gate-slipping

I stay with the stream but slow down a little, reconnoitring the staff arrayed against me. They stand to the left of the barriers . . . electronic gates between me and freedom . . . keeping me from a final goodbye with a cherished friend . . . Four of them. Instruments of the oppressor. Blue blazers and pants, peaked hats, synchronised ties. One of the guys looks like my little brother back in Cape Town — pimples and smiles, just a green kid really. His two mates are black and they're all chatting together cosily, happy as a race-relations leaflet . . .

. . . a picture so PC it's probably orchestrated spin . . .

. . . wouldn't put it past a company like London Underground.

I'm closer now, and I can see the way they're cutting their eyes, hooded by those hats, watching the gates for swindlers. Oh, they may be of us, these four, 'just following orders', but they're enjoying their work, examining the crowd like storm troopers on a checkpoint. I bet they live for the kill, the high break from routine, the shiny stars on their lockers. Privatised pirates.

The fourth inspector, a well-nourished woman almost wider than high, stands off to the right, away from the boys. Surely one of them was stationed beside her but snuck off as soon as he could. No doubt she gets this often, older woman in a younger one's job, spends a lot of her working day alone, no mates to chat with, those wonderful bludges that the bosses can't touch . . .

I bet she can handle herself, though. Keep the lads in line. Perhaps that Stasi-like devotion with which she's watching her gates is brought to bear just as hard on her workmates.

Adjusting her hair like a knight might armour.

I'll have to speed up again soon. Even my small break from beat is confusing the Herd; it tuts as it bustles around me, jostling, bumping, tutting some more. And always the *Sorrys*, the hot-air *Sorrys* like some glib city slogan. I'm a knot in the grain which will soon draw attention, if not from the guards then from cameras in the ceiling, that big Eye that never blinks in the City of Lies—

I jump in fright as a hand brushes my bum too hard. A builder's apprentice or something, in a cocky blue Nike jacket. I wait for a lag in his swagger, for him to turn back around, so I can watch him watch me twist my nose, but he lets the flow pull him on.

Matron's still scouting hard, but even her glacial eye must absorb less than the combined attention of her three brat collegues, so I drift to the right as the Herd divides into rows, aligning themselves with a gate. I slide today's *Independent* out, survey the mounts on offer . . .

The Sikh student in glasses is patting pockets for his ticket; he could baulk at the hurdle, throw me into Matron's ample arms.

Helen the PA in the fawn overcoat appears a much smoother ride . . . but then she looks past her shoulder at me, and I don't like what I see. I bet Helen stands in the front row at Aerobics; is no fan of the Piggy Back.

Which leaves Russell, briefcase brimming with quarterlies, marked for the board and two-time captain of the Hull University pelican-drinking team. A fool for a wiggle and a grin if ever I saw one should it come to that.

My heart's thumping as I match his stride, almost on his heels, bound to his back, a broke blonde limpet. Watch him slide his monthly ticket into the gate's suspicious slot.

Green light, mechanical nod: *Ticket Accepted* — and the gate splits down the middle, slapping itself open.

One last look at Matron, then I'm hard on Russell's arse: into the narrow gorge, reaching ahead with my rolled *Independent*, blocking the red eye on the gate's far side just as Russell draws level with it, my timing better than on other days . . . and the cold, dumb machine relaxes in the knowledge of a single person four feet wide waddling through its gate.

No loud, piercing beep? No smirking inspector ambling over? No affronted civilian drawing breath to denounce me?

It seems not.

Another blow for the people, and I can't kill a grin as I file past Matron, wishing I could tell her the score's 12–0 since Tuesday.

*The talent is an acquired one, and you should ease yourself into it, buying tickets (see **Chapter Six: Child Tickets and Zoning Loopholes**) then promptly forgetting them, slipping the gates as if you're broke. You'll be busted a lot early on but that's part of the fun, watching their faces fall (and this is good conditioning for when play time's over, when you start getting caught for real). Make a game of it, count your score,*

and don't go active until you've successfully slipped twenty
gates in a row.

Out into the cold of the night: Piccadilly Circus, the very maw of the City of Lies. It's a circus all right, but the only carnivores you'll find here wear ties and cufflinks. No need for billboards now: we've got screens the size of bowling greens blazing out above us. This is potentially one of the world's most wondrous cinemas, a forum to reach and woo thousands each hour. And what use is it put to, its sole pupose in life? To remind our kids that Ronald cooks better meals than any mum; to insist we're only free when we're cracking Cokes. All day all year, 24/7, McDonald's and Coke, Coke and McDonald's, brighter and bigger than ever you've night-mared.

Capitalism on crack.

But they're preaching to the converted, because you'd search long and hard to find a brand-free body around here. Kids in Nike trainers, already hounding Dad for the next pair because these ones are so December. Low-slung Gap jeans on Pop Idol wannabes. Tommy hats for the lads — Ali G would've killed him if the branding hadn't killed their irony first.

I fucking hate it here.

I used to love it once. The vibrancy and glamour, the glitz and pizzazz. The near certainty that at least fifty A-list celebs were within a few hundred metres of me. Like nothing I'd ever known, a raw taste of the dream force fed to kids the world over.

The best defence — apart from never coming — is to get indoors as quick as you can, shield that cubic millimetre from the sensory barrage. The Happy Angler is a few blocks that way, and I'm soon halfway there, scooting through gaps in the crowds as they gaze in windows, loiter in doorways, digging deep, shovelling cash right back where it came from, spending their sweat, sore backs, their RSI, on whatever their shot cubic milli-metres tell them to.

Retail-counter terrorism.

There's an old homeless guy begging outside a Starbucks. I stop to give him my coppers and wish him luck, breathing through my mouth against the odorant he's wearing. He looks half dead, and I wonder where he'll sleep tonight. Opulence Central, where some people spend more on lunch than a month in a cheap hostel costs, and this poor bastard'll be lucky if he survives the winter. The years sleeping rough lie on his face like rings in a tree trunk, and I want to know how long he's been out here. He must have had a life once, before circumstance ambushed him. Doesn't he have kids he could turn to? But I can't ask him, and I can't stay either. Besides, I'm interrupting his begging: these minutes could be the difference between his getting food tonight or not.

My phone starts ringing while I'm J-walking Regent Street. It's Katie and she wants to know where I am, why I'm so late.

'Something came up, babe. Don't stress, I'll be with you in five.'

I've barely tucked my phone away when I hear my name being yelled from the far side of the road.

2

The Kiwi dropped something in a bin and jogged on to the road. He crossed four lanes of traffic in neat bursts. Overcoat flapping behind him, brake lights glowing in his glasses, he vaulted the pedestrian rail and landed right in front of where Lisa was standing. Then he stopped and seemed to back off, running a hand through his hair.

Lisa, grinning at him: 'Wow! I feel privileged. Do you do that for all the girls?' *Wish I could remember his name, but.*

He laughed, went to say something, changed his mind, then said, 'Only the South African ones.'

'I'll take you to a Jo-burg shebeen one day; you'll soon revise *that* policy.'

She waited for his reply but he took his time, checking his watch, and then his pockets. At last: 'I'm — ahhh . . . do you know where The Happy Angler is?'

'Oh, you've come for the party also? Cool. Did you get lost?'

'. . . Horribly.'

'Yeah, it's a real bitch to find. You should have come with the others from work, or given someone a call or something.'

Rubbing an eye: 'I . . . ahhh . . . I had to work late and my battery's dead.'

'Well, mister, it's your lucky day.' Beckoning with her head: 'I'll lead, but only if you've got my back.'

'Done.'

She quite liked his smile, a far cry from the half snarl he wore when she'd spotted him crossing the road, but that too was much better than the bland usual. Sharon said she thought he looked cute sometimes, but Lisa couldn't see much of that.

As for his name . . . she'd just have to wing it for a while.

Alex focused on threading through the crowds, glad of the diversion that helped hide how electrically aware of her he was. She was a lot shorter than him but he sensed her presence dwarfing his. He didn't care. She was quite pretty and she bopped along with magnetic pep, turning heads regularly. She was dressed down, skater-girl style, but it suited her well. Her head never stopped, eyes bouncing from person to person, smiling secretly. She made him think of an octogenarian whose youth and looks have been magically restored, all primed to do it again, and to do it much better at that.

What a stroke of luck running into the only person from work who might ease his entry into the party.

Lisa: 'So, what are you up to the rest of the weekend?'

'Working tomorrow, not sure about Sunday.'

'Wow, you're keen. I haven't worked a Saturday since Christmas. What sort of stuff do you and your mates get up to on weekend nights?'

The last thing he wanted to talk about was himself. 'I dunno. Been going to a few — ahhh . . . parties and stuff lately. What about you guys?'

It was as if she didn't hear him. 'So you don't have a girlfriend then? Quiet nights at the cinema? Markets on weekend mornings?'

She grinned a bit as she asked this. He couldn't tell why. One foot in front of the other. He went deliberately the long way around a group, gained some thinking space. *Do I have a girlfriend?* And still came up with nothing.

Eventually, trying for man-of-the-world enigmatic: 'Na, no girlfriend. Not really.'

And straight away he felt the words hit her crookedly. Her hands went up in the air — '*Oooo*, I *see*!' She gave some big affected nods, grin hardening. 'Not *reeeal*ly. If only I had ten rand for every time I've heard a guy say *that*.'

Alex was suddenly mortified. 'What do you mean?'

'I mean that a guy who likes to be known as "not *really*" having a girlfriend either has one — a very *real* one — and shags around on her anyway, or he wants to give himself an easy ribbon with which to wrap up casual flings.'

This appalled him so much he could think of no rebuttal at all. 'But . . . I . . . ahh—'

'My first *real* boyfriend, back in Cape Town, used to do that. I had no idea for over a year. Then one day I phoned him for a joke, spoke through a handkerchief, pretended I was someone else and that I'd met him at the pub the other night when he was hammered. I asked him if he had a girlfriend, and he said, "Not really."'

'I didn't mean it like that, honestly!'

Lisa was surprised with how agitated he'd become; she was only teasing him. Truly. So she laced her tone with way too much sardonicism. '*Sure*, sure, sure, that's what they *all* say.'

His earnestness flared across the gap between them. 'I'm serious! My girlfriend and I — my *ex*-girlfriend — we split up about six weeks ago. She's not even in the country any more.'

For fuck's sake, dude, I was just having a laugh. She turned to look at him fully. 'It's OK, I was just ribbing you.' And in the beam of a Planet Hollywood spotlight she noticed how red his eyes were. It clicked into place. The wooden movements, the awkward speech, the vagueness . . .

Our new boy's stoned off his box!

Her sentiment towards him underwent a seismic shift. She hadn't picked him for a member of the Club, that vast netherworld of drug-based conspiracies and relationships, throbbing and seething just inches beneath the unknowing noses of those not complicit. This made things a lot easier for everybody.

And he still wasn't sure about the girlfriend thing — she could read that much. Better to change the subject before his stoned paranoia got the better of him.

'How much are you paying for your puff at the moment?'

Wary: 'Pardon?

'Your blow, your gear. How much are you being charged?'

Crab in its shell: 'I don't know what you're talking about.'

She was going to push it, tell him she too was a card-carrier, but in the end she just shrugged. It was his business if he wanted to be cagey for a while; he was new on the job after all, had no way of knowing who the narcs were.

Alex wanted to ask her what she meant, but decided he'd come across dense enough for one night. No doubt he'd misheard her, or his slang-savvy just wasn't up to it. He could tell that he'd somehow irked her though. He needed to make up for it, but even without the eccentric tangents she kept firing at him, her voice and accent had his tongue in knots. If only he had a minute to flick through his notebook, it was bound to contain something, something interesting and fitting. Something—

She saved him. 'How long have you been in London?'

'I arrived about two months ago with my girlfriend, but she

hated it, so two weeks later we moved to Coventry where she had some work lined up. Two weeks after that she decided she hated the whole country and wanted us to go home. Long story short: she got on a plane and I came back here. I've been back about a month.'

He expected sympathy — it'd been a trying period — hoped for some too, really. But instead she slapped him on the back and hollered, 'That's makes you a virgin, mister! Welcome to London, party capital of the Southern Hemisphere!'

He found himself laughing with her. And it felt a lot better than sympathy.

Lisa: 'Home of Tony Blair and other fine actors!'

He laughed harder.

Lisa: 'So you're still up in Finsbury, yeah?'

'Yeah . . .' *C'mon, you lame bastard, don't leave it at a monosyllable.* 'Still losing two hours plus on the tube each day.'

Then she blew his heart out of his chest. 'Are you still looking to move closer? It's just that Matty's room round at our place will be empty soon and I'm having a little trouble filling it.'

Ba-bom, ba-bom, ba-bom . . .

He hadn't dared dream so high! What better way to bond with workmates and a new social circle than to go and live with them? With *her*! And to kiss that shit-hole hostel goodbye forever and for longer. All that was keeping him there was the bond and advance rent demanded for every room he rang about. He didn't have a spare six hundred quid right now; was dealing with strangers and so couldn't ask for credit. But these guys — he *worked* with them! They might be willing to waive the bond for the week or two he needed, especially if he offered to pay some form of plus-market-rate interest.

Play it cool, bro. 'Ah yeah, that might be ideal. You guys are quite close to the warehouse, right?'

'Three stops, mate. Ten minutes' travel from front-door to sign-in. On the rare occasions when the trains aren't fucked, that is.'

He tried to piece together all the people in the house from the chatter he'd overheard. There was Lisa, of course. And Matty, soon to be no longer. Who else? Jim, the Tasmanian bloke in the Goods In office. Greg, the Kiwi with Labour Save, fork-lift driver. Katie, Sydneysider in Accounts. Johan, another South African, Labour Save supervisor . . .

Then his soaring train of thought hit a cold trough.

He lived in there too.

The All-Australian Boy. Mr I'm Too Cool To—

A drawl from behind them: 'I want your purse and your mobile, sharpish.'

Lisa spun around. 'Ryan! How the fuck are you!'

'Just as fine as wine in the sunshine.'

Alex, at six feet, was a little taller than Ryan, but he had to fight through sudden, crippling deflation to keep all of his height in use, something he'd trained himself to do a long time ago. Didn't much matter, though, because Alex knew that alongside Ryan's looks and cockiness he could be a seven-foot-two body-builder and he'd still languish in the Aussie's shadow.

Lisa gave her housemate a little hug, then stood back, maybe remembering Alex, wanting to include him. Her posture said it too.

Ryan gave it some seconds before acknowledging Alex with his eyes, sending a wild burst of hope through him. But then no word, not even a nod, just holding the look long enough to milk full value from Alex's position, reminding him of, reaffirming, the pecking order. A bigger insult than ignoring him cold would've been.

A heat welled up in Alex, tried to tug his lips back. How could this guy be such a *prick*? What would an ounce of pleasantness have cost him? *He's got everything in a life over here, and he puts the boot into mine over and over.* In a different setting Alex might have shown old Ryan exactly what such spite could be worth. Given it a go anyway, to hell with how it panned.

Ryan, lifting an eyebrow at Lisa: 'Running late, yeah? Not like our Lisa at all.'

'You seem to be a little behind schedule also.'

'I had to fuck around picking up a leaving present for Matty.'

'Oh right. Anything nice?'

'Na, not really. C'mon, let's get into this joint before they drink it dry.'

He swaggered off, Lisa falling in beside him, and Alex, after standing still for a second, severely wanting just to slip away, caught them up. But there wasn't enough space for three abreast, and he was almost happy for the need to drop back a little.

Lisa felt for the Kiwi, but what could she do? Ryan got like that sometimes. Well, quite a lot of the time actually. It was just his way with new bods. He seemed to have less and less time for virgins. Though not even saying hello seemed a bit extreme, even for Ry.

She needed to get the two of them talking somehow, but the Kiwi, stoned as he was, seemed to have been completely thrown. She dreaded to think how Ryan might maul him conversationally if the Kiwi proved as slow off the mark as he had been a minute ago. Besides, how could she force Ryan's attention on to the Kiwi without either betraying that she didn't know his name or sounding horribly rude? It had to happen soon, though. At some stage of the night the Kiwi had to get talking with Ryan, because he wouldn't get into the house without Ryan's advocacy. Truth be told, she couldn't see it happening. Ryan would be shoulder to shoulder with Matty tonight; he'd have bugger-all time for *any*one else, let alone the virgin here.

She sighed, supposing that an extra tenner a week wouldn't kill her for now. She'd still give it a stir or two, but there seemed little point now in letting the matter impinge on the night's fun.

Then Ryan started murmuring to her about Kevin, and the Kiwi was forgotten.

'So he was round at *our* gaff all evening?'

'Well . . . only for an hour or two. No one was home, so we chilled out and blew a spliff. He wanted to hear that Tool album of yours.'

Bullshit. Ryan knew for a fact that Kevin wouldn't listen to Tool under pain of getting his jewellery confiscated (and Kevin's into garage, where it's kilograms over carats). He'd always suspected Lisa and Kevin had ended up fucking that night over New Year. Now this — Kevin going right out of his way for her whenever Lisa needed to score.

It had sounded unlikely to the others: South African backpacker and inner-London wide-boy. But Ryan for one knew about Lisa's thing for black guys. He probably knew better than she did sometimes. And there was plenty of opportunity for the two of them to be hooking up. Lisa spent a lot her time kicking around town alone these days, supposedly up to whatever leftist shit was the flavour *de jour*, and she could be a sneaky bitch. She had denied it vehemently the one time Ryan asked her about it, and certainly Kevin hadn't offered anything. But then he wouldn't if she'd asked him not to. One thing was sure: if she was visiting Kevin at the estate, Ryan would soon hear about it. But he hoped like hell she wasn't.

A little while later Lisa's phone went off. Ryan couldn't tell who she was speaking with, but she was soon motioning him for a pen. There was one in his bag somewhere, but he couldn't be fucked rooting around for it, so he shook his head. She frowned, then signalled for him to ask Alex for one; then she turned away, speaking intently.

Bitch.

He was going to refuse but decided he couldn't; turned to

Alex. Grudging: 'What was your name again?'

Alex's stride caught, and he stared at Ryan for a hard second before muttering, 'Alex.'

So he has got a pair. A semblance of one anyway. The name thing was perhaps a little harsh, and Ryan felt a prick of compunction, but there was no way he was going to go out of his way to smooth things for the latest company hotshot. Especially a stuck-up mamma's boy like Alex.

'Got a pen on ya?'

Alex pulled one from the pocket of his River Island shirt, moved a beat towards handing it straight to Lisa, then stopped himself. *Yeah, that would've shown you've been listening in on us, wouldn't it, cobber.*

Lisa took the pen from Ryan, jotted a number on a receipt, tucked it away, and kept talking as they walked, though whoever had called her was getting a lot more in than she was — a rarity. The silence between the two guys was suddenly awkward, which wouldn't normally have bothered Ryan with Alex's sort. But perhaps a change of tack might be in order: it was starting to seem as if Alex might not be so shy at holding grudges after all, and there was no need to go making an active enemy of a future boss.

'So how's work treating ya so far, mate?'

Alex hated himself for the flare of excitement the overture gave him. 'Not too bad, I suppose. Getting a feel for things.'

'Yeah, there's fuck all to it really.' Then: 'You'll be calling the shots in no time.'

There was a big barb in that too, and it left Alex stranded for a moment. '. . . Julian's in no rush. I won't be given any responsibility until I've got a thorough grounding of the whole operation.'

Lisa ended her call without saying goodbye. *'Who*'s in no rush?'

Ryan, somehow mocking: 'Juuuu-lian.'

She looked agitated. 'Why? What's *he* got to do with Alex?'

Ryan, surprised: 'Didn't you know?'

'Know *what*?'

Chuckling: 'Well, fancy that. There was a time when a rat couldn't fart in that joint without Lisa Tailor knowing if it'd drawn mud or not.'

Alex was pleased that Lisa wasn't yet aware of the circumstances of his employment, but he was worried what sort of twist Ryan might put on it, so he spoke up first, pride and embarrassment warring in him. 'The company were looking for graduates; they hired me on a management traineeship.'

Ryan: 'He studied neo-fascism — I mean, economics.'

Lisa was silent a while. 'So you're only on the floor learning how it all works?'

'Ah, yeah.'

'Then what?' Sceptical: 'Promoted directly to team leader somewhere?'

'Ahh . . . maybe'

Ryan, gleeful: 'Team leader, my arse. He'll go straight to section manager if he's up to it.'

Fire crackled up Alex's spine, into his cheeks; he hoped it was too dark to be noticed.

But the revelation seemed to have all the impact on Lisa that he'd hoped for. 'Fucking hell,' she muttered eventually.

They crossed another street and there it was, The Happy Angler, music and merriment vibrating through the walls. It looked less of a lion's den than it had earlier, but Alex automatically dropped back to let the others enter first.

Ryan: 'I need quiet a word with Lisa. We'll see you in there.'

Something like fear shot through Alex, and he hated Ryan now like never before. *Think, think, think!* He needed to eat before drinking . . . a sandwich board on the street said meals were served inside. He needed to piss . . . hello, it's a *pub*. He needed cigarettes . . . they probably knew he didn't smoke. He needed . . . he needed to wait patiently out of earshot for the pair, and then follow them in as if they'd all come together.

All this in two heartbeats but even that was too long: they were both peering at him oddly. 'OK, no probs.' But there were probs aplenty.

His hand was on the door when some insurance occurred to him. Over his shoulder: 'What are you guys drinking?'

Lisa, immediately: 'Vodka and lemonade, double.'

Ryan: 'I'll sort meself out.'

I'm gonna hospitalise that prick some day, swear to god.

Anger helped push Alex through the door. Even so, it felt as if the creak of the hinges, the in-rush of cold air, alerted every eye in the busy front room. Even Travis on the jukebox seemed to stop and stare as Alex negotiated the invisible trip-hazards on the floor between him and the bar, engrossed himself in counting coins, unwilling even to check who, if anyone, from work was in the fore-ground. He could feel himself blushing badly.

Reaching the people around the bar, he made sure he wasn't queuing beside a known face, then he tried to camouflage himself among the strangers, cutting his eyes left and right, peering around heads, scouting for enemy positions.

Halfway along the other side of the place, up on a platform with tables and stools, he first noticed Greg, chatting with three others he recognised but whose names he wasn't sure of. He grad-ually began to make out more people he 'knew' up there, and then more and more. Jim and Sharon were at the bar across from Alex, at the front of the queue, waiting for service. She was laughing as she told a story, but his grins were pretty distant; he kept looking for someone further along the bar, towards the jukebox where

Trent was clustered with the Swedish girls from the labelling department and a Spanish guy whose name might've been Chico. The toilets were away to the left, near the entrance, near Alex. He jumped when the Men's door slammed open and Matty steamed out, Frank and Kenny following him. They were all well on the way by the looks, sharing a loud laugh, pickling Alex in the green stuff. He dropped his head, studying his watch as they passed a metre or so from him. But they were soon back within the party on the platform, swallowed by shadows and gaiety.

It was all a matter of timing now, timing Alex had no control of. How long before he arrived at the bar? How long before a staff member served him? How long would Ryan and Lisa's 'quiet word' take? Too many variables. Alex *loathed* such situations: just watching things unfolding, desperately wanting certain results, no real power to influence them. As the minutes ticked by and the bar drew nearer — too hot with his coat on in here — the sweat began to roll off him. The barman even commented on it as he took Alex's money.

Alex turned sideways to watch the door. But there was still no sign of them, even after he'd pocketed his change and knocked back a quarter of his pint. Then he saw Ravi, a Sri Lankan guy from Replenishment, chatting away in a corner towards the platform. Alex had broken a bit of ice with the little man two days ago; could've giggled relief as he made his way over. But when Alex was still ten steps away, Ravi slapped his buddy on the shoulder and walked off, oblivious.

Shit, shit, shit . . . What the hell should he do now? Go back to where he'd come from, pretend to be queuing up again . . . with his hands full of drinks? Head on up the platform . . . ?

But he couldn't bring himself to do either, and in desperation crossed to an empty table and placed the glasses down. Put his foot on a stool and slowly untied his shoelace before retying it again, turning his body until he could see the door.

He'd just changed feet when Lisa popped in, patron saint of all losers. Ryan came immediately behind her. Alex swept the drinks up and took two steps towards them, then disaster struck again: Lisa mouthed something to Ryan and made a beeline for the toilets, while Ryan struck out for the platform, walking like a warlord, shunning the bar because people like him don't need booze to give them confidence.

If he'd been prompt Alex could have headed him off, thought up something to say on the way, however lame it came out. But he couldn't bring himself to do it, just dithered where he stood. Ryan would see him anyway, stop by and collect him . . .

But he didn't. Of course. No doubt he saw Alex, just pretended not to, knowing that would be enough.

And then a triumphal climb to the platform, shaking hands, pointing and winking, laying about with jests. Then Matty's roar: 'Fucking hell, here's my man! Where the fuck've *you* been, ya wanker! Give us a hug, Skippy!'

If they looked his way, Alex would be in full view of them: he stuck out horribly in the open space his table centred. He should look away, bury his head in the beer until Lisa came back, never have to know if his social leprosy went noted. Blissful ignorance: far better that way. But he was morbidly drawn to the scene, a broke kid at a Toys-R-Us window.

Then Ryan had a need to point something out to Matty; several others who were hanging on their words followed Ryan's hand too, looking at something outside the pub, something through a window . . . a window right behind Alex.

He heard Matty's drunken stage whisper, and lost feeling in his legs. 'Hey, isn't that that new cunt from work over there?'

Managed to dump his pint on the table, beside Lisa's pretty little vodka with the lemon twist and straw, and wheel towards the toile—

She was standing right behind him, smile warm enough to singe his spleen.

'Where're you going, Alex? Am I boring you so soon?'

In a stroke he didn't care if a million of them were staring at him, laughing at him.

'I . . . ahhh . . . I just had to use the toilet.' Almost knocking it over as he snatched at it: 'Here's your drink.'

She cocked her head with pleasure. 'Oh, thanks, you shouldn't have. I'll get the next one in.'

This was getting better by the second. What should he say now? Was it too soon to tell her how nice her hair looked?

But she was suddenly business. 'Listen, don't let me keep you from the toilets. You go —' she was steering him towards them, her hand electrocuting the skin under his coat; there was no saying 'no'— 'while I take our drinks into the lounge bar through there. Meet me when you've finished. I need to have a chat with you in private.'

God had supervised the construction of this woman personally; His powers had worn off on her, because what that sentence — *I need to have a chat with you in private* — did to Alex's bloodstream was nothing short of sorcery.

He didn't need a piss, but squeezed out the little he could, popped a couple of breath mints, flattened a clump of hair with some water, lamented the redness of his eyes, then walked out, through a small arch and into the relative quiet of the lounge bar. He found Lisa, in a white sleeveless, sitting at a booth in a corner, and the way she was staring through the window, absently stirring *his pint* with *her straw*, gave him organ convulsions all over again.

She beamed at him: '*Here* you are. Sit down and lose that coat before you roast.'

42

3

Greg: 'Where the fuck's Lisa, Ryan?'

'Dunno, mate. She walked in with me a minute ago.'

Lisa's gone missing, and there are a fair few would-be space cadets anxious for her return. She's switched her blower off, apparently. Can't see Alex anywhere either. What could the two of *them* be up to? I was pretty sure that bit about Alex's job would kill them off pronto. Maybe she's got him cornered somewhere, laying into him with a sermon.

Matty's reaching over and tapping me. 'You coming to the airport tomorrow, bro?'

What the fuck for? So I can cry into a beer with you? Then cry into one with myself while your empty chair laughs at me? 'Yeah sure, I'll be there.' Made that mistake about four times too many now.

The boozy sheen over Matty's eyes clears for a second. 'What's wrong, man? Let's not have a funeral till there's a body to bury, eh?'

'Oh, fuck off, ya cunt. Nothing wrong with me. You're the one going back to a country with fuck-all jobs, fuck-all money and a national rugby team dependent on Islanders.'

That does it. 'Yeah, well at least my home's not fast becoming known as the sunny Fourth Reich. Looks like you blokes have at last found a use for the ninety percent shit that your country's made of, eh?'

Johan: 'Yeah, they gonna exterminate towel-head queue-jumpers in there because the world's press can't stand the flars for long enough to cover the story!'

He gets some good laughs for that.

Sharon's soon jumping in for me. 'I dunno why you Kiwis are laughing. That "ninety percent shit" happens to contain mineral deposits weighing roughly twenty times what your entire country does.'

Matty: 'Add to that all the gold fillings and jewellery . . .'

'Hahahaha!'

Greg, Kiwi: 'And you're soon gonna need every fucking cent of it to pay for relocating your coastal cities, thanks to Howard's and Bush's energy obtuseness.'

Greg's a bit of a closet scholar. You can embarrass all kinds of results out of him by highlighting the pompous flashes in his vocab. Jim starts pulling him up for 'obtuseness' but I steam over him with a better one.

'Don't you guys knock Honest Johnny over global warming, mate. You really think he'd ignore the scientists if he didn't have a better plan than them? Howard's got it covered. He sees global warming for what it really is.'

Matty: 'Do tell. I'm fascinated. What is global warming really?'

'A free and easy way to introduce millions more Australians to the pleasures of beachfront living. No longer will the sea be the sacred preserve of surfie wankers and Gold Coast millionaires. *Oh* no. Every Australian, from stockmen in Mt Isa to skimpy barmaids in Alice Springs will soon get to ride a wave or two after knock-off.'

This gets them going. Think of some icing: 'It's mostly for the Aboriginals though.' They stop to listen properly. 'In global warming Johnny's found a way to shut them up at last too, 'cause how much easier do the tinnies slide down when the ocean's lapping your ankles?'

Matty: 'Wahay! Here's our girl! About fucking time too! Get ya Jaapie arse up here, candy-girl!'

He's too pissed to notice the dark looks a few of the South Africans throw at him. They don't often appreciate being called Jaapies. But Lisa's too far in the bad books today; she stops and winces a theatrical apology as twelve of them line the rail and applaud her. Alex lags for a moment, then leaves her behind, skipping up the steps.

Lisa's too much of a show-girl to let a little lateness keep her down though, and she's soon taking the piss, curtseying, an actress at curtains time, getting clapped like one too. The Poms around us look on indulgently.

———

Alex feels fantastic suddenly! He attributes it to Lisa's invitation that he move into the house. Beer tastes a bit funny, but who cares?

Right, now who shall I talk to? What about that Portuguese chick from the Stock-Control office?

'Howzit going? I'm Alex. I met you the other day. Doug introduced us. Sorry to be rude, but I've forgotten your name.'

'This is not to worry because I forget yours too. I'm Anna.'

He holds his hand out and she gives it a petite shake.

Alex: 'And who's your friend? You work at EUE too, don't

you? Think I nearly knocked you over in the cloakroom the other day. Sorry about that.'

His name is Alonso. He's Albanian.

Alex: 'Are you two an item?'

They laugh.

Anna: 'No. My boyfriend was Nick, a team leader from Replenishment.'

'*Was*?'

A tightness to her smile: 'Yes, was. We split up last week.'

'Oh, I'm sorry to hear that. I know how that feels. I broke up with my girlfriend a short time ago as well.'

Alonso asks if she was a Kiwi too, and Alex finds himself telling them about Jessica.

———

Lisa's flat out for the next ten minutes, sitting at a dark table in the platform's far corner, as far from the bar as possible. This night has been built up for two weeks now, and the Club affiliates are keen to renew their membership. On impulse she decides to cover her additional rent charges by marking the gear up an extra quid or two.

She ends up sitting with a few of the girls afterwards. Of the four of them, Angela's the only non-Club member and Lisa's popularity has her thrown.

'What *is* your secret, Lease?' She's trying hard to make a joke of it. 'Half the party's done nothing but ask after you all night; you finally arrive and it's a *fuck*ing stampede to sit down and say gidday to you!' There are only two occasions when Angela uses the 'f' word: when the conversation around her is riddled with it and she wants to blend in, or when she's arguing with a swearer and gets rattled. Either way, it always rolls crookedly off her tongue, pops up in the wrong place.

Angela's the last person Lisa wants to talk to right now anyway. 'What can I say, Ange. Some of us have just got it, you know?'

'Got *what*?' The big smile's fooling no one. Angela's got a complex about her prettiness/friends ratio being lower than it should. At least that's what she confides to her diary quite often.

The E's kicking in for Sharon already, and she breaks off from Katie to chant to Angela: '*Je ne sais quoi*, that certain something, a little ba-da *bing*.'

Angela's thrown, and Lisa's quick to shift her chair more towards Katie.

Lisa: 'So what are you getting me for my birthday, babe?'

Katie: 'We're thinking of doing a whip-round and booking you in for breast implants.'

Lisa, laughing along with them: 'Ha fucking ha, bitch. You of *all* people should know that breasts don't make the woman.'

Angela, pointed: 'Not even *lopsided* breasts, eh Sharon?'

Sharon: 'Will you shut up about that? Most women's tits are a little different.'

Angela: 'Not to the point where they need dual-cup-size bras!'

'I do *not* need dual-cup-size bras! That's a slur started by Jim because I wouldn't let him fuck me that night.'

Lisa: 'Don't worry about it, Shaz: women like you attract slurs the way lumps of shit do flies.'

Sharon gapes for a moment, then snorts into laughter.

Katie: 'Shut up and listen to this.' Her eyes are twinkling alarmingly; maybe the cocaine.

Katie's Lisa's best friend in London. They met when Katie responded to Lisa's roomshare ad in *TNT*. Katie was fresh off the plane from Sydney, the obedient daughter of strict Catholics. They hadn't gotten along at first, but Katie caught on fast, and within a few weeks she was pretty much out of control. One time she went to an underground rave on a Thursday and sleep-walked in an hour before work Monday morning. A three-month relationship then grounded her a bit, but Lisa's fascinated by the degrees to which people can change in so short a space when transplanted from home and hearth, when suddenly thousands of miles from authority figures and role models.

Katie, leaning into Lisa: 'Ingrid from Stock Control, yeah? Her boyfriend flew in from Malmo to see her a fortnight ago. She wanted to look her best for him so she went for a wax at that beautician's in Fulham — you know the special we were talking about?'

Lisa, intrigued: 'Yeah, so?' Katie can be a minx, and they all hate Ingrid as healthily as most women hate Scandinavians taller and prettier than they are.

Katie: 'So they do her legs, no bother.'

Sharon: 'No bother except that they had to send out for three more pots of wax and a fucking step-ladder.'

'Hahahaha!'

Katie: 'Then Ingrid's decided she wants her bikini line done too. But they're one side into the job and she can't take it any more. The pain's killing her. They tell her to come back the next day and they'll finish up.'

Angela can't hold back a guess. 'Sven arrives early to find his girlfriend's loins a little lopsided?'

'You could say that, but not because he rocked up early. She woke up the next morning and the "smooth" side is all nasty, pussy little pimples. And she can't bring herself to get the other side done.'

Sharon, wincing: 'Oh, fuck me, those things take *weeks* to heal.'

Katie, voice rising: 'I know! So lover boy shows up a few days later, and Ingrid's snatch is modelling the Yeti-meets-leper look!'

This breaks them up for a long time; a lot of the others look over. Then they notice that Ingrid is one of them and they lose it all over again.

Sharon manages to ask, 'What did she do about it?'

Katie: 'What do you think? Got her period early and sucked todger till her gums were raw!'

Lisa starts to feel for the Swede — she met her properly the other day and found her nice — so she waves them off and heads for the bar to get a round in early. This way her next round should get lost in the order as things get messier.

———————

The jukebox goes from The Manic Street Preachers to Destiny's Child and I look around for the culprit. 'Who's the fucking unit who played this?'

Kenny, still in his suit from work: 'I thought it was you, Ryan. I distinctly heard you asking Ravi to slip up there and play this for you.'

He's been getting into the craic a bit lately, fronting me head on with it. Spends half the day up above us; comes down and lords it after knock-off, has his way with the peasants.

Been getting a few too, it must be said, and Kenny's voice has grown correspondingly louder.

Me: 'Yeah, I could see you pining for it, Ken, so you owe me one, yeah?'

Greg starts to say something but Kenny overrides him. 'It's easy to knock girl bands, but you've got to admit the concept's pretty sound. You take four hot birds, plaster them in make-up, squeeze them into skimpy costumes . . . well, it rather falls down at that point, doesn't it?'

The new chick, Samantha from Cairns, is standing near the pillock, and she giggles at this more than the rest do. Fuck, if

Kenny's the first to get her in the sack as well he'll crown himself the new resident quim-ninja.

Jim's having a heart-to-heart with Matty. 'It's worked out OK for you though, man. You heading home with ya missus, that is.'

Me: 'How do ya work that one out?'

'Well, think about it. It's such a massive reality check when what Kiwis call the "Overseas Experience" finally finishes. You've gotta pack up, sever your ties here, try and find a plan for the next few years that won't have you reaching for the Prozac after this, head home and see how much water's gone under the bridge, whether you still know your friends and family — whether they still know you. Especially for a guy: we're so fucking shocking at keeping in touch. And, I mean, hardly any of us make it home with much money intact — that all gets spent on the African odyssey — so you've got that stress too. I imagine life can start to feel pretty fucking lonely, man, inverted culture shock. And if you've gotta face it all alone . . .'

Jim can be a boring cunt when he's E'ed, delving people's heads, seeking tonics for burdens — his own especially.

Fuck that. Life's too short.

So I turn back to Kenny, Samantha and those other two from Kenny's new fan club. Kenny's telling them about his body piercings. His way of proving — along with his tattoos, his motorbike, his drumming lessons — he's as 'out there' as anybody, even if his folks do 'have land'. He breezily comes to the new piercing in his dick, through the tip of the urethra. Samantha gasps, appropriately shocked and intrigued.

Chico: 'What the hell make you go and do something like *that*?

Me: 'Nine Guinness with absinthe chasers.'

Even the fan club have to laugh at that one, and Kenny's grin rots a little at the edges.

He comes back at me as soon as the volume's low enough.

'Don't you believe it, Skippy. You've got no idea what a turn-on it is for the birds. I pulled at a club last Friday, and we were still in bed on Sunday afternoon.'

Too easy, Fauntleroy. 'Yeah, but she told me it only took that long because your prick kept snagging on the duvet, mate.'

That kills them — Jim and Matty look ready for seizures — and Kenny's coerced grin gets drenched by it for a good ten seconds. I throw him a dummy just as he starts to retort. 'You've got something in your teeth, Ken,' pointing at my own, slicing him off, then walking away.

Looking around for someone to talk to, I notice Alex down near the bar. His manner breaks my stride: he's yakking his head off with Murphy and Lord Fuckface Trent, waving his hands, cracking up . . . cracking *them* up too.

So the little Kiwi can hold a conversation down when he wants to.

Lisa bails me up. She wants to say something but skirts around it for a few minutes. I know she's getting closer when she goes all blasé.

'So what are we going to do about renting Matty's room?'

'I thought *you* were taking care of that?'

'Amm . . . I am. I *have* . . . well, kind of.'

Here it comes. 'Oh yeah? Who did you find?'

'Well, I interviewed a few from Gumtree and *TNT* on the phone. Didn't much like the sound of them though.'

'And?'

'And then I heard that someone from work is looking.'

'Who is it?'

'It's Alex.'

'You're shitting me.'

'Why?'

Final: 'No way, Lease. Keep looking.'

'C'mon, Ry! He'd be OK.'

'Didn't you hear me before? He's on a fast track to the ivory tower. He's gonna be our boss in a few weeks. If he's *living with us* he'll know everything we get up to. And look at him: he'd dob on his grandma if he thought there was Brownie points in it.'

'No, you don't understand! He's a stoner. It won't be like that.'

'A *stoner*? *Alex*? Oh yeah, and you're an informant for Special Branch.'

'He *is*, man! He was off his dial when I met him out in the street. He could hardly walk and talk, and his eyes were hanging from his head.'

'You're in fantasy-land, babe. If Alex is in the Club, Molly Meldrum just got a job doing rub-downs for the Parramatta under-twelves.'

'At least say you'll—'

'What the fuck are you playing at, Lease?'

'I just . . . I can't afford the extra rent while the room's empty.'

'An extra tenner a week? Just mark your drugs up another pound.'

She looks away. I know she's already done this. Extra rent isn't the issue here.

As she walks off: 'Well, at least have a think about it.'

Later on some fat bird nudging forty-five with peroxide hair, leopard-print tights and a Silk Cut permanently glued to her fingers comes in and sets up a karaoke machine. She's standard Brit working class: met her husband in the returns queue at Argos; flew easyJet to Italy last year to bail her soccer fan son out of lock-up; has seen every plot device known to man fed through the cast of *EastEnders*. There are ten thousand of her dispersed through the launderettes of the city at this very moment. Seems too downmarket for this part of town, but then she starts singing and she might as well be an albino Aretha. The song menus and fill-in cards are soon flying around, and ten minutes later Sharon's behind the mic singing 'Who Can it Be Now?', Men At Work, a heap of the crew hitting the dance floor and cheering her on. She's pissed or high or both, holding nothing back, and that lets her make a decent go of it, which is lucky for everybody because Sharon normally sings with about as much melody as mating cats.

I've had Samantha alone for fifteen minutes now. She's an educated liberal — and I don't mean Howard's political party — and at one point earlier talk turned to the latest African famine to become fashionable and I declared that I was a participant in the dollar-a-day scheme.

She'd looked impressed. 'Really? Good for you! How's it all going?'

'Not too flash, to be honest.'

Face falling: 'Mismanagement again?'

'Must be something like that because I've been on the programme almost a year now and so far I've only made about three hundred bucks.'

We're still on the platform, the dance floor in sight but far enough away so we can hear each other clearly. I'd cut her from the flock by acting her opposite, talking about kickings I'd had at the hands of 'pissed-up coons', torpedoes that should be fired at 'queue-jumper' boats, exasperating her until she bailed me up in this corner, a genuine Aussie redneck in her sights and all of Sydney Uni morally behind her. So she was taken aback when I told her about an 'aboriginal bloke' I worked with out mining, how he'd not only been my best mate for a year but also been the most popular guy in camp, eighty percent of it rough white guys. Then I told her about Hassan, a runaway from the Woomera Detention Centre who I'd given money and shelter to but now feared for the fate of.

The first story was true, every word of it. The second was

complete bullshit, but it served its function well enough.

It's worth trying sometimes: you give a bird reasons to like you. Then you give her reasons to dislike you too, because bastards are alluring. Sad but true. Then you invalidate the negatives, and if you've sown enough positives along the way there's a fucking good chance you'll soon be inspecting the soles of her feet.

She's telling me about voluntary work she did in Redfern as part of a sociology degree or some shit, and I'm leaning in and staring, nodding, barely listening, when a loud cheer from below goes up.

Murphy's singing 'Warning' by Green Day, and Alex is in the centre of the dance floor, the crew encircling him and clapping. He's banging his head and air guitaring it, spanking the planks something fierce.

Samantha, grinning: 'What's that guy's name again?'

'Alex.'

'He *rocks*!'

Me, stunned: 'Never would've thought he had it in him.'

We're standing together watching Alex, and her hip's tapping me to the beat, and I'd been planning on waiting another twenty minutes but I slip an arm around her back on impulse. She moulds into me a bit, and I'm well in here—

'He's a cracking fuck, love. You've picked a winner tonight.'

I turn around and almost yelp.

Katrina.

She's had her hair done recently, but tears have cut streaks through the heavy make-up. Her eyes are shining and she's beaming ear to ear. Specks of white powder around her nostrils. She looks like some exquisite doll that's been cracked open then glued back together.

'He's not much chop in the size department, but he's knows more positions than the *Kama Sutra*, and he'll say shit that'll have you feeling like the only woman in a five light-year radius.'

Samantha draws away from her.

Me, drowning: 'Wh . . . where have you been?'

Lisa's suddenly there, putting an arm gently around Katrina. 'C'mon, Kat, come and have a drink with m—'

Exploding: 'FUCK OFF, BITCH! YOU FUCKING KNEW AND YOU SAID NOTHING!' Katrina's fists are bunched in front of her face, like she wants to throttle Lisa and is just holding back, and the dressings wrapped around both her forearms are so white they glow.

Me, dizzy: 'What happened to your arms?'

'WHAT DO *YOU* FUCKING CARE?!'

Katie arrives, and she and Lisa restrain Katrina as she lunges at me.

Lisa: 'Ryan, go.'

Katrina, tearing at one of the bandages: 'YOU WANNA KNOW? I'LL FUCKING *SHOW* YOU THEN, YOU *CUNT*!'

And I can't get away fast enough.

———

Angela volunteers to go with Katrina to keep an eye on her, and Lisa and Katie watch the taxi until it disappears.

Katie: 'Man, he *really* screwed her over. It's been months and she's worse than ever.'

'It wasn't Ryan's fault. He never even told her he loved her.'

'He didn't stop her from saying it to him, though.'

Sighing: 'She's a bloody head-case, Kate, she always was.'

'One to be handled with care. Which he didn't do.'

Back in the pub, Katie asks Lisa for a tampon, then walks into the toilets. Someone's singing 'Obstacle One' by Interpol, a song Lisa adores, and whoever the singer is he's doing it justice superbly. Lisa pops another E as she heads to where she left her drink — she's going to need both, and then some, if she's to get revved up again — and gets a shock to see that it's Alex behind the mic. His eyes are closed and he's swaying, but there's no act to it at all. He could be alone. Lisa sings with him under her breath, the haunting lyrics stinging her eyes.

———

Closing time and everyone's gathering outside.

Matty, to me, legless: 'Where we headed now, Ry?'

'I'm going home.'

There's a nightclub beside the pub, two gorillas in dinner suits on the door. Greg struts up to one of them, makes a show of looking him up and down. Finally, implacable, shaking his head: 'Oh na, you're not coming out here, mate. Not with those shiny shoes on you're not. You look like you're stone-cold sober too.' They don't get it.

I scoot up the road for a piss, into an alley.

She must have slashed her wrists. Both of them.

Up the alley a little, into the dark, away from the punters, sober enough for a little decorum . . .

And I've got my cock halfway out when I realise three figures are in here sharing the shadows with me. Young guys.

Youths.

English as fuck, British at least. The clothes tell me that; not sure what else, hard to finger, some sort of cocky carriage, the territorial creature on its own patch.

So long as you keep ya nose half clean, street hassle's rarer than you'd think in this part of town, even at this hour. But you'll get it from this type before you will from others. A mistake walking into their midst in a backwater like this; by the heft of the

Reef bottle one of them swigs on, I reckon they think I came this close as a wind-up. Or a dare.

Or that they're at least reserving the *right* to think this.

Nothing else for it, though, can't back away now . . . Well, I could always use my watch as a transparent sitch-saver, bolt out of here like I'm late to a twelve-pound coke deal. But I'm pissed enough and my back teeth are fucking floating, so I swing away from them and get on with it.

Nothing said for a spell . . . problem is this load's a fucking jumbo, and I'm not even halfway done before I'm worried about the flow I'm sending along the ground, whether or not the lads are downstream of me. Try to go faster.

'No toilets where you're from, pal?'

Oh yeah, and like you haven't done this a thousand times before, ya little cunt. By the rate that Reef's going down, you'll be taking my place before I've zipped up properly.

A laughingly embarrassed 'what-can-I-say, I'm-pissed' apology is what's needed now.

I wonder how close she came to dying.

'None that conveniently materialise outside closing pubs.'

A second: 'Conveniently materialise?'

I sneak a look over my shoulder, get a squiz at his face in the light from a window.

Lifting his chin, drilling me with a stare: 'Well, no, you won't find no bogs on the streets over 'ere, *mate*, but we've got alleys where smart-arse foreigners conveniently materialise right when you're after a little fucking privacy.'

I try not to break the look too quickly, but I don't know how well I did, 'cause under his Yankees cap there's the look of the bad bastard on this one. My piss ices up in me — at least this lets me stop. Shaking dry and I sense one of them shifting around, putting himself between me and the street. His foot scuffles suddenly against the concrete, and, dick half out or not, there's a big lurch in my chest and my flight/flight mechanism very nearly kicks in.

But no, it's not a violent charge, the kid merely stumbled a bit. And yep, he's falling-down-drunk, folks. Which would be good news for me were he alone.

Instead it's a snowball down the back of my shirt.

The one with the coming-soon-to-a-prison-near-you eyes saunters right up to me after I've zipped. Making a yapping mouth with thumb and fingers: 'Always givin it plenty-a this, you fucking Aussies are, yeah?' He manages to impart the direst kind of insult and threat into the clacking of his fingers, big rings sparkling like his gaze. He's shorter than me — he doesn't seem to have noticed — and he's standing so close the bill of his hat's nearly touching my forehead. Menthol fags on his breath, the queasy-sweet reek of the alcopops.

That hand's still yapping, and I'm briefly overjoyed when the little one on my side pipes up, letting me gracefully break eyes with the nutter, as if that's a good thing . . .

Yap, yap, yap . . .

Junior, slurringly strident: 'Yeah, just cos all your criminal granddads came from 'ere, you wankers think you can stroll round our gaff taking the fucking piss, init.'

Time for a 'sorry' for defo now. Probably won't be enough though, and I'm a cunt hair away from bolting — *the whole crew will see me running* — and my hands are raising as I check out the big, lanky third, and the sharp *eagerness* with which he's watching the street — making sure I've no back-up in wait, no coppers passing by — is fucking bloodcurdling.

Stuck in the middle. I hear the crackle of the energy gathering in Yankee's arm, maybe in his knee; that grin's gonna detonate any second now. I pull in a breath to yell HELP, but the crew are too far away to hear me, and all the passers-by will go city-deaf; better off yelling FIRE to those cunts—

A new voice: 'Hurry up, will ya, Ryan. Everyone's waiting for y—'

Matty.

My three little beasts jump like they've been caught flogging off.

Liquid relief, mulled in fire, racing out from my centre. Beats any chemical hit in the whole fucking world.

But then I see it's not Matty at the head of the alley. The wrong Kiwi has come. The wrong one for me right now anyway. Fucking typical.

It's Alex.

Alex, reserved: 'Everything OK, Ryan?'

I hear what I should say. *Go and get help.* Might set the kids off prematurely, that, and needlessly — the façade, after all, is minutely intact. But Alex will have a mob here in under thirty seconds. *Go and get help.* I hear it like thunder.

But if I say it he'll *see* me. And after the way I've treated him he'll unmask me with glee, guaranteed.

Hoping like hell he's listening properly, or can see my face in this gloom: 'Ah . . . yeah, I'm all right.'

I half expect him to shrug and walk away; he's got enough camouflage to pull it off. If I were him, that's probably what *I'd* do. What happens instead slaps me like a warm gust: Alex hears me clear as day. My undercurrents take root in his spine, cranking it straight. And he doesn't bother looking around for allies either, just strides straight in. What's happened to the obsequious little geek who blushed his way around the warehouse these last two weeks? No trace even of the manic teen-at-first-party from a minute ago. Wee Alex suddenly looks like he washes his balls in ice-water. The glasses just make him look more dangerous somehow: scholastically psychotic, Treblinka's resident physician.

Still, three on two. Alex might be up for it — *Surely not, he's gotta be bluffing . . . he's got a rock-solid career in Vegas if he is* — but I sure as hell aren't. They're on the back foot right now though, which leaves me in control again. I don't give Alex a chance to fuck it up.

Me: 'Yeah, just taking a slash, mate. All done too. Let's get out there before the next search party arrives, you know what those pricks are like.'

He shrugs as if he's just as happy to stay and let the chips fall, gives Yankee a long look, then matches my withdrawal step for step.

Back in the bright lights of club-land. They feel warm again. Forgot what that felt like.

Me: 'So . . . when ya gonna move your shit round the house, mate?'

4

MELVYN

Must admit, I noticed the kid as soon as e walked in, even before e went and made a spectacle of imself. 'Fucking pretty lil cunt,' I says to meself, cos when ya get battered in the womb wiv the ugly stick as bad as what I was, the beautiful people-a the world tend to stick out a mile to ya, and forgivin em for it aint always an easy thing. So e ad my goat up just by the way e looked.

Then I noticed who it were e was ere wiv. It were *only* Angelika, Miss Kiev er-fucking-self! She were new round ere, only started workin eighteen, nineteen days ago. Not long, sure, but she were startin to make almost as big a mark on pulling the punters fru that door as Nadia fucking does, and that's sayin somethin.

Now this bird's fucking 'ot stuff. Top-shelf talent. Bit skinny up top, but that's a blessing, cos if her rack was, say, more Nadia's size, she wouldn't be able to go outside wivout bodyguards. She's got that big a future in the industry that unless I'm able to get sum kinda hook into 'er very soon I simply will not be able to keep er ere for more than a monf or two. Sure, she don't know the time in this town yet — first time out ere n that — but some cunt'll tell er to go try out at Stringfellows or somewhere soon enough, one of them top-end joints up town, and that'll be the enda that.

But she's ere now, int she, and between me n the lads it's been a proper stampede to see who's gonna get to tumble er first. I've been tempted to 'extend my protection' over er in fact, but if I done that n got nowhere, they'll all be avin a laugh at me big style. Albeit a quiet one. So instead it's a fucking cock race, and wiv a big possibility that no one's gonna win it, cos this girl is Premier-league pussy, make no mistake, and aloof as hell to boot.

So yeah, I'd already clocked im the second e walks in, apparently alone. Then waddaya fucking know, *Angelika* follows im in fru the door. She catches im up, and then she's *only* gone and whispered in 'is ear and pecked im on the bleedin cheek!

I thought, 'You lucky lil bastard, you just got more than any of us cunts ave ad off've er in three weeks-a solid tryin.'

Anyway, she takes 'is 'and n leads im fru to a table near the cen-a, and by this time even those in ere who didn't know er were staring at the pair-a them.

That were when I looked over at Vernon, and I thought, 'Oh shit: that pretty cunt aint goin ome under 'is own steam tonight,' cos Vernon ad the orn for Angelika even more than the rest of us. And when e gets that look in 'is eye someone's goin to the fucking ospital, minimum (so long as I don't tell im to knock it on the ead, that is.)

So anyway, I've just shrugged and tried to go back to what it was I were doing before they fronted, which was playing a bit of poker wiv Teddy Walker from out Reading, avin a laugh.

But I kept an eye on the pair-a them — mostly cos me own envy wanted me to be looking right at em when she finally tired of prick-teasing and booted im into touch. And the thing about it was, right, was that after an hour-a watchin em, it's gone and become agonisingly obvious to me that she wanted nufin more than to wrap them long luscious legs round 'is waist and fuck im till 'is intestines bled.

I may be an ugly cunt but I know birds, and it were written all over her gorgeous, fragile face. But ere's the thing: e weren't up for it! It were one-way traffic, I were fucking sure of it!

Well, there were only one explanation for that then, obviously. The kid was a botty boy. A bum-drummer. And this explanation pleased the hell outta me. Don't get me wrong, I aint got nufin against faggots at all — long as they keep behind closed doors. Just leaves more muff out n about for us real blokes, init.

Only I *wanted* to believe this, that e were a poo-pusher — I were well made up wiv that — but deep down I couldn't convince meself of it, could I. E jus did'n ave none of it about im, know what I mean? There were nufin in the walk, nufin in the way he drank and smoked, the way he sat, the way he pushed round that fringe I'd give a million fucking squid for. And, sure, it's common among fellas to write geezers as pretty as im off as shit-shovelling bottle-merchants, but that's just a load of jealous old bollocks rushin to that kinda judgement on the strenf-a someone's looks, cos I've known some strikingly andsome men in my time who could batter fuck outta the average geezer in arf an 'eartbeat was they of a mind.

Which they quite often was n'all.

So I finks to meself, 'Maybe e's attached and behaves imself.' I've 'eard that that appens sometimes. But na, I dunno, call me a victim-a me own cynicalism, but that don't wash wiv me. You don't work round clubs for twenty-odd years and come away wiv high regard for the male capacity for fidelity.

Meanwhile Vernon's sat there staring big, bleeding chunks outta the kid's back. E'll stay stiller than an ungry fucking mantis, that cunt will — ide imself in the shadows too — if you catch 'is attention the wrong way. They don't often spot im when e decides to move neither.

I'm wondering if Vernon's hump 'as left im enough capacity for thought for im *also* to be ponderin the kid's lack of interest, but I doubted it.

But as she chats away at him — saying more in a minute than I've 'eard er say in weeks — she starts lookin a lil rattled. She's touching 'is 'ands n that all the time too . . . and he don't seem to be givin much back. I nicked off for a piss at one point, walked past em, and sure enough, under the table she's slipped er shoe off and she's runnin er toes up and down 'is leg. I says to meself, 'Thank Christ Vernon can't see that or e'd likely rip the kid's chair out from under im, then plaster im to my carpet wiv the fucking thing.'

Anyway, I've gone out the back for a spell after that, ad to get a package ready for Dessie, and by the time I got back out there the band's on and everyone's up n dancin. I don't mean everyone as in the 'ole gaff, I mean everyone involved in the lil London tragedy I'd been watchin unfold. Everyone except for meself, that is, so I've grabbed Rowena by the 'and as she bustled past wiv er drinks tray empty, and we've 'it the floor for a bit of a knees-up ourselves.

Because from the way Angelika were slidin and shimmyin up and down the kid, and by the way Vernon were treadin all over some fat bird's feet — e's a rubbish dancer at the best-a times — I could see things gettin proper nasty in 'ere any second.

Vern knows better than to cause grief in the club. Not good for business, that aint. I've warned Vernon about 'is wee tiffs in inappropriate settings, and e listened wiv both ears too, cos even 'is sort can remember what's good for em now n then.

But I know that look, and I know 'ow poor Vernon's memory can be when e's got the ump real bad. And maybe e wanted to be sure of doing the kid in front-a the bird too. Right pain in the jacksy at times, Vern is. But like they say, there's a tool for every task and a task for every tool. And I just never seem to run outta tasks for old Vernon.

So I figures I'll just stay close for a bit and de-rail Vern if need be. Course, I could-a just yanked im aside and told im to pull 'is ead in then and there, but if I'm honest I were quite interested to learn ow much e were willin to disrespect me.

And for some reason I also wanted to see ow well that kid looked after imself. I don't mean ow well e'd go in a proper row, because wiv a bloke like Vernon involved, by the time ya realised that the kid weren't gonna do so well, e'd likely ave a burst eardrum on 'is 'ands or nufin more than bite marks where 'is left nut used to be. Na, I just wanted to assess the kid's . . . *awareness*.

But what, between Angelika tryin to use im the same way she uses that pole in er act — im respondin about as sensually as the fucking pole does n'all — and all the ova punters shakin it up around im, never mind wee Vern a few feet away sucking 'is scent into 'is nostrils, I doubt the kid even knew im from anyone else in the gaff yet.

So while I covered meself wiv a prattle of bullshit into Rowena's ear, I kept one eye well peeled on events and moved in closer to the kid every time Vernon did, who was so engrossed in 'is quarry e adn't even noticed me. Meanwhile, Angelika's slinkin seemed to be heatin the pretty cunt up at long last — if it adn't, then I would-a known im to be a rump-wrangler for certain — and as he moulded imself into her I could see that e ad a bit of rhythm in im imself too, the lil bastard. Nufin near the likes-a meself, but presentable enough.

And what'd I say earlier? About never seeing Vernon when e moved? Well, I went and missed it meself n all this time. Thanks mostly to the strobe coming on, e were on to the kid before I could stop im. Surprised the shit outta me, though, cos all e seemed to do was shove into im a bit. Now I know Vern's no knife-merchant, but I 'arf expected to see pretty boy slump to the wood wiv claret gushing past 'is fingers. But no, e were fine, just a bit surprised.

Then I 'eard Vern growl at the kid, 'Watch where you're tangoing, Romeo. That's strike one, yeah?' As if the kid had bumped into *him*. And then Vern's spun away as if e actually ad some interest on the floor outside of a four-foot radius around pretty boy.

E were right taken aback about it too, the lil pansy. And so he should-a been, cos if e couldn't see what Vern were up to, e were too green to ever be let down the corner shop, let alone in 'ere.

As for me, well, I relaxed right away. Felt a little touched n all, if I'm honest. Cos Vern ad no intention of makin a pig of imself against orders again, ad enough respect for me not to do it. E were just gonna scare the kid off wiv the old 'three strikes' psych-out, show im up for a nonce in front-a the bird. And I ad no bova wiv that.

She surely adn't been ere long enough to see Vern work 'is 'three-strikes' laugh on a geezer, but either one of the ova girls ad told er about it, or someone'd just told er enough about Vern for er to work it out erself, cos she stopped dancin as if er feet was in. The kid were trying to shrug it off, but that were just for er sake, cos if there's one thing I know, it's what fear looks like, and I could see the bottle droppin out of im like e were fucking see-fru. She tried to lead im off the floor, but e made imself pull er back. She fired some words into 'is ear, but e were all soothing shrugs, and a few sentences later e managed to get er dancin again.

They was a shadow of their former selves, though, dancin. She couldn't stop looking round for Vern, and the kid's efforts *not* to look were fucking ear-splittin.

Almost anyone who knows anythin at all about Vernon and gets to 'strike one' wiv the geezer would either streak from the place wivout finishin 'is drink, or at the very least get 'is ead down round a table somewhere. Being a stranger ere, the kid didn't know that, and 'is pride wouldn't let im scarper in front-a the bird. I could see clear as day though that once the pansy reached 'strike two', e'd cut 'is losses lively.

Two minutes later it appened, same as last time, Vern shoving into the kid's back. Only thing different was that when the kid looked round Vern didn't bova snarlin at im again, just eld up two fingers and stared.

That were it for Angelika. She wanted off the floor. The kid did too, only 'is dose of the shits were so bad e motioned for er to wait a minute, and then went over to Vern wiv 'is hands up to make a bit-a peace.

I were pretty close by, and e ad that look on 'is face that's the sole property of poofs, 'airdressers and Eye-talians. My old man pointed the look out to me a long time ago. He never taught me just ow much milkin can be done on those who own such looks — discovered that one all by meself — but e made bloody sure I burned mine nice n early.

Please, sir, I don't want any trouble.

I come in peace.

Take what you like and leave.

I wasn't sure wheva to vomit or jump the queue. As for Vern, when the kid leaned down to apologise in 'is ear, e just stood there relishin every pretty muscle of it, sneaking glances at the bird n all . . .

. . . Which may've been why e never once moved when the kid said, 'Strike three,' and drilled an upper cut fair under Vern's chin.

Arf the club must've 'eard Vern's teeth clackin together, and as 'is legs buckled and dropped im, through my shock I'm thinkin, 'Vern, my son, you and your tongue should be thankful e didn't get you talkin first . . . like you woulda done to im.'

And lookin at im lyin there, so peaceful for once, I thought of the amount of people round London who'd've been very interested to spend some time wiv Mr Vernon Davies right about then. In amongst the open mouths, I could feel a few sets of ears in *ere* startin to prick up n all.

As for the kid, e might not've ad a scooby doo about wot e'd *actually* gone and done, but e were smart enough to know that clumpin geezers spark-out in clubs won't win you favour wiv management too often. Wiv the bird on 'is 'eels, e were marchin imself right past me, 'eadin for the door, when I grabbed im by the arm.

'What's ya rush, son?'

'. . . Beer in here's a little flat.'

'How bout a brandy then?'

'. . . Who are you?'

'I'm the guvna ere. This is my gaff.'

'. . . Are you gonna kill me?'

'. . . Prob'ly not, no.'

'. . . Balloons or high-balls?'

That were the start of it. I got a coupla the lads to whisk Vernon away, and I sat down and ad a drink wiv the kid. Then a couple more — no angle or nufin, just liked 'is spirit. Though it didn't take me long to work out that behaviour like what e'd just shown were out-a character. News that morning of a death in the family back in Aussie and a day spent cryin in a bottle had brought that on.

Anyway, it were only when e quietly let me know that e ad knock-off console games for sale that I ad any kind-a tingle for business from im. So I sniffed some more info out of im, not giving a monkey's what e *thought* we was talkin about.

And whadya fucking know! I've only gone and hit a reef, int I!

5

ALEX

That's something you must always bear in mind with a job, especially one in a big workplace: when the current situation's bad — for you personally, I mean — you should take heart in the fact that the dynamic is bound to shift sooner or later. I mean, I *hated* this place for those first two weeks, loathed the very thought of it. The prospect of another eight hours in here each morning was soul destroying. I would definitely have quit if I hadn't been so desperate for the cash, so desperate for a reason to get out of that hostel. And now — how much later: about a month, five weeks? — now I can't get enough of the joint.

I take out my safety knife and dig it into the layers of plastic wrap holding this pallet of Xbox games together; walk around it full circle, the blade humming sweetly. Rip the plastic off and scrunch it up into a football-sized bundle, hide it behind another pallet. The labels on the sides of the boxes — 15 games per box, 50 boxes per pallet — tell me there's three different titles of game on this one, which means I'll have to split them down in order to make an accurate count. No worries, bit of labour's a good tonic for the cold. There's no way of heating a warehouse this size — three hundred metres by two hundred; no cost-effective way at least. There's a pile of empty pallets on the far side of the Goods In floor, and I head across to them, weaving through the rest of the stock. All this glorious work that needs doing will keep us busy till knock-off, piece of piss.

An empty pallet's reasonably heavy, so I build up some speed as I drag it over, the scrape of the wood filling my arms, warming the bones, briefly drowning out Virgin FM in the speakers nestled high above, amongst the neon lighting, the sprinklers, the security cameras.

I'm halfway through stacking all the Commando-18s on to the new pallet when Harry and Greg come dawdling back from the direction of the canteen. Sixth fag break of the shift for those two. Not that I mind. And they know I don't. Nothing's been said specifically, but I've made it clear enough. I'm the only team leader anywhere near our area on a night shift — never mind the managers, I'd be surprised if there's more than one in the building (back at uni the joke was that no manager worth his salt should get stuck working nights) — and so long as we're on target to clear the floor by sun-up they can take all the breaks they want.

Because when we're snowed under, like last night, they don't need to be told what the deal is.

Harry's an odd sort. One of those thirty-something working-class Poms who still live with their parents. I've met a few of them who do. No ambition to do much more in life than read *The Sun*, watch football, and spend a week each year surrounded by others just like them on a package holiday resort somewhere. He seemed quite baffled when he learned that a kid raised on nurse's wages — me — had found his way into management. He couldn't swallow the concept, kept looking for qualifiers.

Harry returns to the pallet he's nearly finished splitting, and Greg heads for his fork-lift. As soon as they're out of my line of sight I pick up the plastic ball I made a minute ago, harden it up with a few extra scrunches. Harry turns and sees what I'm doing, stands back to adjudicate as I take aim. Good shot too, better than the last one — you don't field at point all your life if you can't hit the stumps now and then — and the ball collects Greg in the back of the scone. He jolts forward, and the cup of tea he's holding spills over his jersey.

I hadn't counted on that, and while Harry hoots up a storm, a shot of regret goes through me. How would *that* look? Two weeks into my team-leader promotion and my horseplay sends one of my charges to hospital with second-degree burns. But Greg's grinning as he turns and levels a dire finger.

'Your card's marked, arsehole. Count on that.' Walking away, slapping liquid off his chest, sing-songy: 'When you expect it least, expect it the most.'

I've seen a lot of Greg since moving into the house, he and I being the only two on nights, and working in the same section as well. He's got a sense of humour and a half. A long memory too: I'll be lucky if I get the better of him tonight. After all, he invented the game. But then again, Greg claims to have invented the phrase 'excuse my French'.

The totals on my pallet match the paperwork perfectly — which is mildly disappointing: tracing discrepancies, my job alone, is a good challenge and good training — and I decide to make the long march to the toilets before beginning another. We're located in the north-western corner of the building, where the stock's brought in through the big doors — a wide yard outside for the trucks to pull into — and where the main entrance leads through to the security complex where the body searches, surveillance and signing-in get done. There's a toilet across from us, on the north-eastern side, behind the multimedia pick-face, but sometimes I prefer to stroll down to the other one, in the bottom corner of the warehouse. It's taking the piss a bit really, the extra walking time, but like I said, we've got things covered for this shift and only one more delivery booked in before knock-off.

Even at 3 a.m. on a sub-zero morning, certain sections of the warehouse are humming. I won't deny it: the sights, the sounds, the smells, the cooperative energy of this place — and there are maybe two hundred people working even on a quiet night like this — get my skin tingling. EUE (European Union Entertainment) is an entertainment goods distributor — middleman to the manufacturer and retailer — and they've got the market cornered. Almost every piece of music, software, every gaming console and game, video and DVD on a shop shelf in this country was fed through the systems of this building. Isn't that amazing? I scarcely believed it when I was told, couldn't credit any one workplace with so vast a claim.

But then I went over the figures, realised it was true.

Arriving at work the next day felt like entering a church.

Long before I crossed the equator for the first time (cracked a single-shot rum in commemoration, the only one awake in the cabin, glued to the progress map) I'd known full well that the industries driving the economy of this nation made our own look rustic. I'd naturally hoped to win first-hand experience of this, pad my CV with distinctions simply not available in New Zealand. It felt elusive for those first few weeks. But then to start work here, to suddenly see all the figures and tables compressed into one steel and glass building — *this* building — well, that had set my head spinning.

I sometimes see life as a figure in my path, twice my size and unyielding. In one hand it's got a big sword resting on its shoulder, ready to swing in an instant. I can't see its face behind the visor, and the suit of armour it wears looks impregnable. Realising what this warehouse stood for was like spotting a big patch of rust in the centre of that figure's breastplate.

But this warehouse — and the countless others like it — offers hope not only to graduates. It's the simplest thing in the world to get a job in here; you don't even need fluent English. The workforce is a visual delight, a human map of the late British Empire, ages along a bottom-heavy spread from seventeen to seventy. And there's the Europeans too, London drawing Continental youth as surely as it does colonial. From St Petersburg to San Sebastian, young writers, skaters, students, ravers, artists, here for their futures or for 'personal development'. EUE gives them work in less than a day if they're not fussy.

As for the colonials, we cousins from the South . . .

Our predecessors laid the groundwork in the seventies and eighties, and now we're a cornerstone of these places. Work as hard as any ex-salt miner, then drink a Dutch DJ under the table. Skimming invisible fences, no concept of any class structure, lacking the social antennae, so not bound by it. And so much in common with the Brits running the show. This ensures that few Southerners who start here remain on the bottom rung for long. A lot of them work as supervisors — supes — for Labour Save, the outfit which provides the shop-floor workers. Some are offered full-time EUE contracts or skilled temping.

And the rest? They just leave. If you've got good English and a reference or two, it won't take you more than four weeks to find a decent job in London.

I see two of the Labour Save supervisors, Murphy and Trent, down the way a little, engaged in a 'focus session' with Justin and Jeremy, full-timers with Allocations. Jeremy's got a pallet of audio CDs on an electric pump-cart, and the two supes have requisitioned it for seating purposes. Night shift or not, this sort of thing's just not on: slacking off for a gasbag in full view of a temp shift hard at it. Not my section, though; they can hold a four-way limbo-a-thon for all I care.

I feel like heading over and joining in for a minute, but Jeremy and Justin are virtual strangers to me, so I quicken my pace, engrossed in the earth-shattering importance of the check-in sheet in my hand—

Murphy, near a shout: 'Oi, Al? What, no toime for the troops now tat you've made the brass, is tat the craic, is it? Fucking shameful behaviour, by Jaysus.'

Trent: 'Yeah, let's not see you go down the same road as the rest of the high-fliers, Alex: scheming your grand schemes' — putting a solemn arm over Justin's shoulder — 'neglecting the beating heart of the company hard at it down here, we who brave the trenches.' He sniffs back a sob, and Jeremy's patting him on the back consolingly.

I'm grinning as my feet change course.

6

RYAN

It's 6.27 by the time I walk through the front gates. Supposed to start at 6.00, when the night shift knocks off, but one of the cool things about starting at bird-fart is that the fresh sign-in sheet at the security window is always empty, leaving me free to put down any time I fucking well like. Go with 5.45 today. An extra half hour's pay, thank you very much. Which, considering the wages I'm on, won't exactly have my bank manager creaming himself any time soon. Not sure why I bother really.

Speaking of which, can't remember if Amy's working Security today so I casually ask Todd about it. He informs me that she's starting at 7.30. Todd's such a dopey cunt I could probably've asked him *uncasually* and not worried about it. If the dude was any dumber you'd have to water him. No departure really: Andromeda, the mob EUE contract their security out to, pay their bottom level less than I make, and as a consequence most of them are thicker than *War and Peace, Large Print Edition*.

Between shifts the place is almost dead. Cunt of a big place, this, and at this time of year, this time of morning, she's as cold as all fuck, the company far too tight to heat it for us, those who matter well sorted in their offices. Trent's writing behind the Slave Labour sign-in desk, and I just rock straight past him. I hear his pen stop scratching as he sees me though.

OK, as the first of the Goods In crew into the building there's a few responsibilities that naturally fall to me. The first is to head down to the canteen and make sure the coffee machine's working. Check. The second is to make sure the heating's on in the smoking room. Check again. In a spurt of conscientiousness, I light up again and monitor the heater for another ten minutes. Then I fire up the lights and heaters in our pre-fab office in the warehouse's top corner before checking the book for any early deliveries: negative.

Excellent.

Out on the floor I ram a pump-truck into an empty pallet, jack it up, then head down to the multimedia pick-face, a long series of shelves, five high. Replenishment load them with stock from the rear and the units roll down to the front as the sheep shuffle around picking them, filling boxes with whatever their computated directives instruct. There's a six-digit number marking each small section of shelf; each number corresponds to a single title.

There's no good reason for me to be here. I sometimes have legit business on the other side of the shelves — bringing priority stock straight down from Goods In, bypassing bulk storage — but the pick-face itself is no concern of mine.

No official concern anyway.

Of course I could easily get what I need from bulk storage, the high racking where the pallets themselves are housed. I spend half my day in and out of there on a fork-lift. But that's exactly why I *don't* claim my fringe benefits from there.

Lesson 34: Shit not in thine own nest.

Numerical inconsistencies discovered here, on the other hand, could've been the handiwork of three or four different departments, any number of people.

I take out a sheet of paper with a few location numbers on it that tell me exactly where I can find the titles I want, the unreleased stuff. I looked them up yesterday morning on a computer, entering the in-house network that we temps aren't issued passwords for, and I've soon built up a nice little pile of games on my pallet.

If they're ever gonna have a crack at an informal pay-rise, working along the pick-face is about the best opportunity most of the sheep in this place will ever get: the supes are made to run too tight a ship for any decent fiddles to develop. Hence the phalanx of cameras jutting from the roof in this area.

But I personally don't give a flying fuck if they're *all* lined up on me.

Well . . . perhaps some of me does. Can't show it though; this is all about lethargy, boredom, yawning, counting fake figures on your fingers, cursing when a tally doesn't match the paperwork in your hands, a 'this-sux, I don't wanna be here' pout. Without the right ingredients at the right mix, without the will not to glance up — *not even once* — or to flinch when a body walks by . . .

And gathering the games is the easy part. A few hours from now and it's time to try and smuggle them out, time to complete the dance, your tango with Security when someone will lead and someone will get fucked.

I'm exaggerating a little. It's not as bad as all that, at least not for me. Not any more. Amy sees to that. But the stakes aren't small — 'Company Policy is to prosecute EVERY act of larceny' — so as soon as Security unmask another tea leaf the Old Bill are instantly summoned. And sure, the Met'll take an hour to show if you're half-conscious and bleeding on a doorstep down Peckham way, groaning into a mobile, but they'll be here to lift a pilferer so quickly the Tardis could be involved. And the first stop you'll be making in the panda car is your humble abode.

And I tell ya, no matter what I happen to be collared with at the time, should the OB ever shake my fucking *room* down, it'll mean a lot more than a slap on the wrist and no reference.

Lesson 37: *Keep your gaff clean.*

A luxury I sadly don't have.

So I run this thing at maximum prudence, stay sharp.

And also because allies in games like this can be mercurial. Few developments in this world will test a relationship better than fixing the prospect of a little porridge to the end of one.

Lesson 38: Trust no one.

Weekly bonus in order, I quit the pick-face, heading back through one of the bulk-storage aisles, high and narrow and camera-less. I throw my games on top of a storage pallet and pretend to write down the location number.

Goods In's still dead. At the corner of our area there's a shady nook between the end of two rows of racking. But for a small door, we've all but sealed it off with shelves and pallets and point-of-sale displays. We furnished it a bit, and as far as havens in this building go, this place is number one by a long shot. I don't care how rotate-able and zoom-able the company congratulates itself on its cameras being, until those super-dicks invest in some X-ray eyes there'll be no perving on what takes place in here going on.

We keep our jackets and shit in here, take most of our breaks here too — both flagrant violations of company policy — but we're careful to hide things, keep the haven free of the signs of habitation, keep the chairs stacked like they're in storage; tend a hidden bolt-hole into the aisle.

Lesson 43: Egress, egress, egress.

Most bosses don't even know this place exists. I don't even think Security know. But our old team leader, Jack, Cardiff's finest, he used to know. It was his idea in the first place. Not cut from your standard managerial cloth, our Cardiff.

Miss the big prick, I must say. I used to wind him up about English subjugation big time, asking him how things were in 'the Principality' whenever he returned from home. Tell ya what, you'll search long and hard to find a Welshman proud to refer to his country as a fucking *Principality*, or to old Charlie as his Prince. What a disgusting piss-take of an anachronism. Poor Taff bastards. Why hasn't all that shit just become unacceptable to the civilised world, the way evolving times left South African apartheid so Dark Ages that the world wouldn't tolerate it any more?

The company uses two team leaders to run Goods In, one in the office and one on the floor. But when Cardiff and Bianca from Accounts started getting it on, the big Welshman lost the plot. Or perhaps he found it. Ran off with her to Oz for some long-term backpacking; chucked in his job and career without a week's notice. Not to mention his mortgage and marriage. Got married far too young anyway, the stupid prick.

Anyway, because this happened at the flattest time of year and we've got a pretty solid crew at the moment, they haven't replaced Cardiff yet. And Tina from Grimsby, our office team leader, is seldom to be seen outside the warmth of her small dictatorship. So the haven's safe for now.

Of course Alex is team-leading Goods In over night shift, and when it picks up again he might end up taking Cardiff's spot on days. Which could suck. Haven't seen much of him since he moved in, but he seems more chilled than I'd picked him. If he's said anything about the fact that the week-night pastime of choice in the house is smoking spliffs and playing hot games and DVDs, then I haven't heard about it (though I doubt he's put two and two together regarding the latter yet). But if he ends up on days with us I'd be very surprised if he'd be willing to let the haven endure.

Because quite aside from whatever petty rule violations the

haven constitutes, if Security were ever to employ someone who doesn't exhibit the symptoms of mild brain damage and he/she were to find this place and spike it with a small camera, before the week was out about six of us would be nipple-deep in the brown stuff.

Inside the haven, I pull aside a life-size cardboard cut-out of Angelina Jolie and climb up and retrieve the box of fringe benefits I just stashed there from the far side.

Late in the day I'm driving me fork-lift past an empty admin desk in Allocations when the in-house phone starts ringing. It's for me. I've no business here except transit. But in-house phones scattered around the warehouse quite often start ringing as I'm making my way past them.

I hit the anchors and pull up beside the desk, close enough to grab the receiver without having to dismount.

'Ryan! My petty pilferer of preference!'

I haven't seen Amy all day — though she's certainly seen me; she's probably watching me right now; I feel like I can feel it — so I have to sit back and feign amusement at her 'how droll and cocky am I?' small talk for a few minutes.

Amy's a league above the other Security muppets: that is to say, her vocabulary extends beyond 'Duh'. She stuck out the bottom level for a few weeks, then fluked a promotion to shift coordinator when her old-fart boss got culled by a company hissy-fit at missing-stock levels. Her rise to 'the top' is deliciously ironic to the few of us in the know, because you supposedly need a spick and span sheet to get so much as a cleaning job with Andromeda, let alone a shift coordinator's gig. Given that Amy's moral code might've been modelled on Fagan's, her promotion is either a black dot on the company's vetting procedures or glowing testimony to her skills.

She gets to the point at last: I tell her what time I did the bizzo on the games this morning (she's no Scorsese with footage but her critics are less zealous) and exactly what time I'm gonna be signing out. She reminds me of the order she placed with me a couple of days ago. You see, Security may have the run of the place — a mandate to snoop wherever, whenever — but they've got no credible reason to spend time handling stock.

Unlike my tireless self.

Symbiosis, huh? Sublime to be a part of one.

Jim's outside the haven door, keeping watch for me. Drop my baggy jeans and tape one game to the rear of my thigh, another to the other thigh (murder on the leg hairs once). Two more games go down the front of me jeans as I pull them up. One each into the jacket's deep pockets, and four into a special pocket I've sewn into the jacket's bottom rear. The last two go into the folded newspaper I'll carry.

I let myself do this just twice a week. It's hard, though. Greed's got a croon like a mermaid's. Back in the days of personal use, when the game's boxes and booklets and cases were surplus, I could get two units out — down my crotch — and barely break a sweat even if Security sprung a body search on me.

How times have changed.

Eleven games. Two for Amy, nine for me. A while ago nine games could have taken me a week to unload, slogging around the city after work on travel cards. These days I'm sitting pretty. Melvyn takes anything unreleased at a set rate. Massive slice of luck meeting that dude.

Jim tells me I'm clear, so I slip out, then turn down an aisle, taking the quietest route to Security and the two curtained-off areas at the bottom of the room for male and female searches. Ring the buzzer and wait. Sometimes — like when a Slave Labour shift has just finished and they're all queuing to be searched — ya can't move in this place, but today it's empty. Knocking off on the quarter-hour ensured that.

Amy pokes her nose through the doorway from Security's inner sanctum. But instead of waving me straight through, she grins a little and her tongue flicks across her lip.

I know that look — and have to fight not to shudder at it.

Because in return for her complicity Amy sometimes demands more from me than just stock and backhanders. Which wouldn't be a problem . . . did the woman not look like she hails from the fiery pits of Isengard.

She ogles me up and down, and my old boy's cowering in a corner in the fetal position, ready to confess to anything.

But as much as it kills me to admit it, sex is at the core of our arrangement; was the catalyst and glue.

Amy flirts more nakedly than any woman who looks like her should ever have the gumption to. Loves the cock and has no dramas asking for it. So from the moment she started work here I knew full well that she wanted into me Reg Grundys. All this combined to see me very nearly come unstuck in the search-room one day. To any normal person the crotches of strangers are off limits, so a CD or two down the front of your daks should survive even thorough pat-downs. But nature or nurturing forgot to equip Amy with this grace, and she was laughing as she copped a full feel that first day she searched me. The laughter froze in her throat when she realised there was more on the go down there than a well-travelled yoghurt-thrower.

Would've been her first bust, and — unsecret admirer or not — she was clearly stoked to be getting her Brownie-point account underway. But, panicking, I seized her arm as she reached for the phone; told her she didn't wanna do that.

She's a feisty working-class cunt. 'Why the fuck not?'

I pushed her against the wall and pinned her. 'Because then

you'll never see me again.'

'. . . So what?'

But I could see her lung-warts fluttering, and with the courage of the desperate I put my hand between her legs, made an educated guess at the doorbell's whereabouts. She gulped. So I rang it again, harder; rubbed my nose against hers.

She broke free, but only to drag me out by my hand, into her office around the corner.

Wasn't that bad a shag actually. Circumstance sure spiced it up: I'd never screwed me way *out* of trouble before. I could've used a pair of dark glasses — if not a blindfold — and I lived in sheer terror of the lads finding out for months afterwards, but to avoid prosecution and deportation I would've been prepared to screw worse.

Maybe.

Our business venture has its roots in that office.

I do all that I can to keep my pants on around her. She knows I can't stand her physically — she may be vile but she's not fucking blind — but she doesn't give a shit about that, and from time to time she'll try and blackmail another bonk out of me. Not often that the male member of the equation feigns orgasm, yeah? Gets headaches and doesn't feel very sexy right now.

It's been a few weeks, and as she stares at me now I'm groping for a convincing excuse. But then I see her eyes flick at something behind me, see her frown — someone else here to sign out — and she reluctantly waves me to the exit.

My narrow escape has me sparing Todd some hearty platitudes as I sign out through the window and walk through the wire, turn for the station. I guess the hard-work bonus I just had away adds to the cheer too. *That*'s more the kind of thing that'll please my bank manager. At least it would if I intended letting it anywhere near the cunt's nimble fingers.

Lesson 56: Bank no funds which can't be legally accounted for.

7

MELVYN

Thing is, I've ad enough, me. That's what it comes down to. I can't complain, I've done better out of it than most of the mugs involved. Done less than four years' bird all told. Worked me own hours, then worked for meself. And had a lot of laughs along the way.

Ad its downs too, of course, like anythin. Getting shot at weren't no lark. Getting hit once were even worse, like getting whacked by a sledgehammer swung by Thor im-fucking-self. Farewellin friends in the courtroom and the undertakers. An OB tail so fucking persistent I ended up invitin em in for tea cos it would-a been out of order not to.

Unable to 'old on to birds I loved cos of all the fucking baggage.

But I've sure as shit got nufin to moan about.

Fact o' the matter is, though, that every ride 'as to come to an end. Sooner or later. You either get off or it throws you off. Kinda like a gun footballer nudgin past 'is early thirties. If e mistimes it, angs on too long, 'is form can slip, 'is fans turn, and suddenly a few let-downs on the pitch finish up being 'is fucking legacy wiv the small-minded cunts. Or e can cop a bad injury, spend the rest of 'is knock in pain, creditors doggin im to an early grave.

But it aint creditors you ave to worry bout in my line o' work. Well, none who rent premises on high streets anyway. The wolves in wait for a bloke of my wee vocation who outstays 'is welcome ride round in panda cars. And the longer you stay at it, the greater the chance of some cozza getting smart or lucky, or some slag pullin a stroke, rollin over or turnin fucking Queen's. Even though I *ave* managed to make a decent bit of scratch at this wivout lettin me profile grow too big — cos, I tell ya, those who let it go to their ead and go the ova way may roar fru life like a fucking sky rocket for a bit, but the crash at the end seldom differs. Na, take it from me, the most successful crooks ave been, and always will be, the last names you will ever 'ear spoken in a fucking 'household'.

So I done what I could to furva meself wivout givin the Met too many reasons to unt me down, but I been workin a long while now, init, and the law of averages alone becomes more of an enemy to me by the monf.

Then there's the competition . . .

Not somethin I like to talk about beyond those I've come to trust more than me own old dear — and that number's a fuck of a lot smaller than the digits on both 'ands — cos this is one game where you do *not* want to be givin the wrong signals. But just between you and me, things 'ere aint what they was. Used to be a code, see. Sure, there'd be tear-ups, but there were certain dos and don'ts, and the trouble most often arose when those who ad crossed a line got sorted for it. We all ad our manors, you worked ya way up, you stitched someone up if you didn't like im or ad more mates than im, or maybe you found a niche of your own that didn't tread on toes bigger than yours, and Robert was your old dear's bruva. Yeah, we ad Chinks, and later on Yardies, who wanted to, ammm, cut a few corners in life — and I tell you this for nufin, you did *not* go messin wiv those geezers unless you was very, *very* sure what you was about — but they ad their flocks to fleece, we ad ours, and rarely would the twain meet, let alone tangle. Even the Pakis and that, the Arabs and Africans, when they began to work ere, old country firms branching out and diversifying — as is their right in my mind: their people, their prerogative — even these geezers showed due respect, kept out of our markets unless invited. Things evolved and re-adjusted wiv the times, but on the 'ole it were business as usual.

But suddenly we've got these fucking Eastern cunts coming out our eyeballs. And these pricks are just arseholes, plain and simple. Ruskies, Latvians, Albanians, all of them former labourers from the workers' paradises. It's like they've been starved of opportunities for so long that they're paralytic drunk just on the air over ere. Like kids raised in a workhouse, then let loose in Willy Wonka's chocolate factory. You don't even ave to give em an inch for em to take ten miles. Maybe the sub-groups operate wiv some semblance of protocol among themselves, but I seriously fucking doubt it.

I don't even like to call em ard bastards, cos they aint. They're just nutters. Hard bastards feel fear; they just keep it on a leash till it's needed. These cunts feel nufin. No problems for em to lure birds over ere wiv bullshit, then lock em in a cellar and make em turn tricks day and night. Slavery in London in the twenty-first century — fucking disgusting. No problems for one of em to get done in a row in a pub, then firebomb the ova bloke's parents' gaff at four in the mornin, or to drag some kid into an alley after work and do him with bricks cos e pinched the wrong bird's bum by the smoko truck.

And this is all first hand.

Don't get me wrong, if you've got the bottle, I'm all for you takin a bigger slice of the pie than society 'as deemed you can ave — we can't all go to uni or slave our way into management, and I aint never bought a lottery ticket in my fucking life — but not at the expense of every ova geezer in the same boat as you.

And these clowns just want more and more.

Unlike the ova migrant crims in London, these guys aren't appy wiv just parasiting off their own kind. They see anybody — *anybody* — as an opportunity. No matter who might run the area, or make up the spread, these vultures will sniff till they find an angle, strong-arm their way into it, then control dissent and competition wiv lessons learned from Comrade fucking Stalin.

I mean, for Christ's sake, who would've thought a decade or so ago that Soho — fucking *Soho*, vice capital of the UK, playground of the rich and unattractive from Dartford to Dreyton — who could possibly've predicted that a little after the turn of the century good old *Soho* would be under the control of Albanians? *Albanians*! It's just ludicrous. 'Ow it was allowed to appen I do not know, but the fucking *Albanians* ave good old *Soho* sewn up tighter than a broke Jock's ringpiece.

And the thing is, if you see em comin and nip it in the bud some'ow, they'll regroup and come back. Then come back again. As often as it takes. These cunts just do not give a fuck.

Even the OB have a shit of a job combatin em. I've seldom in me life rooted for the cozzas — in fact *or* fucking fiction — but they're on an 'iding to nufin so far. Gettin these pricks to grass on each ova is even arder than it ever was in my circles. They speak a different lingo and ave different customs, so it's arder to track em and keep tabs on em. Then you've got these trustafarian wankers wiv bugger all better to do kickin up a civil liberties shit-storm cos the wrong ones sometimes get lifted.

Na, this epidemic has grown well beyond the control of the Met. Even the Yard are stymied. So old muggins ere finds imself avin dealings wiv the cunts more and more by the day.

And I've ad enough of it, int I. More than enough. Time to punch out.

8

LISA

There's so many tourists milling around I'm able to slip the gates at Charing Cross tube without harassment. A quick hike up the stairs and I'm here: Trafalgar Square.

Seems a gross name for such a grand place, because I doubt there was anything grand about the Battle of Trafalgar. At least not if you were a bushwhacked boy tending a cannon with your eyes streaming, your ears battered numb, and burning canvas sticking to your back. Agonising death just inches away. I imagine the officers pulling the strings with four courses and a good claret in their bellies got rather more of a bang out of it though. As did their venerable fathers back home.

Back here.

England continues to commemorate that battle, to *celebrate* it. Is it just me, or is that seriously fucked up?

I do like it here though, one of the few places in the central city free of ads, of technicolour trickery, corporate clone stores. I find the sight of the flag of the Rainbow Nation atop South Africa House comforting as well. Cross to Nelson's Column — you people got *so* ripped off when god was handing out heroes named Nelson — duck under the rail running around it. The first level of the statue's plinth is about five feet high, but I know what I'm doing: get a run up, kick off a low niche and — *youth* — vault my bum up over the edge. Some of the tourists eye me coldly, imagining I'm tarnishing their London experience by breaking the law to get closer than they. A few of the younger ones, though, take my leap as an ice-breaker, follow me up, and I'm happy to share my stage with them.

Four huge lions mark each corner of the plinth. Hilarious how the rarest creature in England remains its national animal, its symbol of choice. It's like Malaysia or Zambia enshrining the polar bear. I walk around to the base's southern edge, careful not to look up; climb up the next two levels, then plonk myself down, dropping the daypack beside me, my back towards a plaque reading: *England Expects Every Man Shall Do His Duty*. I picture the bold souls who issued that proclamation, hard at their own duties in sumptuous state rooms, the finest food and drink and whores the Empire could provide, playing the greatest game ever devised by megalomania.

I fish out my pre-rolled spliff and spark the baby.

There's something really tickling about blowing out in a place like this, a few metres away from one of *the* prime locations on the hit-list of any self-respecting terrorist. The English plutocrats guard themselves with the same reserve they do most things in public: you won't see fleets of tanks and special-force-murderers waving their toys about here. But the net's no weaker for it, I'm sure. The cop cars are numerous enough — and that's just the marked ones; there's usually a chopper or two offending the air overhead somewhere, and as your eye improves you'll see loiterers too sharply dressed to be any kind of loiterer except a secret-section one.

Because as I look up at last and exhale that first plume of smoke, I'm staring straight down Westminster Road, all the way to the Houses of Parliament. Yes, the kilometre stretching in front of me is nothing less than the penultimate nerve-centre of this top-heavy world of ours.

When I first arrived here I dossed in a studio in Camden for a few weeks. I was working at Victoria and used to catch a 24 bus, which stopped outside my door. Just another commuter in the world. Except that my commute happened to take me down through Camden on to Charing Cross Road, past Soho and Leicester Square, around the roundabout enclosing Trafalgar Square, turning right on to Westminster Road, past Downing Street, and then past Big Ben and the Houses of Parliament, all within a few minutes of boarding, traffic allowing.

Twice a day, a pound each way. That was a spin-out, that was. I felt like a character in a Dickens novel.

For about two weeks.

I still get a thrill from this part of London, though. It's just rooted in something less ingenuous these days. Something brooding and foul.

My joint's finished, so I flick the roach and shoulder my bag, everything blowing my mind that little bit extra, a small headache underneath it. I've jumped down from here a hundred times, but I still feel as if everyone's watching me, trying to snag my feet and my balance with their attention. But my soles slam cleanly on the concrete.

Same thing crossing the road, though, checking left and right four times even though it's a one-way system and I've got a green pedestrian light, checking again because my buzz tells me I missed a grey transit van and it wants to bounce me eight feet high. It's not there, and the pressure eases as I bustle past some rich Italians and on to the footpath.

Then a different tension starts singing within me as I start down the road. I'm searching the faces of the crowds, but none of them seem to realise where they are, to hear the silent evil ticking around them. The buildings down here are less flashy than those around the square. They're just as big though, maybe bigger, and a lot more imposing. Except for the windows. You can never see far past the blinds, but they look for all the world like normal rooms, places of carpet and desks, chairs and shelves. There are no runes on the glass, no pentagrams on the ledges. I even saw a woman come to one once, and she looked exactly like a human. They all do. But she was surely one of the Brokers, because offices over-looking this road are not assigned to humans. Humans have no place behind these windows. Any human asked to work on the things that go on in these rooms would leap from the ledge within a fortnight.

There's a dull throbbing beginning in my temples, and a kind of subliminal drone disturbing the air, vibrating between the walls, filling the road with an intangible hum. Ears can't detect it, but my skin and my bones and my spirit can feel it. Far too strong for the noise of the traffic to impinge on its business. And far too sly to rise higher. Not yet.

I can feel my headache feeding off it.

I stop and lean against the cold granite of one of these nameless buildings, and the drone kicks up a pitch, entering me through this direct touch, and my gaze is drawn to the windows, as inscrutable as eye sockets in a skull. I try to read the drone, inter-pret its affairs, let it tell me a little of what its servants in human costume, its batteries, are up to behind their blinds and their curtains.

But the drone wants to watch me collapse, right here, watch my head crack open and spill out across the ancient flagstones. Yes, the drone and its makers run on alternative fuels. So I jerk into motion, trying to strut down the road as if these monsters don't scare me. But there's no escaping the drone; it grows louder with each step . . .

. . . because within a hundred metres I'm opposite *it*. Opposite nothing less than the lair of a coven of supreme vampires Themselves.

Downing Street.

I can remember when that phrase meant nothing more to me than cigars and tea, goodwill to man, the seat of our lords saviour, defenders of the Good. Even when I first arrived in London, came down here to check the place out, I could hear nothing coming out of there but benevolence and concern. Dear god, what a diet of insidious, vile bullshit I was raised on! There's tourists aplenty, pointing and beaming and snapping at this demonically prosaic little courtyard, so glowingly just, apparently, that it needs no more protection than a ceremonial spiked fence with two unarmed bobbies at the gate. The tourists can't notice the tens of cameras up above, the hidden spooks studying the pores of our faces, the snipers in blacked-out rooms. I doubt the tourists even *see* the cameras. These tourists — I can see it on their faces — they see nothing but what I used to, what we're programmed to see and hear. They feel Churchill hatching audacious plots, delivering us from the Evil Hun; they see Thatcher and her selfless suited warriors, thwarting the Red Beast the world over; they hear Phoney Blair and the Straw-man, all earnestness and anxiety, terrified Saddam's unmanned drones will soon be spraying their 'employers' with anthrax.

But we silenced the drone once. Oh yeah, we shut this awful, bone-numbing buzz *right* the fuck up. Two million of us. What a fucking day that was. Right past here we marched. And as each of us drew level with Downing Street we all had something to say to Them.

A middle-aged man with his daughter in a pushchair: '*Not in her name! Don't you bloody dare!*'

An Indian lady in a sari: '*No blood for oil!*'

Me: '*Can you hear us yet, Phoney!*'

God, it was beautiful. Two massive human snakes, one starting at Embankment around the corner, the other at King's Cross, coming together at Piccadilly Circus for the run into Hyde Park, closing the city to traffic for a good eight hours. A total transcending of the class, race and age divides that They rule through. Made one at last by universal outrage, banding against a common threat to common sense, to common decency, to the morals They pay such glossy lip-service to. Banners and placards and chants led over megaphones. Caricature Shrubya and Phoney masks, TWAT, KILLER, LIAR spelt in fitting black on their foreheads.

And every now and then a roar would build from ahead, gather mass as it sped down towards me, a wordless howl of outrage and passion, unity and commitment sweeping through us like a Mexican wave, an inarticulate cry that enough was enough, turning spectacled schoolmistresses into bellowing barbarians just for a second or three. Fading slowly as it powered on down through the millions.

For the first time in Christ knows how long the drone was silenced that day. The poll-tax riots, the miners' strikes didn't bring a shadow of the scare that day caused in them — because on that day we came in numbers.

And we came in peace.

At last the face of the movement defined its inspirations. Not since Flower Power had peace confronted violence so emphatically, and this neo-movement of ours was so much more than its baby-booming predecessor, so caste transcending, the spontaneous subversion blooming all over the world. This wasn't 'a bunch of stoned kids dropping out': this was a broad cross-section of Society

United. The nightmare of the tyrant from hunter–gatherer days.

The drone's makers were rocked that day. They were nowhere to be seen, though They were surely watching, lurking above us, peeping through gaps in Their curtains, desperately plotting how best to navigate this sea of goodwill. This wasn't what They like; Their less subtle tools were useless against it. They lay in the shadows until sundown. Then one of them appeared again, from the sanctuary of a TV tube, telling the world that official figures for the march — therefore the actual ones, the ones for the history books — were 752,893.

But I was in Hyde Park when Jesse Jackson announced the *real* figures. I was there in the dying light and the low cloud and the biting wind, basking in the collective heat pouring off us. None of us had any idea what we had done until he said it. Even then most of us didn't hear him thanks to Their helicopter which hovered above the stage throughout the speeches, the words from the PA sliced to echoes by its rotor-blades.

'Did he say *two million*?'

He sure as shit did, sisters and brothers! And as word was passed around, as it shocked us and rocked us and tried to sink in, the biggest cheer of the day went up. And up. And up some more, until it felt like we would buffet that infernal chopper right out of the fucking sky.

9

RYAN

Until a few days ago I hadn't been behind the wheel of a car in a good two years. Bugger all of us do over here. Too much hassle and expense in a place where public transport can get you anywhere you need to go (theoretically). And so much piss gets consumed that owning a vehicle is just asking for dramas. I think the sheer size of the place tends to intimidate you too. So I felt a bit caught up in a teenage time-warp yesterday — excited at the freedom upsurge, apprehensive at the 'what ifs' — when I picked the van up from Dessie out at Deptford after Melvyn called me and arranged it.

He insisted I pop into the local nick and change me licence over first, though. I didn't see the need for it personally: I've heard that the Old Bill are pretty forgiving with colonial licences. But I wasn't about to argue the toss with the dude, especially since he said he'd throw the costs in on top of me first pay packet.

Couldn't believe it when the guy offered me work. I'd been back to the club three times since the night I laid out that ferret-faced little windbag. Just to shift a few games to Melvyn. I never hang around, though — I'm scared of bumping into that guy again, and only marginally less scared of bumping into Angelika. But I get on good with Mel, and agreed to some cash work he offered me.

The van's a piece of shit by a normal person's standards, but once I got used to the stiff clutch and accepted that my local naivety didn't automatically qualify me for a ten-car pile-up, I was whizzing round town as proudly as Brockie coming down the Mountain into Conrod. Even found meself revving the engine at lights, mock-swerving at sheilas on the crossings. As if they saw something more than a working-class nobody delivering laundry or something.

The fucking traffic signals threw us for a bit. Rounding a bend into an intersection, seeing the orange light and braking like any decent motorist not in a rush . . . only to find that my wheels had no sooner stopped than the lights changed to fucking *green* and there's smoke coming off the tyres of the car behind as he tries to keep from turning my bumper into a back-brace. I soon realised that the orange signifying 'go, unless the view is agreeable and you'd rather hang around a few seconds longer' actually flashes on and off, so you just treat it like a green and gun it.

With that little piece of protocol sorted I got straight back into it, turned my head to navigation. Which was never going to be a problem for a bloke who's been kicking round town as long as I have. It wasn't long, though, before I was facing up to the fact that tubing and bussing and cabbing do not accurate road knowledge make. Especially the tube: a virtual teleport machine really. Unless my destination was well signposted — seldom — I seemed doomed to a downward spiral of wrong turns, wrong lanes and potential nose-to-tails as the wear and tear on the *A–Z* built up exponentially.

Yesterday was the worst. Knocked off from EUE at three and headed up to Watford. Melvyn needed some Amarula brought down. Getting up there was a piece of piss: A40, North Circular, M25, no worries. I've done this kind of work before, and was expecting the Watford address to be some manner of bonded warehouse. Melvyn hadn't hooked me up with collection paperwork or anything but I thought I'd just give him a call from Watford and get him to sort it over the blower with the dispatch team. Only it wasn't a warehouse I ended up at, it was a fucking pig farm. And this big cunt in a flash suit and Ray-Bans, looking wildly out of place, has come bursting out the front door as soon as he hears the van, as if I'm MI5 or something. Just stood there staring, as though he was a second away from calling artillery in on me. I decided to act like I hadn't noticed. Slipped out of the car and said gidday.

'U the fock are you?'

Northern monkey. 'Here for the Amarula, mate. For Melvyn?'

He didn't move for a while, left me kinda stranded by the van. At last: 'The new boy then, I take it.'

The new boy. Didn't like that. On several levels.

'Just doing a little driving in the evenings.'

This seemed to amuse him some. 'All right, Viduka. Open doors and I'll huv it out in a while.'

About ten minutes later I hear the roller door being yanked open, and two guys come staggering out, straining under one end each of a small pallet. One of them's over fifty if he's a day. Place didn't even have a fork-lift. They were small and slight — a little taller than Dopey — covered in dirt and Christ knows what else, looked vaguely Slavic or Ay-rab underneath. I guessed then that it wasn't MI5 the northern cunt was worried about, more likely Immigration, because if these lads were working in a place like this, doing these sorts of jobs — the old boy was puffing, stumbling on the gravel — if they're doing dogsbody work *here*, then they simply don't have visas. Northerner's probably got a staff of twenty of them, takes rent for the decaying caravans across the way straight out of their two-fifty an hour.

Welcome to the Promised Land.

They got it in the van eventually, me making bloody sure no damage was done — to the booze or to the paint. Working fingers, they wandered off and leaned against a wall, lighting a fag each. A moment later, though, they almost shat themselves in their haste to ditch the durries as the office door opened and Northerner poked his head out. He barked at me to tell Melvyn to phone him in the evening. I asked him where the dispatch sheet was for me to sign, and his only reply was to jut his head forward on its neck a few inches and squint. I stammered a bit at that point. Then asked for the consignment note then.

'Consignment note?' he almost jeered. 'What, to make sure a few don't fall out of van before you get back to clob?'

Which is certainly one of the functions of a con' note. 'Amongst other things.'

A nasal snickering: 'You'll find Melvyn has better anti-theft systems than con' notes, kid.'

Didn't want to ponder that overly as I drove back through Watford and on to the four-lane M25. Xfm were doing the damage — Primal Scream, the Kings of Leon, Placebo — as the traffic started thickening, slowing me down to a weaving 70mph, then 50, then 30. Then I gave up on the weaving as first one lane-change went pear shaped and then another. Soon, thirty miles outside the city and traffic's down to walking pace, or sitting stationary for minutes, every car showing just the one head in it. My first London traffic jam. I wasn't much bothered, better than being stuck in a stopped train. But the music was just getting better and better, I had a little hash over from a few days ago, and I thought that if it's going to take me two hours to get back into town I might as well make an event of it. So I blinkered left and into a service centre, rolled up a doobie and smoked it.

And the drive afterwards was certainly more entertaining for a while. Half an hour later, though, I've stuttered towards an accident which has closed off the far lane, passed it, and found the congestion easing almost immediately, open spaces all around. Only now I'm stoned, and just going the speed limit feels insanely reckless. And I've got the prospect of city navigation in front of me.

Just stay focused.

A notoriously difficult decree to maintain for more than a minute or so when the green's residing in your cranium. I was tootling along in the slow lane, watching Lote Tuqiri score beneath the bar, when I realised that my turnoff now lay at least a mile and a half behind me.

No choice but to go with the flow, hoping a place-name I could orientate from would appear. None did. So I just procrastinated . . . and ended up stuck in the wrong lane, committed to some alien exit.

Full dark fell and I blundered along in a haze of hash and remorse before stopping to find myself on the map. It wasn't good. Got my sense of direction back, set off in a general direction. At least I thought I did, so I was more than a little surprised when I found myself driving past King's Cross fucking Station. During rush hour.

And sure, my driving had been getting better, but I wasn't ready for an assignment of this magnitude. Melvyn hadn't given me a time to be back by, but I had to imagine he planned on selling some of the Amarula to the punters tonight, which gave me about two more hours. Half an hour of which I wasted just finding some-where safe to stop and take a breath, read the map again. I plotted a course but got no more than three turns into it when I caught myself half a second away from steaming up the wrong end of a one-way street. I hit the brakes in time . . . and left myself broad-side across two lanes. Slammed into reverse but no cunt would let me back in.

Fuckfuckfuckfuckfuck . . .

Finally I just went, forced someone to stop, and when he sat on his horn as I graunched into first I suddenly found myself halfway out of the window, giving him the pumped fist and slapped bicep, yelling what he could go and do to himself. I couldn't see him past the glare of his headlights, but his door snapped open straight away, and I judged it best to be on me way.

Then, for the next five minutes, the dope had me convinced that he was following me, intent on a road-rage battering, and I could focus on nothing but the twin points of light in my rear-view, locking my doors for the stoppages, darting down side streets until the road behind was finally clear.

At least five times more lost than I had been. As in: middle of the bush, no path, no compass, no food, no idea. Because even if it wasn't that life-threatening on the face of it, the bigger picture was quite a bit closer to the same footy oval. Because if I let Melvyn down on my first job, that'd be that.

And the odds of me finding another cash employer who paid what Melvyn paid were a fuck of a lot shorter than Dopey. I've been sniffing around for one for a long time, found bugger all paying more than minimum wage. And sooner or later I'm gonna lose it and spit the dummy at one of those suited wankers at the warehouse. Or get sprung for an indiscretion, or . . .

. . . or some EUE pen-pusher's finally gonna realise that my work visa ran out over a year and a half ago. Why else they think I've stayed working there so long is beyond me.

And if you think I'm going home after four years based in Opportunity Central, no career in sight, fuck all more to show than hangovers and hang-ups, a few stamps in a passport, a kaleidoscope of female faces . . .

That straightened me up, calmed me enough to let me face the dilemma again. Or rather it panicked me more deeply. More productively. Because twenty minutes later I was coasting down the A40 with a clear run through to Melvyn's gaff, half an hour up me sleeve.

10

MELVYN

So yeah, I've been liquidatin for some time now. The game just aint what it were, and I'm gettin too old for it any road. I don't envy the young lads I know who are startin out. You can't rely on nufin no more, barely a given in sight — a grotty reflection of today's white economy, I spose — but they'll be takin their chances wivout me, cos there's a villa on the Cote d'Azur wiv my name about to be mown into the front lawn.

I've been quiet about it, but loose ends are knittin togeva nicely. Still got the biggest earner at near full volume — the door contracts at clubs. Still packing the punters into the club most nights, and running card games upstairs. Still got birds dancing at private dos all over the city. And still got me contacts wiv barrow-boys nationwide (i.e. buyers for most anything that comes my way). And that's about it really. Couple-a fingers in some smaller pies, and supplyin the gear on a couple of estates.

Still a blindin earner, that one is. Kills me letting em go. Too many wogs on em now, though. The blacks and the Pakis were always appy to work wiv me, and when it bec̶ weren't really needed no more they ad the brains an̶ to buy me out honourably. These Eastern fucks though . .

Soon as there's a decent infestation of em on an estate the̶ freeze out the incumbent suppliers, then fuck over any punter wh̶ refuses to buy fru em. Leaves me the choice of either uppin sticks and lookin the mug, or makin an example-a someone. Only these fucks don't take too well to lessons; they tend more towards comin back to class mob-handed, tooled-up to fuck, and drowning the faculty in the school pool.

No thanks.

Still, wiv young Kev running the show over on Murdoch, I'm appy to keep me 'and in down there a bit longer. E's a business man, Kev, a stand-up guy too. Get the gear to im on time and at market rate and e's made up. Sure, there's a heap of Easterners on Murdoch now — Albanians too, the worst of the lot of em — but Kev's got the smarts and the balls to keep em in line.

That'll change though. But I'll be well shot of the manor by then.

So yeah, unloaded most of me interests, the old nest egg's looking pretty ealthy, and it's soon to be margaritas, senhoritas and an all-year tan for yours truly.

. . . Only I'm like that footballer on the wrong side of thirty-five, int I. The one who knows that even if a bit of coachin or punditry work comes 'is way when the boots are ung up, odds are it aint gonna be nufin like what e's grown used to. Equations flyin fru me ead day and fucking night: ow long I might ave left on the planet; ow much I've got squirrelled; ow much that'll leave me to play wiv per annum; potential medical bills and what not; gonna want some nice motors to get around in too, and what's life near the water wivout a decent-sized boat to fish and ski and fuck on? Day and night, etc, etc, et-fucking-cetera.

. . . And I don't feel like I've got enough yet.

So what I need's a job. A tasty one. A one-off, back-of-the-net, don't-call-us, kiss-my-arse-Josephine type job.

And them don't grow on trees.

Aint been my style since I were a nipper neither. Same in any business: high return equals high risk. Them flash-in-the-pans'll ave an eye out before you can blink. Whadaya think I done that four-stretch over? Learned me lesson right proper that night. Accumulate, consolidate, then speculate from a position of strength. Only reason I'm still ere and at the top of my lil pile.

Sure, occasionally — if I knew the lads workin ad their nuts screwed on — I've sat tight at the ova end, a wee cut for me troubles, ta very much. But wee cuts aint what I need no more.

Only nufin come up, init. You'd be the biggest mug in the world to send lads into a bank these days. Ditto a security van or jeweller's. I needed to think outside the box, and it just weren't appenin.

Then that fucking toff's come into me life, and by the time I realised what e stood for I could've dug 'is Gran up outta whatever marble tomb she's inside of and given er the shag of er after-life outta sheer fucking gratitude.

Melvyn, old son, after the career you've ad, a slice of luck this juicy at the end of it just should not ave arisen. But it fucking did.

And you'd better believe that I know what to do when that appens.

11

RYAN

I'm apprehensive as hell about the night's 'work' ahead of me — heading over to Neasden to pick her up is one of those journeys you wish wouldn't end — and when I turn a corner and see her leaning against a street light outside a sad little estate, my nerves pull themselves even tauter.

We've never met before. I don't even have a description to go on. But my nerves are sure it's her.

She's wearing a long raincoat and some kind of top hat, a gear-bag at her feet. Can't see her face under the hat brim, but her posture seems to say that she's pissed off about something. Maybe the world in general — a big possibility in her line of work — because I'm only three minutes late. I pull up beside her and turn the music down, slipping into neutral. Flicking the interior light on so she can see me better. Leaning across to wind the window down.

Putting cheerful irony in it: 'You wouldn't happen to be Nadia, would you?'

She barely moves, as if even turning towards the likes of me is beneath her. Strange accent, husky voice: 'Who want to know?'

'I'm Ryan.' Holding my hand out the window.

She ignores it, and for a second I think she's gonna snub me fully, go back to staring up the road as if some other 'attendant' will pull round the corner in a bit.

'I never see you before.'

Give her the grin. 'I never see you before either.'

'You take the piss.'

Ball breaker. 'I'm sorry, I didn't mean to. I just fall back on humour sometimes when I'm nervous.'

'You should fall harder.'

I can feel her hostility wanting to become my excuse to abort the job. And that's out of the question.

'OK, *Ryan.* Tell me who send you and I get in.'

'Melvyn sent me.'

'Where you from?'

Now she's pushing it. 'Australia.'

She slinks off. Not far, though. In the rear-view mirror I see her stop, a phone in her hand. I listen hard for her voice, catch a few numbers and some throaty gibberish, then she's pocketing the blower and slinking back.

What the fuck . . . ?

It hits me. She's phoned someone and given them the van's licence-plate number. I've no idea how to feel about that.

She slides in at last. Closes the door. Changes the radio station.

But I yank the hand-brake on. 'Why did you do that?'

Bored: 'I hate that fucking song. I hear it five time today at my friend place.'

'That wasn't what I meant.'

'What then?'

'Why did you give my details to one of your friends?'

'. . . Why you care?'

Righteous: 'Because I fucking do! Because I've been around long enough not to sit back and ignore it when people I hardly know start weaving shit behind my back.'

She faces me and her chin jerks up, the shadow of her hat receding, giving me a clear look at her face. Pale skin, dark eyes and brows. A bump at the top of her nose. Eyes too wide apart, lips a little pinched. Not very pretty really.

I wonder if this is her first gig. If Melvyn's even laid eyes on her before. Further up the logic tree I start to worry about the reaction of the punters when we walk in and I tell them that *this* is their entertainment for the night.

But then she starts firing words at me, and somehow the force of it, the contortions in her facial muscles, give the ensemble something greater than its parts seem to merit. 'Oh, you been round a while and you not guess why someone with my job would get into car with kind of person who usually do your job — some stranger she never meet before — and not arrange a little of insurance for herself?'

Bitten and beaten: 'Oh . . . No worries . . . That's cool. Didn't think of that.'

For a second it looks like that won't be enough. Then she settles into her seat again. 'You may not seem like others so far, Mr Ryan Australia, but *I* been round a bit too. Now drive, for fuck's sake, I hate being late.'

She ignores me after that, finds a song she likes on the radio. Sits back, swaying gently, clicking her fingers and humming, gazing over the hunched figures on the cold, wet streets. Not a bad old track either — Neneh Cherry, 'Buffalo Stance' — and part of me wants to sing a line, let her know she can approve of my tastes, but I'm also trying to feel affronted at her effortless takeover of the operation. Either way, five minutes of silence is all I can take.

Can't think of much to say, though. Another disappointing departure. 'Bit of a shitty night, eh? Looks like the winter's gonna hang around another month or so at least.'

Her fingers stop snapping, the only sign that she's heard me. Then: 'You wish to discuss *weather*?'

I almost giggle at that, see her suddenly as some kind of a gypsy, unbound by our social conditionings. And that she has only to turn her head to stare clean through all of mine. 'Ammm . . . na, I wasn't proposing a discussion. Just making a comment.'

'A comment?'

'Yeah!'

'Well make another then. I hate talking weather. Unless it snowing. Or unless you were walking home in rain and car passed and wet you from the puddle.'

Strands me again. It's this fucking night, this 'job'. It's unnerved me. Can't even hold my own with a pidgin-talking Slav. 'You seem to hate quite a few things.'

'What you mean?'

'Well . . . since we've met you've told me that you hate a song, you hate being late, and you hate talking about the weather.'

'What you mean?'

I wonder if I've scored somehow, or if her English just doesn't include 'What's your point?'

'You just seem pretty hostile, that's all. Not just to songs and that . . . but to me too.'

Satan's handmaiden quotes me again. '*Hos-tile*. What does this mean?'

And I know what she's doing: force-feeding me more rope. Resigned: 'Hostile means aggressive, unfriendly . . . discourteous.'

'One at a time, man!' A different spark there, and when I look at her she's opening a small notebook. 'How to spell it?'

To my surprise I see her writing the letters down as I sound them. Then, to herself: 'The woman in the car was *hos-tile.*' The book disappears and that seems to be that.

A long pair of legs in a miniskirt up ahead, so I turn my head too early, pretend I'm looking at something else and swivelling my eyes, getting a good perv in without appearing to — a move usually reserved for the company of girlfriends, wives and mothers.

Nadia: 'I suppose I are a bit *hostile* sometime. But that just me, yeah?'

I hear myself exonerating her completely.

Me, a little later: 'So where are you from?'

Rummaging in her bag: '*Where are you from?* I guess that a bit more . . . uni-queue than, *Shitty weather, huh?* Not much though.'

Uni-queue. I almost laugh out loud at that, but I reckon she'd take it the wrong way. 'I seem to recall you asking me the very same question a while ago. And it's pronounced, "U-*neek*".'

Ignores me as she pulls a walkman out. Seldom a good sign, that.

Nadia: 'Now I going to be . . . *discourteous* once more. Accept my apology.'

Not a question, but it salves my ego enough to take the crease again. 'You mean you'd rather listen to music than respond to my stimulating conversation?'

No smile, but a bit of a scoff that has me grinning given the context. 'Yes. I want to run over my steps again.'

Run over her steps? Unless she specialises in nothing but very economical lap dances, this smacks of panic to me. 'Have you ever done this before?'

'Once or two.'

'Once or *twice.*'

'That's what I said, once or twice.'

'I mean . . . for Melvyn. Have you worked for him much?'

She's got the earphones in and her thumb's on the play button as she looks straight at me. 'What do you get at?'

And I'd better back off right now or this could get ugly. 'Ahh . . . na, nothing.' Sheepish: 'It's just that I'm hoping you can show me what to do if I need it.'

I'm thinking she's not buying it . . . but then she at least decides to rent for a while; turns away.

I beat her thumb by half a second. 'Tell me where you're from and I promise not to get offended if you ignore me for the rest of the drive.'

'Iraq.' *Click*, and she's segregated from road noise and Ryan.

I can hear the tinny buzz of the music; she's on the full escape and can't possibly hear me mutter, 'Iraq, my arse.' Louder as she shuts her eyes, as the pub gets closer: 'What, do you put on a long dress and veil, do yoga and hope the lads only yell, "Show us ya nose"?' She's moving her fingers and hands a lot. 'Not with that red hair, *baby*. Lucky for me too, 'cause that number-plate phone-in you did would've been setting up a car-jacking at the Hanger Lane roundabout. Load the back up with homemade sarin and do laps of Trafalgar Square.' Then again, who knows? Arabs'll do anything for money. Like that Jemal fuck at work: bullshits his way into a supervisor's gig, then gets done a week later for taxing his workers ten percent of their wages to make sure he puts their names down for work the next day.

Chalk Farm. The pub's called The Victoria (to go with the four thousand other The Victorias in Greater London). The car park's pretty full, and it's a daunting symbol of the crowd awaiting us. I quietly drop a couple of speed-bombs as we get out. She doesn't seem half as anxious as I feel. She takes out her bag, then locks the door. The only tools I'll be needing are deep pockets. Melvyn said it's just a matter of liaising between the publican and the bloke throwing the party. And that he, Melvyn, knows the publican anyway.

She gives me a CD in a case as we reach the door. I'd love to dawdle and let her walk in first, but that's a big no-can-do. I find the door locked, and have to phone the publican — an aging, pock-faced geezer named Trevor — to let us in. He's got a big smile for us, and he shakes my hand and prattles off a long welcome. I tell him I'm called Tom, which he immediately extends to 'Tommy'.

He slides his hairy hand out to Nadia. The obligatory tones of the sleazebag male to the 'industry girl': 'Or-wight, darlin?' She barely bothers looking at him, and the sincerity in the tap she gives his hand is, if anything, worse than the cold indifference she earlier gave mine.

Me: 'What sort of crowd we got in tonight, Trevor?'

'Thirtieth birthday. Bloke from the rugby club down the road.'

I give the word a twist; express contempt for the sort with my fellow grafter here: 'Toffs?'

His flabby lips curl predictably: 'Mostly' — as if they're the mugs and his sort the ones to watch.

I often wonder if Elizabethan dung collectors used to stand back and chuckle knowingly at the dolts clattering past in their ball gowns and carriages. Mind you, I reckon a lot of this moronic condescension comes from the perceived 'hardness' gap between the classes, as if anyone brought up in a house with a separate toilet and bathroom must by default be a nancy-boy. A theory that certainly deserves a little credence here and there — tough streets make tough people — but you don't wanna go taking it for a rule.

I certainly don't. Not any more.

Like all these corn-fed apes in here: at least a hundred of them, suit and tie all week, bloody battle on the Saturday, then drinking games to make a Roman senator chunder first.

The braying laughter and chat die down as Trevor guides us in.

More file in to the main bar. Attention's never really thrown me, but given my role here tonight, the quantity and 'quality' of tonight's regard have me feeling like a dero.

Or a pimp.

. . . But it's OK, 'cause I'm from the *colonies*, mate. That's right. And we may have been your offal once, but now your toilet shits all over you, and you fucking know it. The weather, the athletes, the beaches, the babes. And because we were once rubbish to you pallid sardines, sewage to be flushed Down Under, as our way of life evolved we put distance between it and your own, and ours sure as fuck didn't feature the need to ram a carrot up your ring before speaking if your dad happened to have a few bob. Yeah sure, you get a few tossers from politics and arts and shit who still eye you lot up, but they're just a drop in the billabong, mate, more often derided than deferred to, and you can bet they'll be rejoining the real people once we get around to fucking off that eyesore royal family of yours.

'How y'all doing tonight? I trust you've saved me a Four X or two?'

I watch the words in their stares retracting.

No, I'm *not* some commoner from Clapham sliding round fringe London on his tongue and his testes. A jackal at a Great Dane show. Sniffing for angles. No, because *now* I could tell you that I'm the son of a grease monkey or the heir to a mining lease, and you wouldn't have a fucking clue either way, would you.

A few female faces in the crowd, and that relaxes me further. Because the person they *thought* I was might have no greater a chance with fanny like this than a shit-faced lay and a mumbled 'I'll call you', but all bets are on for us raiders from the South. And their presence should help keep the lads semi-civilised too—

Fuck, I'd forgotten about her. She's walked past me, and Trevor's pointing out the sheilas' dunny, and no one's looking at me any more. The toilets are on the far side of the floor, and as she carves a smirking corridor through the punters some amused muttering starts up.

Exaggerated disbelief: 'That can *not* be her. *Surely*.'

'Who arranged this? Andrew? Well, he always *was* barking bonkers, wasn't he?'

Forbidden relish in the slur: 'What is it — a bloody *Paki* or something? Sand-nigger?'

You fat, rotten bastard. Wouldn't be heard for dead saying those words in public, would you, but once the ranks close with the Chivas flowing, you're as bigoted as any estate yob.

Only you should know better.

'And to think, my wife flat out *barred* me from coming tonight.'

There's a big chance that she's hearing them — I wish I was the type to get her attention, then stroll up and smash one of them fair in the mouth — and maybe there's a missed beat in her walk too. But she keeps her poise and gets through the door.

Stage whispers turn to stage voices — one of the birds gets a fair old chuckle by reminding Andrew that she'd offered to perform *gratis* herself tonight — and all my concern is suddenly for myself again. Trev puts a pint in my hand. I feel like knocking it back in one and ordering another with a bourbon chaser, but I'm fucked if I'm gonna let these smug tossers see me do it.

So I get to 'work', asking Trev to point Andrew out. But right then Andrew comes up to me himself, wanting to haggle boring old money away from his exciting young team-mates. He's so short he has to be the team's half-back. There's a quiet determination under his rapidly thinning dome, though: got the look of a lawyer. Shaking his head, saying this isn't what he had in mind at all, that he'd booked something tasteful from a young . . . hottie.

He was going to say 'white girl', I'm suddenly sure of it.

'What are you trying to say?'

'She's just not up to snuff, mate.'

'Look, pal, we've come all the way out here on a job. Our boss is expecting us to hold up our end of the transaction and remunerate him with your end upon our return. Out of that we both get paid. Now if you think I just gave up my Friday night for nothing more than a wet drive and a free pint of Becks, you've been on the wrong end of too many head-high tackles.'

'But the service supplied differs markedly from that offered. In fact—'

'You're in no position to make a claim like that until you've seen the act. Beside the point anyway.' Raising my voice with each sentence: 'Now if you can't afford to honour the agreed transaction, that's fine. No problem. What's gonna have to happen now is that I'll address all these good people, tell them what's transpired, and organise a whip-round to cover your debts. No worries. Should only come to a few quid each.'

By the time I finish he looks set to reach up and clap a palm over my mouth. This is enormous fun, and I'm partially hoping for him to go another round or two. Five seconds later, though, there's a roll of twenties in my palm and Andrew's sidling back up to his pals, erupting with them to a punch-line he can't have heard the set-up for.

Trevor's got a gleam in his eye. 'Nice job, mate. I had the skin-flint cunt knock me down fifty squid for hirage of the pub because there weren't enough fucking tables.'

I count the cash quickly and pocket it, then stand at the bar and shoot the shit with Trev for a few minutes. He's got another pint poured for me before the first's three-quarters cut. My phone goes and it's her, telling me she's almost ready. She wants to know if everything's prepared. I'm not so sure what 'everything' is.

Covering the phone: 'Everything ready for the show, Trev?'

'Sure is, geez. All the lights are lined up on the bandstand. I'll whack 'em on and kill the mains when you say. There's a chair up there, like I were told, and a jug of water. All I need is the music.'

I tell her to come out as soon as she sees the lights go down. Hand Trevor the CD. He slots it into the stereo behind the bar, passes me the remote control, pointing out buttons.

Some bloke gets my attention and asks what the hold-up is. His tone's relaxed, though, so I walk over to him and joke about how five minutes ago Andrew was so keen to get things rolling he tried to have the show cancelled.

'Well, she might not be what we were expecting, but that's no reason not to take a closer peek.' A bit of mischief round his eyebrows. 'Never is in my book.'

A bird standing nearby notices and heads straight over, marooning some steroid-freak in mid-sentence. Cocking her head: 'Where's your little friend, then?'

Me: 'Now, now, let's exercise a little patience, shall we? Good things come to those who wait.'

Eyes wide: 'More like those who wait never get to bloody come!' Tossing back a slug from her champagne flute. She's had more than a few, and a small trickle dribbles down her chin.

The guy, to the chick: 'Inspired by the Derek and Andrew reception committee, Sophie, he didn't think interest in his . . . "colleague" was running very high any more.'

Wrinkling a pretty little nose: 'Oh, pay no heed, not a fucking filament. Most of us quite appreciate a dab of exotica in our erotica. It's not like she's *black*, for Christ's sake.'

The guy pulls a scandalised face at me over her shoulder. I feel myself wanting to like him; suck in my cheeks.

Sophie: 'Besides, catching a crap show can often make for better entertainment than a good one if the audience has bottle enough to speak up about it. You should have seen us at the Comedy Club a few weeks ago.' Her face goes mock stern as she holds up a thumb and inverts it slowly downward. 'This coliseum can be a trifle unforgiving, I'm afraid.'

'Don't be afraid, Soph: you're among friends here.' I give her just the hint of a grin, but my stare's on middle stump and going nowhere. 'Anyway, you aren't the type I'd normally expect to see at a strip show — i.e. you have breasts and look good in a dress. Yet you sound quite the connoisseur.'

'Not half as much as you are, I'll warrant.'

It feels good to drop her eye first.

Me: 'Anyway, chap and chapess, how about I get the good times a-rolling?'

They 'hear, hear!' me as I turn back to Trev, flick a finger over my throat. He dips the main lights right down until the spotties form a bright circle over the front of the bandstand. A cheer goes up in the near-dark. There's more than a little irony in it though.

She comes out, forces a path through the middle again. Whispering, murmuring, scattered barks of laughter, and it's an ugly sound to me, as if they're as hungry for humiliation as anything else. And expecting to get it. I can only see the hat at first, but as she mounts the stage I see that she's dressed exactly as before . . . though if those slits up the sides of her raincoat were as high then I certainly didn't notice.

She sips from the jug of water and paces around the stage a bit, maybe measuring its dimensions, absorbed enough to be alone. A few voices start to call out. She moves to the back of the stage to get the chair, and almost disappears in the shadows before placing it in the centre of the cold, bright light. Then she stands behind the chair and straightens. Stares into space, erect and still.

I'm suddenly quite sure that she hasn't looked any of them in the eye. Not once. And with the light the way it is, she won't have to either.

Something warm on my arm. Sophie is letting her shoulder

graze me.

Nadia holds her pose for almost a minute, as if she's getting off on the vibe, feeding on the temperature burning hotter against her . . .

Or like she's frozen up, gone tharn, the cone of light around her headlights on high beam.

But at last her hand starts tapping a beat on her thigh, and immediately I cue the music. A hauntingly groovy bass-riff starts throbbing through the room like a pair of sick hearts, slicing the voices off clean. Bodies fall into time with the beat. She lets it repeat itself maybe ten times, standing, staring, tapping . . . long enough for the music-induced mood swing to start wearing off; voices rising above it, sceptically demanding . . .

Then she starts to dance.

Two minutes later and nobody is speaking. Or even moving much. In five minutes they've remembered where they are, and they're dancing and cheering, yelling comments at each other. Without even glancing at them, Nadia pulls them closer, and ten minutes after she's started the space around the bandstand is a pulsating press.

She's taken off nothing but the hat.

She draws them out for the best part of an hour. She and the music complement each other flawlessly. The medley of song sections could have been written for just this point in time and space. There is sex in the beat, always in the beat, or at least sensuality on crack, but it's the wailing of the indie guitar, the tears of the blues mamas that lets Nadia prise them open. Hers was the first form captured on canvas. But she is abandoned and cold; her glare is a disguise. She will regroup, though, always, and she will fight to the quicks of her toenails.

But she is incomplete and she is doomed, because all men are bastards.

And when she's half naked on the floor, hugging her knees, it's seeming as if they've had enough, that she's pushed that button for too long and will lose them, when a soft techno beat starts to build. It nurses her; she lifts her head again, rises to her feet in stages. And by the time the music reaches its crescendo, crashing over the crowd and re-igniting us, she's been found by He of the White Charger, and any man in this room could be the one at the reins. The clothes she sheds now are for him and no one else.

But she's too much the artist to leave them like that. Without slowing, she and the music change, tell the saga of the demise of the knight, tossed into the mass grave of the Nice Guy minority. But this time she wants revenge, and when the rock guitars kick in — two of them, flirting around and around each other — she's preparing for battle herself. The guitars heat up, and by the time they're fucking the music and the dance are pure raunch. She's fighting all right, with a weapon as ancient as Eve. She unshackles the troll in them.

But this weapon is not enough. Its essence is its undoing. She knows what Man will trade in the sordid quest for his desires . . .

. . . and she knows that once she's fed them, her spell will be as broken as her heart is.

Because all men are bastards.

So by the time the cheer for the final layer of underwear fades, she's lost again and the music is all jagged piano chords and eerie violin, jerking her about like a cruel puppeteer. She struggles to break free but she's ripped off her feet, landing with a thud.

Twitching like a corpse as the final note fades.

The applause is thunderous, and though I barely know her I'm so fucking proud my eyes are watering. Suck on that, you secret-hand-shaking wankers! Old Trev behind the bar looks like he just watched his team lose the Cup final from three-nil up. I drop a look to the Sloane Ranger beside me, and I can tell that if Sophie wasn't at least bi-curious before this she sure as shit is now.

Nadia stands up at last, and the ovation swells again. At one point she'd thrown her head right back and drunk desperately from the jug, letting most of it spill over her, and her short red hair is standing up in spikes. There's more sweat on her than water though, and her lean muscles are glistening. She's got good tits — they almost look plastic, but I know better — and I'm trying not to stare at them. There's no trace left of the Victim, the Woman buffeted through the ages by the caprices of Man — she left Her dead in the fetal position — but I still can't bring myself to really *perv* at her. Now, as she collects her things, ignoring the applause, there's only the pride and resolution, the endurance and independence. And *the power*. She's all *the power* now, and how did she ever convey to us its innate fragility? She's naked still, but her composure could be armour. She wants nothing from any of us but to never see us again.

She mocks them with a bow as the coat closes, and they bay as if she's invited them all home. She confiscates a lit fag and disappears into the Ladies'.

There's almost a sense of release as the main lights blink back on.

As the chatter restarts, Andrew sidles up to me again. He's asking for an 'encore'.

I just laugh at him. 'Like fuck, big man. I'm taking her home right now.' *Make what you will of that, cobber.* 'You've already had ten times what you paid for, and you fucking know it.'

But his smirk soon tells me that I'm back in his domain. He

scoffs at the thought of not 'reimbursing her adequately', as do a few of his cronies who have crowded in around him. I stare into their eager faces and decide that this was the group of teens who once paid bums to fist-fight each other; who left shit in the sheets of the family villa, giggled as the maids arrived. Her act didn't touch them at all, not like it touched most of us.

They start reeling off what they want in this 'encore'.

You get a lot of 'shows' like this back home, skimpy barmaids taking cash and heading to a house with a crowd in tow. I went along to a couple but never stayed long. I can barely believe, after what we've just witnessed, they'd mention Nadia and these demands in the same breath.

I laugh in their faces. 'Aint gonna happen, boys. Best you all be loading up the Jag and heading back down to King's Cross. You'll get your needs met there right enough.'

But then they start swinging their money around, and if the power Nadia depicted is ancient and awesome, this one is not much less so. They do a verbal whip-round, and by the time they're done I'm hating the part of my brain that's calculating my cut, cold as coins under my outrage. The boot's on the other foot now, and these cunts are driving it straight up my arse.

Surely, though, she could use the money too . . . and I almost cut over them with a counter-offer — way too high, even for the exorbitant field they've set, but leaving me some sweet middle ground to corner them on. But I could work on my speech for a month and not find a way to bring this up with her, to tell her what they're willing to pay to watch her—

My phone rings and I gladly put Andy and co. on hold. But it's her. Nadia. She wants to know what they're saying to me. I look over at the Ladies' and see the door's open a crack.

'They want an encore.'

'What an *encore*?'

'Another show. A more revealing one.'

Not surprised: 'How do they offer?'

'. . . A lot.'

'How much, Ryan?'

And the sound of my name from her throat makes me want to tell her to forget it and hurry up out. 'I think I could get them over a thousand.'

'. . . One thousand pounds?'

'Yep.'

'What would I have to do?'

I tell her.

Her contempt crackles over the air-waves. 'No way.'

'Thought you might say that.'

But she tells me what she *will* do, and the minimum she wants for it — she's done this before — so I end the call and go to work on the lads.

The lap dance is a sticking point — they want her starkers on the birthday boy, and she's outright refused — but in the end a deal is struck. Five hundred quid on top of the regular fee.

I feel oddly queasy as I tell her the score over the phone. She tells me to get out.

'What do you mean?'

'I want you out. Out of bar. Stay out until I call you.'

'But . . . but I have to stay.'

'I take care of myself.'

I don't doubt it either, but she ends the call before I can tell her that.

Sophie follows me through to the side bar, and we chat and drink as the music cranks up again. I'm fully on auto, though, barely registering what I say to her. I try to roll a smoke but sweat from my hands kills the paper and the tobacco drops out.

Sophie, enjoying herself: 'You look like a groom whose bride's out on her hen night!'

'Fuck off. Just concerned.'

'I'm not surprised. Sounds like a Serb paramilitary booze-up in there.'

The music finally fades. Nadia summons me back in.

But there's something wrong.

The main lights are back on. She's wearing her coat, and she's standing by the bar, Andrew and ten others fronting her with smirks smeared all over them. The rest of the room seem to have detached themselves from the clique. Andrew's talking to Nadia — he's all smug eyebrows and shrugged shoulders — and she looks well pissed off. Of course she's never come over as jovial, but there's something blazing now.

I'm straight over to them.

Me, to Nadia: 'Everything cool? You ready to split?'

Some cunt: 'She was splitting a minute ago, pal, believe you me! *Right* down the middle!'

His snigger spreads. 'While pulling a bloody hand-stand!'

Nadia, to me, reluctantly: 'They won't give me money.'

Eh?

'What's going on, Andrew?'

'What's going on is that she hasn't fulfilled her obligations yet. We can't pay her until she has — it'd be ghastly form. She hasn't given the birthday boy his lap dance.'

Nadia's face contracts. 'What fucking *lap dance*? I make clear I not *do* this!'

There's a bit of doubt visible in the lying prick now, and he can't help flicking me a look. 'I'm afraid that's not the agreement I remember making.'

Me, pointed: 'Is that *right*, Andrew?'

'*Yes*. That *is* right.'

'Fucking arse. You know damn well what the deal was.'

Gazing at his cronies, guileless: 'Whatever are you getting at? It's his *birth*day, for god's sake: we can't let the stripper leave without a lap dance. What kind of a friend and host would that make me?'

'One who doesn't embarrass himself by trying to cheat people.'

'It was a rhetorical question.'

'Don't you think I know what a rhetorical question is?'

I just can't believe I'm hearing this. Shouldn't surprise me, though. These kind never play it fair or straight. How else have they skated above the masses for centuries? You pulled a stunt like this in a pub in the Goldfields — or down the East End, or anywhere else real people drink — and your own friends would queue up to have a swing at you.

'This is fucking bullshit. We had a deal.'

Prim: 'As a barrister, I can assure you that the terms of our "deal" have *not* been transgressed. I have ten witnesses who will verify that.'

I'm so surprised and offended by all this I can barely think of what to say next. The way Nadia's weighing me doesn't help. 'Ten witnesses, eh?' Looking at them: 'How much honour have any of you got?'

A few look down, but they've come too far to break the silent pact.

Nadia, nearly shouting: 'What about rest of you?' She means the ones pretending they're somewhere else. 'You know what going on here. You enjoy my dancing? Yes? But what, not enough to be decency when this piece of shit friend of yours take piss out of me?'

But no one will look our way. They're not going against the grain for a migrant stripper and a smart-arse Aussie. I'm sure there are codes they live by among themselves, but when it comes to their 'lessers', if it's not illegal, it's not unethical. And if it *is* illegal, pay someone to change that.

Someone like Counselor Fuckface here, who's suddenly looking indignant. 'Who are you calling a piece of shit, girl?'

'Who the fuck you think, you bald little *cock*sucker?!'

His mouth purses, and I step between them. This is getting settled one way or another; I'm not walking out of here and sitting in the dark with her while the silence jeers at me. But with Nadia dissing this midget in front of his crew, my options just got reduced big time.

Signal for her to chill, then beckon Andrew in. He looks like he wants to hold his nose, but he comes.

Me, low: 'Do you understand exactly what you're doing, Andrew? Who it is you're ripping off?' Sounding scared, concerned for us both: 'Who we work for?'

Shakes his head, but I've got his attention.

'Well, I won't mention his name — he doesn't like that . . . but let's just say that if you *cheat* this guy, Andrew . . . it won't be a courtroom you meet him in.'

I gaze over at Trevor. Bless the old geezer, he's read things, and as Andrew turns his eyes to him Trev gives two of the most dire head-shakes I've ever seen.

Wee Andrew, barrister, backs off real quick after that, then tries to hand me the cash. But I point my head at Nadia instead. He baulks for a beat, then pays her and shuffles off. A lot of them are looking at me, but I'm only interested in her.

'You ready to bail?'

'. . . Bail?'

'Yeah. Leave. Get the fuck out of Dodge.'

'You bet.' She picks her bag up and follows me to the bar, where I say a goodbye to Trev. He offers me his number, which I put into my phone because you just never know. Then he wants mine, but I assure him I'll call him. He beams at Nadia, thanks her for changing his life, holding his hand out, and this time she not only shakes it properly, she leans across and pecks the old glass-wipe on the cheek.

Trev unlocks the front door for us. But just as I stand back to let Nadia out first she dumps her bag in my arms and walks back in.

'What's up?'

Ignores me, keeps walking. Then she slams her palms against a table — loud enough to draw attention — and vaults herself on to it, springing up straight. Everyone stops to stare, and this time she's staring back, commanding the scene again.

She doesn't yell, but she doesn't have to. 'This from the Sand-niggers of the world. Put it with rest. Look like you need it more than we.'

And she hurls Andrew's roll of money over their heads.

It disintegrates in mid-air, and the collective hiss seems to waft the falling notes. In another crowd the scramble would be on, but none of this lot takes so much as a step as she soars to the floor and strides from their lives.

I may be in shock, aching to scuttle shamelessly among their feet, but I try to force myself to give them a grin and salute, and to drawl 'Don't spend it all at once', before walking out airily. Instead I wait till the door swings closed behind Nadia, then instruct Trevor to put the money on the bar one night and to call me when the piss-up goes down.

12

MELVYN

Don't get me wrong, most of the punters who end up round the table upstairs on any regular basis are usually worf a bob or four. Always new money though, init. Spose the odd younger toff might spend some time up ere, lower emselves for the adventure of it, but discretion's vital for them older boys breakin the rules, and they've got their own clubs. They aint ruled this land and any other they could conquer or buy for a thousand years by trustin cunts like me to help em let their hair and their pants down and not then turn round and wring every inch out of it later. Na, you won't find too many plums in the throats that call the bets round my tables in an 'urry.

But this one cunt — mid-forties if e's a day — e's only gone and become a fucking regular!

Was Nadia what done it, god bless her slinky, haughty arse. The amount of good that angel's done me wivout even knowing it, when I finally pension meself off to the land of the winter tan I've arf a mind to set er up in er own little place somewhere. Maybe she'll finally throw a fuck my way n'all.

Not sure when e first come in — even Vernon couldn't remember, and that cunt's got a memory like a fucking man-trap. One night there e just is, sat by imself at a table in the middle ground, sipping Johnny Walker *Blue* Label, waiting for Nadia's set to start.

I'd had Blue Label Johnny on the menu for over a year wivout anyone ever orderin one. So I've gone down and introduced meself. Now I like to dress a bit snappy most of the time, but the suit this boy were in made me feel like a Bethnal Green hobo. We chatted a bit, then Nadia's come on, and I've ceased to exist for im. Guess e's ceased to exist for me a bit then too, cos I could watch that angel dance every day for a year and not get bored of it. Then e's asked me to invite er over to 'is table. I reluctantly told im, 'Fat fucking chance, mate', cos she don't do nufin like that. Never. Won't even sit wiv a bloke and lead im on while e runs up an ealthy bar tab for me.

Then e's finished up and thanked and farewelled me, perfectly polite but cold as crystal, generations of in-bred class layerin every word and gesture.

Nadia took a fortnight off to study for exams after that, but e musta rung and found out when she were next on, cos I'd forgotten all about im when, lo and be'old, ten minutes before she's due to dance again there e is, same table, same tumbler full of Scotland's finest.

This carried on for a good while, me tryin to spy in chink in 'is Savile Row armour — cos fish as fat as I was guessing im to be don't swim into my wee pond very often — but all of im were cased in plate.

Except for one lil hinge that flapped open as soon as e walked in.

Nadia.

I begged, bribed, cajoled and enticed, hour after hour, for er to play a lil ball for once, but she weren't avin none of it. Weren't till a couple of friends of ers from back ome — illegals, straight outta the container — needed somewhere to lay low that I finally found a gap in *er* armour. I put em up in a two bedroom in Euston, and she agreed to ostess round a table upstairs a couple-a times.

E'd previously turned 'is nose up at invitations to sit at a game, but when I mentioned that Nadia would be up there this one night, the toff cunt were up them stairs so fast you'd've thought e moonlighted at Blackpool Casino. Course you woulda changed ya mind soon as you saw im play, cos e were fucking abysmal. The size of the whiskies she poured im didn't elp either, and e were down two large in an hour and an arf. Coulda taken im for more, but I pulled the plug soon after. You can shear a sheep many times but you'll only skin it once. And if I got the chance to skin this arrogant prick, I wanted to come away wiv one big enough to carpet a fucking hall wiv.

E's back again a week later. Got shit-faced, lost money, drooled over Nadia (she were polite enough to im, and for er that's really somethin), then e went ome when she disappeared. Same again next week. And the next. He sure ad a taste for fine sauce, not the best ead for it though, and I gently confirmed my suspicions: 'is powers of recollection when shit-faced weren't exactly photographic.

I can sometimes unlock a person fru one weakness. Give me two and it aint often that I can't spill 'is belly out all over the fucking floor if there's a reason to. So I've filed it away and bid me time, thanking me lucky stars that Nadia's friends stayed dependent on the Euston gaff.

Then, woddaya know, the toff's only gone and 'anded me a *third* chink! E's started 'angin on after Nadia's cleared off and pawin up the ova birds. Then e stumbled off to a room wiv Loretta one night for a bunk-up.

HOWZAT!?!?

I paid er a good rate but didn't charge im.

This entered the pattern.

Then it appened. Bout three monfs after I met im, four in the mornin, e's blind drunk and bettin small, when Beth's popped in and whispered that I were needed downstairs. Fast. The club were closed and dead. The problem were Loretta, in the dressin room, all by erself. 'Cept for those upstairs, she, me and Beth was the only ones left in the buildin. Beth ad gone to check on er when she adn't come out in a while.

Loretta ad told me she were off the skag, and she adn't been lyin at the time cos I know the signs well. But either she'd fallen back into it recently or she'd been tempted to do a one-off hit. Upshot is that she's lyin on a couch wiv a needle in er leg and blood all over er mouth and nose. Starin at nufin. And she's been dead a while cos she were stone fucking cold.

I liked the girl, but she were brown bread and there weren't nufin no one could do for her. Beth I know I can trust. So I've gone back upstairs and slipped a Mickey into the toff's Blue Label, then cleared the others out soon as e's 'it the table snorin.

E's woken up two hours later in a backroom bed wearing nufin but a condom.

Next to a naked dead girl.

Game over. One-nil to Melvyn.

I were waiting outside the room when e started yellin. I went in, seen that e'd killed a girl I loved like a baby sister, and lost the plot big-style. I bounced im off the walls for a while, im screamin and beggin to be believed that e adn't done it. Then I've wrapped me fingers round his throat, and held on till I smelled shit. Great rule of thumb, that one. Then my fury faded and the grief took over.

Leavin im in a corner, I've taken Loretta's ead into me lap and wept.

Then I've pulled out me mobile and asked to be put fru to the cozzas, cos an omicide ad taken place on my premises.

E flew across the room, knelt at me feet, and swore 'is soul to me in a most convincing wheeze. I urled the phone against the wall, smashin it to pieces cos she were like family to me, and it took im arf an hour longer to convince me it'd be worf my while to put love aside.

Far as e knew, she'd end up in a shallow grave somewhere wiv his shirt beside her, just in case 'is commitment to my grieving process should appen to waver. E showered, then went ome.

The ambulance fronted up a while after Beth and I realised poor Loretta ad been lyin dead of a smack overdose in the dressin room all mornin. We thought she ad left hours ago.

13

ALEX

Saturday. We bust arse all morning and most of the work's polished off by eleven. Things slow down then — too much talk about today's rugby semi going on. A bunch of the crew had approached me midway through the week about an early knock-off today, and I cleared it with the relevant managers. By quarter to twelve there's still a bit left to be done, but none of it's priority stock and I'm happy to leave it for Monday.

A lot of Labour Save temps have lunch passes, keen to take their breaks relaxing in the park and the new spring sunshine, so there's a big queue in the security area as they get searched. Takes us nearly ten minutes to get to the head of it, and Trent's starting to worry about missing kick-off, wants us to jump the queue. We'd get away with it too — temps rarely say boo to us — but I never let myself be seen taking liberties, and the other guys hang back for once.

Security search none of us anyway, wave us straight through.

At the window we direct another guard to our names on the

log. While we crowd around, pointing out our monikers on the sheet, Ryan walks out, head down, daypack slung on one shoulder. A strange silence falls over our group: you can tell they're not going to say anything to him . . . unless he says it first . . . which some of them kind of want him to do. But he doesn't, just gives a flick of the eyebrows as his eyes meet mine. I smile. Ryan doesn't bother lining up to point his name out: as he passes, Donald simply nods that it's under control, and Ryan's away, up the footpath beside the wide driveway.

Jim: 'Was Ryan in the queue behind us?'

Trent: 'Don't think so.' He gives me a pained look but it's sarky as hell. 'Not everyone keeps company with conscientious bosses.'

I still get a jolt of pride to hear myself referred to as a 'boss'. We're signed out ourselves now and walking to the road. 'I wasn't stopping you from jumping the queue if you wanted to, Trent.'

Jim: 'Oh yeah, Mr Manager, that's what ya say now, but we know your type, matey.'

Katie: 'Fuck yeah, we're fully aware of the dirty little dossier you're compiling on each of us, assembling ammo for when the time's right.'

Greg: 'Yeah, why else do you hang out with us after work when you could be snorting charlie in hotel dining rooms, those places with more rich white chicks than the lifeboat deck of the *Titanic*.'

This is fast becoming an old wind-up but I grin wide with it every time. 'Once I start getting in*vited* to the Ritz, believe you me, folks, I shall be consorting with your type no longer.'

We're out on the road and milling around the bus stop. There's an electronic board telling us one is due in two minutes. I can handle that, as can our one o'clock kick-off.

Ryan comes out of the corner shop thirty-odd metres away — he never gets the bus from here — and starts walking away from us. I'm thinking about how he is around the warehouse, always getting through his work on time and well, but keeping to himself all day, staggering his breaks to be alone with a book. He comes and goes from the house at all hours, eats in his room when he's around. Never comes out on the lash with us, seems to spend time only with Lisa really. Not that he's actively rude any more, he just seems listless. Voluntarily lonely. He's walking quite slowly now, almost aimlessly, like someone who wants somewhere to go but doesn't have anywhere.

Not sure what I'm doing: 'Just gotta remind Ryan of something.' And I'm jogging down the road. 'Ryan!'

He stops and turns back, impassive but swaying a little with surprise. I draw level and he starts walking again, silently inviting me to fall in with him.

And I've got nothing to say. But he just keeps walking, as if we go places together often. I finally settle on: 'Aren't you watching the game, mate? I thought you liked your rugby.'

'I do. And I'm sure as shit watching the game too.'

'Where? We're heading to The Crown, closest place with Sky. You should come with us . . . you might miss kick-off otherwise.'

'Na, mate. I'm watching it somewhere else.'

I glance back over my shoulder. They're all lined up, watching us.

'You ahh . . . ya want some company?'

The reply's so quick, so unexpected, I get a small head-spin from it. 'Yeah, no worries.'

Then I'm torn on how to walk out on the others so unceremoniously. I decide to send them a text later, but feel the Judas big-time.

Ryan says nothing to me. I should be feeling awkward — he and I have rarely spoken — but I've felt a thawing from him. And watching him ghost around work has me viewing him as much less the social autocrat. There's something about him, though. Maybe it's just the pictures the old stories conjure. Whatever, I'm suddenly looking more forward to the rest of the day than I had been. As wingman to Ryan, I might even end up with some crumbs trickling my way, break my Northern Hemisphere duck.

Ryan: 'So you've been kicking round with those guys a fair bit?'

He's pointing *down* the road, and I'm confused until I realise they just went past us in the 256. And it must seem like I cold-shouldered them twice in minutes. Maybe I'm being too complacent, shunning a good group of mates like that. Because if they decide to shun me back, I could end up where I was a few weeks ago.

'Yeah. Been running amok actually, out on the tiles every Fri and Sat at least.'

'Good nights out?'

Chuckling: 'Shit yeah. Couldn't be better really.' *Except for the way they* haven't *concluded.* 'Big wear and tear on the wallet and liver though. Should try and rein it in a bit.'

'You and ninety percent of all the other Antips in town. That's what we come here for.' Somehow enigmatic: 'Isn't it?'

'. . . I s'pose. What did *you* come here for?'

Harsh: 'To fuck as many foreign women as I could possibly lay my glands on.'

I'm taken aback by that. But not in the usual way, like when a proven playboy starts relaying feats he knows I've no hope of matching.

Me: 'How did that work out for ya?'

He walks a few steps in silence, then turns and smiles. 'Not too sure really, mate. Bloody good question.'

I've rarely seen him grinning before. His whole face changes. His whole *character*. Imperious prince to benevolent bandit. Maybe it just hits you all the harder for its scarcity. Could be he understands the power of it, keeps it in ambush for the optimum moment—

Shit, do I smile too often?! Walk round grinning like an idiot all day?

We get to the tube station, go through the barriers and climb to an open-air platform, a Tescos below us, some soccer fields on the left.

Ryan gets a text, smiles as he reads. 'From the old man. He finally faced his technology phobia for long enough to learn how to text. Now ya can't shut the old prick up.'

'You get on good with your dad?'

'Oh yeah, he's like a father figure to me. You?'

'Aint seen mine since I was twelve. Not in a hurry to either.'

A train pulls in and Ryan helps a black woman lift her pram out. He nods at her thank you, then enters the carriage and spreads himself over two seats. I take the seat across from him as the train starts moving. Ryan picks up a discarded newspaper, throws it back, tries another, settles in with it.

The train reminds me of a funny story I heard. Ryan doesn't seem interested in chatting, and it takes me a while to get up the gumption to speak. When I do his eyes stay on the paper, as if he's going to ignore me, but just as I'm about to trail off he looks up.

Me: '. . . so he's totally hammered, eh. He gets on the train; it's the last train of the night and he's stoked to have caught it. He's got a long a way to go, though, and after a few stops he falls—'

'He falls asleep. No offence, mate, but I've heard this story about a hundred times. He falls asleep; next thing he knows a tube worker shakes him awake and tells him he has to get off 'cause the train terminates here. He looks around and realises he's slept past his stop and all the way to the end of the line: he's at fucking Epping or somewhere, stranded till morning unless he can shell

135

out big coin for a taxi.'

Me, deflated: 'Ahhh, yeah. That's about the sum of it.'

A few people board. A girl with dark hair piled up on her head, some stray bangs hanging in her face, takes a seat down from Ryan. She's young and pretty, done to the nines too, as if for a wedding or something. She glances at him as he reads his paper, and I'm checking her out with no restraint, jealously certain her attention will linger on him, when her eyes flick across to me. Busted big time. Still, it's only a few seconds before my eyes are drawn back to her. Shock horror: she must have picked me for a leerer, because she's still looking and I'm busted again. But then her lips crinkle up in a smile that's so surprising my body goes into shock for a second before belting me with a charge of raw delight. I make myself smile back — it feels lopsided — before looking away.

I try to wait for the semblance of an assured, confident period, make myself count slowly to ten. She's picking lint from the shoulder straps of her velvet dress. God, what a honey! Again she looks at me, and as we stare off it's like I'm clinging to a low-voltage electric fence. Smiling shyly, she looks down, but darts another glance at me almost straight away. We carry on like this, and by the time the train stops again I'd trade my index finger just to drink her bath water. I'm about to say something, leaning forward and shaping my mouth — her eyebrows raise receptively — when I realise I don't know what I should say. I pretend I was just readjusting, read an ad above the windows, flay my brain for a decent opener. She's still waiting when I look again, but I'm as blank as a Hollywood bullet and dying a hideous death each second.

Ryan turns another page.

Two more minutes of glancing and grinning and social ineptitude, frustration and something close to outright terror . . .

The train stops again. She stands, shouldering her bag, and a black hole opens up in my stomach. One last smile from her — I think she thinks I didn't *want* to take things further — then those delectable legs take her from the train, my self-respect pinned to her shadow. I almost hope she won't, but she smiles again as the train passes her, flicking a little wave.

Staring dumbly around the carriage, I feel like lying down, burying my face in the worn cover of the seat cushion. Maybe some obese builder will come along and not see me past his belly, sit on me and end this fucking misery.

Ryan, from the depths of the sports section: 'Hope you've got a short memory, dude.'

'. . . Why's that?'

''Cause otherwise she's gonna haunt you till your coffin lid closes.'

We de-train at Shepherd's Bush and step on to a long escalator.

Ryan: 'You know what you should've said to her?'

'What?'

'"How's it going?"'

Not many bushes or shepherds on Shepherd's Bush Green today. The area, like most London suburbs devoid of real investment, is ugly and squalid. Brown faces in the majority, drunks everywhere. Dodgy stalls outside one-pound shops hawk everything from freshly pirated DVDs to mobile-phone chargers. Shops sell food from all corners of the old Empire — spices diluting the smell of stale urine that clings to the streets — but I wouldn't eat from them if I was coming off the forty-hour famine. Antips are drawn here by the pubs, though, and there's so many around I feel oddly at home.

We wait for a green light on a pedestrian crossing, then Ryan stops to use a cash machine. I stand around, watching events on the green. Bum Central over there. Even if their clothes don't give them away, you can spot a bum by the drink in his hand: supermarket vodka or extra-strength lager, the cans that cost about ten pence each, pack a thirteen percent wallop and taste like bad port cut with grey-water. I bought one once, looking for a catch-up kick-start to a night out, and got through all of one sip. Atrocious stuff. Small wonder that sort are too eternally pissed to ever get a job: they need to stay drunk just so they can get the next swig past their tongues.

It's not even dawn on the party-goers' clock, but the footy's already drawn a big crowd into the Walkabout. A couple of Maori bouncers on the door insist on looking in Ryan's bag. For a second he seems reluctant, but then he opens it. The bloke barely glances inside, and I follow Ryan in.

Unless I'm a real regular I always feel insecure walking into pubs, as if management don't actually want my presence and my money, as if I'm somehow trespassing. Maybe it's more to do with the other punters, the ones who pause and stare when they hear the door opening. Then there's almost a guilt/embarrassment thing at having chosen the same place as them in which to seek a good time; like they've got a monopoly on it and might not want me joining in. Those first few steps I always make through treacle.

The sensation barely lasts a second in here, though. The place is too big and full, far too many personalities bouncing off each other already for anyone to care about more trickling in. Southern 'chic' all over the walls, TVs every five metres. At the end of the bottom level the roof opens out into a hall, a dance floor and band-stand with a massive big-screen above it. Almost uniform young Antips and Saffas. Later in the day the reputation of this place draws others in, but not at a lunchtime footy session.

I follow the path Ryan cuts through the bodies, have to brush across the back of a blonde in a tight T-shirt; cut an eye back at her, and *yep*, she's hot, and *nope*, she is not aware that I exist. We go up a cramped staircase, to where the bar upstairs has more room and more sun, a balcony looking out over the dance floor.

I'm wondering whether Ryan will consult me on where to make camp. I'd rather he didn't — I really don't care — but neither do I care to follow his lead too meekly, so I duck the moment by getting the first round in. A dude with a bone-carving around his neck pours me two pints of Kronenberg. I feel like saying to him: 'Shit, are you from *New Zealand*, man? *Me too!*' But I'm nowhere near drunk enough to take the gamble on his sense of humour.

I spot Ryan behind a pillar — good spot too: TV on the wall, enough elbow room to swing a pint. On the screen, and over the PA now, we're treated to the spectacle of a panel of English pundits dissecting the Southern game. Will Carling wrinkles his nose as he talks of our 'new habit of gang-tackling'; Dan Luger seems distressed that Southern teams with their 'frothy' back lines are sometimes scoring four tries in a game and still losing.

Ryan calls him a wanker, and we go off on one about the dreary Northern game, the pretentiousness of its administrators and media. I relay a couple of my own favourite quotes from that quarter . . . then I notice my beer's half gone and that we've been yakking full on for a good five minutes. That kind of shocks me, drives my next sentence away. Then a cheer goes up, and we look at the screen to find the wise men gone and the two teams jogging on to the Ellis Park cauldron.

14

—Would've thought you'd be more into your Aussie Rules, Ryan, being from West Aus.

—Used to be. Don't mind me rugby though now. Half and half, I reckon.

—We play quite a lot of Aussie Rules in New Zealand.

—Really?

—Yeah. But we get the girls to wear little skirts and give them a round ball to piss about with.

—I'd like to see ya say that to someone like Barry Hall.

—Barry who? What's an Aussie doing barracking for a Kiwi outfit anyway?

—They're not my main team, of course, but my best mate of a couple of years out mining, Kiwi guy called Frankie, he was mad for the Blues, never shut up about em, and I ended up getting brainwashed. Soon I'm calling the Blues 'us' instead of 'them'. In any New Zealand–South Africa clash, I always cheer for the Kiwis anyway. In fact, unless you lot are playing an Aussie side, Aussies almost always cheer for the Kiwi team, no matter the sport. Not like you bastards. You *never* barrack for us, not even when we're playing the fucking Poms.

— That's because we've taken so many pastings from you pricks down the years, and because of how much your players love rubbing it in.

—Whatever. Oh, for fuck's sake, ref, he was off his feet, surely!

The game's tight, scores locked with some penalties traded. Alex and another Kiwi are ganging up on a Saffa with some good-natured wind-ups. A cut-out pass from the Blues halfback, quick hands in the mid-field, and the winger's into space. Does his opposite, and he's off, flying down the touch line. Everyone's suddenly yelling.

Alex: 'Go for the corner, bro!'

He does, but the fullback is quick enough and good enough to smash him out over the flag. Half the house groans; the other half roars. Alex and Ryan swear in tandem but can't keep from grinning.

Both sides score tries in the next ten minutes and the atmosphere revs higher. This is Alex's first big game in these parts; he's never before stood in a pub watching sport with support evenly split. Geography usually makes it one-way traffic. It certainly spices things up, the banter whizzing round, loud mouths drawing hecklers, flinging it back, a few Kiwi lads chanting a haka, the Saffas telling them to shut it because there are more Islanders in the side than Maoris . . .

Half time, and it was very nearly a three-pint half. Alex hasn't eaten much and he can feel the strong lager warm in his veins. In his tongue too, and he stands at the urinal talking rugby league with a burly bloke from Toowoomba, Cowboys fan.

There's a deep queue around the bar, so Ryan starts chatting to a Kiwi bird beside him — *Enjoying the game*? She's off to Egypt in a few days and swore she wouldn't blow any money this weekend, but what can ya do when your degenerate flatmates crank up the pressure on both rubber arms? He laughs obligingly, then out of habit he thinks of a question that'll get her talking a lot, a topic he can restart her along easily — *There's so much to do in Egypt. What are your plans once you get there?* — then he switches off. He's drinking in the atmosphere around him, wondering how he could have forgotten it so completely. He hasn't been in an Antipodean theme pub in months. It's common for a lot of London's Southerners to disparage these pubs, declare it sacrilege to relocate halfway around the world then stick to places that could as well be a mile from your parents' house. But even these types invariably have a ball whenever they venture back.

By the time they reach the bar, the Kiwi girl's on about taking a felucca down the Nile to Cairo after she's finished in Nubia. Ryan's wondering if Alex has been introduced to Mr Snakebite yet, doubts it, decides it's high time he was, and orders two of them. He gives the girl a fitting farewell platitude — *Might talk to ya later* — and she's like, *Yeah, mate, no worries*, without seeming too fussed, and Ryan decides then that he probably *will* talk to her later.

—What are these?

—Snakebites.

—What's in 'em?

—Depends where you're at. In here they're lager, cider and red flavouring.

—Sounds appalling.

—You'd be surprised, mate. Not for no reason is this a Southern piss-head London staple. Have a lash.

— . . . Tastes better than it sounds. Sweeter than beer. Pack much wallop?

—Amm . . . yeah, kind of.

—What's the damage on a pint of . . . Jesus, what do ya wanna kick it from there for, man?! Prime attacking ball and he kicks it away!

Alex sits on the Snakebite all second half. A good thing too, because he soon needs to piss again but there's no way in hell he can leave with the game so delicately poised. The Blues number eight goes from the ruck, breaking a tackle, making good metres. Two more hit-ups from the forwards, then quick ball back for the drop-kick. It doesn't look clean enough but it limps the distance, skidding over, sending the Blues ahead by two.

Ryan: 'You little *ripp*er!'

Three minutes to play. Alex wants the Blues to shut up shop; Ryan says two points isn't enough, that they've gotta try and score again. The Bulls win a dubious penalty near halfway and their kicker lines up the shot.

Ryan: 'Whatcha up to the rest of the day?'

Kicking for a big one with you? But he's not about to extend himself so baldly. 'Not too sure really.'

Ryan: 'Tell ya what, mate, I'm overdue a bender, so if we scrape through with a win here we'll see if I can't show you your biggest night in London Town so far.'

Alex looks at him sharply. Then he feels jealous, wishing he too could say what he felt so unselfconsciously.

'You're on there, mate. Always happy to fall in with a seasoned campaigner.'

'Let's see if that's still a motto of yours by morning.'

Then Alex wonders what will unfold if they *don't* scrape through with a win here . . . and as the kicker starts his run-up he feels like he's got fifty quid riding on it.

Distance won't be a problem . . . but he's put a small hook on it, and the wind carries it still further . . . It hits the upright and bounces away. The Kiwis and Ryan go mental . . .

. . . The rebound is gathered in by a Bulls winger following up, the angle of his run wrong-footing tacklers, and he crashes over under the bar.

Ryan waves in disgust and heads for the bar through the cavorting of every Saffa in the house. Alex trudges to the Men's. The urinal fills up with near-silent Kiwis. Alex wonders what might have been. He's not happy about the footy either. Realises he can still hear the commentary and looks around, spotting a TV in a high corner. Watches the conversion go over. There's a queue for a urinal now, but Alex can't bring himself to rush things, that emptying/relief sensation about all he has left to savour. There's a ledge in front of him and he wishes he'd brought his drink in.

A voice from further down the toilet, yelling loudly: 'Go wide, go wide, go wide!'

Commentator: 'Time's up on the clock, next stoppage will end it. That's nine phases now for the Blues though.'

A big jolt in Alex's chest. He looks at the screen to see his team in possession near the opposition twenty-two. Surely not . . .

The forwards keep it close but that's nearly twenty phases; they're bound to make an error . . . The toilet is shouting exhortations, advice; Alex realises he's facing the room with his dick in his hand; zips up without looking.

'Send it out *now*!'

The ball takes an age to be recycled. The first-five gets it, passes and doubles around, takes the ball again . . . running sideways . . . throwing a pass so long the ball and the clock seem suspended, spiralling through a world of possibilities . . .

. . . The Blues centre enters the image out of nowhere, hitting the ball a metre from an intercept, crashing into the fullback, stretching out an arm . . .

'YEEEEAAAASSSSS!!!'

Alex pushes free of the bedlam in the toilet. Ryan's standing alone, one fist held up. His flinches as Alex throws an arm around him; then they're yelling at each other.

15

RYAN

The last time I was in a Walkabout there was a loud Aussie guy standing at the bar. He was wearing an Adelaide Crows T-shirt and drinking VB stubbies at two quid a pop. Powderfinger were on the stereo, and the bloke was bopping along, singing when he wasn't talking. He'd just returned from the classic Southern 'van tour' of Western Europe, Amsterdam to Pamplona to Oktoberfest, the horde partying every night, alienating every culture they came across. Two friends from home had just arrived and moved in; they'd brought Twisties and Bundaberg and were throwing a boozy barbie tomorrow arvo. The tour company, Down Under Up Top, were taking them up to Hogmanay for New Year's, and if they had a good time with DUUT, they were going to book with them for the tour covering the Gallipoli piss-up next year.

He's not bad company, young Alex. Got a bit of craic in him; a bit twisted, but I'm all for that. He's friendly enough too, but I can't see him ever kissing much arse. Quiet with strangers but getting more chatty as the drink goes down. I got some grub in him from the bar kitchen, then steered us into a circle; he left all the talking to me — it was getting a little embarrassing — but he's pitching in more now. Getting some laughs too.

Alex, to one of the guys: 'You're a chef? How come you're not wearing your hat then? Ashamed of your profession, are you?'

That one doesn't go down so well. Then one of the girls brings up Geri Halliwell's name, for Christ's sake, something about another comeback, and I'm disappointed when the others pick up on it. This goes on for a minute or so, and I can see Alex has something to add. I'm trying not to sigh as it looks like he's going to reveal himself a pop-freak as well.

Alex: 'An interesting fact I heard about Geri Halliwell: she actually shares a Christian name with a fellow called Jerry Mouse . . . who played opposite Tom Cat in the animated cartoon series, Tom and Jerry.'

A few of us break up over that. The others chortle along for form's sake. Not too sure how long he's gonna be able keep it at this even keel, though; he's on his fifth pint already. It's the girls that worry me. The way he's ogling them on the sly, staring them down when they're talking. He's so transparently keen I've gotta guess he hasn't had one in a while. It almost looks like he's dealing with the Northern duck syndrome: yet to get off the mark in these parts, no mileage on the cock, shot-selection suffering for it.

One of them seems mildly interested in him, but as Alex gets more juiced he's gonna blow it for sure.

Happens a lot with shy guys. Use booze to shed the shell for a while, drink themselves beyond prime-inebriation point, and suddenly they're slurring and yahooing, blind to the signals they should be sifting for. Sure, they should still have a good time, but that don't count for much when you're a single man out on the pull, and the next thing you know the sun's in your eyes and there's nothing in bed but you and a crusted hanky.

So I pull him aside. 'Nice day out there: let's go and lap up some sun on the green for a while.'

Frowning: 'Are you kidding me? This is cool, bro . . . Those guys are good value.'

He can't even tell me he wants to stay because he's on first base with some girls. 'They'll still be here when we come back. They'll be steaming by then too.'

We head out and amble back the way we came, stopping at the first shop.

Alex: 'Gotta love that about this country: walk into your average dairy and walk out with a bag full of piss.'

Dairy. Pretty fucking Kiwi term that one. Luckily I've kicked round with the sheep-shaggers long enough; I'd need a fucking translator otherwise. 'Gotta love that about this *con*tinent, mate.' I get a can of Becks. For a second it looks like Alex is eyeing up the hot stuff above the counter . . . but he settles on two cans of Amstel.

We're crossing the road to the green as Alex lifts his first lid and drops a good swig. Comes up smiling. 'Gotta love *that* too, the lax street-drinking laws. Do this on a city street in NZ and the first cop who goes past is gonna want a wee word.'

'Yeah, same in Oz. Different drinking cultures, though. Only drunks and teens and Southerners take the piss and get tanked in public here. If you let everyone do it back home, the streets'd be fucking mayhem.'

'Oh hell yeah. You'd have a riot every night of the week.'

Me: 'It's frowned on, though. Drink in public and you're a cunt hair away from being classed as a bum. You'll get the wide berth from a fair percentage.'

I see that this shocks him a bit. He says nothing as we walk on to the green. Looks at the can in his hand. Runs an eye over his clothes. Then a group walk past us and you can see him trying to read the nuances in their looks. He holds the can subtly after that, behind his leg, Southern style.

We find a spot on the green as far from the huddles of drunks as possible. A few of the geezers around the park have taken their shirts off, though it can't be much above 20 degrees. You can tell when spring's arrived in the UK by the blinding flashes of white you're suddenly assailed by. It's like people use public disrobing as soon as they humanly can as a finger in the face of another winter survived. It's different on the Continent. I remember walking the Ku'Damm in Berlin one May, singlet and thongs, shorts and sunnies, still sweating, and barely spotting a single bared limb anywhere around me. I couldn't for the life of me work out how these people weren't passing out. Had a few drinks in the arvo with a fraulein I was staying with, and ended up yelling to a square full of jackets, 'What the *fuck* is *wrong* with you people!'

The sun feels mint today, like it's filling the skin with nutrients, revitalising dormant impulses. Alex is into it too, downing his beer at a rate that depresses me, cracking his second already. I was hoping there might be a game of touch happening that I could get us involved in, but everyone seems content just lounging. So it looks like I'll be shepherding a drunk around tonight, until the early start floors him and I have to carry him home . . .

Fuck that. I don't need it, and he needs it even less.

Go through my pocket until I find the right bag, take it out casually. I made a few speed-bombs earlier — quarter grams wrapped in tobacco papers — and I make sure he's looking as I pop one in my mouth, washing it down with the Becks. From behind my sunnies I watch him stare for a few seconds.

Finally: 'What was that?'

'What was what?'

'That thing you just ate.'

'Oh, just a bit of speed, mate. Bit worried at how pissed I'm feeling. Keen to try and get laid tonight; that's not gonna happen if I'm stumbling and dribbling shit by sundown. So what time did that call from—'

'And how does speed help with that?'

'It just does.' I've no right to take this gamble, but fuck it, he deserves to know anyway. '*You* should know.'

A frowning smile: 'How would *I* know?'

Puh-lease: 'You've had it before.'

'Oh no I haven't.'

'Come on, man, no need to bullshit me. I'm not gonna ring ya old girl and dob on ya.'

'I've got no idea what you're talking about.'

'Like fuck you don't. You were on it that night in The Angler, up Picc Circus. You were fucking *steaming* on it, mate. On fire.'

'*Me*?' Swigging at his can again. 'I've never *touched* drugs.'

I kill my dubious smile too suddenly, like a man spotting a snake and jumping back. 'Oh right. Never mind, my mistake. I might go and get another—'

Sharp: 'Na, what? What made you think that?'

I make like I'm going to play dumb . . . then sigh. 'Sorry, man, I can't tell you.'

But that's bait few can turn their backs on, and he's having none of it. I stretch out his coercing me for a couple of minutes, then: 'She said she told you. She fucking *promised* me she told you about it. Oh man, she's gonna *disembowel* me for this.'

Alex, a roiling ball of intrigue, leaning into me: '*Who*? *What*?'

'. . . Lease.'

'Lisa? What *about* her?'

Lying back full length, as if the words drain me: 'She put speed in your drink that night. When you first arrived.'

The silence stretches out, but when I look it's to find Alex staring into space, a look almost of rapture about him. His voice rings with it. 'Hooooly shit. You don't know *how* many questions that answers for me.'

Me, sitting up: 'What do you mean?'

His face explodes into a grin. 'I was near sober when I walked into there, nervous and shy amongst all you pricks. Then I've had a pint with Lisa . . . and just fired into it like you were all long-lost mates! I usually have to drink four pints before I'll come close to relaxing that much. But *that* night . . . It didn't feel like drunk-talk . . . and I wasn't drunk anyway, I was sure I wasn't, not for ages.'

I'm brightening by the word.

Alex, staccato: 'I barely stopped to think about it at the time. Just pulled up once in a while and marvelled at how much fun I was having. But in the days after . . . That night made everything fall into place for me; I was really struggling up till then. Jesus Christ, *speed*? That never *once* crossed my mind.' Sobering suddenly, a rueful chuckle: 'I'd convinced myself it was some innate quality that came to my rescue; the resilience of the born go-getter. Twat.'

I feel sudden pity for him.

Then he's marvelling again. 'So *that's* what speed does?'

'What'd ya think it'd do?'

'I dunno . . . thought it made you aggressive, violent; thought the addiction bit in after one go on it.'

'Until you invariably found yourself doing houses and muggings in an ever-descending cycle?'

'Something like that.'

'Too many Ministry of Health pamphlets for you, old son.'

'So it's not dangerous?'

'Of *course* it's fucking dangerous. Just as dangerous as that thing in your hand right now.'

He looks at the beer can dubiously.

'It all about balance, mate. Drugs give you highs but there's

151

always a corresponding low to be repayed. The higher you go, the lower the crash. Just like a hangover being equivalent to how pissed you got. Take too much and the low kills you. Do it too often and you lose touch with the median altogether. Which might well kill you too. But booze makes life better sometimes; and other drugs are the same, just different effects.'

'I've met lots of Southerners over here who do drugs but seem completely different to the druggies I knew back home.'

'Yeah, sure. It's part of the antipodean landscape here.'

'Why?'

'Hard to say. Variety, quality and price are much better. Then there's the fact that most of us are here for a good time, not a long time, and we're a long way from people whose disapproval you can do without. So when you arrive and the mate who barely even smoked joints back home is popping pills or doing lines, having a ball but still getting to work every day . . .'

'I would never've believed that, but *fuck*, that was easily one of the best nights I've ever had. And I walked into the place alone and lonely . . . Why did she do it though?'

Not too sure about that myself there, chief. 'She just thought you'd make a cool housemate and wanted you to bond a bit more.'

'That little *bitch*.' But his face says he views her as anything but.

I silently hold the bag out to him. He reaches, then hesitates.

Me: 'You're not alone and lonely now, mate.'

That does the trick, but I feel a sudden weight on the moment as I watch him cross a very big line.

'What do I do with it?'

'Just wash it down . . . Now forget you ever took it.'

We stay on the green a while longer, talking about nothing. Then it's time.

Alex: 'We going back in?'

'Na, fuck the Walkabout. Let me take you on a pub crawl up the Uxbridge Road, see where the winds blow us.'

Alarmed: 'But what about those chicks?'

There you go, kid! Coming round already!

'A mere drop in the dam, brother. If you haven't forgotten their names by nine, I'll tattoo a silver fern on me foreskin.'

16

Alex asks Ryan what all the shit between him and Trent's about.

Ryan had arrived back from snowboarding in Andorra one Friday night. The house seemed empty, the whole crew partying in The Bed Bar. Texts and calls assured him that if he chucked a no-show he'd be woken by a twenty-body pile-up somewhere around three. But he was up for it.

Showered, then entered his room wearing just a towel; found Jennifer sitting on his bed. She hugged him a welcome home. She was wearing a miniskirt, and it rode up even higher as she sat down again. She had great legs. He'd told her that often. She was dossing in Lisa and Katie's room while she waited to go flatting in Richmond, and she'd stayed behind to make sure Ryan didn't weasel out of coming to the bash.

Ryan had struck out in Andorra, and Jen was more than shag-gable. She could be a shit-stirrer at times, but she made no secret of it, and he found the combination pretty horny.

He sat beside her, not bothering to dress, and asked her about

Trent. She'd hooked up with him the night before Ryan left, and he didn't know if anything had come of it. She said nothing had.

He stepped up the flirting then, but he knew the result and wasn't getting much from it, so he leaned over and kissed her within a minute.

—So what happened then? After you fucked her, that is.

—We caught a—

—How many times?

— . . . Two. So we're mini-cabbing to The Bed Bar. On the way she told me that her and Trent were 'perhaps' a little closer than she'd let on.

—Bitch! Did you feel rat shit?

—Guilt factor high but not hellish; she'd deceived me into it.

—Doesn't sound like your interrogation was Inquisition-like though. You knew she was dodgy, eh?

— . . . Yeah, maybe.

—At least you secured plausible deniability.

—That's a bit harsh, man.

—If you say so.

Another housemate, Jackie, a real mouse, had been in the next room the whole time. She'd heard their voices, heard the music for two hours, then innocently asked them about it in front of everyone in the bar.

Wasted and caught by surprise, Ryan finally came out with a story about showing off travel souvenirs and photos, but Jen gave it away with some terrible acting. And Trent went mental. Ryan denied it, but he and Trent were close enough for intuition to be slicing clean through Ryan's hot air. Trent disappeared, then bailed Ryan up at home.

—Rightly so too, eh?

— . . . Yeah . . . under the terms as he was seeing them.

—So what did ya do?

—I told them.

—That you had plausible deniability?

—Oh, fuck you! Go and get another round in, ya sheep-shagging prick! Sort these dudes out too. They got our last one.

But it wasn't enough, and Trent had moved out by dawn.

— Then it *all* turned to shit.

—How do you mean?

—Well, you've got this big circle of friends, yeah? A lot of them centred on work. Then there's workmates and shit thrown in: people you work with but who you just know you're never gonna hang with by choice.

—Sure.

—Oh, fuck it, man, no more shop talk. Hate cunts who—

—This isn't 'shop talk' and you know it.

—Sorry, but I'm telling tales out of school here. What's the world come to when Ryan Miller gives up gossip to the brass?

—I don't wanna be looked on as 'brass' by anyone . . . but I'll promise you, anything you say to me in confidence won't go any further.

—I should just look at you as one of the boys?

—*Yeah*. When you work with friends, your loyalty to them should take priority over the company. It has to, or you'll turn into a prick!

—I'm not sure I trust you enough to swallow that verbatim, but let me ask you this . . .

—Shoot.

—After the promise you just made, what if I was to tell you

156

about people you like getting up to bad shit at work — straight-up sacking offences?

— . . . Depends what it was, really. But unless it was something heinously unsafe, or unless they were making me complicit in something, I'd ask you to ask them to stop doing it . . . and then to say that if they *didn't* stop doing it, I didn't want to hear anything about it ever again.

— Not sure that I'm prepared to take it to the bank just yet—

—Shake on it, bro.

—Yeah, whatever.

Ryan and Trent weren't talking, but with lots of mutual friends caught in the middle, they'd end up together a lot. Most people teased Ryan about what he'd done, but few were calling for the lethal injection.

—Then what?

—Then *Morris* stepped into the picture.

—Who's *Morris*?

—This fucking Glaswegian piece of *shit*. He'd started a few weeks before, Dispatch team leader.

—What was his story?

—He was a pretty . . . gregarious type, yeah? Loud, out there, whatever ya wanna call it. He took advantage of his station as hard as he could too, so it didn't take him long to fall in with the regulars. I didn't like him much.

Morris was super-smarmy, making friends just to get nearer others. Treated his temps like shit, except for the young ones with pussies. Then one day Matty and Ryan were chatting with Alonso — Albanian kid down in Replenishment. Morris appeared and bollocked Alonso for slacking off. But Matty took the blame, effectively telling Morris that Alonso was one of the crew, that Morris should lighten up. But Morris ignored him, told Alonso that if he wasn't back at work in ten seconds he could go and sign out with Security one last time.

Ryan's first line was, 'You do a half-decent job of convincing people you're not a complete cocksucker, Morris, but don't you think this is letting the old guard down a *mite* too far?'

Morris bit back right away, and Matty judged Ryan the winner with a fourth-round knock-out.

—So where does Morris fit into the whole Trent–Jennifer–Ryan love triangle?

—You taking the piss?

—Just a smidgen.

—You're lucky I can live with that. Well, I guess you could say that Morris made the triangle into a parallelogram.

—I think you mean a quadrangle or a rhombus.

—No, I mean a parallelogram, mate, 'cause this was one of the most skewed things I've ever found myself caught up in.

That happened a week before Ryan left for Andorra. Back five minutes and he'd fallen out with Trent and began feeling some uncharacteristic coldness from a few of the crew. Noticed how cosy Morris and Trent were becoming, then started to hear from better friends that the two of them were slagging Ryan big time.

Ryan decided that if people wanted to let some poisonous fuck twist their opinions of him, they weren't worth the head-space anyway. So he ignored it. He weighed pulling Morris aside one night and snotting the cunt, but Morris was a team leader . . . and, according to Morris, an ex-schemie wide-boy from way back. And with Matty and Cardiff to large it with, the anti-Ryan camp was never going to get too big anyway. Then Cardiff got caught by his wife with Bianca, chucked his job in without notice and fucked off to travel the world with her. Then Matty's two-month trip through India rolled around . . .

And suddenly the number of people talking to Ryan when the gang were out was half the size of the circle across the room.

—. . . So you pulled out?

—Almost totally.

—What happened to Morris? He's not there any more.

—Well, cobber, I know fine twists and Hollywood endings aren't often synonymous, but this tale has both.

—Spill it.

Turned out Ryan's mate Alonso was more of a dark horse than anyone realised. One night everyone bar Ryan was at the local. The publican finally got them all out near twelve. Some hung about in the park beside the pub, carrying on the party. Morris was hitting on a Bulgarian temp who Alonso's mate had recently broken up with. Morris had been working her for a week and was getting somewhere. Only Morris either didn't understand the waves he was causing or he wrote the Albanians off as featherweights, because when he ducked behind a building for a piss, Alonso walked off in the opposite direction, rounded the building, then snuck up behind Morris and twatted him with a Jim Beam bottle.

—Fucking hell! . . . Was he all right?

—Hospital job, mate. They kept him there three days, and afterwards he was so fucking spooked he disappeared off the EUE radar completely.

— How come Alonso didn't get in shit for it?

—Because no one knows he did it.

— . . . How do you know?

—Because Alonso told me.

— . . . So now I know too.

—You've been on the Smarties again.

—What a *mad* little prick! Bit of a pussy or what?

—Don't think so. It only went down like that so he wouldn't get sacked. Besides, I don't much subscribe to the 'dirty fighter equals coward' thing. It may not take much balls at the time, but you've gotta have the balls to face up to the all-out revenge you're gonna get thrown at you. And you've gotta be willing to face a stretch inside over it too.

— . . . I dunno. Seems like a shabby way—

—Enough of that shit anyway. Get your game face on: Amber and Debs are coming back. Amber's yours. Remember, we're in a band and you're the singer/songwriter.

—I certainly am.

—Give it half an hour, then go up and do your thing on the karaoke machine. You'll be in like Flynn after that.

17

MELVYN

Thing is — and you will *not* believe this — the toff cunt didn't ave no money! Well, e ad money, enough to let im live like e'd been brought up to live, but bugger all more. Bit of a black sheep, see? Daddy cut 'is umbilical quite some time ago. I figured e'd ave investments all over town, been on a good salary for years, but no. A kid and a bitter ex-wife. Didn't even own 'is own gaff no more.

I'm a reasonable judge, and 'is sob story were convincin. But I weren't about to watch my golden goose turn to lead wivout testin the waters. And e passed. My deadline expired, e's made no attempt to 'ide, and even when Dessie ad the 38 to his temple and to all appearances were under firm orders to squeeze, the toff ad nufin for me but snot and tears.

Well, not entirely. Said e could come up wiv three undred large and anuva two undred in a few months, and I were tempted to take it.

Didn't, though. I've seen the arvest of a fair bit-a blackmail in me time, and when things get drawn out like that, the more time the patsy 'as to contemplate a future of avin 'is plates of meat swept out from under 'im every time e looks to be staggerin back up again, someone often dies. That someone is usually the patsy, of course, by 'is own 'and. But toffs have friends in 'igh places. And even if they don't — or if they can't bring emselves to ask a favour for some reason — an undred grand-plus in sterling will buy you some very dedicated 'employees'.

No, in my manual blackmail 'as to be a one-off or nufin.

So I tells im I'd try to think of some alternative arrangement.

I already knew where e worked, but it weren't till e were vomitin every inch of 'is life on to the table for me to go over wiv a microscope that I realised this well-spoken goose still ad one very large golden egg left inside it after all.

———

Alonso knows a guy over here from his home town, back in Albania. Actually, he knows quite a few guys over here from back home. There's this one guy though, Dimitri. He's on the dole. He's twenty-seven. He lives alone, rents a penthouse suite in Holland Park. He wears designer clothes and three-hundred-pound sunglasses. He hangs out in the high-roller rooms at casinos. Dimitri drives a new Mercedes, midnight blue. He cruises with the top down on sunny days, the wind in the hair of whatever girls are riding with him. He has a facial and a trim on a Tuesday, jets to Europe on Thursdays, then stops by the DSS on a Monday to sign on.

Back in Tirana, Dimitri worked for Alonso's father as a roofing apprentice. Dimitri doesn't lay roofing tiles any more. He helps people enter the country illegally, people from the East. As part of the service he then helps most of them into work and accommodation. He knows the men who own the labour agencies and the houses: they pay him by the body. They don't pay the bodies much, what with rent, insurance, administration fees and ten other bills they only ever hear of. Some know people here already; they usually leave quickly. Others can stay or go on the streets. They usually stay.

Dimitri's little brother is a good friend of Alonso's, lives next door to him, and Dimitri comes by the estate to see him once a fortnight or so, stepping his Guccis around the piss puddles in the corridor. Dimitri leaves his Mercedes unlocked in the car park downstairs. The car is never touched. Crime in the area is rampant.

Alonso and the boys like it when Dimitri comes: he hands cash and drugs out like his grandmother once did sweets. Dimitri doesn't deal drugs, though, says it's too hard to keep your hands clean. But he moves a lot of stolen property; can shift most things in a matter of hours. He laughs endlessly and yells his jokes for the whole floor to hear.

Stories are told about Dimitri, not just among the Albanians in London but back home as well. He hasn't been back in three years, but word of his deeds has spread. Albanian boys used to worship KLA fighters and soccer stars. Now their idols are men like Dimitri.

Most of Alonso's contemporaries are the same, both here and at home. They want to be Dimitri.

Not all do, though. Claudian, Dimitri's brother, just wants to marry Arjana and buy a small flat somewhere; maybe save up and bring her mother out. But Arjana won't marry him until they have a few grand for a deposit. He makes four-fifty an hour, before tax. Kreshnik was smart in school and wants to study. He makes six pounds an hour. He'll have to pay all of his uni fees himself; pay them up front, at that: migrants don't qualify for student loans or benefits in the UK. Fernando wants to get out of London: the city gives him migraines. He wants to buy a small plot in Dorset and start a market garden. He's a fifth-generation produce grower; he grows vegetables in the sun boxes outside their tower-block windows. Fernando has never been to Dorset.

But Alonso wants none of this. He doesn't want to be Dimitri either. He's thinks Dimitri will be dead soon. What Alonso wants is very personal to him, embarrassing almost, and he talks about it only with his closest, and only when he's wasted. Alonso is in the West: this is a dream in itself, because dreams come true in the West, ask anybody. He's no idiot, though, thinking that getting here is enough, that the West will do the rest. That myth he had seen exposed in days.

And Alonso didn't come here to let complacent white wankers order him around for the rest of his life either.

Dreams can indeed come true in the West, but only if you can snatch them from the sky.

Alonso's dream is to play guitar.

But Alonso doesn't just want to *play* the guitar, as in strum a few chords and lead sing-alongs. He can do that already. No, Alonso wants to play the lead, be the axe-man, make that bitch fucking *talk*; cut an audience to ribbons with picking and power chords. Fuck Dimitri; Alonso wants to be a post-folk Bob Dylan; he wants to be Slash, Angus Young, John Frusciante.

There was a guy at the protest, the night they occupied Parliament Square, Alonso dragged along by his friend Lisa. Wild blond afro and jeans. The guy's friend had wheeled a barrow with two amps and a car battery on it. They took up station on the plinth of the Churchill statue. The guy cracked open a case and drew out a twelve-string Gibson. Alonso's heart sped up when he saw it: matt black, so dark it seemed to soak up the light like a small black hole. The guy plugged it in.

Then he started playing.

Alonso's seen a lot of good guitarists plying their trade since arriving in London, but *this* guy, without a note of accompaniment . . .

With the chanting and the yelling, the sit-ins closing the roads, the autocrat and his court plotting war right there, the cops getting rougher, the atmosphere in the square had been tightening. The guitarist popped that mood all by himself, with a plastic pick and four fingers. He popped it, then gathered up the fragments and wreathed himself in them, jacked up even tighter. He *ruled* that place for the hour that he played. A thousand-odd years of class and tradition, prestige and power, and this grinning lout turned it into his own backyard. Even the police faltered, as if they'd run up against a power higher than that which fed their babies. Alonso saw policemen tapping fingers against riot shields. He fancied he could see the warmongers themselves lining the windows of the Parliament, eyeing the guitarist like he was a piper on a battlement. Younger hearts knew the words to the songs, and the older ones — some eighty and over — clapped and grinned like teens.

Word came down that he had to go — this was going to spread: the city would be a bonfire by midnight — and a squad of truncheons and shields peeled off and closed in on him. The guitarist mocked them with a bow, then cut into 'All Along The Watchtower', the music jerking his body. A fat Cockney put himself between the minstrel and the closing cops, joined a second later by a crew of white students in Arabic fancy dress, then a line of middle-aged women, mixed race, calling themselves 'mothers against murder'. Alonso had to run, but he got there as it kicked off, as the demonstrators linked arms, defending their talisman as if he were a five-year-old named Sayeed under cluster bombs. None threw blows — it would have betrayed all they stood for — but the police stood for no such thing, and they were pushing with shields and jabbing with sticks. An older woman beside Alonso screeched and fell out of the line, hunched up on the ground. The sound hit a primal part of him, and he was glad he hadn't brought Fernando's gun along. Instead he leaned across to the sneering boy — who'd complacently left his visor up — and deftly poked him in the eye. He dragged the woman clear as the cop squealed and his colleagues faltered, tasting the fear that they had owned up till then.

He shouldn't have done it, but he was no peacenik. Where he came from, to fight without weapons was to eat without teeth. To oppose *the state* without weapons was to tie your own noose. The woman was OK — seething but grateful — and he could still hear Lisa in the line, hollering into police faces. The guitarist was hurtling through a solo, the notes crashing over the stand-off, but when Alonso looked up at him he was looking straight back, and he gave the next twenty notes to Alonso alone.

Alonso left after that. He was new here, but he knew better than to hang around with the state's blood on your finger. He lost himself in the crowd, then slipped from a quiet corner of the square, took a taxi to Victoria and tubed home.

Three days later he and Claudian took down an estate agency in Chiswick, making off on a stolen motorbike that they ditched in an alley. Claudian's share went into his marriage fund. Alonso brought a twelve-string Gibson guitar, black as the gulf between stars.

Alonso doesn't fear the law in this country. Not really. He grew up in a land where torture is used as often as search warrants; where the state can kill you with or without a mock trial. He doesn't really fear the prisons here either: he's sure he can get by Inside, keep his head for a few years. Besides, unless he's pinched for something very serious, he'll probably suffer nothing worse than deportation.

No, what Alonso fears most about this country is turning forty and still pushing a trolley around a warehouse, a pimply young Paddy yelling at him and timing his breaks. His kids playing football outside crack dens. Avoiding the movies that seduced him as a child, that sold him the infinite possibility of life in the West. But he knows he'll never be a sports star, like Jamie Foxx in *Any Given Sunday*. Or a High Court barrister, like Ben Affleck in *Changing Lanes*. He'll never be on ten million a picture, like Julia Roberts in *Notting Hill*.

He knows what the typical first-generation migrant is supposed to do. What the Indians and the Pakistanis — and lots of others who didn't have the brains or the English or the cash to study for better — did after arriving and taking stock. They worked their fucking arses off at whatever they could find, squirrelled every cent, invested it in low-risk, low-return businesses. Then made sure their children grew up with the benefits that this country had excluded them from. And good on them too: with a surgeon in the family, or a broker, they're now reaping comfortable retirements and cracking the middle class wide open, achieving in a few decades what the white masses here haven't managed in millennia.

But that's not for Alonso. He's never fantasised about being Parminder Nagra's dad in *Bend It Like Beckham*.

He wants to be a Mark Wahlberg in *Rock Star*. Sees no real reason why he can't. No reason not to *try*, anyway. And to try with everything he's willing to do, every line he's willing to cross.

He has a great ear and knowledge for music; original tunes bouncing round in his skull, humming in his throat, beginning to break out of his guitar. He's got no idea if he has an innate gift for it, or if you absolutely need to have one before you'll get anywhere. But he's owned his first guitar for a year now, and he's come a long way in that time, sucked up most of what the few free teachers he's found can give to him. He's a late starter, though. He's well aware of that. So what he needs, along with the best tuition he can find and afford, is time. The time to study, practise and play every day. All day. The time to go to gigs most nights, to jams, to scout out the scene. And he knows what can buy him that time.

The same shit that buys most things in the West.

He thinks about thirty thousand sterling should do it.

18

RYAN

This is the fifth time we've worked together now. I've driven a couple of other birds as well; took three of them to a stag do in Surrey the other night. Those shows were more in keeping with what you'd expect. Long nights too, with some of the girls turning tricks afterwards. I'd rather not be a part of that, but it snuck up. Melvyn was busy when I went to complain to him about it and come Friday a healthy cut from all supplementary transactions was in me envelope.

I didn't fancy trying to give the money back.

No matter what the other girls get up to, though, no one affects a crowd the way Nadia does. She's cagey about where she learned to perform: 'gymnastics' and 'too many Madonna videos' is as much as I've gotten out of her. You can see that the thought never crosses her mind, but I tell ya, if *she* wanted to stay clocked on afterwards for a bit she wouldn't have to live on this estate for much longer. I've had some fucking ludicrous sums drooled at me. I don't tell her that, though. She's thinks I'm a wanker as it is.

Still, she actually invited me up for a cuppa last week. Mustn't have felt like being alone. Well, she didn't really *invite* me up, it was more an order. 'Come for a minute; drink a tea,' as the car door shut and I was shifting gear.

It's a pretty small estate this one — three storeys, perhaps fifty-odd units all up — and she says it's hassle free pretty much. I caught her up as she was unlocking her door on the third floor and walking inside. There was this sudden thudding from further in and I felt a presence, some darker shadow. I freaked, almost yelled, thinking we'd sprung a burglar. Then this shadow started whining, and I knew it was just a dog. She patted it in the dark for a moment, thumping its rump hard. Then she flicked a light on, and I almost yelled again.

For this was no dog. This was a carnivorous horse.

Some sort of Rottweiler-cross. Crossed with a bear or something. But the way he snuffled at her, ears fawned back, crocodile tail hammering the wall, relaxed me just as quickly. He was obviously a big softie, and I've never been scared of dogs anyway. So I stepped inside.

Which was when he noticed me. Nadia ceased to exist for him, and within half a heartbeat I was wondering how I'd ever thought he looked placid. The ears snapped forward and the hackles went up, and he was going to eat me, no doubt about it. His head looked like a boar's; chest and shoulders that could play chicken with a Volkswagen. Tall too, as high as her waist nearly.

He's in his prime and hale as hell, but there are scars all over his face — scars from fighting, surely — and the combination was fucking satanic. I waited for her to intervene but she just stood back and watched. Then he's padding towards me, growling like an idling tank, teeth starting to show, sixty-odd kilos of focused butchery.

I was a cunt hair away from leaping backwards and slamming

the door — I wasn't sure it would stop him — when she said one word, very soft. 'Sa-la.'

He flinched and froze in mid-stride, a few feet away from me, one paw in the air. Daring me closer.

Nadia: 'It OK. He will not hurt.' Amused: 'Not right now anyway.' And she walked inside, left me facing him in the hallway.

I did what anyone who knows dogs does. I gently gave him my hand to sniff. He barely even looked at it. Even when I patted him, he just stared and waited. He might not be allowed to kill me but I was on his patch and things hadn't been cleared with him.

I was hoping she'd come back, but then I heard cutlery rattling in a drawer. So I massed my nerve and squeezed past him. He shifted a bit and jammed me against the wall momentarily.

Nadia and I drank tea and chatted. Or rather she tossed bored questions at me and I answered them. The dog sat on his haunches and glared at me. Why did I come to London? How long had I been here? Had I studied anything? Did my family miss me? Did I miss them? She wouldn't answer any of mine, though, didn't even acknowledge them, and I submitted to her rules pretty quickly. Ten minutes later she said she was tired and that I knew where the door was. I had no idea what I'd said wrong.

The dog saw me out. Then he put his paws up on the door so he could look at me through the window, and stared me down the stairs.

He was still staring as I passed out of sight. I checked.

It's a long drive back to hers, half an hour or so, and she doesn't say a word the whole way. Just watches London blink by. I don't either. I never do any more, not until she does. The stick of rejection beat that rule into me. I dunno what the silence is like for her — perfectly fine, I guess, given the company — but it's awkward as fuck for me.

She doesn't say goodbye as we pull in and she gets out. But I'm slow about pulling away, watching her sidelong, and my heart leaps to an alarming height when she stops and mouths something. I try to wind my window down casually.

'What was that?'

Puzzled and impatient: 'You coming in?'

I shape a frown that I hope conveys indecision, but when she shrugs and walks off, the next thing I know I'm skipping up the stairs behind her. The same routine with the dog, only this time he doesn't rush me. It's a nice lounge: deep carpet, big chairs and sofa, TV, computer, posters of wildlife and album covers.

The dog settles down only after I do. There's too much sugar in the tea, but I don't say a word as she fires up the computer and stacks on a play list.

'Any requests?'

'. . . "Loser", Beck.' I'm certain she'll have it. She knows her music in and out, makes the medleys that she dances to herself. She has it sure enough, and she smiles at my choice.

I barely know a thing about her. She's from Iraq; all right, Baghdad. She's been in the UK a year or two. Beyond that I know nothing. She sits down and I'm waiting for the questions again, determined to do better this time. But she says nothing, closes her eyes as she smokes. I can't handle another interminable silence — I'll leave before she puts me through that again — so I ask how she controls the dog when they're out; he must have a pull like a tugboat, outweigh her by near ten kilos, and what was that word she said that set him off me the other night? (And where the fuck did all that come from?)

This time she responds. His name is Saladin, Sal to his pals. Said the European way, which butchers the Arabic diction. I ask how this goes. In answer she stands and walks across to me, bending her head down to mine. Like she's going to kiss me.

Flusters me so totally I almost lift my chin. But she just whispers in my ear.

'Sa-la-ha-deen,' or something thereabouts. I move to practise it, but she snaps a finger to my lips, shakes her head, then returns to her seat. That's his real name but I'm ordered never to utter it while he's around.

He knows he's being talked about. He even stops glaring at me and pads over to her, rubs against her leg till she strokes him. Fixes his eyes on me again.

He was about one when she met him. She was short a place to stay and ended up on a couch belonging to a Syrian guy, Ali, sometime boyfriend of a friend of hers. The dog was his. It wasn't long before she decided that Ali was a prick, 'a fucking *cock*sucker': she says it with real venom. Ali only ever spoke Arabic to Sal. Beat the shit out of him at the slightest provocation, had done from day one. He used a belt, buckle side up, swung at his head, yelled abuse. Justified this by pointing out what a handful the dog was going to be once he had his full growth. He didn't look like he was going to be a handful to Nadia. Sal and she were friends, though only while Ali was out, and it'd taken days of patience before the dog had let her touch him.

He was kept in a tiny kennel in a tiny backyard, so scared of Ali he had to be whacked before he'd come inside. Then he'd tremble in a corner till he was sent out again. She never once saw Ali pat him, and his friends who came round were just as bad — jeered at the dog, called him *Salha*, like calling a Robert Roberta. Nadia decided there was no rhyme or reason to the punishments, that Ali was just a sick fuck. She was wrong, though; she pieced it together by listening to him with his friends. Ali had known both the dog's parents, and Sal was the pick of the litter. He was going to be immense. He was going to win Ali a lot of money, more than Sinbad had before he finally lost. But Ali could barely control

Sinbad by the end; hated turning his back on the dog. This time would be different.

The day before Nadia was due to move out, she kicked in a rotten part of the back fence, then took the dog to her new home. Made sure she got back after Ali was due. He was just setting off to search for Sal.

He never found him. Nadia made sure he never learned her new address.

'He never fought then? The scars are from the beatings?'

'Yes. He never fight. He cool now too — you can see. This was two year ago. He not scared any more . . . until he hear Arabic. I have to lock him down hall if someone come who does not have English. But—'she grimaces — 'this is how I control him when nothing else will do.'

'By speaking Arabic?'

'Yes. Just the first part of his real name usually do it. Then he listen.'

And I'm just sitting there gobsmacked by this. No idea how to feel about the brute (who's fallen asleep, which is progress of sorts on my part, I suppose). Sure, I feel for him — I'm a dog man from way back — but what kind of demons are lying dormant in him?

Fucking London, man. You couldn't script what's around the corner. An Arab stripper with a stolen dog bred to fight that could kill her in a heartbeat . . . keeps it in line with two syllables.

'Does he let other people pat him?'

'Most can if they approach easy. He quite like it some time.'

'He's never bitten anyone?'

'Once or tw— . . . once or twice. And I tell him to both time.'

She gets a call from overseas a while later, puts the phone down long enough to shut Sal down the hall, then spends the next ten minutes giggling and jabbering in Arabic. The contrast between this her and the aloof dancer is dizzying.

She finally ends the call, blowing loud kisses into the phone, then hanging it up. She tells me it was her friend from home who lives in Dubai now and is getting married tomorrow.

Me: 'Is it an arranged marriage?'

'Kind of.'

Impulsively indignant: 'That shit really sucks. Why did you sound so happy for her?'

Frowning: 'It is not as bad as make out here, you know. People forget that West always been ruled by a class who use arrange marriage. And still is.'

'. . . That's true.'

'Arrange marriage not as simple as sounds. Our parents love their childs as much as yours do, this is number one. Number two is that parents want marriage to work — big mess if it doesn't — so couple are not often strangers. All of this considered before matches are made. The kids often have much input.'

I'm surprised by this. It makes a lot of sense, though.

I lose track of time as we talk. I get a txt from Alex at one point, thanking me. He'd been down in the dumps since that Amber chick he'd been rooting semi-regularly went home to Aussie last week when her visa ran out, so I lined him up a blind date with this Polish girl I know. Doesn't sound like he got his dick wet, but they're going to the movies on Wednesday. I make tea a few times and Nadia drives the music, pausing our talk regularly to write more new words into her notebook, and it's going on three when she says she's off to bed. I'm yawning myself; been up since seven.

I'm checking for the car keys as she takes a duvet and pillow from a pile of bedding in a corner. Drops them by me.

'You too tired to drive. Sleep here.'

Before I can answer she's off down the hall, Saladin trotting after her.

And I'm so going nowhere, hound of hell in the house or not.

Woken by something. Dunno what. Where the hell am I? The room's almost dark, but I place it as my head clears — *FUCK!* A white flash of terror and I almost unbalance the couch as I recoil from the dog. He's right by my head — *right* by it! — staring impassively.

Weak as prey: 'Sal . . . ahh . . . good boy?' Dead eyes in the gloom. Dead eyes in that huge, scarred head.

Should I call for her . . . ? Try to get up . . . ? Close my eyes again . . . ? I try to pat him . . . oh so slowly . . . and he lets me. Motionless as my hand rubs the hard muscle at the hinge of that awful fucking jawbone.

'You all right, mate? . . . What can I do for you?'

He kicks my heart again as he wheels around suddenly, trots to the door. Thumps it once with his nose; stares at me like I'm an imbecile. My stomach unknots.

'Oh, I get it. You want out, don't ya?' Which presents another dilemma. Because as much as I'd love to, there's no fucking way I can go freeing her dog on my own initiative at five in the morning. So I utter my most grovelling apology and bury my face in the pillow. I hear nothing, but a spot on my head gets steadily colder, and then he nudges it, sending a long shudder through me. I try a fake snore, but he nudges again, and as soon as I look up he skips across to the door and bangs it once more. Another stare — but he ruins the glacial effect this time by blurting out a long whimper.

Spur of the moment, I swing off the couch and his whine slices off. 'If this thing goes tits up, it was entirely your idea, OK?'

He doesn't answer.

'*OK?*'

No answer again, but he looks away first, and that's good enough for me.

I write her a quick note — *Out whoring and drinking. The boys.* — then pick up the dog lead hanging by the door. This sobers him: he takes two steps backwards and eyes me with real calculation. Shrugging: 'Your choice. I was happier in bed.' But then he seems to shrug himself and he's back nosing the door. I unlock it, pocket the key, twist the handle . . . and he slaps it out of my hand, surging round the corner and out of sight.

Oh, you big cunt! I'm frantically locking up behind me as I hear him avalanche down the stairs. I'm never gonna catch him — and I'm surely as dead as disco — but I take the stairs full speed, shove the door aside . . . stop. He's peeping back round the corner of the building, twenty metres away, dead still and giving me the idiot look. But he's off again as soon as he sees me.

In stages like this, he takes me to the park.

There's light in the sky and we're both fucking filthy by the time we get back. Yahooing through dark muddy parks will do that for you. I've got some breath back from the walk home, but his tea towel of a tongue's still down near his chest somewhere, and he's panting like a steam train. I made sure of that, throwing a stick, then hiding while he tore around hunting for me, shaking the earth like a war-horse. I haven't had a workout like that in months; feels fucking brilliant. Old Sal's had a few though, fit as farm dog, the big bastard.

My clothes are slick with mud and slobber but I've got a spare set in the van. I've got a towel and a water bottle too, so I try to make Sal presentable.

Against my ardent wishes he trots merrily down to the bedroom for de-briefing the moment I let him in. I don't think she wakes, though, and I settle into the bliss of the duvet to the sounds of Sal drinking somewhere . . .

His tail's vibrating through the couch springs as it thumps the floor. I don't open my eyes.

Nadia, to Sal: 'What the hell is *this* then? How long you been out *here*?'

Whump, whump, whump. He must be lying on the floor below me.

She doesn't speak for a long time but I'm sure she doesn't move either. Then she does move, and I hear her jingling the lead. 'You coming or not?' The tail picks up speed but he stays where he is. 'You *must* be kidding me? Right?' Something clicks. 'Oh, *I* get it. You been cheating on me, Sal?' *Whump-whump-whump* . . .'After all we been through, me and you? Walking away: 'Shame on you, big boy. Next time tell me so I stay in bed.'

I give him a blind pat as her door closes.

19

LISA

Estate. Only English rulers would have the temerity to take the name they use for their private pleasure-complexes and fix it to these huge, grim cabinets in which their worst and dullest are filed. Polar opposites along the opulence scale — obscene abundance to minus-bare-minimum — but carrying the same name. 'Estate'. Honest mistake, really.

There's a primary school across the road, a frigid thing of concrete wrapped in barbed wire, not a blade of grass on the whole campus. An assembly line for waitresses and solo mums, armed robbers and janitors. But as Kevin himself told me, the kids round here barely bother learning their ABCs. Survival for them has a different alphabet: GBH, HIV, DOA . . .

One of my first friends over here — Tracey from Liverpool — gave me her address and invited me round one day. 576 Mile End Rd, Mile End Estate. I read that and thought, 'Shit, young Trace is a bit of a dark horse, or what?' Took a bus round to hers, expecting to see an Edwardian mansion, rolling hills, game keepers prowling for poachers . . .

Not quite.

Looking back, hers wasn't all that bad. Comparatively. In comparison, that is, to *this* one. This one's a *name*. Mention that you live here, and the person you're speaking to will likely leap back two paces, check pockets for valuables, then quietly call Security.

I've been here a few times before and it's getting easier, but I've never come this late in the day. It's getting on towards dark. I'm supposed to phone Kevin when I get this close, and he sends someone to escort me in, but my fucking mobile's out of battery. Can't even raise Kev's number long enough to write it down and pay-phone him. Standing at the bus stop by the entrance, I take it out again for one last try, and I'm cooing and pleading with it when three youths emerge from the gate and stalk towards me. Black, medium build, hoods up. A description to match ten thousand appearing in unsolved-crime statements. I gulp, quickly pocket the phone — to them the equivalent of two fifty-quid notes. I'm glad that my feet are at least three sizes smaller then theirs. Then they're past me, and the twilight seems to brighten a shade.

And even if it *had* happened, it'd be more my fault than theirs. They're as conditioned by multi-media glitz and peer pressure to covet the baubles of consumerism as much as any of us are. Only they can't legally earn them, so they resort to alternative means of acquisition. They're as much creations of the consumer society as the trendy kids on the high streets.

Another minute of coaxing earns me nothing more than four seconds of a functioning phone. Fuck, fuck, *fuck*.

I know exactly where to head to in this labyrinth of misery and crime, but the place is fucking massive, and Kev's right near the centre somewhere. I'm going home. This is beyond stupid. Ten minutes along the walkways, through the underpasses, past the doors to the rubbish chutes and boiler rooms, visible to hundreds of windows. A plump lamb waddling the Masai Mara.

Feet slapping corridors, down fire escapes, a quick rap on a door in passing, streaming through the byways, sealing off escape . . .

I'm a true believer in the essential good of humankind, but these poor bastards are the fluff girls of society. Of *white* society anyway. They're not likely to wait long enough for me to win them with some Chomsky or Mandela. Especially not in an accent like mine.

Not gonna happen, Lease. Here's a bus, and I'm so on it . . .

But I've got orders for the weekend coming out my ears already. And this is the only chance I'll have, because Kev's away from tomorrow till Sunday . . .

Doesn't matter. Well, it *matters*, but not that much . . .

Fifty in the black so far . . . no, sixty-five with Willie's order, perhaps another thirty on spec in the Castle on Saturday . . .

Fuck this phone!

. . . Fortune favours, says Ryan. Fortune fucking favours.

Crossing the threshold feels like passing through a membrane, the sounds of the city seeming to dull behind me, to fade far quicker than they should.

Forcing my feet along the path, fear cold in my chest. I'm surrounded by shadows deep enough to hide neon bulldozers. Music filters down from somewhere above, the throbbing of the bass about all I can make of it, like a tribal drum in the Congo. This is about as far from Simonstown as it gets. There's not a body in sight, but such solitude in so densely populous a place just screams ambush. I know the protocol — it's the same wherever predation happens: the more confidence your body radiates, the safer you are — and I fight to put some pep in my step, scanning the shadows with just my eyes, head angled forward as if I couldn't care less what's around me.

I find myself preparing different strategies for the various racial groups I'm likely to be accosted by. I once spent an afternoon talking with an old English woman on the floor down from Kevin's. She's lived here half her life, and she told me that when it opened almost the whole estate was working-class white. But over the decades the dynamic shifted. Blacks from the Caribbean were the first migrants in, ruthlessly derided and persecuted by the incumbents. Then came the Sub-continentals, then African blacks, and the whites were suddenly the minority, those who remained beginning to reap what they had sown. Most of the 'Pakis' had moved on by the time the Eastern European influx began. A few Poms still cling on, a harried look about them, too weak, too poor or too broken to uproot and break for the border, stranded now in a hostile enclave.

Dropping Kevin's name should see me given safe passage by most of the blacks, but the Easterners will be a harder sell. Kevin's crew partly transcends race — he sees ethnic feuds as internecine — but opposition exists.

A figure pops into view from around a corner, turning briskly down the path towards me. The walk tells me it's a guy, even if the size doesn't. Not a black guy either, pretty sure of that. My feet freeze up of their own accord. His don't, but there's definitely a glitch as he becomes aware of me. But then, if anything, he's coming at me even faster.

And then about five more shapes appear from the same direction, falling in behind the first.

My courage expires at the first real test, feet performing an instant one-eighty, and I'm only a hundred metres away from the estate gates and the relative safety of the bus stop and the people gathered there, and with the forty-metre head start I've got on the gang I'm going to make this, piece of cake, no need to stride even, just play it cool, but just a quick check over my shoulder —

My heart slams into my ribs: one of them — I think the first one — is well ahead of the pack, the distance so narrow he may well have been running while my back was turned. Panic close to the surface now, wanting me to run, but that'd be madness, so I let my feet speed up to only half of what they're pleading for. About halfway to the bus stop now, at the worst I'll be able to scream for help, even though—

My bowels ice over as a big red bus sighs to a stop, collects all the people — while disgorging not a single soul — and takes off again, out of sight in three seconds. I can hear his footfalls now, he's definitely running, and my only hope is that it's not me he's after at all, which is entirely possible, isn't it? Of course it is, the guy could have any number of pressing engagements, and my walk slows to the pace of a woman attempting the fetal position while standing upright, and Kevin's name is gonna burst from my lips as soon as a finger is laid on me—

So close to my ear I'm biting back shrieks: 'Boo.'

Spinning, readying a knee for his groin, or a scream, or a plea, or a name drop, all at once, none at all—

Relief like a tepid tidal wave: '*Alonso*!'

His cherubic face wears a grin even wider than usual, but it soon ruptures, hilarity doubling him over.

'You fucking little piece of *shit*!' I'm relieved and angry and embarrassed and grateful, and then I'm hugging him, cackling into his shoulder.

When we can talk he asks me if I'm fucking crazy or just stupid, coming here alone at night? There's ire in his tone about my placing myself in danger, and I love him all the more for it. I apologise and tell him about my phone and my need to see Kevin.

Alonso: 'Yeah, well I care not if you need heart transplant and donor is in there, do not fucking do this again, Lisa, please. This not good place for you.'

I assure him I've learnt my lesson.

The group who were behind him catch up; they're all black and don't seem to have been with Alonso at all. His back straightens a notch and his grin disappears. He gives a measured nod as they pass; two of them nod back.

He says it's my lucky day, that he'll escort me up to Kev's.

For form's sake: 'But aren't you going out? I don't want to trouble you.'

Peering up the road: 'No, it is no problems. Have to meet someone else out here too.' He puts down the large leather bag he's carrying and unzips it. I sneak a look inside, and my stomach jolts: it's full of console games. Full of them. Alonso removes a polystyrene cup from inside the bag, then closes it again. He walks over to the iron fence that circles the estate, climbs up it a bit, then impales the cup on one of the spikes along the top. He comes back, and I squint the question at him.

He smiles softly. 'Sign language. Fernando is buying again.'

'. . . Buying what?'

With thumb and little finger, he makes the sign of a telephone. 'Oh.'

A dark Mercedes pulls up. Alonso tells me to wait, picks up the bag, then opens the back door and slides into the car. The door closes with a muted *shunk*, the distinctive sound of quality. I try to get a sly look at the driver, but it's too dark and the windows are tinted. Alonso exits a minute later, minus the bag. The passenger door opens, and an older guy gets out. He's all tattoos, long hair, leather. The boot pops open, and he takes out a guitar case, then closes the boot again. The car eases out on to the road, its low purr quickly swallowed by the traffic.

The muso doesn't smile as they join me, but he looks me up

and down twice, then stares till I look away. Alonso doesn't introduce us.

We run into Gideon on the stairs. Alonso lives in a different block from Kevin; he tells Gideon to take me the rest of the way, then puts an arm round my shoulders, saying he'll see me at work tomorrow. The muso gropes me with another long stare, then follows Alonso out of the stairwell.

Alone with Gideon, I feel a brush of anxiety. I barely know him. He never seems to say much or smile. On top of that he's one of the most peculiar-looking people I've ever encountered. His features and build are as thick and negroid as they come, but his hair is bright red and his skin paler than mine. I've never asked about him, but he must be an albino. It's the only explanation. Maybe that's why he doesn't smile or talk.

He leads the way silently. As we walk down the corridor towards Kevin's, a raised female voice filters through a door. She sounds angry about something. Then a male voice, louder than hers. Can't make out any words, the language African or the accent too thick. She yells back at the man . . . then a screaming grunt from the woman, and the thud of a body slamming into the wall. A child's voice then — no words, just a high squeal of anguish. I shrink back from the wall, spinning towards Gideon for an idea of what we should do—

He hasn't missed a step. He might as well be deaf.

I catch up to him as another masculine roar, a loud slap, coat me in goosebumps. More thumping and scraping from the inside of the wall, the wail of the child cutting off abruptly . . .

Jesus fucking Christ!

The rapid, discordant thump of a garage track — *oh, that poor fucking kid* — leaks into the corridor from inside number 1018, Kevin's crib. I've never been able to get into garage, it seems to lack all rhythm and melody to me. Then again, my mum used to say exactly the same thing about — *what the hell is happening to them?!* — heavy metal, so maybe I'm just getting old.

Gideon raps a beat on the door, repeats it once, then changes it a little. The sound of several locks unlatching, bolts drawing back, and then it swings open and Gideon waves me in. Tabo welcomes me warmly, then shuts the door on Gideon and re-secures all the locks. The usual smell of pot and crack — *someone needs to call the fucking cops* — but wholesome, yeasty food scents underscoring it all today. There are a couple of other guys I don't know standing around in the corridor. Tabo takes me through to the lounge.

It warms me how the interiors of these rooms always seem so cared for and inviting, so stark a contrast to the awful monoliths in which they lie. Kevin's is all leather furniture and thick rugs, plants and fish tanks, entertainment systems and black and white photography. He's on the couch, sitting between two girls in miniskirts — one looks Asian, the other's white — and as he sees me a beam creeps across his face until his teeth are dazzling.

His voice sounds like the engine of the Mercedes from outside. 'Leeee-sa. Well-cum, girlfriend. Where you been so long?' He rises to his feet and pads across to me. But then he frowns, holding me at arm's length. 'You no look so fine, girl. What da matter?'

'Ah, na, I'm cool, Kev. Just need to use the toilet.'

'Hey, you help yourself. My place your place, you know dat.'

The seat's up, and for once I'm glad for it. I drop to my knees and spew into the bowl.

I wait another minute, retching on some bile, but nothing else wants out, so I wipe my mouth, work the flush and walk out. A shaky grin for the guys in the corridor, then I'm feeling better and through to the lounge again.

A spectacularly fat older black woman in a dirty apron

emerges from the kitchen, tells Kevin the food is ready. He steeples his fingers and bows his head, smiling enough gratitude for her to have just delivered his first son. 'Makesa, you are a *fine*, talented woman.'

She scoffs, feigning imperviousness, pockets some crumpled notes he hands her, then bustles out.

Kevin: 'Lee-saa, you eat with us, of course.'

I'm not at all hungry, and I tell him I can't hang around. He holds his hand to his heart as if this news deeply troubles him, cocking his head and staring, wordlessly imploring me to reconsider. I understand the act but still feel foolishly flattered. 'I can't, Kev. Got to see a man about a dog.'

A sad sigh: 'Then next time, I hope.'

'I hope so too.'

'Come through.'

I follow him through to the bedroom as the girls start whispering to each other. He shuts the door and tells me to relax, pointing vaguely at the futon bed. I opt instead to sit on his weight-training bench. Some kind of tribal music is playing on the stereo. It's not up very loud but the stereo is a class unit, speakers all around the room, and the sound quality is sublime. A false panel at the back of a wardrobe slides down, and he works the combination of a safe.

I'm not sure why he's stopped bothering to hide its location from me. I'm not sure how I feel about it either.

He pulls out a shoe box and comes to sit on the floor in front of me. Inside the box are plastic bags of pills and powder — enough of it to make me shudder. All I can see is solidified jailtime. There's also a big spliff in there, pre-rolled, and Kev lights it and passes it to me.

But that's not a good idea. 'No thanks. Not smoking today.'

'Just hold it for me, please.'

I do, freeing his hands as he takes my order, weighing out the powder on a small electronic scale, making up bags of pills, another bag with an ounce of hash, half an ounce of skunk . . .

It's quite time consuming and I'm half stoned before I really realise I've started puffing. Then I know I'm properly stoned when I take the money out of my pocket to make sure it's all there, counting it three or four times.

The deal's done and Kevin's locking up again, smoothly slipping his shirt off. A hot bubble travels through me. He's not especially tall by the standards of his kind, certainly shorter than a lot of the guys he runs with, and not nearly as bulky as some. But by the cut of his muscles it's obvious that seating is a secondary function of the work-out gear in here. As he reaches up to replace the shoe box, the muscles around his shoulders and back writhe. My chest tightens as he pads back to me, but he just takes the spliff and turns away again, standing by the stereo, raising the volume and smoking deeply, eyes closed.

His head starts to nod, humming along with the voices. It's an evocative image: this half-naked warrior from the Serengeti, transplanted to deepest, darkest London, smoking ganga and rocking to the words of his ancestors. A young chief of his own domain in time and space. The voices and drums assail me from all sides until I feel I'm at the centre of their parade ground, surrounded by the tribe. Then Kevin's singing with them, lifting a knee high and stamping his foot, flourishing an imaginary spear, eyes closed, shimmying and stepping.

I'm so high and transfixed I get a bit of a shock when I realise how close he's getting to me. I swore I wouldn't let this happen again, but by the time he's standing over me, invading my physical space with his body and his dance, I'm so fucking horny it's like my insides are being microwaved. I'm not even sure he wants me to do it, but when I tug his trackies down the end of his cock is poking from under his briefs. I softly lick the bead of spoof from the tip of it, and he's suddenly groaning and not singing. Four more times I flick my tongue across it, and I break him totally: he hauls his pants down and steps out of one leg. Holding my head still, bending his knees, sliding his dick into my mouth, expertly stopping at my gag point.

I let him fuck me in time to the drum, then I lead him to the futon by his cock.

20

The canteen's almost empty and Ryan's alone at a table, a hot chocolate in front him, nibbling a sandwich and reading *The Sun*. He wouldn't buy *The Sun* if there were nude shots of Cathy Z. Jones in it, but there are always ten copies lying around the canteen by nine o'clock. And sometimes it's just too intriguing to resist. How a newspaper, even a tabloid, can become a sloganised propaganda sheet, shamelessly, blatantly manipulating mass consciousness in the interests of a small group of people, is fascinating to him. *The Sun*'s editor is a regular at Downing Street.

If ever a better symbol were needed of the imbecility of the British working class.

Today it's the Liberal Democrats getting the treatment. Given the indistinguishability of the Tories and the 'Labour' Party, and the flak mounting against the PM's dripping hands and scaly tongue, the Lib Dems have been charging up the polls. Their leader is starting to seem to many like that rarest of unicorns: a trust-worthy politician. Their candidate unseated the 'Labour' stooge in a by-election over the weekend, and *The Sun*'s in damage-control mode. The Lib Dem leader's face is leering out from the cover — airbrushed into an expression that suggests his pants are down and your four-year-old is in front of him — underneath the thought-provoking headline: *THIS MAN WILL RUIN YOUR LIFE!*

On page two (the page-three girl is nineteen and from Middlesborough) there's a story about a report charting the ever-rising levels of school-yard bullying. It's followed on page four by the results of a poll where readers were asked to vote by txt for their favourite humiliation TV programme.

A door bangs open and a temp shift files in, about twenty of them, words in exotic languages flying among them. Ryan barely notices, but a few seconds later their mood jars him and he glances up. They're standing around the coffee-machines, not heading to the tables. There's no laughter or smiling today, no relaxing, making the most of a brief break. Ryan understands not a word, but the collective anger filling the room needs no translation.

Another shift enters, then another, these guys aware too of the emotion among the first lot, but obviously not a part of it. Then some of the full-timers come in, and with temps at all of the tables by now, they head straight for Ryan's.

Ryan: 'What's the sitch with those dudes, Nick?'

Nick's a *Sun* buyer. 'What dudes?'

'Never mind.' He turns to Katie: 'Do you know?'

'Na, I don't.' She's craning her neck, checking out the kerfuffle. 'Something's a long way up their arses though.'

Murphy knows one of them and goes over to talk to him, just as Lisa and Trent walk in. They're arguing, and Lisa looks more pissed off than any three of the temp shifts combined. Trent tells Lisa that there's jack-shit to be done about it, turns his back on her cry that 'This is fucking *bull*shit, Trent!', and heads into the smoking room.

Katie: 'Lease! Sit your arse down, girl. Tell mama your troubles.'

She takes a seat beside Nick and puts her face in her hands. She doesn't even notice Ryan reading *The Sun*, a near capital offence usually.

Ryan: 'What the fuck's going on?'

Tired: 'Lynn came down to me this morning and told me to take the chairs away from the labelling tables.'

Three of them grimace.

Nick, puzzled: 'So what?'

Ryan: 'What did Lynn say?'

Disgust energises her again. 'The cold bitch. She breezed about a company research wing in New Jersey that found that labelling crews standing achieve three percent higher productivity than crews sitting down. The results were passed on and a directive was issued: no more chairs for the labelling shifts.'

She makes it sound as though Lynn had ordered hourly birching. Ryan realises that's not so far from the truth. The job description for a temp in Labelling reads: take a box of units; place a price sticker on each unit; replace box. Repeat for eight to twelve hours.

About as stimulating as playing triangle for the Backstreet Boys, but there are people who will take jobs like this. And even for those needy and tough enough to keep at it, being allowed to sit while you work is no luxury.

Katie, to Lisa: 'What did you say to her?'

'I said it could cause major problems, so I'd monitor the productivity figures and tell them that if they slipped below such and such—'

Ryan knew Lynn. 'She insisted?'

'I appealed to a better nature we all know she hasn't got. Then she fucking dis*missed* me! "Thenk yew, Lisa, thart will be awl." Can you believe the gall of that *bitch*?'

Ryan shakes his head. This is typical of EUE, typical of the corporate world in general really. Some of the labelling crew in the canteen are still clamouring, but a lot of them are just staring blankly now, contemplating a working day with chronic pain added to chronic boredom. What a cocktail. And then there's Lisa. She treats her shifts like a hen does chickens, defends every inch of the few rights they have, and often manages to win them a few that they haven't. Every Slave Labour temp in the warehouse wants her as a supervisor. And she knows that if they don't get enough work done those rights will evaporate, so management generally appreciate her too. Now, lamenting with Katie, Lisa looks like a mum with a kid facing expulsion.

Ryan: 'There is one thing you could try.'

'What?'

'Or rather, one *person* you could try.'

———

Alex spent the first part of the morning tracking down lost stock, units not where the computer said they were. He'd become something of an expert at this. Having wondered why no one had ever bothered putting together a standard operation procedure on it, he'd done one himself and updated it regularly.

Three temps from a Dispatch shift hadn't turned up today, leaving an urgent order for HMV in danger of missing its deadline. In addition, a health and safety stand-off had recently inflamed relations between crew and team leader, so Alex was asked to spend the rest of the morning down there making sure the job got done. He worked alongside them until the order had left the building with time to spare, then rewarded them with a two-hour lunch break.

Then he made himself a coffee and sat out in the sun of the

loading yard with some of the Dispatch crew and some contractors repairing floodlights. One of the contractors was from Newcastle — Alex thought his accent was priceless — and they bantered about the Rugby World Cup. Ten minutes later he noticed Greg out in the pallet farm, struggling by himself to set up a load of empty pallets needed at the Slough warehouse. Alex jogged over, took off his tie and went hard lining them up for Greg to stack with the fork-lift. They had it sorted in twenty minutes. Alex was sweating by then, so he had a wash in the Men's, dosed himself with Lynx and threw on a clean shirt.

He was sitting in on the Replenishment weekly meeting — he was required to sit in on all weekly meetings — working out a safer method for reloading the highest shelves when Lisa approached the window. Beckoned to him. He excused himself and went out, quietly admiring the clothes she was wearing, the scarf in her hair. But his cheer soon froze.

'What's wrong, Lease?'

It took Lisa two minutes to bring him up to speed. He seemed to stiffen the further she went, and for the first time in hours she started to feel some hope.

He said nothing in reply; went inside and excused himself from the meeting, then came back out and said, 'Come on.'

She fell in beside him like an officer's batman. She enjoyed watching him go about his work — so unruffled and decisive, always cheery — but was surprised to find that this mood she had put him in now was almost arousing.

They found Lynn holding court in the smoking room with some of her office staff. Lynn was infamous for not wanting work matters brought to her during breaks.

Alex: 'Can I have a word, please, Lynn?'

Lynn, a cold eye on Lisa: 'Does it involve work?'

'Yes.'

'Does it perchance involve this place grinding to a screaming halt or burning to the ground?'

Her staff tittered.

'. . . No.'

Final: 'Then it can wait until I'm back on deck in a few minutes' time.'

Alex: 'That's fine. We'll meet you in your office.'

Lynn: 'I can guess what this is about.'

Alex: 'Look, Lynn, the last thing anyone wants to do is interfere in your—'

'Seems to me that that is pre*cisely* what you're doing.'

'I'm just here to talk. I'd just like to hear your reasons f—'

'I've no obligation to tell *you* my reasons for *anything*. I'd be happy to discuss it with another section manager, yes. But that's not you, is it, Alex. In fact, you're not even a genuine team leader yet.'

Lisa: 'He is so. He's been bailing out team leaders left and right for the past—'

'Have you no work to do, Lisa? Are your friends now capable of supervising themselves?'

Lisa stares.

'Because if they are, then you're obviously surplus to requirements. Adding that to the written warning you received last week for lateness and absenteeism, and now this . . . disobedience. Going over your manager's head—'

Alex: 'She didn't go over your head, Lynn. As you said—'

'Very well, going *under* her manager's head. Amounts to the same thing: insubordination. Either way, it's counterproductive and shan't be tolerated.'

Alex: 'It's OK, Lease. I'll speak with you soon.'

Lisa's only too happy to leave. Out on the floor she can't face the labelling team, so she heads for the sign-in desk, logs on to the computer and starts tallying shift requirements for the next day. A task she's able to focus on for no more than a few seconds before drifting off and stewing. At least she looks busy.

God, I'd love to . . . As a pacifist she's not sure just *what* she'd love to do to Lynn fucking Sanderson. Perhaps pacifism needs an exception as much as any rule. Or she could give Lynn's BMW a thorough keying. Block the exhaust pipe with Poly-fill. Drop a couple of acid tabs into her tea . . .

Her loathing of Lynn goes back a long way. When they first met, Lynn spent the next few weeks peppering her talk with Lisa with casual racial slurs, as if Lisa's being a white South African made her a bigot by default, someone Lynn could drop her guard around. Lisa *despises* that: small-minded people pre-judging her views on race through her nationality, the liberals acting cold and superior, the bigots treating her like a partner in prejudice.

At last Alex comes out, and she hurries to him. Freezes at his appearance. He looks ready to do the things she has just been fantasising about.

'What happened?'

'Nothing happened.'

'What do you mean?'

'I made no further progress than what you saw. She just refuses to discuss the matter.'

A clenched sigh: 'That fucking slag.' But she's not yet ready to face the new status quo, so she says, 'Never mind, Alex. You achieved all you could. Thanks for—'

'Oh, this isn't over yet.'

That's my boy! 'Really? What do we do now?'

'Go over her head.'

'Who to?'

'Who do you think?'

'Flannery, the new site manager? But he's at a seminar till Friday.'

'I wasn't thinking of him. He's scared of Lynn anyway; he'd side with her if she wanted to *chain* them to the table.'

Lisa's at a loss. But the look behind Alex's glasses is scaring her. 'Who do you mean, Alex?'

He breaks the stare and looks suddenly daunted himself. '"If a job's worth doing . . ."'

Lisa's mouth falls open. 'You're going to go to *him*, aren't you?'

A shaky smile: 'Him?'

'. . . Julian Rutherford.'

'No, I'm not going to Julian.'

'Thank Christ for that!'

'*We're* going to Julian.'

She steps back as if he's pushed her. 'No fucking way, Alex. I've never set foot in that place in my life, and I'm not starting now. Especially not like *this*. That prick will sack me just for entering the same room as him.'

'He's not that bad, Lease. He's only human.'

'Oh, no he fucking isn't. He's one of *them*.'

'One of *what*?'

Homo superior. A drone-maker. They of the red right hands. 'One of our overlords. You don't just march in and start shouting the odds to one of *them*.' Suddenly Lisa doesn't care so much about her shift's sore feet. She's surprised it means this much to Alex too.

'Number one, we won't be shouting any odds at anyone. We'll be requesting a quick chat about a de-stabilising operational development.'

'Forget it, Alex. I can't thank you enough for try—'

'Number *two*: he's the one who hired me, and he told me I was welcome to knock on his door at any time . . . Number three . . .' He grimaces, then shakes his head. 'We have to try something . . .

because Lynn's gonna sack you over this. She told me.'

Lisa's head levitates an inch off her shoulders. The air solidifies around her; eases away; closes again.

If Alex felt bad enough before this, seeing the shock upon her is like a kick in the balls. He puts a hand on her arm and tells her not to worry about it, that they'll sort it out. He only half believes it. He thinks there's a good chance they'll *both* get sacked. But it was his misplaced arrogance that got her into this.

'If we can get him to overturn Lynn's decision, then there's no way she can sack you.'

She's staring at him but he doesn't think she's seeing him yet. He takes a grip on her other arm.

Greg whizzes past on a fork-lift. 'Hey, I've been rooting for you kids, but get a room, for fuck's sake!'

Alex feels a blush war with his anxiety for a second.

Lisa, finally, breezy: 'Well, that's that then, isn't it?'

'. . . That's what?'

'Let's go swim with a crocodile.'

21

He waits for her near the doorway through to Security. They'd decided not to bother asking Lynn's permission for Lisa to leave site. Technically it's a sackable offence. Practically she's sacked already. She's about ten minutes late, and agitation gnaws at Alex as he half watches a strange woman walking towards him. *Hurry up, Lisa, for Christ's sake.* Things are already about ten times more delicate than he ever likes to let them become; they sure as hell don't need Lisa's bad habits weighing in against them too.

At another time he would be checking out the woman coming up the walkway — would be helpless not to — but he's peering past her already, down into the warehouse, sweating on Lisa.

'Well, it's nice to see you, *too.* Arranged another date already, have we?'

He looks at the woman properly, gets a jolt. He hadn't recognised her. He's never seen her like this before. 'Holy shit. No wonder you were late. Always keep a set of posh clothes at work, do you?'

'Hardly. The skirt and stockings are Diana's, the shoes are Penny's, the blouse Anneke's, the handbag Katie's, the jewellery's from Fatimah in Stock Control, and the scent —' she steps in and stretches her neck for him — 'is from Emaleen.'

For a second the whiff of perfume turns his lungs to concrete. 'And who's the hairdresser?'

'Sabrina. She did the make-up too. What's the verdict?'

'. . . Ten to fifteen: conspiracy to pervert the course of injustice.'

When you look good you feel good. But in this case, *her* looking good had *Alex* feeling suddenly surer. An unwarranted boost in the wider scheme, probably, but hey, as Ryan said, enough confidence can win you anything. And they were in no position to be shunning allies here.

'You look ravishing, babe. Only a blind man wouldn't stare.'

He's wanted to call her 'babe' for as long as he can remember; wanted to close that familiarity gap. He'd come close a few times but bitten the word back. He barely registers himself using it now.

She takes the compliment lightly: 'You're too kind.' But he thinks he sees some extra satisfaction about her.

They sign out and walk off-site in silence, turning left along the busy road. The high heels of Lisa's new shoes clack above the traffic hum, the beat stuttering and scraping when her balance wavers. They walk parallel to the warehouse, along its length, isolated from it by the high wire fence. The sun's out and sparkling in the mirrored glass of the round tower set beside the far end of the warehouse, looming over it grandly. The disparity between the two — the warehouse's undressed concrete, grimy piping, barred-over windows — is as stark as the two ends of the class divide. Just looking at the tower firms Alex's resolve. An eight-storey monument to success and prosperity.

It's hot in the sun, a light breeze ruffling the blossoms of the trees beside them. The blue of the sky reflected in the mirrors of the tower seems somehow deeper and richer than it does on its own.

And Alex knows that the mark of the winner is taking bad events and spinning them into good. Making priceless pots from inferior clay. And maybe the shoddy clay that the morning served up to him is in reality an opportunity. He understands that no one gets ahead in this world by beavering away, head down, waiting for the breaks to come to them. Especially in *this* part of the world. It just doesn't work that way. Perhaps it *should* work that way. When he lets himself, Alex certainly wishes it did: he's never been comfortable seeking attention, thrusting his hand up high. But that's the stuff of dreamers and followers, not doers and leaders.

It hadn't crossed his mind when he resolved to visit the tower — the decision then was mere desperation — but maybe today is exactly what he needs. What he's been looking for.

It looks like an illusion to Lisa. The sparkles and reflections. Like a tower from a fairy tale: a fortress of black stone cloaked in enchantment spells. It doesn't scare her though. Far from it. If They *are* manipulating reality — and she knows that They are — then she too is part of the saga. A simple girl from a faraway land, in the armour of her times, entrusted with a duty she's neither sought nor wants. Handpicked by powers unfathomable but inexorable.

She swaps smiles and small talk with the tower's security guards as Alex signs them both in. Then a moment of doubt as he leads her to the doors and they pass into the tower's shadow. Her stomach begins a slow somersault. Then she catches her own reflection in a glass panel, and she lets the vision settle her again.

But the girl behind the reception desk has other ideas. The girl in the Chanel power suit with the eighty-quid hair. Her work face kicks in immediately — *I may be paid to smile at you but I can see that you're not worth a real smile, and I want you to understand that* — a frigid crinkling of the lips which is nevertheless tinged in some authentic amusement by the time Alex and Lisa reach her.

Amusement at Lisa's hodgepodge of clothing, her hasty make-up and hair.

A few deftly tweaked facial muscles and Lisa feels like a street tart in a state ballroom.

———

Julian's barely done a thing in hours. In days, really. He's got the promotion on his desk in front of him, along with the files of the three employees still in the running for it. But he's stalled in whittling the list further. They're all capable of doing the job. That's barely an issue. In fact, the weaknesses of the potential candidates have played a bigger part in the assessment than their strengths have.

A much bigger part.

All men. Well, all *boys*. Only a male will do for this role. Plenty of women around who'd stir up a world of shit to that contention should he voice it near them, but Julian's sure he could, if forced to, make them see his reasoning in a few short minutes.

He wants to give it to Willoughby. He's perfectly suited. But he knows the lad; knows his father anyway, and that really would be ghastly form. He's emptying the last of the Scotch into his glass when Rose comes through on the intercom. A management trainee from below wants to speak with him. Just turned up without an appointment. Quite remarkable in itself, that. He gets the name, then quickly places Alex from his interview. Respectful and keen, inexperienced but bright enough. Desperate for the job — that much was clear — but conducting himself with that odd colonial pride that Julian has always struggled to fathom. Quite disarming at times . . . and as intriguing to Julian as most things disarming. Alex had needed the job, but Julian had been morally convinced that should he, Julian, overstep some mark, Alex would've told him to shove it and strode away. It was difficult to finger, this conduct of the classless, the style of these Southerners.

But it was what had got Alex the job. And it helps get him the appointment now. Julian needs distracting.

———

Lisa's seen him before — in the flesh once, from a distance, and frequently in the monthly company magazine. She's put the receptionist behind her and let the quiet command and opulence of this place steel her again. She can hear the drone now, a deeper throb beneath the hum of the air-conditioning. Alex is on the edge of his seat, gives her a weak grin. She ignores it, has no time for anyone except herself.

Then His door opens and He comes bustling out. A real live specimen of *Homo superior*. Receding hair ruffled. Tie loosened, sleeves rolled up. A little younger than her father, she supposes. Same tall height, though. Face too craggy for handsomeness. *Far* too craggy.

He walks right over to them, smiling, a real one too. She's not sure what she expected. Certainly not him coming to them. Without so much as a hint of blood around the mouth.

Looking like Alastair Campbell on Ecstasy.

Alex is on his feet, returning the hearty handshake. 'Afternoon, Mr Rutherford.' He hadn't expected this welcome either, and doesn't know how to handle Lisa's presence. He'd been going to present her as soon as they walked into his office, Julian behind his desk, hard at work and not overjoyed at the disruption. Lisa stays seated and Alex resolves to get whatever small talk Julian offers out of the way before acknowledging her.

It's not to be.

Julian: 'And who might this be? I don't believe we've met.'

She stands up now, but more slowly than Alex would have liked. Not a shred of warmth in her stare either. *What the fuck is she trying to do here?* Alex waits for her to hold out a hand.

She doesn't.

He has a polished speech prepared about who she is and why anything about her should remotely warrant his bringing her here. 'Ahhhh . . . this is Lisa.'

Julian takes her hand — practically has to lift it up for her; says he's delighted to meet her.

Lisa: 'Not the exception then.'

Julian, mildly taken aback: 'What exception?'

'The exception that proves the rule.'

'. . . What rule?'

'That people are invariably delighted to meet me.'

And Alex suddenly wants to throttle her.

He watches Julian blink and frown . . . but then a grin breaks out again. 'Well . . . I . . . ah . . . I can certainly see why.'

Lisa: 'Meaning?'

Oh, you stupid, ungrateful little cunt! Alex is close to calling off the whole thing, admitting that it's all been a big mistake, salvaging what's left of his own job.

Then he notices how Lisa has made no move to retrieve her hand.

Julian gives another stunned grunt. Then he looks into the air, twiddling the fingers of his free hand, openly groping for a response. 'Ammm . . . meaning nothing,' he declares at last. 'It was merely a false, jocular compliment to match your false, jocular conceit.'

Lisa just drills him with her eyes.

Alex waits for the detonation. He knows from talk that this is *not* a person to fuck with.

But then he realises that he's become the invisible man again.

Lisa finally lets her lips twist a little, and takes her hand back. 'Nice to meet you too, Julian.'

He gives a wobbly grin to Alex, then turns it on her. 'Please, no need to stand on ceremony: call me by my Christian name.'

'Fine. And you may do the same.'

He leads them through to the office. Lisa, bringing up the rear, feels like she's been sucking pure oxygen. She could've ruined everything then. *Should've* ruined everything. Not once had she considered acting cavalierly in here. Her task called for a lot more tact than that.

It was his manner, she thinks. His behaving so far out of character. Called for some serious ad-libbing.

Julian waves them to seats in front of his desk, then disappears into a back room. Lisa's near the window, and from up here the warehouse looks even more monstrous. Alex starts whispering furiously, but she cuts him off with her hand. He tries again — she's never heard him so agitated — but he shuts up when she says loudly, 'Please, Alex. Not now.' She can see an afternoon temp shift queuing near Security; a few workers out in the yard; someone on a fork-lift, perhaps Greg, stacking pallets. They look like ants. Less industrious.

She'd love to bell Greg on his mobile and tell him where she is. He wouldn't believe her, so she'd tell him to do something at random, then report back to him what he'd just done.

She imagines Julian sitting up here and reaching for his phone. Calling Flannery and ordering a fire drill. Watching his ants — four hundred of them — flooding the yard. Telling Rick to move them to the northern corner. Then to the southern.

Julian comes back and sits behind his desk. Alex instantly recognises his mouth-wash. Plax Ultra. What Alex himself uses. For an inane moment he wishes he could point that out somehow.

Lisa hasn't acknowledged Julian's return; gazes through the

window like a bored tourist.

Julian: 'Well . . . nice to see you, Alex. Something of a surprise, though.' Was there some censure in that? 'Still, as I told you, my door's always open.' *Phew*. 'How are things going down there?'

Alex, gladly cutting to a measured speech: 'Mostly, things are fine, sir. I *have* identified certain areas of the operation that I believe would benefit from some retuning. A lot of micro-managing taking place. But that's beyond my sphere right now and I certainly wouldn't be here troubling you with that. Ammm, I don't wish to keep you any longer than necessary — and Lisa and I have a lot of work to get back to — so with your permission, sir, I'll get right down to it.'

Julian steeples his fingers in front of his face and leans back in his chair. 'Fine. So long as your narrative goes some way toward clarifying the presence of this intriguing young lady here.'

She finally shifts her attention to the talk, a beat before Alex can kick her. She smiles slightly at Julian's remark, but Alex doesn't give her a chance to speak. He tells Julian what her position is, then gives him the morning's events concerning the Labelling department, half expecting to be silenced at any moment.

He's a few minutes into it when Lisa cuts him off. 'Julian, it just seems so fucking *senseless*.' Alex winces at the expletive, darts a look at Julian. 'I realise these workers are highly expendable, but that job really is so *mind*-numbingly boring, it's tough to keep them focused when they *aren't* in pain. So quite aside from the decency element being trodden on here, it's bloody bad business also. I'm not sure if you realise, but a disgruntled worker down there can quietly create havoc, sometimes going weeks without getting caught.' She breaks off to sigh. 'I tried explaining that to Lynn, but she can be extremely inflexible. I pointed out to her that productivity was as much at risk here as morale—'

Alex: 'Not to mention health and safety.'

'Not to mention health and safety, and all I proposed was that we leave them in their chairs, tell them what's at stake, then closely monitor their productivity rates, making sure they continue to perform above expected norms.'

Lisa suddenly realises that this is all completely needless. Her being in here. Her going to Alex. Her remonstrating with Lynn in the first place. Her trying to impress this *Homo superior* wanker with her vocabulary. All Lisa had to do was quietly tell the labelling crew to stick out a few days on their feet but slack right off the rate of work and quality.

Stupid bitch.

. . . Never mind. If she'd thought to do that, yeah, her job would still be safe . . .

. . . but she wouldn't have got a look at this view.

Julian: 'You know what I would have done were I you, Lisa?'

The first time he's used her name. Something about that makes her shiver a bit. 'What?'

Deadpan: 'I would have led a conspiracy whereby your shift contrived to lower its output until their chairs were returned to them.'

Lisa's temperature drops several degrees.

He holds his mask for a few seconds before smiling. 'I'm joking, of course.'

She makes herself smile back. 'Of course.'

Julian, summarising: '*Right*. So you've politely told her that she cannot be fucking serious. That this is a gratuitous maltreatment of workers, and that they should be granted the chance to prove some Yank *think-tank* wrong before being subjected to its draconian findings?'

Alex sneaks a peek at Lisa; she looks like she's holding herself together in the face of Julian's shift better than Alex himself is.

It smells like a trap.

Lisa: 'Ahh . . . *yeah*. That's about the sum of it.'

'And she told you to fuck off?'

'Correct.'

'At which point you took the problem to Alex?'

'Correct.'

'And Alex? You enjoyed no more success than Lisa?'

'Worse, actually.'

Small frown over the steeple: 'How so?'

This was it. 'Lynn was so incensed at my involving myself in her affairs — and at Lisa for going around her — that she decided Lisa had to be . . . let go.'

Julian opens his mouth slowly; gives a theatrical 'Ahhhh.'

Alex knows he's speaking too fast, can't help himself. 'I realise this is way beneath you, sir, but Lynn's decision is effective as of tomorrow. It was my meddling that put the camel in the spinal unit with Lynn and Lisa, and with Irvine and Rick both away for another week I couldn't think of anything else to do.'

Impossible to know what Julian's thinking as he quietly questions them further, and even Lisa is knife-edge obedience by the time Julian lifts his phone off its cradle.

'Lynn. Glad I caught you . . . No, no, nothing to do with that . . . Your decision regarding the labelling operation . . . I don't think that's overly important at this stage, Lynn.'

Alex inwardly cringes.

'I'd like you to reconsider your decision, Lynn . . . Yes, I'm aware of the findings. I'm also aware, as you should be, that every operation has its own idiosyncrasies, and research findings — those from abroad particularly — need to be taken with a grain of salt.'

Lisa's picturing the rouge in Lynn's cheeks as Lynn tries to keep her voice down.

'. . . I'm sorry, Lynn, but I disagree. I believe an alternative course was mooted to you by a supervisor down there? . . . As I've *said*, Lynn, that's not the issue right now.'

Lisa feels herself grinning; sucks her cheeks in.

'What is is that I see no harm whatever in putting her alternative into effect for a trial period.' Julian holds the phone from his ear, rolls his eyes a bit, re-igniting Lisa's smile like a switch. But then Julian's posture stiffens; Lisa feels the change come over him almost tangibly.

'Agree to disagree? Awfully sorry, Lynn, but I'm afraid that's rather not good enough.'

Conscious of the awkward position this conversation will leave him in, Alex is nonetheless thrilled by the result of his decision to come here. Thrilled too at this measured glimpse of Julian's power. Plotting in the workplace is counterproductive, he knows, but it is also practically essential in getting ahead. Pictures himself in the chair opposite, freshening up in his own bathroom, making calls. He looks to Lisa, wanting to share the moment . . .

She doesn't notice him, riveted to Julian, her tongue resting against her top lip.

Julian: 'Here's a better idea, Lynn: let's agree that you agree to agree with me . . . Splendid.'

Alex is glad when Julian puts the phone down.

22

Ryan walks into the club. He sees the far corner occupied by a large group of rowdy friends and workmates. *Too* rowdy for a Tuesday. Alex is up at the bar, chatting with a couple of suits. He sees Ryan and yells across the room: 'What's ya poison, Skippy?'

'Pint of the black stuff, mate.' Ryan swings past the fag machine and into the toilets. He comes back out to see Alex deposit an armload of drinks in front of the gang, then head back to the bar for more.

Ryan, hailing them all: 'How are we, people?'

Everyone stops talking to greet him. Lisa and Katie shift their chairs out so that he can slot one in between them.

Ryan: 'You lot are in fine form for 5.30 on a Tuesday. What's the occasion? I was halfway home when Lisa txted and ordered me down here.'

Murphy: 'You didn't hear, ten?'

'Hear what?'

Greg: 'At long fucking last, one of us becomes one of them!'

Lisa, rubbing her hands: 'I've finally infiltrated a plant. Now we can *really* get to work.'

'A-fucking-men, baby!'

A cheer is taken up. A few of the locals glance over, but it's good-natured appraisal. They know from experience that the local Southerners are as harmless as they are mad.

Ryan: 'Can someone translate, please?'

Katie: 'Alex got promoted!'

The cheer had almost died, but at that it revives again. Alex arrives with another improbable number of drinks in his arms; adds them to the stockpile on the table, his grin splitting wider as they drink to him.

Ryan's happy for Alex. It's no real surprise to him: it was on the cards in Al's terms of employment, and Ryan has seen what a great job he's done around the place since he made team leader. He speaks up when the volume level lets him, smiling himself now. 'So we're looking at the new Goods In section manager, are we?'

Lisa, rapt, leaning into Ryan: 'Like fuck! He's been made warehouse *personnel* manager, man!'

Jim: 'With duties upstairs as well!'

'An executive cadetship!'

This takes Ryan so far aback it's almost a physical slap. 'Jesus Christ.'

Greg: 'No, I'm afraid it still just plain Alex McConnel for the moment, but give the lad another month or two . . .'

More cheers.

Blushing garishly, Alex plonks a pint of Guinness in front of Ryan and perches on the arm of his chair. Ryan's input to the cater-wauling is sluggish: camouflage while his brain reels. Then he manages to gather enough of himself to shake Alex's hand and congratulate him.

It's an hour or two before Ryan finds Alex with a moment alone. He wants the full story.

Ryan, marvelling: 'Fucking hell, she was gonna *sack* her over it?'

Alex: '*Yeah*. End of story. I went in there to try and breathe some reason into the labelling situation, and the ground under my feet just crumbled.'

Ryan knows there's a history behind Lynn's decision, and that it's a lot longer than one morning. Lisa's running crying to Alex was just the final straw. He doesn't say so, but Alex going to fucking *Julian* over the dismissal of a temp with a badly flawed record was, in Ryan's estimation, idiotic.

But . . . who was the idiot now?

'So you went to Julian?'

'Yeah. There was no one else to turn to. So I took the gamble.'

'And collected big time.'

A giggle: 'Sure looks that way, dude!'

He fills Ryan in on events in the tower.

Ryan: 'I can't believe he sided with you.'

A little hurt: 'Why not?'

Because Lynn's been with him for more than eight years and always seemed on top of things. Because Lisa's late to work every other morning, averages one sickie a week, deals drugs on site, buys stock off the company through the five-finger discount scheme (though not as successfully as others who shan't be named) has had more final warnings than David Boon played final cricket tests, and has taken every chance that's ever come her way to wind Lynn right up. 'Dunno, just seems a little odd.'

'What, you can't see the sense in what I said to him; where we were coming from?'

'. . . I can, but the sense is pretty minor from a management perspective. They don't usually burn their own on the strength of such things.'

Alex: 'We're not in the Dark Ages any more, Ry. Anything to

the good of the operation has to be held above cronyism.'

'Why did you take Lisa up there with you?'

Alex ponders for a while. 'I dunno really. I think mostly because I couldn't face him alone. And I was irrationally gutted with her for getting me into this too, so I figured she should pitch in.'

Ryan, staring at Lisa as she and Katie boogie beside the pool table, shaking it up to The Cure, balancing drinks in one hand: 'You sure there wasn't a "power of the pussy" thing there? She looks great when she's done up like that.'

Alex, wistful: 'She looks fucking great *all* the time, mate.'

Ryan glances at him sharply, but Alex doesn't notice. The Lisa Ryan knows would have gone to lengths to get out of having to enter the tower in the first place, not gone to lengths to blend in with its inhabitants.

Alex, musing: 'There was more to it, though . . . just not like you think. I wanted Julian to see who it was getting screwed. I wanted him to meet her and listen to her.'

'So what happened after you got back?'

'Lynn must of gotten off the phone from Julian and confirmed who she thought it was that'd gone over her head. She called us in as soon as we got back.'

'How was she?'

'. . . Cordiality personified . . . with a high-jump bar rammed up its ring.'

'I'd do murder to see her like that. How was Lease?'

'"Pig in shit" ring any bells?'

Lisa's got a small crowd around her; she's gleefully relaying the same story. 'Then as we walked out of the office, I said, "Well, at least we're all in *agreement* with each other now, Lynn!"'

Ryan: 'She's gonna be gunning for you, dude.'

'In the words of the great George Walker Bush: "Bring it on".'

'Bet you didn't think that at the time.'

'Na, you're right there. Thought I might've written a cheque my job description couldn't cash.'

'Until?'

'Two-thirty this arvo. I'm ordered back into Julian's office. I'm guessing Lynn's rallied her power base and stitched me up regardless. Julian's formal as fuck, sits me down.'

'And?'

'And he proceeds to tell me that he's just finished on the phone to Brighton, speaking with Flannery about my performance to date. Spoke with a few others in the warehouse too. Which I assumed was for reasons not positive. Then he starts talking about how he's been looking at creating a personnel managership downstairs for some time. But the successful applicant would need to have an interest in working upstairs a lot too, getting accustomed to upper levels of the operation. He's grim all this time, and all I can hear is the swish of the axe.' A big smile lights Alex up. 'Swear to god, bro, I was *this* close to saying, "Save your breath, I'll get my coat", when he starts talking about how all the reports on me, coupled with what he saw of me this morning, left him confident in my ability to carry out the role.'

'You must've almost creamed yourself on the spot.'

'Almost *shat* myself, more like it. I was so shocked, mate, I actually managed to look like I mulled on the offer before accepting it.'

They clink glasses and drink.

Ryan, smiling: 'You remember your first week on the job?'

Grimacing: 'Only in nightmares. No one smoothing anything for me. Not quite rude, but just . . . just not being arsed . . . Except you.' Grinning: 'You cunt. You were just rude.'

'. . . S'pose I was too. Didn't want any new friends then, 'cause all me old ones had either bailed or turned on me. And look at you now. Fucking massive effort.'

23

RYAN

I've learned a bit about Vern in the months since I met him. In the months since I *decked* him, for fuck's sake. Not from Nadia though. She rarely dances at the club: turns up half an hour before her slot once a week, then buggers off again. Most of the staff are dark on her, truth be told, think she's a stuck-up bitch. I mostly avoid the place too, and I've never seen her there.

It didn't take me long to start patching together the truth regarding Vernon though. There were no words to go on at first, just ominous omissions. But I needed to know how Vern might react if we ever ended up together, in spite of Melvyn's reassurances.

Snotting him like that was fucking madness anyway. I still can't believe I did it. I've never been one to, shall we say, approach violence proactively. Pre-emptively. As long as there's a chance of talking me way out of it — and until it kicks off there's always a chance — igniting things myself was simply beyond the bounds of my courage. Fuck 'was': *is*, mate. Unless I know for a fact that the guy's not much chop.

But there was something different about that night. I'd had news that afternoon of my Granddad's death. It'd been on the cards for a while, but it still came as a shock. One of the hardest aspects of it was that I knew I wouldn't be going home for the funeral. With my visa expired, once I leave the UK I won't ever be allowed back here to work, and calling it curtains to be at home for a single occasion just wasn't practicable.

Sorry, Granddad. I reckon you'd understand though, mate.

I had to give him me own send-off, though, no choice in that matter; and I knew damn well that the only alternative that would sit well with him was for me to go out and get maggoted on top-shelf Scotch. I obviously wasn't about to let the gang see me grieving, so I just started mooching around the West End pubs by myself, drinking Glenfiddich, Johnny Black, all the big guy's favourites (didn't let himself buy them very often but he never said no when I showed up with a bottle). He barely touched a drop in his younger days, but Nana reckons the young man who came home from the war was young in age only.

Anyway, I'm three sheets in a pub in Leicester Square, Granddad's favourite spot from his London posting, when the mobby starts buzzing. It's Angelika, who I'd met a week before round at Kevin's crib. She's asking me out for a drink and I found myself agreeing.

Not sure if it was sympathy I wanted or what. I remember wanting to fuck her as soon as I heard her voice, though. Cheat death's chill with the act of life. Sounded plausible then. But by the time I was sitting with her in the club it just felt like Ryan trying to cop off again, business as usual, on the day his granddad died. She was fucking gorgeous and I hadn't had one in a while, but the notion went sour for me quick-style.

She'd wanted it too. I wasn't sure at the start, but my lack of response soon got to the heart of the matter. That can often work wonders. Hardly the optimum course, but you'd be surprised how many cards it might draw. There she was, cracked open by intrigue and self-doubt. And I hadn't even been trying.

I was getting drunker though, and that mixed with the grief had me mood-swinging all over the place. She'd been trying to get me up to dance for about an hour; I wouldn't have a bar of it, but then I contemplated the way I was treating her and felt a right cunt. So up I got.

And then Vernon's started up with that three fucking strikes shit!

I made myself shrug it off, shrugged off her efforts to get me off the floor too, shrugged off the fear in her eyes; coaxed her into dancing again.

And thinking of my granddad, the blood of friends on his face that would never wash off, standing against arch-bullying . . . And here's Angelika, suddenly dancing like Worzel Gummidge, shooting looks over my shoulder. Hailing from one of the countries to suffer most at the hands of my granddad's enemies.

I didn't know much at that point, in that state, but I knew that that wasn't right. Not today.

Then 'strike two', and Angelika's joined the refugees; a boy of eighteen's howling 'FUCK YOU!' from a fox-hole as a Stuka screams in . . .

. . . and then Vernon's flopping at my feet.

Crossed a line that day. Didn't decide to, though, because I'm not my granddad and I never will be.

But the people I met working wouldn't talk about Vernon much. It was like his name was English for Sauron. I'd push it and turn conversations into half-crushed crabs. There was a lot of looking at me too, whispers and pointing. Like I'm some outta-town heavy-hitter brought in for a sort-out.

It was only Melvyn who kept me coming back. His is a

presence that inspires complete security in you. He told me about some bloke he let go recently because he couldn't get along with another employee. Mentioned it casually, but I got the picture.

Then I got to know Dessie, and he filled me in. It wasn't pretty.

I stayed on, though. Fuck, how could I not? Guaranteed custom for every fringe benefit I could get out. Getting paid three times what I'd accept just to drive dancers around; watching others watching me get paid to do it. A 'company car' among the perks. Hints about work that would let me leave this glossy, grotty noose of a city on terms I could face.

Besides, it kept me seeing Nadia.

And the work itself, the driving, meant I seldom had to set foot inside the club anyway.

Then I was asked to follow Dessie up to Manchester one day; he was delivering an old Rolls Royce, mint condition, to someone up there and needed a lift back. Anyway, there was a pile-up on the motorway as we headed back down. A three-hour trip became five, me and Des killing time with yarns but getting well fed up. Then we're crawling past a service centre near Milton Keynes and we decided to see the congestion out in a pub, jump back in the motor once the traffic eased. It didn't happen though; still down to jogging pace as our fifth pints sailed down, so we made a session of it and kipped in a B&B around the corner. Fell in with some locals lads and had a grand time, top night all round.

Except for Dessie's Vernon CV.

Then we've walked into the club the next morning. I'm shaken by what I've heard, big-time bricking it, and I'm there only for me last pay packet, an agonised-over resignation speech set to play for Melvyn. The dark wings of the club now looked like Ugandan jungle, but it was a Monday and I hadn't seen Vernon in there since I first 'met' him, and there's no way he's gonna be around at half ten on a Monday morning.

Melvyn, in a tracksuit and sweaty, sipping on a tomato juice, booms out a 'Gidday cobbers!' from behind the bar.

Vernon's in a cheap suit. He swings around on his stool and points this sugary grin at me. My feet seize up as Des passes me.

Melvyn: 'C'mon, Viduka, don't be shy. If I know Des, e roped you into a pint or nine last night. Get over ere; I've got the perfect angover cure.'

I was obviously safe for the moment — thanks to Des and Melvyn — and that's all that enabled me to cross the floor. Vernon gave Des a matey slap on his big shoulder, then turned to me. I'm not a great believer in auras and shit, and if I hadn't heard the things I had I reckon it would've been different, but those bulbous eyes fairly sparkled with malignant, playful genius.

Vernon, far shorter than me on his stool: 'Aw-wight, Ryan?' He held out a hand to me, and I expected it to suck all the heat from mine; crush it like a compactor. But it was warm, a little sweaty, the skin smooth. It was small too, much smaller than mine, the fingers tapered, and there was no grip to speak of. His hand sat in mine like a jellyfish fillet. And stayed there for much longer than etiquette required. I hid it, but holding that position brought my stomach higher each second.

I ended up on the stool next to Vernon. As soon as I could I began an apology — *Look, mate, about that other night . . .* — but Melvyn cut me off, dumping a cocktail of fruit juices in front of me, extolling its curative powers.

I'd never experienced cold sweat before that morning. I thought the term fuck all more than a linguistic liberty. How wrong I was; I lost what felt like a litre in the ten minutes I was forced to sit there, listening to their matey small talk. I think I even spoke up a couple of times — answered some questions at least — but I've got no idea what I said. My brain was far too busy careering through possible words or actions that might get me out of there.

Melvyn's wonder tonic had all the taste of low-fat water. A total, spineless retreat was frankly weighed, I remember that, a full-noise sprint for the door.

Ctrl+Alt+Del! Ctrl+Alt+Del!
Ctrl+Alt+Del! . . .

My heart began to beat again only when it became clear that Melvyn had business elsewhere and that the gathering was ending. I started hollering silent prayers that Vernon would leave the back way, or need to take a dump — anything to stop him being near me when I got outside.

Then Melvyn dropped a strange set of car keys on the bar. 'Favour from ya, Ryan?'

I nodded dumbly.

End of story. Before the favour had been named. Melvyn's good at that.

'Another couple-a hours work for ya. Vernon needs a lift up Swiss Cottage, and then e'll be stoppin at Burnley. Take the Lexus out front. 'Ang on to it afterwards. Phone me on Thursday. Ta ta, gents.' As cheery as if all he'd just done was push me back to deep fine leg.

My only hope is Dessie, and Dessie's my man, after last night particularly. He won't leave me to—

'Ay up, lads. Be seeing ya's weekend. Drop that game off to me, Ryan, if ya get a chance. My young un's clamouring for fucking thing.'

I could only glare at his back.

Vernon, easy: 'Yeah, see ya, Des. Regards to the missus, mate.' Then, to me: 'Nuva drink, Ryan, or shall we hit the frog and . . . ?' And what wasn't being said hissed like a fucking tidal wave.

I really don't remember anything from that point until we're in the car together. Honestly. Something like absolute terror cauterised the part of my brain that was supposed to hold those imprints.

Next thing I recall is Vernon twisting to me from the passenger seat, an elbow on the back rest. I had a smoke in my mouth, a Dunhill; he must have given it to me, 'cause I've never bought Dunhills in me life. 'OK, Ryan, listen. You and I need to clear the air a little.'

I started babbling a sorry, but he cut me off with a finger. Cringing in the far corner of this strange seat in this strange car, I must have looked about as hard as a Ken doll.

Vernon: 'No, son, I won't have you apologising. I was out of order that night and got my dues. I was . . . I was . . .' He looked down then, shook his head a bit. 'I was jealous of you with that bird, that big Yugokrainian bitch.' Bit of appeal now: 'I'd been workin on her for a couple-a weeks, mate! Christ, I'd been having dreams about her n all! Then you've ambled in and . . . What can I say, mate . . . I was a twat. I'm sorry.'

At last: '*You're* sorry?'

'Damned right I am.'

'Ah . . . OK.'

He nodded gratefully and turned away, snapping his seat-belt on. 'You was well within your rights reacting like that. Won yourself a ton of respect in there that night. And with none more so than me.' Then the gleam stole back into his eyes. 'Cos you should fucking see what *I* woulda done to some cunt what took a liberty like that.'

And I believed him. I really did. I took him at his word on this version of his feelings on the matter. I was too stunned to even feel a great deal of relief right then, but it seemed the kind of twisted logic that might make sense to a certain psyche. If only for cast-iron prudence, though, the me I thought I knew would have played along while clinging to the conviction that Vernon was just scheming until he could somehow get me out from under Melvyn's wing.

But I didn't.

Thing is, I've seen quite a bit of Vern since, and things have been sweet. He even jokes about that night, how I pre-empted him with the 'strike three' call; treats it like a grand laugh. He even tried to saddle me with a new nickname for a while: Umpire. Thank fuck it didn't stick.

I dunno, though; sometimes it seems like he's dwelling on it too much. The cringe factor for me in him so much as alluding to the incident is fucking acute, and I reckon he understands that. Vernon's no Rhodes Scholar, but he's got deep cunning oozing from every pore.

Or is his appreciation of my awkwardness just a benign breed of revenge, a harmless piss-take? Or perhaps keeping things light is his way of dealing with what he sees as his own failure? What if —

Jesus, I sound like fucking Alex here!

Anyway, Melvyn's been teaming me up with Vernon a lot lately. Dessie's almost always with us as well though, thank Christ. Vernon doesn't drive. That's right. Useless prick never even learned how to drive an automatic. And Des likes his bevvies too much to drive all night: one thing Melvyn won't abide is drink–driving on the job.

Vernon's nostalgia aside, it's the easiest coin I've ever made. Easier even than chaperoning dancers, because I rarely have to get out of the car on these jobs. Not sure what they do at these addresses I run them too, they never stay long, but I'm not worried. Melvyn's a bit dodgy, but his stock income seems to be nothing more pernicious than security contracts. Well, bouncing contracts anyway: you won't find his lads in yellow vests guarding building sites, but he's got blokes on doors all round town.

And when they're not needed elsewhere, Vernon and Des run around keeping an eye on things, stopping off at clubs on Melvyn's books, troubleshooting.

We're in a new MG tonight, and the thing runs a dream, glides across the bitumen like a puck on ice, that low growl throbbing through my foot, demanding more gas the way big Sal tugs on the leash.

Stopped at a crossing, and two obese women waddle past us. Vernon: 'The things you see when you've got a gun, eh Ry?'

Yeah, funny prick.

The club's down in Clapham and there's a queue thirty-odd long as I pull in to the curb beside the door. No need to search for parking spots in this line of work. I gathered from the phone call Dessie took that the lads on the door are on to a dealer working the club. An unsanctioned one, I guess. Either they can't pinpoint him or accosting him is too iffy, so Melvyn's sort team's been called in.

In this car, parked so brazenly, we stick out like dog's balls, and the punters are checking us out closely as we step into the night. I've got no intention of going inside — I never do if I can help it — so I tell the guys I'm over the road for a takeaway and will meet them back here.

As they close around a big black dude wearing a headset, two birds halfway down the queue get my attention.

'Oi, can you get us on to the guest list?'

'What's in it for me?'

'Anything your diseased mind can conceive of!'

Toffs n'all. Sloanettes. 'Tempting, ladies.' Taking a gap in traffic, over me shoulder: 'Very tempting.'

The Moroccan joint's a tiny, squalid place, a wizened old bloke cutting the meat, more sweat dripping off him than grease off the meatloaf, and a balding slob on the till with a great gut straining at his filthy apron. He asks what they can do for me, and I very nearly ask for a murder/suicide pact. Get a kebab instead and wander outside.

I've often wondered how anybody with a jaw smaller than a reticulated python's is supposed to consume one of these monstrosities on the move. In the fashion in which they're designed to be eaten anyway. I'm leaning against a wall, close enough to the club to see if the lads come out, peeling the paper away, catching the first handful of meat and onion that tries to escape, stuffing it into me gob, reeling with luscious pain from the super-strong chilli sauce—

A bomb inside my cheekbone, another almost instantly as my head cracks against the brick wall. Food shooting from my mouth, from my nostrils, the soles of shoes slapping the ground around me, more thuds in my face, on my head — no contact, just stunning, internalised noise — trying to reel away from it, tripping on something — *thud, thud-thud* — my knuckles scraping the dirty concrete beside my eyes — *thud thud* — the kebab crushed inside my fist . . .

. . . sucking in breath to scream with; a jolt in my ribs ripping the wind out again . . .

. . . my Mum fading away in a hospital bed; my Dad sacked from a job for the first time in his life, crying softly as he cooks my dinner . . .

My mind screams Vernon, appalled at myself for underestimating him.

A voice from high above, chillingly urgent: 'Get im intae the alley! Drag the cunt in!'

Groping for something to hold, anything, as my legs are hoisted and I'm moving, shirt riding up, bare spine scraping the pavement; hand finds a grip on something, something thin but fixed, a pipe maybe, and I'm not letting go of this if you hook me up to a fucking bulldozer, but the giants brace themselves and rip me away, and I'm off again, building up horrible speed — they must be running — helpless as the degree of light lessens in a heartbeat, as the traffic I couldn't hear before fades sharply, completely helpless, another thud in my head . . .

. . . then a face thrust in mine, rays of light from the road several miles away glinting in its eyes . . .

. . . but it's not Vernon . . .

. . . not with that mouser moustache, as thin as a teen's . . .

The lust of the rapist: '*Mister* Ryan Miller! Fork-lift driver *ex*traordinaire!'

'. . . Mister Morry McTavert. Prick.'

Exultant: 'Now, now, my bronzed Southern reeder. Is that any way tae greet yer old workmate and drinking buddy? How the fuck would ye be oan this *fainest* of evenings?'

Words blunt from the blood in my mouth: 'Yeah, good, mate, tickety boo. Cheers for asking.'

Fucking London, man. We're three and a half boroughs from where I last laid eyes on this piece of shit. Several million souls between there and here. I could prowl the streets for him for a decade and not find so much as a sniff.

This is a Lotto win minus the money.

I'd never really bought into Morry the Hard Man. Glasgow wide-boy. Ex-borstal. I guess my needs of the time just couldn't countenance it. There's at least four of them in here with me. This is bad. This is one I might not walk away from. There's no fear, though. Not really. Just this tundra-cold resignation.

And the interior of a human body with no hope left inside it is the coldest thing you could ever imagine.

Morry, blowing his shark's breath all over me: 'Ever the fucking smart cunt, eh?'

A lick of hope then, Dad's words ringing down the years. 'And to think: people used to speak of you as though you were a bad arse.'

A bark: 'Meaning?'

'You forgot to mention you were only a man when it was four on one.'

But Morry's not just half a cunt. 'I'm ten tames the man of that prick who boattled me.' End of. Then he takes me by the throat. 'Now, surfer boy, you're goany tell me exactly who it was who done me.'

'Now what would I wanna do a thing like that for?'

Acerbic pondering: 'Well, let me see now . . .' Gazes up at his boys, like they might have answers. 'Can you lads guess why he mate wanna dae a thing like that?' They snigger, and his eyes flash wide as a fake penny drops. 'Here's a reason! So that yer legs are still functioning when you're discharged fae the hoaspital!'

'What the fuck makes you think I've got a clue who did it anyway?'

'Because you ken every fucking thing that goes doon in that place!'

And either I'm hallucinating or Vernon's slipped into the alley. Standing at their backs. He's far shorter than any of them, only visible to me between bodies. Dead still. Just looking on. Drinking it. Loving it. A whimper from me as I cut my eyes around, praying Dessie's come too.

He hasn't.

Vernon's eyes gleam like black candles.

And now I *know* I'm dead. One man's bane is another man's boon. Vernon got here too late; sorry Dessie, sorry Melvyn. He chased them off but my head was just mush by then.

And Morry punches me in the face, a measured *Behave, bitch, or worse will follow* of a punch that I don't even feel. My eyes are locked with Vernon's. Old Morry has no idea how hard he's really hit me.

Vernon, casual: 'You three on your feet. Leg it. Five seconds.'

But they're all on their feet once they've landed from the jump Vernon startled from them.

Morry, covering shock with defiance: 'Who the *fuck are you*!?'

Vernon doesn't look at him. Same tone: 'You three. Jog on. Sharpish.'

And it's just comical, this curly-headed leprechaun, dressed for a funeral, drawling orders like there's ten of him. High farce.

Not to me though.

A crew-cut: 'And what if we tell ye to shove yer orders up yer soft southern erse?'

Vernon steps in and slaps him. That's all. Just a slap. Across the side of his head. But there's almost no sound as it lands, like a ruler landing cleanly on a table, flat side first. *Pwoof*. More a puff of air than any substantial noise.

So why does the guy scream in a long, shrill wave? Buckle at the knees, clutching his ear?

Vernon: 'You two. Scarper.' Matey chuckle: 'And this really *is* your last chance.'

Eyes leaping from stricken friend to midget undertaker . . . One of them mutters, 'Fuck this,' and darts away, his friend following.

Morry, backing off as well: 'You win, mate.'

But Vernon's got him by the wrist in a twinkling. '*You*, my jock friend, are going nowhere.'

The guy on the ground, thick with pain, disorientation: 'Jesus fucking Christ! What have ye *done* to me?'

'Ruptured your eardrum. Nothing a fearless northern monkey like yourself can't deal with.' Addressing the rest to Morry: 'Nice little trick a cousin once showed me. Interesting quirk of physics, yeah? Hope he enjoyed that last sentence of his, cos thems the last words he'll ever be hearing through that ear. Now, depending on what Ryan wants, I think I might do that to *both* of yours.'

Only then do I accept that I'm off the hook. My saviour was dressed as my nemesis. Funny old world.

Funny old city.

Floating to my feet cleanly, blinking, taking a breath because hunger in my chest tells me to.

Morry's cringing against the wall, wrist held fast in Vernon's dainty little grip. Morry's not done, though; his litany of pleading weirdly composed. 'Please, man. Ryan had it coming. I swear on mah mother's eternal soul. I'll take ye to the cash machine reet now. I've goat two grand ye can have. He boattled me from behaynd a few months ago. I'll give ye mah pin number and mah car keys. Mah flat keys too—'

Vernon: 'Do me a favour, Ry. I can't listen to this much longer.'

24

ANSWER

—Speak to me.

— . . . Err . . . is this Lisa Tailor's phone?

—It most assuredly is. And this is her majesty herself favouring you with her priceless attention. And who might you be?

— . . . I'm sorry to phone you cold like this. I got your number from the Labour Save people. I hope you don't mind.

—Sorry, mister, but you'll have to tell me who the hell you are before I'm in a position to answer *that* with any degree of sincerity.

—Yes, of course . . . It's . . .

—Spit it out, dude, I don't bite. Well, I sometimes do. First thing in the morning usually.

— . . . It's Julian Rutherford.

— . . .

— Are you still there?

—Ahhm, yeah. Ju— . . . Mr Rutherford. What a surprise.

—Standing on ceremony now, are we? I think I rather preferred Julian.

—OK . . . Julian . . . How might I be of assistance?

—I wondered if we might talk.

— . . . Oh Christ, you're going to sack me, aren't you. Lynn convinced you t—

—*Haha*. Déjà vu. Seems you and Alex have something in common. No, Lisa, I'm going to do nothing of the sort.

— . . . What then? . . . You're going to *promote* me?

—Afraid I haven't called to do that either. That wee slice of history shan't be duplicating itself twice in the same month.

—What do you need to talk to me about then?

— . . . Well . . . that's just it really.

—That's just what?

— . . . What's making this so fucking awkward. . . . I'd like to talk with you about nothing . . . and everything.

— . . .

— . . . Would you care to say something? I've never dealt especially well with suspense.

—I . . . ammm . . . I'm pretty busy right now. I'll call you back.

—*Ah*. Famous last words. I'm very sorry to have bother—

—Is this number OK to phone you on?

— . . . This number is fine.

—OK. *Na razie.*

—Excuse me?

—It's Polish: see you later.

—Oh, I see. *Dziekuje.*

END CALL.

25

RYAN

I haven't seen her for a couple of weeks. She has exams soon and has cancelled all her evening work to focus on study. I thought she might be too busy to take Sal running and might call to see if I'd do it. She hasn't. But I'm gonna head down to Richmond Park this afternoon for an eight k run and I don't fancy going alone. Just started out as a good excuse to get fit, taking him to parks and that, but now I'm used to having a dog with me again. Jogging or walking in a park without a dog to play with is a bit like washing dishes without music cranked up. I'd forgotten about that.

```
Goin runnin ths
aftanoon. Sal wanna
come?
```

She hasn't replied half an hour later when I fire the van up and head down to Waitrose with Greg, Alex and Sharon for the weekly shopping run. There's a car wash set up in the far corner of the car park. Greg christens a little black guy washing windows as 'Chammy Davis Junior'. One of Chammy's co-workers is a blonde in a pair of tiny shorts, tanned legs stretching from here to Helsinki, and Alex reckons he's totally going over to talk to her after we finish. He won't though.

She still hasn't replied by the time we hit the meat section. We're standing around trying to plot our way through personal house meat-boycotts (Lisa don't do Brit beef for mad cow reasons; Katie don't do Brit chicken because she once worked in a Midlands poultry factory; Jim don't do turkey because he thinks it tastes like shit) when Greg comes haring into the aisle riding a trolley skater-style. Waving an arm grandly at the shoppers: 'Make way, commoners and guttersnipes! Make way, I say!' Then he's past them, and yelling it at us too, acting like he doesn't know who we are. Grabbing a baguette out of our second trolley, Alex stands at attention . . . then tries to jam Greg's front wheel with the baguette in passing. The breadstick snaps in half, but it skews the trolley to one side and Greg stacks it into a Chicken Tonight display. It's not pretty, and we walk too casually away, snorting behind hands.

Alex and Greg split in the opposite direction, and she still hasn't replied when they hook up with us again in the booze section. They're all off to a barbie round at Choco and Anneke's gaff in Acton, then about ten of them are going to the Ben Harper gig. There's a spare ticket floating around, and it's starting to sound well tempting. I really can't be fucked running today anyway, so I throw a carton of Grolsch on the trolley.

I'm on the phone to Choc about her saving the ticket for me when a txt comes through, so I say I'll phone her back.

```
He want 2 no what tyme
you pick him up?
```

And looking at the sun beating down out there, it really would be a shame to waste the arvo drinking. Plus there's the consistency factor in getting fit: if I skip it today, it'll be easier to skip it next time. So I cancel the ticket and put the beer back.

I've gotta be smelling like a shit-house in apricot season after that effort, so I stop in at home for a shower before dropping Sal off. He's well knackered himself, but struggles out of the car and comes in with me, jumping up on the couch beside Katie and laying his head in her lap. They're deep in conversation as I head upstairs.

Aside from Katie the house seemed empty, so I get a bit of a shock when I'm shaving in front of the bathroom mirror and Lisa steams in.

'Oh shit, sorry, Ry! I didn't know you were home.'

'Likewise, my dear, likewise. Don't let me be the fly to your ointment, though: shed those trappings and let cleansing commence.'

'Yeah, you wish, baby . . . Where are *you* going tonight?'

'Nowhere special.'

Scoffing: 'Yeah, right.'

Frowning: 'Why? What are on about?'

'Ryan, you never wear CK One when you're up to "nothing special", and you shave with a blade about as often as Katie does her underarms.'

'. . . Well, D. I. Tailor, I'm willing to take a polygraph on this.' Then I notice the clothes she's holding. 'What about *you*?'

'. . . I'm going to the theatre with Stacey.'

'Oh cool. Have a good one.'

It's going on 8.30 by the time me and Sal turn up on her doorstep. He whines and jumps all over her, and she indulges him for about a minute, ignoring me.

'OK . . . I better get going. Don't feed him too much tonight: him and Katie pigged out on leftovers.'

A stern shake of the head, some kind of tension about her: 'No. Come in for while.'

'Well . . . if you insist.'

As Sal walks around the corner he suddenly seems a little tense too, and I learn why as soon as I follow him into the room. There are five people in here already. Five men. Twenty-some-things. Their talk freezes. They stare at me.

They're all Arabs.

The dark complexions, the hooded eyes, speak instantly of honour killings and terrorist plots. A little hasty, maybe, but they certainly don't speak of a welcomed interruption from an imperialist oppressor. Nadia makes the introductions, and I make the effort to shake all their hands, but the mood doesn't thaw at all.

I feel like a teen caught hanging around bushes outside a girl's bedroom window. By her psychotic father and brother.

This is suddenly the last place I wanna be. I open my mouth to make my excuses, but Nadia says she'll bring me tea, shuts Sal down the hall, and disappears into the kitchen. There's no room to sit, and I'm left in no-man's-land. They're still staring at me. I got a cold 'hello' or two over the handshakes, but I'm not sure if any of them speaks English.

One of them, Faisel I think it is, stands up from the couch and gestures. His English is very neat and precise. 'Sit with us, Ryan.'

But I'm not about to give him the upper hand, so I politely decline.

'Please. I insist.'

And there's not much recourse left me after that, so I nod cold thanks and take his place. He pulls up on the floor. Then he gives me a long, open stare which I've no idea how to read. I look away, then look back; he's still staring, and he smiles slightly. I force one back, and his eyes shift at last.

The silence holds, the seconds stretching out; they look as uncomfortable as I feel, though I'm guessing for very different reasons. Whatever is was they were discussing — camels, sand, beheadings —they're not about to continue with me in the picture. I notice then how well dressed they all are; no Savile Row budgets, but tidy pants and collared shirts to a number. Then one of them mutters something to Faisel in Arabic.

That dodgy smile: 'Ryan, Ibrahim wishes to know if you are an Englishman.'

What the fuck business is it of his? 'No, I'm not from England.' He waits patiently for me to expound . . . and I crack a long time before he would have, I'm sure. 'I'm Australian.'

A murmur runs through them.

Nadia comes back out, handing me a cup of tea, and Faisel's smile raps something at her in their tongue. A few of them grin.

Nadia, to me: 'They want to know if I know what happens to those who feed the enemy.'

Jesus Christ, what do ya say to that? But I have to say something, because they're all waiting. 'Ahh . . . you guys are all Iraqi?'

Faisel, Ibrahim and Dawoud are Iraqi; Mohammed is Syrian; Tariq is from Lebanon. It doesn't help me frame an answer though, so I just nod dumbly.

Then Dawoud starts talking in Arabic, quietly at first but getting steadily louder, eyes flashing at me, lingering on me. Faisel and Nadia sound like they're trying to calm him down but his anger seems irresistible. And it's swelling too, showing teeth as he growls the harsh sounds, the hand gestures all blows and grips.

Christ only knows what his problem is, and a chill creeps over me as I realise there's a very real possibility that someone he knows was killed by Australians in the war. People die in war — the Aussie SAS are reportedly pretty good at making it happen — and few killed aren't survived by people who loved them.

Dawoud's not getting any happier. I shouldn't be here, and she needs her fucking head read inviting me in (needs her head read hanging round with these cunts in the first place). I've never thought of how often this must take place in London — someone from a country that's suffered at the hands of another coming across a nationality they consider to be an enemy. Must happen all the time. Another exhibit to go with the multitude attesting to the luck-by-birthplace of we Southerners: the only citizens we're ever going to encounter in our travels with whom we might hold a grudge worth bringing up are . . . well, no one really. Unless you've got a long memory and count the Frogs, and no Aussie I know ever died from Mururoa fallout.

Then Howard jumped into that fucking 'coalition' and conceivably gave all kinds of people around the world compelling reasons to seek out a 'wee word' with *me*, given the chance.

And this Dawoud guy looks like he's got more on his mind than a 'wee word'. Fuck knows how I'd behave the next time I came across an Indonesian should my dad be killed in his home by a bomb from Jakarta. And you have to imagine that this guy is much more conditioned to violence that I am. A smack in the face isn't likely to satisfy someone from a land where cluster bomblets lie on footpaths.

Now Faisel stands up, trying to make himself heard without shouting, not enjoying much success, hands resting on Dawoud's shoulders. Nadia's standing beside them too, talking rapidly, and things look to be turning to shit real fast. And then the anxiety in the frown she throws at me cranks my alarm dial up viciously. The other three guys haven't said a word — which can only mean that they're in sympathy with the nutter — and the only reassurance is the presence somewhere of Sal.

But that's not enough. Standing: 'Look, Nadia, I'm just gonna leave. I shouldn't be here.'

Then Dawoud's on his feet, and they're holding him back, but he's getting closer to me, and I'm backing off, and, oh fuck, that face — I thought he was handsome at first — is absolutely riddled with rage. He stretches out an arm to point a trembling finger at me . . .

. . . and I feel like I'm in some kind of lunatic dream as he starts grinning and pidgin-singing an Aussie anthem. 'I meet a strange lady. She make me nervous. She sit me down and she give me breakfast.'

Me: 'What the *fuck*?'

The tension leaves the room like air from a burst balloon, and they're all falling about the place.

Dawoud, an arm on my shoulder: 'Oh fuck, man, I sorry! I could not resist!'

It's only then that I realise I've had the urine extracted from me big time. I don't know whether to laugh or storm from the place.

Me, waving a fist at Nadia: 'You nasty, *nasty* bitch.' I feel myself smiling though.

A while later Faisel explains something to me. 'Ryan, we are Arabs. We do not judge an individual on the action of his leader. Dawoud is Kurdish. If that was the way, he would have tried to kill me many years ago. Tariq is Lebanese; the Syrians, Mohammed's people, have invaded and killed in Lebanon many times.'

Dawoud: 'This how we begin, anyway. People with brain. Otherwise we would be in fight every time we walk outside. We wait to know them before we judging.'

Ibrahim, grinning: 'Then, if we do not like them, *then* we blame them!'

That sets them off again.

Someone asks Nadia what she's preparing us for dinner. She just deadpans him and points to the kitchen. There's a joke in this somewhere, but it's sailing over my head.

So I just ask.

Tariq, dreamy: 'Let me draw you a picture of the perfect Arab woman, Ryan. She is polite and quiet. Very, very quiet.' Their laughter punctuates his points, Nadia enjoying it as much as any of them. 'She obey her mother-in-law in all things. *All* things, Ryan. You understand? She has never made the sex before. She has never even *thought* of the sex until she put her eyes on me for first occasion. But she has friend who is slapper, and this friend now tell her how to make the sex *veeeeeeeery* good. Good for *me*, that is.' Curt: 'Then she tell slapper she never want to see her again and she not welcome in my home.' Nods sagely as the laughter rings around him. 'This woman, this *perfect* woman, she never want to leave house without me. World is too much for her . . . without me. She believe in Allah, and she pray to him every day to give her ten strong sons for me. Her grandma and her mama, they teach her how to keep house *perfect* . . . at *all* times, you understand? And, most important, they teach her how to *cook*.' The men's eyes mist extravagantly, hands rubbing bellies. 'And I mean *cook*, Ryan. Falafel, dolma, kebab, kuba, all of these and more she can cook like a chef, cook for me and for as many friends as I come home with each evening. Then she make tea, wash up the dishes, prepare the dessert while we talk or watch football—'

Muhammad: 'Or build bombs.'

'Or build bombs. Then, when my friends finally leave, she dance for me — in the old style, of course. Then we make the sex for as many times as I have energy . . . and she fall pregnant with twin boys, big, strong, handsome and clever.' Emphatic: '*This*, Ryan, this is the perfect woman.'

Faisel, sighing sadly. '*Then* . . . then you have Nadia.'

Ibrahim: 'Nadia, when she have her first son, she will kill him.

238

Just as revenge for baby girls killed in world because they had no dick.'

That one really tickles her.

Gallows humour? This is more like gas-chamber humour.

Tariq: 'Nadia, she not dance like harem girl for all the silk in Babylon.' Grimacing: 'She dance like fucking Madonna.'

Dawoud: 'Nadia refuse even to get on her knees and pray to the real gods in her world, the Red Hot Chilli Peppers.'

Muhammad: 'Nadia's mother-in-law will last two minutes in room with her. If she ever come back, it will be her taking orders.'

Faisel: 'And the slapper, the one who teach the perfect wife how to fuck?' Nodding sadly: 'Nadia *is* that slapper.'

They dissolve over that.

Tariq: 'And when Nadia go into the kitchen to make falafel, dolma, kebab, kuba . . .'

Dawoud: 'She come back out three hours later and serve you burnt Weetabix.'

Me, when the laughter dies down enough: 'You know what all that makes her, don't you?'

'What?'

'It makes her the perfect *European* woman.'

And that brings the fucking house down. I may have made the joke, but I'm only getting a smidgen of it, I'm sure.

Faisel: 'Which, Ryan, was really just a very long way of telling you that if you are a man and you wish to eat in Nadia's house, you had better put the apron on and get to work.'

Ryan: 'Fuck it, let's just go and get some takeaways then.'

A quiet comes over them suddenly. I'm about to make the suggestion again when something clicks.

Maybe they're all skint.

I give it a few minutes, then tell them I'm off to the shop to get some fags. Dawoud asks if he can come for a mission. I can't say no.

There's an Offspring tape in the stereo. I had the volume pumped when I got here and it catches me out as I turn the key. I get the volume down, then eject the tape.

Dawoud, tentative: 'Would you mind if I listen? I not hear that song in more than a year.'

Me, blinking: 'Really? Yeah, sure. I didn't think you'd like it.'

Big grin: 'You kidding me? Those guys were my *favourite* when they come out!'

'Where were you then?'

'Baghdad.'

'People listen to the Offspring in *Baghdad*?'

'Of course. You could not find in many shop though — especially back then, through the embargo — but people would have some sent to them and sell them to friends. You like the heavy metal, Ryan?'

'Yeah, sure.'

'Me too. It was me who teach Nadia. I used to have the long hair and everything.'

'Really?'

'You see?' He takes a photo from his wallet. 'This me, in centre.'

There's a bunch of maybe twenty young people sitting on rocks beside blue water, huddled up for the photo; a few tennis rackets, a soccer ball in mid-air, a girl in the front row cradling a guitar. Not a can or bottle to be seen, but by the grins they're all having a ball and a half no matter. Two of the guys have long hair; Dawoud looks like a young Geronimo in Oakleys.

He grins: 'I need to be careful though, with the long hair. Late at night, if I walking home from party, I need to avoid police.'

'Why?'

'Because if they bored, maybe they take me to station and cut my hair off.'

'No shit?'

'No shit, man. Ask Nadia. One night I leave her house, looking like Kirk Hammett; next morning I see her and I look like a fucking neo-Nazi.'

'Bogus.'

'*Most* bogus, dude!' And he gives a Ted 'Theodore' Logan riff on the air-guitar.

Which spins me right out. I cover it by asking where the photo was taken.

'In park beside Tigris, outside Baghdad. Young people would go there to play and to swim . . . But not any more.'

'Why not?'

'American planes blew up tanks there. They use the poison bullets. Some friends went back, after the war . . . They all sick now.'

It takes me a second to make the connection. 'Depleted uranium?'

'This is it.' Without warning he turns to me fully, almost imploringly, as if I can give him an answer he's been searching hard for. 'Why do they do this, Ryan?'

'Do what?'

'Use the poison bullet?'

'. . . They say because they needed to.'

Growling: '*Need* them?' And this anger looks nothing like the fake stuff he gave me earlier. 'Like they would lose without them. You can never know how easy it was for them, this "war". Ryan, they have more weapon than Shaitan himself. But they hit *every*-thing — even empty things — one hundred time harder than they need to. I do not understand why. Their soldiers in more danger from their own team than from the scared boys they burning. But still the poison bullet. And still the cluster bomb. My people, they die from this for many more years.'

Dawoud hits the volume as the opening drum riff to 'Come

Out and Play' comes through the speakers, tapping it perfectly on the dashboard. I shift into first and floor it, burning a little rubber before the tyres bite, and we look at each other, chanting the first line.

We walk back in with two pizzas and a bucket of K-Fried big enough to drown someone in. No potato and gravy, though: you won't find any in European KFCs. First time I rocked into one — Lavender Hill, South London — I asked for a three-piece pack and a medium potato and gravy. The dude behind the counter asked me to repeat my order. Then he asked for it again. Then he asked his mate to come over and translate.

But it's a good ten minutes before I can get any of them to start eating. You'd think I was deep in the red and had been moaning about it all day. Nadia finally clears it up with a burst of Arabic; she tells me later that she could only bring them round by saying that I owed her some money and this was part of the repayment.

She's got a play list going and 'Hotel California' comes up, taking me right back somewhere, somewhere good. Then Don Henley starts singing, and all six of us are accompanying him. They reminisce in between verses, and I see that it means as much to them as to me. Jesus, is there anyone in the world who doesn't have a memory to this song?

Nadia's sitting close to Faisel, on the floor in front of his chair, leaning her back against his leg. I notice the contact suddenly and get a cold jolt; wonder how long they've been like that.

Later — now she's sitting beside him — I silently ask her if it's OK to spliff up round these cats. She nods, so I break out a quarter I had floating in the glove box. They won't hear of it, though; and two of them produce stashes of their own. I try to insist, but it's six on one and they seem well serious. Nadia fluffs around for a while, assembling the pieces of a huge hookah bong, filling it with water.

I'm praying she won't, but when she finishes she folds herself into the space beside Faisel again, resting against his shoulder. His arm slips around her as naturally as the moon rising, and I'm feeling sick as someone hands me the hookah's mouthpiece.

The pair of them fit together like pie and mash, like cigarettes and beer. I want to hate him, to write him off as a thief and a prick, so that I can compete somehow, fight for what he's taking from me . . . But I just can't. And there's much more to it than the fact he's holding all the cards in this setting. There's something about the guy's bearing, something deeply pensive, melancholy almost. Something principled too, a suggestion of virtue leagues above the hollow mantras I pretend to live by. And there's no knowledge anywhere in those eyes that he's holding cards over me, or even that there's a contest taking place.

Yet he must know why I'm here.

I'm soon stoned, and that helps me deal with it, helps me tune in to the stories the others are telling. Tariq was six and taking food to his father in a field above their village in southern Lebanon when Israeli jets attacked it. He says there is nothing in the world to make you feel smaller than the sight and sounds of a jet closing in on a bombing run. He says your instincts makes you run — even though you can feel in your bones that feet cannot help you now — and that your panic feeds on the running and can drive you mad even before the earth begins to buck. Dawoud was in Baghdad at the time of Bush Snr's war. Electricity was the first thing to go, and for a week afterwards his whole suburb was a constant party as people tried to eat the food from the freezers before it could spoil. He has never in his life experienced such a spirit of community and goodwill. There is no such thing as a stranger inside a city under assault. Ibrahim's older brothers made a lot of money smuggling opium across the Syrian/Turkish border. It was the easiest thing in the world: they'd travel to Turkey and buy semi-wild camels from Kurdish tribesmen, then herd them back to Syria. The camels would be loaded with bags of opium and set free near the border around sundown. The boys would then ride motorbikes back across the border crossing, and, once in Turkey, intercept the camels as they neared their old grazing lands. It was their tradition to free a camel for good once it had success-fully 'muled' for them four times.

It's getting on a bit, and a couple of the guys start to doze, Faisel especially. Some things just transcend language, and when Nadia tells him in Arabic to go down to the bedroom I understand every word. What's about to take place between them grows more solid by the second, bearing down on me like a jet-fighter made in America. But hope springs eternal in the soul of the scoundrel, and as Faisel says good night and leaves the room I'm trying to convince myself that my instincts were wrong, that it's just platonic. Then, as I head down to the toilet I glimpse them through her bedroom door at the end of the hallway, and they're standing there holding each other, as silent and still as the last two people on the face of the earth.

I stare at myself in the bathroom mirror, amazed at the self-pity sloshing inside me even after everything I've heard tonight.

Dawoud's still wide awake in the lounge, and bored as well, so I suggest the two of us hit a Soho metal bar I know. He beats me to the car by ten strides.

He loved the joint. Everyone halfway into that kind of music loves the joint, but for him it was a glimpse of nirvana. It's a converted cellar I discovered by accident, two flights underground, all ancient brick, low ceilings, deep booths hewn into the walls. And freaks of many descriptions playing in the shadows. Dawoud took over the dance floor, head-banging with the locals through the dry-ice smoke, howling out lyrics. I couldn't get him away long enough even to get a drink inside him.

Not that he needed it.

Slipped him a speed-bomb though; dropped one myself.

Later this tall Danish bird in PVC I spoke to took a shine to him, and we ended up sitting in a booth with her and her friends, passing spliffs around, and Dawoud and the blue-haired Amazon fell into each other with some of the raunchiest tongue-kissing I'd seen in yonks, and I slipped my hand around the thigh of the girl beside me — she had a light chain running from her earlobe to a piercing in her lip — and she didn't respond for about a minute, just chatted away in German with another bird on her far side, and I was thinking about either backing off or upping the ante when she turned around and licked me from jaw to temple with just the tip of her tongue, and then they've found out that Dawoud's Iraqi and two of them have wanted to talk politics, and I can see that he can't be fucked right now, and neither can I 'cause that shit can polarise instantly, and we've already said we'll drive them home, spare them the reeking anarchy of the night buses, so we could well be on for our own breed of *pole*-arising — if ya take my meaning — but one of these bitches was insistent, so off it starts, but it all looks good for a while, no knee-pad conservatives in the group, and my fingertips have just started brushing the skin above the top of the German's stockings when the other girl, Dawoud's bird, said that she thinks the wall in Israel is a great idea, and Dawoud's stood up, pocketed his fags, knocked his drink back, grabbed his jacket and just started for the fucking door.

And I doubt I can convince him to come back — I'm starting to know the look — so it's either follow him and blow this gaff, or hang around, get the drinks in, and start laying fun foundations with these four hot fucked-up Euro-sluts whose house I'll soon be inside. And there's no fucking choice here, not tonight, none whatsoever . . .

'Oh, you fucking stupid, *stupid* cunt.'

I turned to the German and snogged her so hard and suddenly — she had what felt like a blunt sliver of glass pierced through her tongue — that she lost all her breath, then I pulled away and went after the fucking stupid cunt.

The blue-haired thing followed us to the stairs, then yelled up that we must be faggots, and if he heard he didn't falter, but I looked back and blew her a big kiss while I mimed giving his arse a good kneading, and outside he didn't even look all that pissed off, like he quite often blows off prospects like that, and he wanted to know what a faggot was, and I told him to take a guess, but he said he didn't have one, so I told him I'd give him a clue and diverted us into this gay bar down the road — you can tell them by the black windows, an unsubtle code for straight folks out of their hood — and I got the pints in and stayed deadpan as we stood at the bar and started drinking, and Dawoud gazed around, oblivious and mystified for about two minutes, and then he clicked and just keeled over in mid-chat, laughing like a lunatic.

Afterwards we decided to stay and finish our pints for entertainment value, and about five minutes later the barman brings me another beer, and I told him I hadn't ordered one, and he pointed out some bald body-builder in a Wonder Woman costume who's staring at me, said he'd bought it for me, and I felt weirdly flattered, so I lifted the pint and nodded thanks, but then Dawoud asked what was going on, and when I told him his face went dark, and he said I was well out of order in accepting a drink off the guy.

'Why?'

'Because you and I might be together, he not fucking know! You disrespect me, both of you! What am I, some *object* to you?'

So we pretended Wonder Woman had caused a tiff between us, stood there bickering like a couple, getting louder. Finally I exasperated him too much, and he minced out of the place, lacking only a handbag to throw over his shoulder. Linda Carter tried to intercept me as I went after him, and I gave him a grimacing smile for the wank-bank: *What can I do? He's a slag, but I love him.*

I caught up to Dawoud a safe distance down the road, and we giggled like Gatling guns all the way to the car.

It made me feel like London's biggest loser but I decided to stay at hers when we got back, pulling up on the floor among the bodies. Big Sal carved out a space for himself, then flaked out beside me.

I wake up a bit later. Sal's got his head on his paws, staring intently at something in the corner. As my head clears I realise that it's a body, kneeling, face pressed to the floor. It straightens slowly, whispering, then prostrates itself again.

It's Faisel.

At first I feel contempt, a reflex reaction from the Muslim/madman thing I've been conditioned to, from my contempt for religion in general, from my haste to have something over the bastard. *What kind of man leaves the bed of a woman like that to suck on Allah's tool instead?* But I can make that last for just a few seconds, because there's nothing remotely insane, gullible, weak about the image he projects. I can't stop watching, and I'm soon feeling a voyeur of the worst order. The quiet dedication, the service to something higher, fortifies the inferiority he stirs in me. He continues for minutes, so calm and controlled, but charged by some invisible force.

Then his eyes open and he looks straight at me.

Fuck.

But again he surpasses me, smiling that fathomless smile as if he can't tell that he's made me feel like a tramp caught dick in hand.

Hushed: 'I'm sorry to wake you, Ryan.'

'You didn't.'

Standing up: 'Will you take tea with me?' ·

You prick. Wanna rub some salt in before fucking her again? Why don't you just ask me if I've got any condoms handy? Every fibre in me wants to say no, I'm too tired, to lash out with the only weapon I'm ever going to have against him.

. . . But it's not every fibre.

The 'yes' still sounds resigned, though; and as he brings two cups of tea, sits on the floor near me, even the way I sit up to face him makes me feel like I'm following orders.

—Do you believe in God, Ryan?

— . . . No.

—Neither do I. Not really.

—Then why do you pray?

—I have only started to pray recently. I pray because I am scared. Scared for myself. We all need a god when we are scared. And I pray for my people who have died in this war, and those who might die in the future.

— . . . What about your people killed by Saddam? Did you pray for them?

— I never knew anybody killed by Saddam. A cousin of mine disappeared before I was born. He was a member of an underground socialist group.

—Really? What about the mass graves?

—Saddam was an appalling leader, Ryan. But the short history of Middle Eastern nation states is full of bad men in power. It still is. And you know who made them? You know of colonialism? Post-colonialism?

— . . . A bit.

—Few in the world knew Saddam's name until the invasion of

Kuwait, even though his worst crimes were committed before that. Suddenly his is a household name. Up there with Castro and Ho Chi Minh. Do you know why this is?

—I think so.

—What do you think?

—Saddam's most dangerous crime, at the end of the day, was to tell Uncle Sam to go fuck himself.

—Western governments did not condemn Saddam for the gassing of the Kurds in Halabja. They sold him the weapons. Then, in the run-up to this last war, you do not hear a politician speak without bringing the massacre up. Fifteen years late. The image the world has of Saddam was drawn by spin.

— . . . But even so, don't you think your country's better off without him?

—The whole war was a lie, and to kill for lies only breeds more evil. Yes, a democratic, stable Iraq would be a much better place, but we have a saying: better one year of tyranny than one day of chaos. This may sound strange to your kind, it may sound weak, but you do not know what that day actually looks like. There is nothing worse, Ryan, than coming home and finding your brother and sister dead in the school with twenty other children because a bomb brought down the roof of their classroom. Who should I speak freely to then?

— . . .

—But you are right: Iraq has a chance to become a fine place to live now. For many reasons it should never have been done — even the reasons sold at the time have fallen flat. But it is done, and we have this small chance.

—You must live in the present.

—Yes. But I tell you, Ryan, the rest of the world does not suffer from the delusions you in the West are force fed. We have not one ounce of trust in America, in anything that it does. We will never accept a government that answers to Washington.

—What will—

—But here is the crucial factor, Ryan, the thing that terrifies me most. Iraq is *full* of weapons. *Full*. Thanks to Saddam and his former friends in the State Department and Home Office, in terms of weapons, Iraq makes Afghanistan look like a paint-ball park. And we have millions of trained soldiers, many of them highly trained. All of this spread out through three major factions who were only ever held together by dictators . . . *Democracy?* There is only one Arab democracy, Ryan, Lebanon, and it is unstable and it took fifteen years of civil war to make!

—Everyone deserves the chance to be free though.

—There are many kinds of freedoms. Yours took centuries to evolve. We have always had more important things in our lives than the ideals of Thomas Jefferson. We did not even know what a nation state was until Western surveyors drew them up for us.

— . . . You guys are on the brink.

—We are on the brink of a black hole that will make people pray for life under Saddam. Civil war in Iraq will turn into the most bitter and bloody in modern history. You have heard the commentators saying that the West is headed for another Vietnam?

—Yes.

—How do you think *I* feel when I see these highly paid people in make-up speaking of this? However bad Vietnam was for America, it was about one million nine hundred and forty-four thousand times worse for the Vietnamese.

— . . . How do you think it can be avoided?

—Until America relinquishes control it cannot be avoided. But there is only one way this will ever happen before it is too late.

— . . . What are you going to do about it?

—What would you do if the Chinese occupied Australia,

smashed your army in a few days? If they killed tens of thousands, including civilians, while losing less than a hundred of their own? If they were building a puppet government to make sure Australia served China from here on? If hundreds of your people were being herded and killed and abused by the Chinese every night?

— . . . You know what I would do.

—Of course.

—But how can you fight from up here?

—I cannot.

— . . . Fuck, you're *leaving*?! Going *home*?! *When*?!

—Tomorrow.

—Jesus! And you're going to fight? To join the insurgents?!'

—Yes.

— . . . Fucking hell, no wonder you're praying.

— The final straw came a few weeks ago. The mujahideen had a successful week, and the US began conventional bombing again. How can a bomb distinguish between a fighter and a civilian if searches and checkpoints cannot?

— . . . It can't.

—I sat in front of the TV and listened to some sixty-year-old *cunt* in a uniform brag about how they had decided to use a sledgehammer to break a walnut. These were his exact words. All I could see were my nieces and nephews playing football in a back yard . . . and this *cunt* strutting for the cameras with his medals and his tough-guy scowl. This is strategic murder, Ryan, nothing less. This is true terrorism, by every definition. I can watch this no more.

— . . . Can you . . . ? Have you killed before?

—I was staying in a village near the Highway of Death in 1991. US jets incinerated the retreating Iraqi army without opposition. Miles of cars and trucks and conscripts. Flat desert, nowhere to hide. Planes filling the sky. No enemy aircraft, no anti-aircraft fire. The soldiers were trying to surrender, we could hear them on the radio in my uncle's truck, begging to be taken prisoner. First they clogged the road. Then they strafed the column, hundreds of them, one after another, all day long. In my head I could hear the yelling of the pilots — fly boys, Tom Cruise fans, with real targets at last. I could hear them whooping with each other as they coordinated the slaughter. In the years since, pilots who took part have lost their minds . . . and they never saw it from the ground. But I did. My uncle and I went looking for survivors a day later.

—What did you find?

—Hell, Ryan. We found hell itself . . . I am not a violent person, I have seldom punched in my life, never mind shot. But you must believe me when I tell you that I would kill an American in uniform on Iraqi soil with a butter knife if there was nothing else. I fear what will become of me. But I fear for my people far worse.

— . . . You're leaving tomorrow?

— I fly to Jordan. From there by bus to Baghdad.

— . . . And then?

—We shall see.

— . . . What about Nadia?

—What about her?

—What will it do to her if you die?

—She will be upset, but I cannot shirk this because of that.

—So . . . you two aren't all that serious then?

—What do you mean?

— . . . She hasn't been your girlfriend for long?

—My *girlfriend*? Haha! *This* was what you thought?

—But . . . but you just slept with her.

—I have slept beside her more times than I can remember. But actually *sleeping* with Nadia would be like sleeping with my sister.

— . . . Oh.

—Hahaha, *no*, my friend, I'm sorry, but Nadia is *your* problem.

—What do you mean?

—What do you think I mean?

— . . . Has she . . . has she said things about me?

—Hardly a word. And this is how I know.

—How?

—Nadia is a rebel, Ryan, a rebel against her culture, against the role of the women in it especially. But she is also a product of it. And our young women do not do talk about the men in their lives to other men. Even to me, who she trusts perhaps like no other. I am an Arab man, therefore there are things she cannot say to me. Of course she knows I too am different — we could never have become friends otherwise. She is not scared of what I would do or think, she is just embarrassed. Ashamed, maybe. For no real reason except what is hard wired inside her.

— . . . So because she kept me quiet, you're sure she likes me?

—And because she invited you in here today. While we were here. This was harder for her than you can ever know.

— . . . I dunno, mate. She barely looked at me all day. I felt like I was here on sufferance.

—And you thought her and I were shagging! You poor bastard! Hahaha! It's lucky you did not run off and fuck someone else for revenge! Though I doubt Dawoud would have let such a thing happen.

— . . .

26

LISA

He'd wanted to take me to the fucking *Dorchester*. He finally got around to asking me out; I said where; and his first suggestion was the fucking *Dorchester*. As if I'd sit there and be impressed by him talking over the wine waiter's painstaking routine, rejecting a bottle because the nose wasn't right.

'Sorry, not really my scene.'

'OK. Where might be more in keeping with said scene?' That fucking accent, man. So airy and bored; every syllable just the right side of sarky. And then again, maybe he wasn't so much trying to impress me as trying to get me out of my comfort zone and off balance.

So I very nearly told him I wanted us to meet at the Redback. Now that would've been just total quality, him in his suit and cufflinks and ten years older than anyone else in the house, the Southern hordes debauching themselves around him, Lisa shaking it with everyone who had the balls (or the ovaries) to come close enough. Absolute class.

Couldn't do it, though; way too close to home.

But it was the kind of thing I wanted. So I told him how to find this salsa club in Paddington I've been to a few times, a wonderfully atmospheric Cuban joint.

I was pretty nervous about what I was going to do to him, so I needed some sustenance. A pill was too dangerous: not the occasion to be infusing oneself with false love. Speed would have had me shooting off at the mouth. Acid he would have seen straight away — seen something anyway, even if he couldn't place it.

So I made an exception and armed myself with some ching.

I hooked Alex up with a couple of grams earlier in the week — first time he's ever asked me for *that* — and levied a little taxation on both bags, leaving me with a juicy quarter-gram. I've got the first line ready to go inside a compact, and as the train terminates in Paddington, I dick around until I'm the last one left in the carriage, then hoover the baby up through a tenner.

The others have gone to the Walkabout to watch rugby but I wasn't interested. I hate sport. Professional sport anyway. With the globe in so parlous a state, that so many millions of hours of emotion and thought and creativity are expended on *sport* is something I find viscerally offensive.

On the concourse of the station. I'm only a few minutes late, so I pick up a couple of Bacardi Breezers and loiter. There's a brass band and choir group performing, about thirty of them, and I know the coke's hitting me because I hate the song — 'In the Mood' — but I'm tapping away to it despite myself, leaning against a divider and letting the sounds wash over me as I sip. One of the British Rail staff is pissing about by a ticket machine near me, and he's singing along with the band, seemingly to himself but very loud, giving it the full warble too, getting right into it. He's old enough to have a thing for the song, I suppose, but I can't tell from his tone whether he's singing derisively or not — maybe they've been here for hours and they're starting to piss him off — but either way it's funny as fuck, and I'm giggling every time he starts heading toward a big note. He notices me laughing at him, so I clap the beat and grin at him, and he winks and goes back to work, singing even louder, getting the face right into it too, lilting over the last syllables, and I'm just fucking dying here, and a lot of people are starting to stare, and I don't really give a shit about that right now, but I get up and split anyway.

Then I realise I've left the station at the wrong exit. Nothing looks familiar, so I fire straight back into Paddington, waving at my aging serenader again. The place is a bit of a maze, but I spy a WH Smith over the way and head across to it, remembering that Zenab, a girl I know from EUE, started working here a few weeks ago.

I inquire after her but the lady says she's quite new here and Zenab's name rings no bells with her. She asks for a description of Zenab, and I say mid-twenties, tall and slim, curly hair pulled back in a bun. Then I'm about to say that she's black, but the word lodges in my throat. Change it to 'coloured' but that lodges too . . . She's looking at me oddly, and in the end I just tell her to forget it and walk away.

Fucking *apartheid* hangovers. I should've put on a false accent before opening my mouth — I do a good American and a passable French — but hadn't thought that far ahead.

I hit the maps section of the bookshop and grab an A–Z, tracking down the right page. A staff member is looking at me a bit warily as I take out a notebook, so I beckon him over, ask him about some non-existent book he pretends to have heard of, then chat with him about nothing. He's up for a chinwag so he's not about to complain when I start transposing a precis of the map I need into my notebook right under his nose. I finish in a couple of minutes — it feels great flirting with him while Julian sits alone waiting for me, glancing at his watch, a vodka and lemonade untouched beside his Long Island Iced Tea — then I offer the guy a go on the Breezer bottle. His eyes narrow, then he sneaks a peep around, grins and downs a swallow. Then he gets another shock as I throw him a cheery goodbye and leave him standing there. But he calls me back, saunters up to me all cool and casual, and asks for my number. Bless him. I've got no intention of going out with him, but I give him the number on the condition that he phones me some time tonight.

Back on the street, and the hit from the warm night air, the heat left in the tar seal by the setting sun, intensifies the coke somehow; I can fucking *hear* it surging through me, my synapses firing like machine-guns, and I feel like I could dance down the middle of Praed Street, on to Edgware Road and Park Lane, all the way to Tower Bridge, traffic giving way, gathering a retinue a few thousand strong.

I piss around and yak with people on the street as I dawdle towards the club, and it's another fifteen minutes before I see the red star of Club Cubana blinking ahead of me.

Then the excitement/nervousness ratio that the cocaine had been ruling with a puffed chest takes an alarming swing south, making me stop and blink, so I duck into a phone booth and crack my second Breezer.

. . . But fuck that, what am I worried about here? I leave the drink untouched on the phone for the next lucky punter, and I spy him through the window . . . and he looks far from uncomfortable. How he quite achieves that while sitting alone and staring at nothing I'm not certain of. Still, he looks far from enthralled either, finding himself immersed in revolutionary bric-a-brac, Fidel and Che smiling from every wall, the staff with red stars on their black T-shirts.

But I'm not sure if people like him are ever enthralled by anything.

And I can't see myself staying here long anyway, so in I go, trying out some Spanish with a guy on the door, keeping it up until I'm sure he's seen me, then keeping it up for a few minutes more. Then I walk over to his table, feeling like every eye on earth is fixed on me.

  — He doesn't seem aware of the fact that I'm almost an hour late.

'Ermm . . . sure you wouldn't care to eat?'

'Positive.' I'd told him earlier that eating was off the cards.

'No problem. I wasn't sure what you cared to drink . . .'

'They do a wonderful Long Island Ice Tea. I'll nip to the bar and get one. How's yours?'

'No, please, I've begun a tab already. I'll order through the waiter.'

'No thanks. I'd rather keep track of my expenditure. On a bit of a budget these days.'

This seems to fluster him a bit; he's not sure how to respond. I'm happy that I've made him wary of saying it. 'It's quite all right, you know. I did invite you here; don't see why old-fashioned rules need not apply.'

Pretending to ponder the statement: 'Old-fashioned rules need not apply? Afraid I'm not that great a fan of old-fashioned rules.'

'. . . Me neither, really.'

'That's settled then!' And I disappear towards the bar.

Like most London clubs, the bar in here charges like a wounded bull and the whack on a Long Island Ice Tea is fucking frightening. But I bite the bullet and get one . . . then bite down harder and get him another Pina Colada as well.

Which has the desired effect when I casually slide it in front of him.

—*What did you guys talk about, Lease?*

  —*He tried to avoid what was basically a cringing physical presence*

at the table with us by asking me travel questions almost straight away.
I wouldn't have it.

—What did you do?

'So, Julian. What's going on?

'Ermm . . . concerning what or whom?'

'Both, I guess. Why did you ask me here?'

He blushes. He actually blushes and needs to pick something from his eye. 'Ermm . . . I fail to believe that men don't ask you out on a routine basis, Lisa.'

'You mean you asked me out because you want to fuck me?'

And there's no blushing now, rather a whiff of the steel that came over him when Lynn told him they'd have to agree to disagree. That's not why I lighten the barb with the hint of a grin, though. This man does not scare me.

'Well . . . I'm going to have to request you slow down somewhat. I require rather more wooing than one Pina Colada in a hotbed of red sedition.'

'The exception then.'

Been here before: 'The exception that proves which rule?'

'The rule that most men will happily fuck a woman they're attracted to without so much as a word exchanged if the opportunity arises.'

'I can imagine that particular sentence sounding thoroughly vulgar on the lips of another.'

We'll have none of that. Charm = non-violent manipulation.

'Well . . . I do get asked out a bit . . . but not by men like you.'

'You mean men old enough to be your father?'

'How old are you?'

'Forty-eight and counting.'

'You're not old enough to be my fucking father then. Don't say that again.'

'Done.'

'But yeah, men of your age group. Men of your . . . vocation. Of your . . .' *Class.*

'Lisa, if you dare use the "c" word in a place like this, I'll—'

'You'll what? Denounce me to the cunts in black sedans and jack boots?'

He sits back in his chair as if I've pushed him; laughs long and loud. A rich, resonant sound I wouldn't have credited him with. A lot of people sitting around us glance over, the cheer in the sound bringing smiles to their own mouths.

I love seeing that.

Julian, at last: 'You've just answered your own question with more fullness than I could have ever.'

'You thought I might make you laugh?'

'Yes! Make me laugh, make me snap. Just make me *something.*'

—*I dunno about you, girl, but that'd go some way towards charming the panties off me.*

—*You're such a slapper, Katie.*

—*That's so not true. I made Matty take me to three movies before I let anything happen, and I thought he was* well *fit.*

—*You jerked him off in the cinema before the opening credits for the third were even finished!*

—*Yeah, but I made him buy me a sit-down Indian afterwards.*

—*And then you brought him home and made him—*

—*What happened, my mother just walked in? Fuck the old news, gimme the new, girl. Did you chill out a bit then, or what?*

—*I interrogated him on his domestic status.*

—*Oh, you so did not!*

—*I so did.*

—*And?*

—*Separated from wife—*

—Heard that one before.

—Yeah, handy word.

—No ring then?

—No.

—No white mark the exact same size of one?

—No.

—What happened then?

They'd talked for an hour or more, Lisa keeping the tone one of gentle sparring, Julian not offering much counter-attack. Then they'd heard the salsa starting up downstairs, and Lisa felt a hard glee as she told him they were going down to dance — she would've put money on him having two left feet — and then led the way without waiting for a response. She'd have lost her money, though. She knew a few salsa steps from previous sessions here, and her natural rhythm and exuberance made up for a lot of what she didn't know, but her anticipation at Julian's discomfort melted just a minute into it, because he was pretty good. And a certain foppish nonchalance, an air that implied that winging was part of the fun, drew smiles and encouragement from dancers around them.

She tried another tack, spinning away from him and dancing with a flamboyant Latino guy. But when she risked a glance at Julian he was waist to waist with a handsome brunette, making her laugh as she threw her long hair side to side.

—Did he ask you home for 'coffee'?

—No.

—How did the night end?

—With him flagging me a cab, thanking me for a great time, then walking off with his jacket on his shoulder.

27

ALEX

Ever been out in public somewhere and had the lights go down on you? Full-moon fever?

Thing is, it's usually just one person who starts it. Loses it, or just decides to. And then it spreads. It's a bloody weird feeling, and entirely distinctive, one you can feel even if you arrive during a lull in the madness. Your brain smells the fear and aggression like your nose smells sulphur.

And fear and aggression are highly contagious.

I'd seen the lights go down back home a few times. Argument in a pub gets out of hand. Feuding factions ending up at the same party. Down go the lights, and people you've never even clashed openly with might wander up and unload on you. People unable to do the right thing because others around them aren't doing it. Or suddenly feeling that they're *allowed* to do the wrong thing, again or for once or at last.

Wouldn't have guessed the night would end that way. Sitting around a table in the club after work on a hot Friday, about ten of us, pints flowing. Basking in the peace of a week's work behind us. Friday fever, half drunk and getting drunker. One of life's real pleasures, yeah?

Bit different for me; I was working the next day, but work for me by then was a lot more rewarding than it was for most of the others.

Johan, out of the blue, speaking up to the whole table: 'I remember when I first went to Aussie. I'd been in London about a year, me and some mates saved up for a surfing safari, Indonesia then Australia. Went down to STA Travel, booked the tickets, then the girl asked me what kind of insurance cover I needed. I said, "Well, what do you suggest? We're going to a place ridden with weird diseases, a homicidal police force, rampant corruption from the very top down, an appalling human rights record . . . oh, and we're going to Indonesia also."'

Even the Aussies laughed.

One of the Dispatch full-timers was turning thirty and having drinks at a pub in Hammersmith. Half the warehouse were there already, but it was 7.30 by the time our lot split; six of us just walking out with our pints in hand. Tough drinking from a glass while you're walking, but Ryan had the solution. Every so often he'd yell, 'Stop!' and we'd freeze until he yelled, 'Drink!', and we'd drink until he yelled. 'Walk!' and off we'd go.

'Stop! . . . Drink! . . . Walk!' A few cans from the offie were floating around now too. A new girl was with us, Malena, just started in Dispatch — Italian and pretty, a real retinal massage. Her English was none too flash, though. She laughed at our drinking game but joined in with ball-tingling gusto. Jim asked her who she supported in the *Serie A*, got nothing but a blank look. So he asked Ryan to try and get her talking.

Ryan: 'She won't understand a word I say, mate.'

Me: 'Trust me, Ry, in your case that will be *no* disadvantage.'

Katie got her started though — 'Stop!' — asking her what had brought her — 'Drink!' — to these parts. Turns out — 'Walk!' — Malena's here looking for nannying work, is having a little trouble getting started, came to the warehouse to tide herself over.

Lisa, portentous: 'Looks like we've got ourselves a case of Hot Nanny Syndrome, folks.'

Sharon: 'OK, I'll bite: what the hell is "Hot Nanny Syndrome", Lease?'

'Think about it. Who does the hiring of the nanny? The wife or the hubby?'

Angela: 'Not that I've ever hired one, but—'

Greg: 'That don't surprise me, Ange: hips like yours, you should count yourself lucky being able pass wind, let alone an ankle-biter.'

Ang: 'Fuck you.'

'Stop! . . . Drink! . . . Walk!'

Lisa: 'No, the mother usually has more to do with the kids, so she makes the choice. Now, what woman in her right mind opts to put a young, hot piece of femininity under her husband's nose twenty-four bloody seven?'

Ryan stops us all, makes a show of looking Malena up and down. 'A word of advice, *signorina*: reassess your career options.'

She wants to know why we're all laughing at her, but no one's game to try and explain. Then Alonso, smiling, sidles up — 'Stop!' — to her, and — 'Drink!' — starts rapping away in — 'Walk!' — Italian. She soon snorts into giggles; throws Ryan a grin. But she's found someone she can relax with now and she and Alonso fall into chit-chat.

A few of us guys stop for a piss behind a skip. Amazing how the frequency with which ad-hoc urinals present themselves in London corresponds precisely with the amount of booze you consume. By the end of the night you can almost always find one within a few feet of you if you know how to look. We catch up to the others, but we're still a good hundred metres from the bus stop when the bus we need whizzes past us. A half-hearted jog, but there's no chance of all of us making it. Then Greg grabs me and we're both sprinting up the road, leaving the rest behind. We arrive as the bus does, and jump on. Greg's counting out change for the driver when he sucks in an almighty breath, clutches his chest, and keels over backwards. It's so unexpected I get a genuine jolt, but then I'm kneeling over him and the driver in the turban's yelling to know what's wrong, and Greg's gasping, 'Asthma! Asthma!' I'm hollering down the bus for someone with an inhaler, and people are standing up and crowding around. I shake him, take his pulse, yell for an inhaler again, slap his face, and I'm running out of things to do when the gang files on to the bus. Greg dusts himself off, and leads our merry way upstairs.

The tubes are running smooth and the train's half empty, and we're soon pulling into Earls Court. There's a gang of lads in Chelsea colours on the platform right beside us — shorn heads, a lot of tattoos, drinking, singing football songs. Their aura of latent menace erects a five-metre buffer zone around them. The most dangerous caste in the UK, this type, far more likely to attack unprovoked than any other. Probably the most chilling sound in the UK too, a drunken football chant in the throats of a group coming towards you. Most of us instinctively look away as their stares scan for something to lock on to.

Jim got done by a pack like this outside White Hart Lane stadium on a match day about a year ago, for no reason at all, and he actively despises the type now. The Chelsea hard-core are infamous for far-right connections and 'beliefs', and as there's a lull in their singing, as the doors slide shut and the train begins to pull away, Jim starts yelling through the crack of an open window at them.

'Hey ladies! The sequel to *Mein Kampf* 's just been published! Guess what happens at the end: THE ARYANS GET THEIR FUCKING ARSES KICKED!'

Recovering from shock, a few of them keep pace with us, thumping on the windows and screaming murder. Jim puts his face on the glass and blowfishes it, holding the middle finger of each hand up, and as the train speeds up more of us start to taunt them. Greg drops his arse out in a brown-eye, and we're in hysterics by the time the tunnel swallows us. Most of the strangers around us smile, give thumbs up, but we pipe down too quickly, and for the rest of the journey I sense that most of us are irrationally scared that the gang might somehow beat us to the next stop. But we're soon piling unmolested on to the platform at Hammersmith.

Alonso and Malena had been riding some way down from us. As they're de-training she calls out to him and points to a bag on the seat that he must have left behind. But he shakes his head — it clearly contains just rubbish — and she follows him out. But then Alonso stops on the platform beside the window of the carriage. The doors close. About five of us look back at what's keeping him. He taps on the glass until a middle-aged white woman inside breaks off from her talk with the man beside her and looks Alonso's way.

Alonso's still smiling, but it's somehow different now. Much sharper.

Much weirder.

The woman frowns a question at him. He points to the unattended bag on the seat. She realises he must have forgotten it, but the train's moving now, Alonso walking with it. She stands, but her helpless shrug is half hearted — *Sorry, kid, can't help you, and not really my problem, don't you think?* But Alonso shakes his head to show that she doesn't understand. He lifts his wrist, and with the

266

other hand taps the face of his watch, counting off seconds for her. Suddenly he throws his hands up, eyes bulging as his head snaps forward, miming a shock . . .

. . . Miming an explosion.

He points at the unattended package again. Smiling like a shark. Big, slow nods.

The woman frowns on for a moment. Then she whirls towards the bag and collapses from view. Reappears further up the carriage, falls again . . .

We're rooted to our spots as the train vanishes, Alonso catching us up.

Greg finds his voice first. 'Ammm . . . that *was* just rubbish . . . wasn't it?'

Alonso, no smile at all for once: 'Of course.'

Lisa's cackle is so sudden and loud I jump as if it were a bomb blast. Greg joins in; I feel as sick as Katie and Jim look.

He doesn't run, but Alonso's almost at the escalator already. We do run, following him as he climbs the moving stairs. Halfway up it I see the funny side . . .

. . . and three of us are still pissing ourselves as we clear the station and spill on to Hammersmith Broadway.

The ones who hadn't seen what happened want to know what's so funny. Katie, who hasn't laughed at all, starts telling them. A minute later seven of us are doubled over, enjoying the biggest laugh of the night. Alonso hasn't waited, striding briskly across the road. We catch him up; he's still not smiling, and Ryan asks him why he did it.

'I did not like what they were talking about.'

Lisa: 'What were they talking about, Alonso?'

'Anti-terrorism.'

Lisa's in absolute tears, losing it again every time it looks like she's got control.

Greg, crowing: 'What a night so far, eh? Jim gets us on the hit list of the Chelsea skinheads, and then Alonso lays a false trail for MI fucking 5! This is shaping as a classic even by London standards!'

The pub is supposedly on Blacks Road, but we can't locate it. Ryan says he has it covered. He walks into another pub and asks the oldest-looking guy in it if he knows where The George is. No luck. So he asks the man who looks the second oldest and gets a result. It's down the way a little and across, the entrance in a mews off the main road.

There's an aging tattooed Northerner on the door, looking weedy and worn but somehow the harder for it. Low-brow sort of joint — pool tables and jukeboxes, 2-4-1 alcopops, St George flags on the walls — but we know most of the people. A few of Alonso's Albanian mates are here — they chat with us a lot and smile, but when you look closely you see that their faces are much different when they're talking among themselves.

Quite a lot of geezers in the house too by ten or so when we're really starting to large it. They don't mingle too well with our crowd, never tend to really. In ones and twos they can be good value — or if *we're* in ones or twos — but when there's a group of them they seem to regard us with this condescension laced with more and more enmity as the pints go down. Not sure what their problem is. Sometimes it seems as simple as not liking to watch others have more fun than them. And we *always* show these prickly pricks how to party.

No different tonight. We've got the place singing and dancing and laughing to bring the walls down. I even seem to be getting somewhere with Malena. Well, she's asking me all sorts of questions about myself, so that can't be bad. I've laid off the pills tonight, don't fancy work in the morning on a come-down. Murphy tries to talk me into it one, tells me the secret to pilling is to budget an extra ten quid for the next day so you can ease the blues with a few cans and a spliff or two. Could use a little speed, though; beer's lubricating the tongue but you can't beat a touch of the goey for a talk turbo-charger. Murphy's says he's not holding any, tells me to hit Katie up. She slips me the bag and off I go, signalling to Ryan. He's keen, following me into the bogs.

The urinals are all blocked and near overflow point, and there's an anti-domestic-violence ad on the wall, a woman with a battered face holding a toddler to her chest and staring at me.

A short guy comes in, staggering around the urinals one by one, then declaring, 'Tey all seem to be on a slow drain.'

Ryan: 'Yeah, if you wanna avoid splash-back, you'd be better off slashing in the basin, mate.'

The Paddy casts a doubtful eye at them. 'Too fecking hoigh for the loikes of me, so tey are.' And he walks out.

We duck into a shitter together while the place is empty, and lock the door. I rip the bag open and spread it on my palm, and we dab away at the powder, washing the acrid taste down with beer. Someone knocks on the door; I yell that it's occupied. Then they try to open it, and I tell them to use another one. We're left in peace then; finish dabbing, then walk out.

The bouncer's leaning against the basin waiting for us. His folded forearms are part sinew, part Indian ink. He's half our size. He looks like he could be a foot shorter and still have us both without chewing.

Implacable: 'You two, clear off. You're out and don't come buck. No drogs allowed in here.'

I get a flash of panic. Speed and piss have got me in as prime a pulling state as I get, and Malena said she would wait for me to come back out. I just can*not* be bounced from this place right now. I'm about to tell him that, actually, drugs aren't allowed *anywhere* but that doesn't stop anyone. My next impulse is to offer the prick a ten-quid backhander, but Ryan beats me to it.

An odd lisp in his voice, some embarrassment too: 'No, sir, you've got the wrong idea: we weren't in there to take drugs. You can check our pockets.'

'Oh right. Why else do two men enter a focking cubicle together then?'

Good question.

Ryan sighs, then mutters at his shoelaces: 'We're gay. Our friends don't know. We just wanted a minute alone together.' Looking up, appealing: '*Please* don't tell anyone!'

This really throws the guy, and I'm trying to arrange my face into anxious and mortified while a standing ovation for Ryan takes place in my head.

Bouncer, at last: 'I wanna see you two kiss then.'

Shit. Nice comeback.

We look at each other, but this is checkmate.

Then Ryan grabs me and spins me away from the bouncer in a wee dip, ducking his head into mine until our mouths are a millimetre apart.

Shock or disgust or hilarity almost snort from me as his eyes bore into mine from a range male eyes should never reach. But I hold it down, even manage to wiggle my head a little. Seconds feel like hours, and there's no way this bastard's gonna buy it, but this is desperation time, and I tangle the fingers of one hand in Ryan's hair, give his bum a squeeze with the other . . .

And the bouncer groans in genuine disgust. 'All right, all right, that's enough, for *fock's* sake!'

He's about four steps further from us than when I last saw him. 'No focking more, though. You fairies wanna tog each other off, do it in someworn else's pob.'

He walks out, a visible cringe running through him. Sudden silence. Then my 'lover' and I are cackling like deranged things.

The pub starts to clear out at 10.30 or so, everyone off to a house party nearby, but with work tomorrow I'm going to head home straight from here so I stay on. Malena's working too — thank god! — and we're getting on great (as great as near-pidgin talk allows) and she hangs around, saying she'll catch the tube with me. Lisa and Ryan are finishing up, then going to the party. Alonso and a mate are playing pool against two geezers from a group, and if there's resentment between the geezers and the Southern crowd, you should feel the vibe between this lot and the Albanians. Every shot is discussed and weighed like a military manoeuvre.

Lisa's pissed and dancing round the table, bumping hips with Alonso as he picks some air guitar on his pool cue. Not many more girls left in here, and she's very much the geezers' focus. She's not said a word to them all night; they've clearly assumed she and Alonso are going to hook up, and their sullen stares are branding her a race traitor. Alonso breaks off to take his shot, and she places her drink on a table and heads for the loos.

She has to pass close to the main body of the geezers, and as she does one of them yells, 'Show us your fucking fanny!'

His wit earns him an uproarious laugh. But Lisa stops and walks back to him. 'What did you say to me?'

The lanky kid hesitates, but all his boys are looking on. On a spurt of drunk bravado, leaning into her: 'I said, *show us your fucking fanny!*'

'Hahahahaaaaa!'

Lisa: 'OK, I will.'

'. . . *Huh?*'

'I *will* show you my "fanny", show it to you and all your mates . . . just as soon as you show me your prick.'

He gapes at her. Then scoffs, waving her away.

Lisa, staring up him: 'No, I'm serious. I promise to show my fanny if you drop your dick out first.'

Everyone's watching, and the geezer goes slowly red, trying to grin and not succeeding. At last: 'Na, you aint worf it, don't wanna see yours anyhow.'

'Oh really?' She runs her eyes over the others. 'You guys think I'm worth it? You wanna see my pussy?' They loudly assure her they do. 'The power's in your mate's hands then. If he shows first, I'll show mine.'

This turns them, and they're egging the lad on, yelling at him to do it.

Agitation mauls him, caught between a cock and a soft place. Finally he hisses a 'Fuck off' at no one in particular, power-walks away, a jeering cheer chasing him.

Lisa then bops to the toilets with a saucy victory wiggle.

He's alone and sulking over the jukebox at the far end of the pub, where the toilet doors are, when she emerges right beside him. If she sees him she ignores him, but he calls her back. I can't hear what he's saying but he's standing over her, anger shot through his posture. She doesn't back off an inch, and whatever she says seems to piss him off further. I'm about to head over, but Alonso's ahead of me, moving quite fast, the geezer's mates shifting closer too.

That's when I feel the lights going down.

I quickly look around to see how many of us are still here — about eight — and then I notice Fernando, a friend of Alonso's, taking his shoe off.

. . . *Taking his* shoe *off?*

Then he takes his *sock* off too . . .

Then he takes the purple four ball off the pool table and drops it into the sock.

The smell of a fight had pumped me; now my marrow turns into hoar-frost.

By the jukebox Lisa's sneering and waggling her little finger in the geezer's face. He pulls a hand back, maybe to slap her, but Alonso arrives in time to shove him away. Alonso points a dire finger at him and shakes his head, throwing a quick look over his shoulder . . .

The geezers are closing in, maybe six of them . . . Some of them are holding pint glasses and ashtrays.

Time slows. I'm paralysed by what's about to happen. It's not supposed to be like this.

Then Lisa's victim lunges at Alonso, but Alonso twists away, sends him diving at nothing. The mob of geezers charge at Alonso, and he must have known they would because he sprints for the far exit immediately. Fernando, DIY mace in one hand, pool cue in another, dashes past me to a window up from the far exit. He shoves the butt of the cue through the window, smashing it, and Alonso, drawing level outside, snatches the cue from his friend's hand.

Spins around and swings it full force at the nearest geezer. I'm a good ten metres from the contact, but easily hear the awful *CRACK* as it lands.

Lisa, dropping to her haunches, starts to scream.

It got well ugly after that.

Fernando ran outside after the geezers; gave it to one of them from behind with the mace, dropping him clean. Managed to drop another one before they turned and smothered him.

Inside, a bottleneck at the back door between more Albanians and geezers quickly turned into a brawl, then a geezer further inside the pub turned to Johan and tried to ram a pint glass into his face. It missed and hit the wall; Johan threw a headlock on him, and they went to ground, wrestling desperately. Greg was backing off towards the front door when a geezer bumped into him more out of accident than anything; Greg started swinging punches in a panic.

Alex hadn't moved at all. He looked like a man in meltdown.

Ryan was almost out through the front door when he happened to catch sight of Lisa, hugging her knees in the far corner, not even watching the punches and glass filling the air around her. He nearly left her to it — he would have left almost anyone else — but found that he couldn't, and turned back, terrified. Ducking between the fighting, keeping as clear of it as he could, shoving bodies away, ten seconds that felt like a million.

He scooped her up and shouldered through the door into the Ladies' and relative quiet.

'You OK, Lease?'

She turned her face to him, and her puzzled expression scared him further.

He shook her. 'It's OK, babe! Speak to me!'

'Did Alonso sink the seven? It's all set up from there. If he sinks the seven he should win.'

Bodies smashed into the toilet door, knocking it half open, and Lisa scrambled away.

The two fighters stayed by the door, buffeting against it, one of them growling in Albanian; the sounds coming through every time the door opened were like a soundtrack from hell. Ryan wasn't going out there again, and he was just as certain Lisa wouldn't either, but the mayhem could go on until the cops arrived, and it could spill into here any second.

Lisa was gulping deeply, back against a wall, then she vomited a glut of liquid down her chest.

There were windows big enough to climb through, but they all had security latches stopping them from opening more than a crack. Ryan wanted to break one but there were no implements to do it with. He couldn't bring himself to punch at the glass, and they were too high to kick.

The door crashed open again and a geezer charged into the

toilets, one eye a purple mess, hand clenched round the stem of a broken bottle. He ignored them, turned back to the door as it swung shut, waiting in a crouch and roaring, *'C'moooon, you fucking wog wankerrrrrs!'*

Ryan bundled Lisa into the farthest cubicle. She hugged him, shaking into his chest, and when another fighter was heard charging in, Ryan saw the answer staring straight at him. The porcelain lid of the cistern. He had it off and through the window in one motion, and as soon as Lisa saw the night gaping at her she launched into it. He was out on the street beside her in no time, and they held hands as they crossed to where Ryan spied a knot of the others. Battered by shock, wasted, they were milling like the lost, girls hugging and crying, guys itching to go back but not having it in them, people screaming into phones at the cops.

No one bothering to ask where such-and-such was, because they all knew exactly where the missing were.

Ryan handed Lisa off to Malena before crossing back over. He wasn't going to get involved, not directly anyway, but now he could make sure he kept a passage to flight open, and he might be able to do *some*thing. Jim followed him.

Things seemed to have lessened inside the pub a bit — Jim told Ryan that some black bouncers from up the road had gone in a minute ago — but out in the alley, where Alonso had made his stand, it was still blazing. There was no sign of Fernando, though there were several bodies strewn on the ground, and Alonso was backed against the pub wall. The pool cue was broken, but Alonso held geezers off with its point, stabbing and lashing. Someone had Alonso's back, was standing beside him, flinging combos from a boxer's stance, and Ryan blinked when he realised it was the Northern bouncer.

Six on two. Ryan wanted to go in and even the numbers a bit, but it was just an abstract desire, a forlorn longing, because placing himself in danger like that was the last thing his instincts were about to allow.

The bouncer caught a left that staggered him, and two of the geezers dragged him clear. One of them sat on him while the other went back to Alonso. Alonso sent another geezer spinning off and squealing with the stick, but then he was engulfed and thrown down beneath the broken window. They closed over him with blood-curdling cheers.

Ryan heard Alonso's voice; he sounded like he was still smiling. 'You better kill me.'

'No farking problem, you li'l wog *cunt*!'

Then they started kicking chunks out of him.

Ryan's and Jim's eyes met, loathing and revulsion seething between them, and it was as much for themselves as for the scene, because all they were going to do was watch, and they both knew it.

Jim moved in a little and screamed for the geezers to stop, but there was no place for words inside their red mist.

Sirens getting closer . . .

. . . and then Alex leans out of the window and smashes a glass pitcher over a geezer's head. His shirt's in tatters, more of a cape than a shirt; hair in mad clumps, glasses gone. He leans out further and grabs another bloke with both hands, snarling and hauling him in. The guy puts a hand in Alex's face, trying to shove him back, but Alex gets a mouthful of fingers and clamps down. The geezer screams, Alex locked on and going nowhere . . .

And then *Jim*'s in Ryan's picture, tackling a geezer away from Alonso, scrambling on top of him and driving punches into his face, and Alonso's dragging himself up the wall, and then cops are suddenly everywhere.

28

Ryan gets home at eleven o'clock Sunday morning. The place is pretty quiet; only three people have surfaced so far, and they're all in the kitchen. Katie and Jim are on fry-up detail, Lisa's on hot drinks. There's a real art to running multi-person activity in the small kitchen, a system of tacit give-ways and red lights. Ryan stands in the doorway yakking for a bit, amused at the three-body pile-ups, a hard night showing clearly in the missed steps of the kitchen-shuffle.

Autumn's bearing down and migration season's in full swing, that time of year when most of the Southerners whose time in London has ended choose to move on, milking the most from the summer, then fleeing before the cold and dark set in again. Most of the gang had been at yet another farewell party the night before.

Katie: 'Where did ya get to last night, Ry?'

'Just working.'

Jim, breaking eggs: 'The mystery moonlighting gig again?'

'No mystery, mate.'

Lisa, too blithe: 'What *is* it that you do again, Ryan? I've forgotten.'

'Just do a bit of driving for these rich twats. I've told you that.'

Jim: 'So you're like a chauffeur? Have you got any training in that, or do they hire any bloke with a licence?'

'Was just a mate of a mate thing. So—'

Katie: 'How come you always get home so late?

''Cause they like to stay out so late, then I sometimes have brekkie with em. When are you off to Trinidad, Jim?'

'Six days and fucking counting. Not a second too soon either. Three weeks away from terrible weather and terrorist wars.'

Katie reminds him to bring her back a Trinidadian pebble. She collects pebbles of the world in her handbag.

They ask Ryan if he's eating with them; he says no, but he sits next to Lisa when they're in the lounge and picks at her plate. She wants to know why Ryan's still hungry if he ate breakfast with his 'rich twat employers'.

'. . . You should see the size of the meals dished up round there. No wonder these clowns are loaded.'

Katie: 'You've been up all night then?'

'Yeah.'

'That's funny, you don't look tired at all.'

'I snatched some sleep waiting in the car.'

Lisa: 'But—'

'What is this, the Antipodean Gestapo?'

He flees to his room and starts making a CD for Nadia, mostly Aussie music that she can't find on the net. Lisa comes in later, lighting a joint. She's dropped the work wind-ups, and he gets an intelligence report on the thrills and spills of last night. Not much news except that Greg was last seen getting into a taxi with a Dutch bird he met, and Alex got a call at ten o'clock and ditched them without saying where he was going.

'Is he back yet? Me and him are gonna go to Highbury this arvo to try and get tickets for the Arsenal match.'

'He came home at some stage but he got called into work this morning.'

The sounds of a housework detail start reverberating through to them, someone banging the door too hard and too often as they hover down the hallway.

Ryan: 'Think she's trying to tell us something?'

Lisa, curling up on his bed: 'How the fuck would I know? I fell asleep half an hour ago.'

He finishes the CD, then goes downstairs and spends an hour and a half in the kitchen, washing dishes, cleaning the benches and stove-top, mopping the floor . . .

Greg comes home. By his apparent flatness Ryan knows instantly that he got some. Greg's modest to the point of not kissing and telling for hours unless somebody asks him. He *wants* to tell you — loves telling Ryan especially — he just hates risking coming across as a blow-hard. Thing is, he sometimes puts false claims in too, and Ryan's worked out that if Greg's volunteering carnal information without prompt it's a sure-fire bet that he's bullshitting.

Ryan gives him what he wants, asks if he got his end away. Yes. Three times (he hesitates a bit, so Ryan downgrades the claim to two). She gave but wouldn't take on the oral, but Greg aint big on drinking from the bushy bowl anyway. Her bedroom light was on a sound switch — clap your hands to operate it — and Greg reckons that at one point they were banging away so hard the light kept flicking on and off. Good looking? Oh yeah, not too bad at all (but Greg's got a pxt phone and doesn't offer a photo, so Ryan's sceptical).

Murphy had crashed in Greg's room, and by two o'clock six of them are veging in the lounge, feeling worse for wear, and

Murphy declares that there's nothing else for it but for everyone to check themselves into retox. Angela and Jim look nauseous at the prospect; two others are keen; and another two let themselves be talked into it, joining the trek down to the local.

Alex, who hasn't returned a missed call Ryan gave him earlier, comes home around three: plenty of time for them to make it to Highbury for kick-off. But when Ryan tells him they have to get moving pretty soon, Alex seems at a loss.

'Oh shit, man, sorry. Forgot all about it.'

'No worries. Heaps of time left.'

'Ahhh, yeah . . .'

'What is it?'

'Oh na, it's . . . it's just that I've gone and said I'd do something else.'

'Oh right. No worries. What are you up to?'

'. . . Franz Ferdinand gig, Brixton Academy.'

This sounds better than football all alone. 'Sweet, I forgot about that. I might as well come with you.'

'Ahhh . . . I don't know if we've got any tickets spare.'

'Sure I can scalp one if it's a sell-out, don't mind paying extra. Who are you going with?'

'Oh, amm . . . just a couple of people from work.'

'Who?'

'. . . Tina, Liz and Kenny.'

'. . . Right. I'll leave you to it then.'

29

The incoming txt beeped on Lisa's phone just as Jim and Katie went in on a round of shooters, making a show of getting one in everybody's hand.

> **READ**
> Left dinner early,
> bored silly.
> Passin by, remembered
> you were inside.
> Thought u mite fancy a
> drive . . .

Her thumb was above the 'lmn' key, first letter of a curt 'No thnx' . . . but her fear of regretting it a minute later wouldn't let it fall.

Alex: 'What are we drinking to?'

Lisa: 'Here's to mushroom clouds over Washington!'

Even those who normally wouldn't were drunk enough to

chorus it.

She tried to make herself make him wait, but txting 'I'm coming' felt too fucking obedient, and not replying ran the risk of him thinking she wasn't attending her phone. In which case he might just drive off . . .

Or *come in*.

She hurriedly began concocting a story that would secure her an early exit, but it was an uphill struggle — they simply wouldn't let her leave unless she said she wasn't feeling well, and then someone would insist on escorting her home — but then Alex's turn on the karaoke machine rolled around and everyone cheered, turning towards the stage. Lisa took it as a sign and just slipped away.

He was parked opposite the pub, close enough for them to spot each other, distant enough for none of the others to clock him by chance. She crossed with her arms folded and leaned down to the open passenger window.

Neither of them spoke for what was definitely way too long.

Lisa: 'I shouldn't really, you know. I drummed up a house party back at ours. Not a good look if I then pull a no-show.'

'Yes. Duty. Obligation. On the other hand, if you don't *wish* to come, you need only say so. The last time I checked, this *was* a free country.'

She was pissed enough to bite straight away . . . which was probably just what he wanted. 'Free country. I believe that all depends on how many freedom tokens you've got.'

'Freedom tokens?' He turned more towards her, settling in, as if cars weren't whizzing right past her arse.

Lisa: 'Yeah. If you can work out what they are, then I'll get in. If you can't, then you're being obtuse and I'll go back inside because the bullshit will be less claustrophobic.'

He laughed, and she struggled against grinning. 'Well, I shan't be seen keeping truck with that kind of carry-on. If that interested me I would have remained in the company from which I've just absconded.' He makes a show of pondering. 'If pressed to guess — which I patently am — I would hazard your "freedom tokens" to represent . . . money?'

Even drunk, the false indifference to the traffic — never mind the fear of one of the gang suddenly tapping her shoulder — had been an effort, and she's relieved to get in. 'Drive.'

'At once, marm.'

She tries for a posture of accidental sauciness in the deep seat; shuns the seatbelt because it would kill the look and because he's wearing his.

'I like your skirt.'

'No you don't, you like the thighs that the skirt shows off.' She's pretty fucking wasted, and there's no fear at all in belting him with brashness. She knows that if she pisses him off too much he could make things difficult for her at work — to say the least — but the whiff of that only heightens the fun right now.

Julian: 'Those too. Although I think you're selling your calves and knees rather too short.'

She lifts a leg and pretends to examine it. 'Well, they *are* rather too short, aren't they? I'm not exactly of Amazonian proportions.'

'A dammed good thing, if you ask me, otherwise you'd have to get used to mincing around in high heels all the fucking time.'

She doesn't get it at first. Flash: 'You mean the way so many tall woman seem to obsess on making themselves even taller?'

'*Seem* to obsess, my arse. Most would wear bloody stilts if it wouldn't kill their head clearance through tanning-clinic doors.'

She can't help laughing. 'Do I detect bitterness? Was your ex-wife tall?'

'A modest five feet eleven.'

'Bitch. Did she wear heels a lot?'

'She practically cooked with the fucking things on.'

'They made her taller than you, did they?'

'. . . A little.'

'Lucky me, I guess.'

'How so?'

'If she hadn't given you your fill of tall women, I doubt I'd be cruising through London right now in a late-model sports car. Not quite as much fun as the tube, but it's up there.'

'You consider this luck? Getting harassed by an inarticulate old man?'

'I don't find you inarticulate at all, Julian.'

He drops down a gear to beat an orange, the acceleration pushing Lisa into her seat.

Julian: 'So it's the age thing then, is it?'

'So *what's* the age thing then?'

'The reason you don't want your friends to know we've been . . . talking.'

She gets a txt from Alex; doesn't bother reading it.

'Actually no. Older men I have no problem with, only shorter ones.'

Stopping for pedestrians in a most un-*Homo superior* fashion: 'Then what is it?'

'Appalling things can happen to collaborators and fraternisers.'

'So I'm informed, but when I last looked we weren't living in occupied Hungary.'

'This war's far more ancient and enduring than that one.'

'Oh.' A touch of scorn: 'You can only mean "class war".'

'Compliments on your lack of obtuseness.'

'But "collaboration"? I don't understand. You're the warrior; I just happen to be one of those being made war upon.'

'Fucking bullshit!' Crossing her legs, twisting to face him fully:

'God, I *hate* that!'

'Care to translate?'

'*You're just the ones being made war on*? Oh, you poor, aggrieved dears! That's just another of those mighty Machiavellian myths cynically manufactured and disseminated by you and yours for the purposes of steering the consciousness of the masses away from the rotten fucking truth. That really is a beauty, that one is!'

'Afraid I'm still not with you.'

'Say "class war", what do you see? A May Day marcher throwing red paint? A lesbian hawking the *Socialist Worker*?'

'. . . That about covers it, yes.'

'Such telling, harrowing blows! How *do* you rich and mighty endure?'

'. . . Genetically enhanced fortitude.'

'Ha! Now let's examine your counter-thrusts, the war you make on *us*.'

'Whatever are you talking about?'

'Hereditary peerdom, campaign donations and lobbying. Queen's Counsels and public inquiry whitewashes, insider trading and "creative accounting". What else? Non-tendered contracts, labour union crushing, trade protectionism—'

Warding her fervour off: 'Enough! I'm not sure what creative leap you're making that allows you to class all this as warfare, but—'

'Creative leap, my arse!' She barely weighs the decision before lighting a fag without asking if he minds. 'Now you *are* being obtuse. You know that the few examples I've mentioned form part of a systematic institutionalised programme whereby the rich consolidate their positions at the expense of the poor. So, if I'm a class warrior, you're a fucking class *war criminal*.'

His only censure of her smoking is to open his window a few centimetres. He focuses on the road, and, as she's interested in his response, she has to bite her tongue to keep from pressing on.

Julian, finally: 'I can see how it might appear that way to someone on the outside, someone suffering from the politics of—'

'If you dare use the "politics of envy" cop-out you're gonna get my "politics of greed" riposte broadside.'

Grinning: 'And there was me thinking that was precisely what I was enduring.' But he takes a moment to rephrase, and Lisa sucks down smoke in contentment. 'The thing someone lacking perspective on this may be unable to see is that nobody implicated in any of your charges is consciously trying to abuse those further down the ladder than they. They are simply thriving as best they can within the system in which they find themselves. And, let's face it, while the system cannot function in a fashion which allows everyone to be fat, it's also the only thing keeping the non-fat from terminal malnourishment.'

'Oh, fuck off! How the hell do we know that? Aside from total-itarianism, it's the only system the modern world has ever been allowed to try! And it was created by you and yours, for you and yours, so that you could hold on to your privilege when social evolution made guns and bondage untenable. You took the shackles from around the proles' ankles and placed them around their brains.'

Raising his eyebrows: 'Now *there's* a conspiracy theory to inspire—'

'When enough evidence accumulates, a conspiracy theory ceases being a conspiracy theory and instead becomes a plain old conspiracy. And isn't it priceless how theories criticising your class as a whole are derided as the brainchildren of paranoid losers, yet for *decades* you rampaged around the world, murdering and robbing and highjacking nations, as you kept us all safe from the fucking global *communist* conspiracy.'

'. . . You don't believe the Cold War was worth winning?'

'I don't believe the fucking Cold War was anything more than the same type of blank cheque that the war on drugs *was*, and that the war on terror *is*! I bet the very term "cold war" was conceived by a glorified advertising company!'

Tinged in pity: 'You're a very cynical young lady, Lisa.'

'You'd be cynical too if you were in your twenties before you realised that your perceptions of Washington and London holding the monopoly on the words "freedom" and "benevolence" were nothing more than the product of exactly the type of culturally imperialistic multi-media mind-control campaigns that you were programmed to believe were the sole preserve of presidents with unpronounceable surnames and/or combat fatigues.'

His sudden laugh — the one she likes so much — punches the air from her lungs. Fighting off a grin: 'Don't fucking laugh at me!'

'I'm not laughing *at* you, Lisa, trust me on that. I just found that sentence thoroughly delectable.'

'. . . You did?'

'I did. Though strictly on a linguistic level, of course.'

'Oh, of *course*.'

A red light brings them to a halt, and when his hand reaches across to her a grenade of conflicting emotions goes off. But he's only opening the glove box. Removing a silver hip-flask. Green light, and his knee holds the steering wheel steady for a moment as he unscrews the cap and takes a good-sized swig. Takes another. Offers it to her.

The liquid has all the kick of strong spirit, but the aftertaste is better than mouthwash. She downs a bigger slug. 'God damn, that's scrumptious.'

'The spoils of war, my dear.' His tone is oddly cheerless and ironical. 'Class war.'

This excites her enormously. His face in the street lighting seems pensive suddenly too. She lets him think, and plays with the space-age stereo until she finds a good song. Grinds her fag butt gleefully into the virgin ashtray.

Julian, distant: 'The thing is, Lisa, you're not the only one brainwashed by her elders. We all are in some way, to some extent.'

This is getting better by the second.

'I grew up in a house with more baths and fireplaces than people, the help notwithstanding. Cars that were lucky if they were driven twice a year. I absorbed this with my mother's milk, yes, but it wasn't long before I was wondering about these homes we'd drive past, the ones little bigger than our Retriever kennels. Or the children my own age walking to school in the rain and snow. My father told me that they were the lucky ones, that they enjoyed carefree, wild existences, loaded with choice, while something called breeding — the tireless, selfless toil of my forefathers — had singled me out for special duty, for the burden of leadership. Only *I* could steer these feckless, lovable clods through the tempests of economics and nationhood. Because there was only so much food to go around in the world, and left to their own devices the clods would end up starving themselves. Our privileges were simply sustenance against awesome obligation.'

Jesus Christ. This was like listening to Hitler brand himself a mad racist.

Julian: 'Now I know all this sounds grotesquely condescending, but this takes place at an age well before children have lived enough to form any equitable sense of justice, when concepts like leadership and duty are deliciously romantic.'

She finds herself thinking of James Bond movies. Her father had always been a vocal fan of them, and Lisa used to defend the films against critics. Then one day she realised that she had never really watched any properly. So she watched some. And they were awful. 'I can understand that. But you've been a big boy for some time now . . . and your programming's stayed intact?'

'No, not at all.'

'Pardon?'

'High school began to wake me. I felt what it was to find oneself at the wrong end of a hierarchy through no real fault of one's own. Then music began to unpick me properly.'

Giggling: 'Oh right. Well, Mozart *was* renowned as something of a rebel. All those rousing overtures set you foaming at the mouth by a barricade, did they?'

He smiles, taking the flask back. 'That really is rather ignorant of you. Quality modern music is *not* the inalienable right of the great unwashed alone. I can't stand classical.' The fingers of one hand race across buttons on the stereo. The radio slices off, and some soft acoustic guitar starts seeping through the speakers. Julian nods along with it. Then a harmonica joins in. The tune tugs at Lisa's memory. She can't place it, but it brings on a faint foreboding. The name of the song pops into her skull — though this is an unfamiliar version of it — but she hopes she's wrong; it wouldn't do for it to be that song . . .

He sings the first line, insisting there's some way outta here.

She's helpless not to provide the next, about the joker and the thief.

He doesn't look at her as they sing the rest of the verse, no gloating or irony on him, like he's refusing to defile the song and the memories it stirs.

Someone calls her and she puts her phone on silent. '"All Along the Watchtower". But who's singing it?'

'Bob Dylan.'

'When did he cover it?'

'He didn't. I'm not sure that Dylan ever covered a song. He wrote it in 1968 for the *John Wesley Harding* album. Hendrix covered it that same year.'

It's a far softer version, just Bob with a gat and a mouth organ.

Lisa, with heartfelt interest now: 'What happened to you?'

'I switched my degree from commerce to arts, sending my father incandescent. A condition not helped much by my branding him a patrician gangster and telling him to shove his disownership threats up his parasitical, exploitative ring-piece. I grew my hair long, smoked dope openly, traded the Aston Martin I got for my twenty-first for a Norton. Ammm, what else? Got briefly engaged to a penniless solo-mother from Malaysia, became a card-carrying member of CND, backpacked a swath of the Third World, managed a rock band from Hackney—'

Lisa feels like part of her is becoming unmoored. 'You're not fucking serious?'

'I fucking well am.' He sounds equally proud and chagrined. He still won't look at her as his fingers play Led Zeppelin's 'Houses of the Holy', one hand and one foot drumming in time with John Bonham.

Lisa, slapping the dash of the car, flicking one of his cufflinks, almost yelling: 'What the hell happened to you?'

He grimaces on a belt from the hip flask. 'I turned thirty-five.'

She waits for him to go on. When he doesn't, mordant: 'Oh right. *Comprende*. Say no more.'

He stops at a red, and fixes the full force of his memories on her. 'I'd never really gotten used to slumming it. When you've been weaned on veal and sautéed salmon, pot noodles tend to grate, even at the most idealistic of moments. None of my ventures had hit any pay-dirt to speak of. My mother had quietly propped me up more times than I care to think of. Then she died.' He blinks several times. 'Then I celebrated my birthday at the Glastonbury Festival, and . . . I guess you could say I underwent something of a reverse epiphany.'

'What happened?'

'I was near the front of the crowd, head-banging, when one of my favourite bands of the time came on, Rage Against The Machine.'

The name of that band through the filter of his cut-glass diction sounds nothing short of preposterous, and she laughs scathingly, relieved to find firm ground because this could only be a lie.

But there's sudden steel in the clench of his jaw. He floors it as the lights change, dizzying her a bit. He drops another hit from the flask, passing it to her, before his fingers work the stereo again, twisting the volume dial.

Something like nausea as the intro to a song she knows word for word crashes through the car. In time with Zach, Julian hollers about another *booooomb* track, the beat running through him, face screwing up. Under the age and the refinement, she sees who he was like a demon clawing for the surface.

She turns the volume down. Earnest: 'I'm sorry.'

His stare is hard enough to scare her again. Then it melts. 'So am I.'

'Keep talking. Please.'

'So there I am, and it's all: fuck them, I won't do what they're telling me, when it suddenly struck me: I was at least five years older than anyone around me, and ten, fifteen, even *twenty* older than most.'

Cold with empathy: 'I've begun to notice the same thing, and I'm only twenty-five. All the most inspiring subversive music is enjoyed and followed mostly by kids. There are few over-thirties in the mosh pits.'

Julian: 'I wondered what had happened to them all. Why weren't they here? It was like they'd reached the age where their capacity to force change increases . . . and then they stop listening to what's been their heart and soul for a decade or longer.'

'I fucking hate that.'

'I felt alone. More incredibly alone than I ever had before. What was the point resisting if it was going to leave me a lonely, broke anachronism in a sea of affectionately patronising children . . . who weren't going to last the distance themselves?'

She can see him standing there, slowly going still as Zach bounced round the stage, lithe young bodies slamming into him.

'That night I listened to the statements round the camp fires, hearing near-mirror replications of the same grievances and protests that I'd been making for fifteen years . . . and I knew that neither I nor anyone else I'd kicked around with had struck the slightest real blow. If anything, things had got worse.'

'And they're even worse today. So what did you do?'

'I decided to do what everyone else had done: start building as strong a castle for myself as I could.'

More red lights. Arab youths squaring off against blacks outside a McDonald's. A mixed-race couple walking a dog. A woman sitting alone in a gutter with the stillness of someone about to vomit seven Bacardi and Cokes.

Lisa: 'Where are you taking me?'

'I'm just driving aimlessly. I know you well enough to know that you go where you want to go, not where someone wishes to take you.'

'Where do you *wish* to take me?'

'. . . Somewhere quiet.'

'How far away is your place?'

'Fifteen minutes.'

She imagines what his flat looks like. Shag-pile carpet. A porter on the door. Chrome fittings in the kitchen. She wonders how long the enemy remains the enemy once it's been slept with. Crystal decanters. Heated towel racks. Four-poster bed. She wonders how well her friends of today will recognise her in a year's time. Wonders how well she will recognise *them*. Everyone changes, everyone evolves.

Don't they?

'I've done some things I'm not proud of over here, but I promised myself I'd never do this. . . . But I imagine you always get what you want in the end. Denying you that is starting to feel like a waste of energy, like a battle I can't win.'

Wry: 'There you go with that sweet talk again.' Then he sighs. 'I always get what I want? You really think it's that simple? That happiness and money are interchangeable?' He scrubs a hand across his face. She has to strain to hear him. 'I never wanted my father to be a whore-mongering cunt, to set girls up in bed-sits all over London. I never wanted an underfed coffee-coloured boy to stand outside my school for weeks claiming to be my half-brother. I never wanted my mum to crawl further into a gin bottle as dear old Dad's façade grew lazier; for him to screw the lid on behind her . . . For her to shoot herself with his favourite Purdy on their silver anniversary night . . . I never wanted to be woken in my boarding school bed with a prefect's cock in my mouth. I never wanted to be denied access to my daughter on the strength of belting my wife the day I caught her and her yoga tutor *at it* on my dinner table. I never wanted—'

'Shut up and pull over.'

He stares at her, open mouthed. '*What*?'

Louder: 'Stop the fucking car, Julian.'

Shakes his head sadly, does as she's ordered, parking outside an animal hospital.

She thought she was ready but her nerve fails her at first. Then she jumps into his lap.

He gapes as if slapped; stiffens as if she terrifies him. '*This* was why you wanted to stop?'

'Yeah. Now kiss me while I'm feeling treasonous.'

He looks old and haggard as she's never seen him, like an

abused loner, a fifty-year-old virgin. Like a tramp in gentleman's clothing, unable to rob a girl of breath if his very life depended on it. But when his big palm presses against her cheek, his mouth closing on hers, she feels as if she's kissing a power socket.

She finally pushes his head away, holding it hard against the head-rest, examining him. He seems to have dropped twenty years in twenty seconds. An almost maternal sense of satisfaction wells up in her. 'Was it worth the wait?'

The vibrations from his laugh tingle right through her. 'Oh, dear god yes! But now you're in terrible trouble because that was more addictive than angel dust.'

Lisa, a while later, panting: 'Please don't try and fuck me. Not here.'

He touches his nose to hers, grinning like a child off a roller coaster. 'Oh, Lisa, to make love to a woman like you in a car would be like . . . like eating Lobster Thermidor from a paper bag!'

He kisses her again, and he feels as warm and solid as a fireplace in a castle.

30

RYAN

We hadn't been up here before. Hampstead. Toff fucking central. I parked down a bit from the house, and Dessie got out, leaving me alone in the new Alfa. At least the car camouflaged. Des didn't. Oh, his clobber looked smart enough, but the walk and the posture, the eyes that never rest — more nervous round these parts than in a Brixton market — they all named him impostor, a tradesman in disguise.

But Dessie's not here to fix the plumbing.

The door in the big, spiked gates was quite a while opening after Des spoke into the intercom. In fact I could see him push the button again and give someone the hurry-up after the first minute. Then he was through, leaving me alone on the dark street. A cold wind whipped dead leaves across the car's bonnet.

Dessie's back in fifteen minutes, looking somehow heavier. Climbs in, sinking into the seat.

I drive off. 'All good, Des?'

He doesn't even grunt. Not like him to ignore me. I sneak a

look at him but I can't read a thing.

Five minutes later I pull into a dead car park beside a Shell. Head in and buy three cans of Red Bull, getting stuck behind some muppet in an anorak as he carefully counts change for the Paki behind the counter. Loses count and starts again. Then he drops a couple of coins. Fucking UK reactionaries: what good does copper do these days, apart from turn you all into coin counters? I used to give all mine to beggars or just biff them away.

Uncle Arthur finally gets his change right, shuffles home to his slippers and his Horlicks. I do my business, dropping half of the first Red Bull can before I'm back at the car. Opening the door, bending down . . .

. . . freezing solid.

Because there's a gun on Dessie's knee. Very black against the white cloth it rests on.

I'm stuck half in and half out of the car, like some abstract sculpture.

Doesn't look like a very big gun. But size isn't really the issue when you chance across a snake either. It seems highly polished, pin-pricks of lights sparkling in it.

I've never seen him carry a gun before.

I've never seen *any*one carry a gun before.

He looks up at me, apparently confused. 'What the fuck are you waiting for, man?'

Next thing I know I'm sitting beside him. I don't drive, though, and he doesn't ask me to. Just stares at something I can't see.

I can't speak for a long time, scared words might act on him like movement might on a snake. But the silence gets heavier and heavier . . . until I feel I have to end it before a slab of it shears off and lands on me. 'Nice gun, Des.'

Waking up: 'Hmmm?'

'Ahhh . . . that thing on your leg. Nice gun.'

He looks at it in seeming surprise. Then: 'Nice? You think?'

'Ammm . . . dunno much about them really.'

'It's a 38 snubnose. Small enough to disappear in a pocket. Big enough to punch a slug clean through breastplate or skull.'

'. . . Why have you got it?'

Sighing: 'Tool of the fucking trade, mate. Other people carry calculators, wrenches.'

A surge of terror as he shifts, picks it up, looks at it. He doesn't seem to notice the claw around my windpipe. When he offers the gun to me hilt first, the fear settles enough for me to breathe again.

Des: 'Go on. Take it. You'd best be getting used to it.'

Horribly at a loss, choosing words like choosing footsteps in a minefield. *What the fuck does this cunt want from me?! Ctrl+Alt+Del! Ctrl+Alt+Del! Ctrl+Alt+Del!* 'I . . . Ahhh . . . Don't really want to, Dessie, mate. Not my sty—'

Just the hint of a snarl, but it's louder to me than a whip crack: 'Take the fucking thing, Ryan.'

It's in my hand. So unexpectedly heavy I almost drop it.

He grunts approval, but there's some kind of knowing, nasty glint to his eye that I've never seen before. I have the gun, but Dessie's in total control.

Des, loud: 'First lesson: never carry an automatic. Always a revolver, like that one.'

The weight of the thing starts to feel like a tangible chunk of power. Like a big, black line. 'Why no automatics?'

'Automatics can jam, revolvers can't, and Mr Murphy's is not the best law to fuck with when in situations requiring the use of a firearm.'

'But don't automatics hold more rounds?'

'Yes, and they look the bollocks too, but if you can't hit your target with six you're not going to hit it with fucking sixty. Nor do you deserve to. We're not storming mosques in Fallujah.'

'What's the range like with the barrel so short?'

'Pathetic. But someone sitting across a table from you would disagree passionately.'

I examine it more closely, find that the drum unlocks easily. There are no bullets inside it. Give it a good spin, mesmerised by the intricate simplicity of this awesome machine. Imagine it: the power to erase someone from the pattern just by pointing at them. Cocking the hammer—

Yelping when Dessie plucks it from my hand.

Des, disgusted: 'What are you fucking doing, boy?'

Scared again: 'Ahhh . . . sorry, Dessie. I was just checking it out.'

'Not that, you stupid little cunt!' Wrapping it in the white cloth, pocketing it. 'What do you think you're doing with yourself?'

Back in the minefield. 'What do you mean?'

'Sitting in a scummy car park in the company of a known undesirable, fondling guns and talking about killing people. What's the fucking matter with you? If you were my boy I'd belt the living shit out of you and send you to live in the country!'

Gobsmacked. That dark gleam in his eyes makes much more sense now. Struggling for an answer: '. . . I need the fucking money, Des. I could lose my job any day, and I don't have a work permit any more.'

A scathing sneer: 'Oh yeah, the money's lush all right, init? Few quid here, few more there, little bit woo, little bit wey, plenty of charlie and totty?'

'Ahhh . . . yeah.'

'Let me fucking tell *you* a thing or two.' He draws a deep breath, calming down a little. 'Done my first job when I were twenty-one. Started out like you did, hanging round faces, doing odd jobs. I thought they were the bollocks, them blokes, flashest cunts around and no one saying boo to em. Then I needed some cash for a new motor. Next thing I know I'm tearing down a Leeds high street in a stolen Escort with three blokes in masks and a big bag of cash in the back seat. Larged it till the wee ones. Didn't go to work next day, or next — didn't need to. New motor, tidy lassie. Two more jobs in next month. Another lass. Running round town like I were the hero in a fucking song. Some old villain pulled us aside and give me this very same speech. I laffed at him, bought a cigar that I couldn't pronounce, still fucking can't . . . Two years later I were in Parkhurst, maximum security. Since then I've done fourteen years all told. The money? I've been flush at times — in between playing cat and mouse for a giro — but all in all, if I'd learned to use a socket set instead of a shooter, I would have *tripled* what I've made, piece of fucking piss. The totty, the type of birds you meet? Slappers and gold-diggers, man, after ya for the easy money and the easy respect, worse fucking head-cases than the men, most of em.'

'Nadia's not.'

Cocking his head: 'You're dead right there, son. She's in a different league all together, that one is.'

'Why didn't you pull out, Des?'

'Who were gonna hire me once I'd been inside? Besides, when you've tasted easy money, going back to earning the stuff honestly's like trading ya Harley for a pushbike. Once you know things too' — staring at me hard — 'there's folks who like to keep you close. Give it up, Ryan. Walk away. You're a good lad, you're not cut out for this. You need to think long and hard about that, how it is that you're sitting here right now when anyone can see that you don't have it in you. They don't call us villains for no reason, son. Go home and start again while you can.'

I thank him for his concern, and tell him I'll think about it, but by the time we're parked outside the club I've recovered from the fear, and from the shock of hearing him speak so candidly. I'm not about to broadcast this to Melvyn, but I've done nothing wrong yet, knowingly broken few laws. Another few months of this and I *will* be able to go home. With my tail in the air, not between my legs.

I explain some of this to Dessie.

A light goes out. He says nothing, just shuts the car door and walks inside.

I shouldn't have done it. What right did I have? What did I hope to achieve?

She was dancing for a crowd of pissed accountants. They had about as much rhythm between the fifty of them as she has in one pubic hair. I was standing down the back, praying they wouldn't chip in for an extension, wishing terminal herpes upon them.

Her bag by my feet. Her mobile in a side pocket I'd seen her zip it into.

It felt like stealing food from an orphanage, but I took it out. Paranoid glances at the stage, though I knew there was no way she could clock the spy at his task. The intellectual property thief.

There were ten txts in the inbox. Seven of them in Arabic, the script so appealing to the eye, so exotic and artistic, so incomprehensible to a monolingual dunce like me. Three were in English. One from Beth, requesting confirmation of Nadia's availability for tonight.

Shame seeping deeper into me. Almost stopped then, stopped my tongue probing for a sore tooth that wasn't there.

The second was from someone called Rahael, asking if Nadia was free for a study session Sunday afternoon.

And then I put it away. Needing to leave her one last secret, leave that last slice intact. Because once I'd gone all the way, with the line fully crossed, there might be no reversing back over it. Trespassing each time her back was turned. Buying a phone that supported languages, forwarding her Arabic txts to myself on the sly — *She operates on prepaid, she'll never fucking know* — then having them translated.

So I put it away and leaned back against my wall. Cringing at the childishness in the core of this twenty-eight-year-old man who could do things like that to a woman he hasn't even kissed.

Watching her reach the halfway point of another creative gem, a physically operatic masterpiece that only the crudest and dullest of perverts could ever consider 'erotic'. . . Perverts like the fifty in this conference room with me. Like the one who suddenly jumps up on stage with her to the howls of his colleagues. He's a big bastard. Pretty too. And drunk as a priest. Shimmies up to her, then jumps back a step as her eyes flash, raising his hands, exaggerated innocence. She holds an arm out, pointing to the floor, but the position of the arm leaves her looking a little like a woman ready to dance, and he lets himself be fooled, grabbing the hand and pulling her into a tango clinch, head whipping to one side, all theatrical machismo.

She rolls her eyes, but there's a hint of amusement too, and she chooses to patronise him, a hand on his hip, her head miming his. The accountants raise the roof with the loudest cheer so far.

Nadia tangos the male-model rugby-star arsehole fucking cunt a few steps down the stage, leading in a way to send a *gaucho* livid, her legs and arse in the g-string that his hand rests an inch above, the sexiest sight ever sculpted by DNA. Then they do the classic 180-degree turn, the crowd baying again, cheering their hero on. One more reverse, and she's tangoing him along the edge of the stage, bodies in synch, cheek to cheek.

Then she suddenly pulls away, catching him by surprise, and shoving him mercilessly off. He collects a couple of his mates on the way down, and they end up in a heap, me the only one not blowing in a hurricane of hilarity. Even Nadia laughs a bit, her face showing more enjoyment in the last thirty seconds than it usually does in four whole shows.

And the phone's in my hand, and that last txt is from Dawoud, my bro from the Soho gay bar . . .

. . . and I wish to fucking god I could take it back out again as soon as my brain starts making room for it.

I don't feel much like talking on the way back to hers. Don't feel much like breathing. Driving like a novice.

She usually emanates quiet satisfaction after a show, once you know her enough to read it, but she seems much more bubbly tonight, babbling about a friend riding a bus home from work after her shift at Bayswater McDonald's the other night.

Nadia: 'These four boys, young and drinking, come and sit behind her. They laughing and being silly, being wankers. One of them pull her hair. She say nothing, hoping they leave her alone. Then he pull her hair again. She turn round and tell him, "Behave".' She sips from a bottle of water, lounging in her seat. 'So, all cool then, nothing for few minutes. She read her book and drink her milkshake. Then he pull her hair *again*.' She hasn't noticed my glacial cool at all, wrapped in her own perfect little world. 'She turn round, tell him again "Behave!" And the boy say, showing off for his friends' — a petty sneer — '"And what are you going to do if I *don't* fucking behave?"' Looking at me: 'So what does she do? Can you guess?'

'Na.'

Scandalised delight: 'She put her book down, take top off her milkshake, and empty it over the little prick's head!'

'Really? Wow.'

'. . . You do not sound very wow.'

And even now I can't bring myself to disappoint her. 'What happened then? How did he react?' *Fucking loser.*

She's a few moments in accepting the offering. '. . . He go bloody crazy. It was Friday night, he in nice clothes and hair gel, now he covered in chocolate milkshake. He scream at her to clean it off. She say, "Sorry, I forget to bring mop and shampoo with me." He say he will kill her, so she talk to driver. He call police and boys run away.'

'She could have got herself into a lot of trouble.'

Shrugging: 'She Sudanese. Trouble for her is rapists with AIDS and the slave trade.'

Back at hers. I don't park; pull up with the engine idling.

Gathering her things, frowning at me: *'Yallah, habibi, ta'ali.' Hurry, my darling, come.*

But I don't let it flatter me overly: she calls lots of people *habibi* . . . all people she likes, admittedly . . . but still . . .

A little hurt now: 'You have to go? You busy tonight?'

'. . . Ammm . . . No, nothing important. See you inside.'

Big Sal hears me enter and charges, whining and leaping up. I get on my knees and head-lock him, but he breaks out easily, and then we're off, playfighting across the lounge. I only came in to see him really, give him a goodbye. People should choose their friends from the canine world more often. You always get what you see with a dog.

She makes tea and we settle down on the couch. She throws on a film — she's downloaded eight of them in the last few days, five of them yet to hit cinemas — but I'm not watching very closely, more occupied with past scenes in this room that my mind can see like ghosts. Or that my hand, resting on Sal's neck, can feel inside his brain, his memories, ones I'm sure he would share with me had he that power.

Him and her. Drinking tea. Smoking pot. Dancing. Kissing.

Smiling over her shoulder as she walks down the hall . . .

Sudden, scrutinising each muscle of her face: 'Have you seen my buddy Dawoud recently?'

Her head snaps towards me before guile arrests it. 'Pardon?'

Oh, you heard me just fucking fine, you devious cunt. 'Have you seen Dawoud recently?'

Pretending to ponder: 'Ahhh . . . no, not for a few weeks.'

She should ask 'why?' at this point; that she doesn't showcases not only her guilt but also how rocked she is. But I'm not sure how to take her to task over this without revealing my theft. Have to try, though: she needs to know that the fault is all hers. A minute later: 'I wonder what he's up to tonight?'

'. . . Who?'

'Who do you think?'

'. . . Dawoud?'

'Correctomundo.'

But where I expected a charade of innocence and denials, I get tell-tale petulance, the resentment of the criminal too tired to run. 'Why sudden interest in him?'

'You tell me.'

'No, you fucking tell *me*.'

'. . . Someone I know saw the two of you together.'

'How this someone know what I and he look like?'

'That's not important.'

She's holding my eye defiantly. But then she blinks and looks down. Looks back at me, and something has softened and sickened. 'You looked in my phone, didn't you?'

'. . . Yes.'

Hurt: 'Why would you do that?' Trying to diminish her own sins with a guilt trip.

But with my confession made, I find that I feel fully justified. 'Because I was worried I was wasting my time. And I was dead right. I'm glad I looked.'

Feigning fright: 'Wasting your time? What do you mean?'

'How long have you been screwing that prick?'

Weak as piss: 'I didn't screw him.'

'Don't fucking lie to me, Nadia!' Sal gets up and trots into a corner, settles his head on his paws. 'You've made a wanker out of me already, don't—'

'It was just twice. Once before that night you met them all, once afterwards.'

Part of me had been hoping I was wrong. The txt left little room for doubt, but denial's made a fine refuge for many a loser. And there's a big difference between knowledge and acceptance. I feel it now, though, a lead sinker falling slowly through my stomach. 'How many others?'

'. . . Two.'

'Who?'

'You don't know them. A tutor from uni . . . and a guy I gave my number to from a show I did long time ago.'

Now the sinker wants to be vomited back up. Standing: 'I'm leaving. Take good care of that dog.'

She's on her feet too, holding my wrist. 'Don't go. Please!'

'I have to.'

'Why?'

'Because I've broken a cardinal rule.'

'. . . What rule?'

'Sluts are great fun . . . but don't ever fall for one.'

She hurls my hand away, straightening and flaring. 'Do not call me a slut!'

'Why the fuck not? I've kidded myself for months that you could do a job like that and be something but.'

Seething: 'You son-of-a-bitch! That not fucking fair!'

'Oh, *come* on! Why would you get naked in front of strangers if you weren't getting off on it?'

Her stare's hot enough to cremate with. Five seconds. Sal whining softly. Ten . . .

The words leave her like dysentery. 'OK, sometime I *do* enjoy it! All *right*?! You fucking *happy*? A part of me fucking *loves* it! Maybe you would too if you grew up in place where you could not leave the house with knees and elbows showing. Where six men once held your head under water and beat the shit out of you because you were seen holding hand with a boy. *Ha*?! I was never allowed to ride bike or horse through my childhood. You know why? In case I break skin on my pussy and *ruin* myself!'

I can say nothing to this. Just wither under her wild eyes. Wishing I could remember what my righteousness had felt like. Sal nosing her hand timidly. She notices him, gives him a pat, her anger deflating a little.

But there's nothing but steel in her gaze for me any more. 'I come from a place where men have so much power that when a girl gets raped she will dare to say nothing. Why? Because best way for men of her family to stop the shame and rumours is for them to just kill her. They will be admired for it. Now I am in place where I can turn room full of men into dogs with one kick of my leg, and they cannot do so much as raise a fucking *finger* at me afterwards. *Yes*, I enjoy that.'

I can't understand why I hadn't seen this before. 'So *that's* why you do it.'

Sneering: 'That is not *why* I do it, you idiot. I do it because I can work four hours and earn what I would working forty in other job. Leave my time free to study. I do not have good English. I do not have qualification or experience. What else am I going to do? Wash dishes? Clean rich men's toilets? All week to meet my bills, and kill myself trying to study as well?' A rare flash of weakness: 'I want to *get somewhere*, Ryan. Sand-niggers have dreams too, you know.

But I barely knew a word of English when I arrive, and I cannot yet write much better than ten-year-old. How can I turn down short-cuts?'

I hate myself more than I do her right now. But she'll destroy me fully me if I stay. 'You're still a slut if you fuck around like that though.'

Shouting again, as much appeal now as anger: 'Like *what*? Three men in nine months? That make me a whore? Where *I'm* from it make me a whore — a fucking dead whore if I caught — but *here*? Why should I not enjoy the rights that you people do not even appreciate? And Dawoud is an ex-boyfriend: you know how easy it happens with exes.'

Feeling so pathetic I can barely say it: 'If it's something you wanted or needed . . . why didn't you come to me.'

'I cannot sleep with people I do not trust. By the time I trusted you . . . I was scared of you.'

'Scared of *what*?'

'Scared you lose respect, lose interest. Scared you would hurt me. I do not fucking know, I just did not know what to do!' Then something telling occurs to her, pumps anger and strength back. 'Anyway, what fucking right have *you* to punish me for this? I have seen the way you are with girls! Maybe you have fucked more people since I meet you than I have in my whole life! How *dare* you—'

Acutely embarrassed: 'I haven't so much as kissed another woman since I first laid eyes on you.' But proud in a way that feels completely empowering.

Her scoff's enough to rattle the windows. '*Fuck* off, you lying prick! Men all same, men like *you* especially!'

'I swear on . . .' Stop to ponder the thing most dear to me, the thing to lend greatest weight to the oath, the thing that would sadden me the most if it were ripped from the world tomorrow.

'I swear on your life that it's true.'

She had been raising her hand to gesticulate, but it freezes in mid-journey. Almost a whisper: 'You swear on what?'

Why she should find it convincing I have no idea, but it feels good to say it. 'On your life.'

She stares at me so long the room starts to feel like a stopped clock.

Then her face crumples, and my heart and my anger and my jealousy alongside it. She drops to the couch, hiding in her hands. Sobs rippling through her.

And I'd do anything to keep her from ever crying again, absolutely anything. I'm down on my knees in front of her, pulling her hands away, and the liquid on her cheeks might as well be my blood.

Nadia, squeaky with tears: 'I'm sorry. I'm so sorry. I never dreamed you would wait. I—'

Covering her mouth with mine; sliding off the lip of a waterfall.

31

ALEX

It's got to stop. They barely bother hiding it from me any more, just a keeping up of appearances thing. New games and music and DVDs popping up in the house almost daily. Lame cover stories given the few times I've inquired about their origins.

Form's sake.

Good old Alex. People's manager. Our man on the inside.

But it's gone too far. Security are crap, but management's eyes are more open than they think. The shit has got to hit soon, and some of it's bound to stick to me. I *live* with them, for fuck's sake.

Friendship versus career.

But if their friendship is worth my silence, why isn't my career worth their consideration?

It didn't take me long to cotton on to the haven when I started here, back when I was team-leading at Goods In. I knew it was against the rules, but it seemed no more pernicious than a place to take tea breaks more relaxed than those the canteen afforded. I could lump that. In fact it seemed productive. I was fooling myself though, wasn't I. Hiding the lack of confidence that stopped me from cracking down — the need for acceptance — with a neat little self-deception.

Because there's more going on in the haven than sandwiches and banter, and there always has been, I'm bloody sure of it now.

I gave them all as full an unofficial warning as I could two weeks ago, mentioning to a group including six of my prime suspects that we managers were coming under pressure to crack down on theft; slack of any kind would no longer be given. They heard me loud and clear too, I saw it on their faces.

But observation since tells me that I changed nothing.

I can't go to Security or Julian, though. I need to stop this quietly. So today, a few minutes before lunch, I make sure I'm alone and unobserved in the storage aisle beside the haven, move a few boxes aside at a B level, then jump up and slide into it. Then I pry a small gap into the point-of-sale displays that seal the haven off.

And wait.

Lisa appears first. She's got no idea she's being watched, and the first thing she does is give her nose a good picking, wiping the yield on the underside of her seat. Opens a nearby paper, but I don't think she's seeing much of it because she's murmuring to herself ceaselessly, one line seeming to be recurring, choreographed facial expressions to match. I try to make out of the words:

'You'd be fucking clinical too if ******* before you realised ******* Washington and London folding the monopoly on the words "freedom" and "benevolence" were ******* product of exactly the type of culturally imperialistic multi-media mind-control campaigns that I was programmed to believe were the pole reserve of residents with ******* surnames and/or combat fatigues.'

To have memorised something that long and wordy she's been relishing it a *lot*, and I find it weirdly comforting to learn that I'm not the only loser in the world who likes to relive past verbal *tours de force*. But as queasily fascinating as spying on her like this is, if I thought I could slip from my post undetected and leave her to it I'd be off in a shot.

It's a relief when Greg joins her a minute later, kicking back and tucking into a full English, Lisa cheekily bludging a sausage off him. He offers her a piece of bacon too: she bites half of it, then hand-feeds him the other half, a look passing between them.

Hello, what the hell's up here?

I wouldn't leave now for another promotion, and I curse silently when Ryan ambles in. Alonso and Katie soon follow, then a couple of others, and they have themselves a right little tea party for a while.

My hip where it rests on the slats of the shelving is murdering me by the time most of them have drifted away. It's just Greg, Ryan and Alonso left now. It's obvious nothing's going to happen, and I'm wishing they'd all get back to work so I can as well before someone finds me here, when Alonso, in mid-conversation, takes a tray full of Playstation games down from a shelf and starts gutting them, placing the CDs and inlay covers to one side and the empty cases to another.

Ryan: 'You gonna take em out now, Alonso?'

'Yeah. I have lunch pass. You know who on security?'

Greg: 'It's only mad Magda.'

Alonso slides a stack of CDs down the front of his pants, slides another stack down the rear. 'What she like?'

Ryan: 'No dramas, dude. If she even bothers searching at all she'll just pat your pockets.'

Alonso has his shoes off, placing inlay cards along the bottoms.

I hadn't really formulated much of a plan beyond maybe observing something incriminating and weighing what best to do with it later — certainly hadn't planned on revealing myself as a peeping Tom — but this is too good a chance to pass up.

Alonso I can sack.

So I push the wall away fully and start sliding out.

Alonso may be the one caught in the act, but he handles it far cooler than the other two, turning smoothly away while Ryan and Greg leap up.

Greg: 'Alex! What the hell are you doing, man?'

'I think it's Alonso who needs to be answering that.'

Ryan: 'Were you fucking *spying* on us?'

'Alonso? What have you got to say?'

Slipping his shoes on: 'About what?'

'Those games down your pants.'

Ryan: 'C'mon, Al, we're all friends here.'

'That's not good enough any more. I warned you guys the other day. You're all pushing it too far, and when one of you gets busted I'm gonna get tarnished by association.'

Greg: 'No you wouldn't. It's got nothing to do with you.'

'It has. I live with some of you, I hang out with others. Eyebrows are going to raise. I don't need that. I've got far more than anyone else to lose.'

Ryan: 'What? A job?'

'. . . You know my job's not like yours.'

'You mean you're going places and us losers are just treading water?'

' I wouldn't put it like that.'

Greg: 'I would. So how can you blame us for trying for a bit extra here and there?'

Alex: 'C'mon, Greg. That doesn't excuse theft.'

Ryan: 'Oh, don't be so fucking sanctimonious. We're not burglarising houses here.'

'What's your point?'

Alonso: 'Point is that the only people who will not steal from someone who has a million of them are just those too scared to try.'

Ryan: 'Exactly. Despite the charade played in public around here, there's no moral question at all and everyone knows it.'

'. . . The company keeps you guys alive. You need to have its best interests at heart as much as I do.'

Greg: 'Why? We're not gonna cause it to go under, and you just admitted it's giving you far more than it gives us.'

'. . . Look, I'm not having this conversation. I warned you all on the q.t., but you chose to ignore me. And I've seen how bad it is first hand now.'

Ryan: 'What the fuck are you gonna do to us?'

'Nothing to you and Greg because I didn't see you commit any crime. But Alonso was about to steal two hundred quids' worth of stock.'

Ryan: 'You are *not* going to call the cops. . . . *Are* you?'

'. . . No.'

Greg: 'What then? Tell management?'

'I *am* fucking management, Greg. Your refusal to accept that is why I'm in this position . . . But no, I won't pass this further up the chain because that'd see the police involved and charges pressed anyway . . . But — and I'm really sorry to have to do this, Alonso — as of tomorrow your services will no longer be required.'

Ryan, incredulous: 'Alex, he's your fucking friend, man!'

'I know. But until I make an example of one of my so-called friends, you guys are gonna keep taking the piss until some of it splashes in my face.'

Alonso: 'Alex, you have my word that this will not happen again.'

'I'm sorry, but that's not good enough. My hands are tied. Don't come to work tomorrow, and for fuck's sake don't steal anything today because I'll be ensuring Security give you a good shake-down on your way out.'

Alonso, looking more shaken than any of them have ever seen him: 'Alex . . . I *need* this job. I am asking you please now.'

'I can't help you. If your theft was just for personal use I might have given you a final warning. But larceny on this scale is highly illegal and causes all manner of headache.'

Alonso, caught between anger and worry: 'We have been through things, Alex, you and I. This not the way to act. I owe you, but do not square the debt like this. This is not right . . . But I will not beg you.'

'. . . I've made my decision.'

———

—You can't sack him, man.

—I already have. I've told Labour Save I don't want him back.

—How can any of us trust you any more?

— . . . On matters like this, you can't.

—Don't you see? This overlaps into all sorts of things.

—I've got a career to think of. There has to be balance.

— . . . You just don't fucking need us any more. Now we're more numbers on the company calculator.

—Bullshit. If that was that it, I *would* have gone to Julian with Alonso. You got any idea how much currency showing that kind of loyalty would have earned me? Don't play the victim, Ryan. What you guys do is out of order, and you know it.

—You hypocritical cunt. How is this any different to you scoring coke in the toilets off Jeremy?

— . . . It's a lot different.

—How? They're both sackable and prosecutable offences. So your mentor would be spewing if he heard about us stealing. Would he spew any less if he heard you ran round here making drug deals?

—This isn't open for discussion.

—Why should we let you sack us for shit and then keep quiet about your own felonies?

—Is that a threat? . . . You wouldn't do that, would you?

— . . . No, you're right, I wouldn't. Because I'm not management material.

—Look, I've known you've been on the take for ages. You and Greg were as guilty as Alonso was this morning; you didn't bat an eyelid. But I didn't do anything to you.

—Why not?

—Out of friendship. I barely know Alonso really.

—You know he'd take to someone with a cricket bat if you needed him to.

— . . . That's not the point.

—That's completely the point. And for deliberately missing a point like that, what you need to do right now is go into the toilets and fuck yourself in the arse. Or even better, go upstairs and let Julian do it for you. That might earn you some currency too.

—There's no need to get offensive.

—There's every fucking need. If you go through with this don't bother coming to me for anything ever again.

— . . . Consider it done.

32

RYAN

It's been a grand old night. Melvyn called me down to the club. I asked if he had work for me — I still socialise with these guys as little as possible — and he said no, just a gathering of inner employees to celebrate a good run. That said, I would rather not have come, but you don't say no to Melvyn.

Dinner in a classy Japanese joint in Knightsbridge, me throwing back the sake, Melvyn bringing some bum along to do the driving. Vernon was in fine form, Dessie a lot quieter. The table across from us included a couple of birds from a girl band on the downward plummet of its three-month shelf life. Melvyn knew their promoter from way back and got them over just as the sushi was served, and we cut up some lines of coke on a mirror the manager brought out for us, snorting away openly.

More lines at the opening night of a new club on Bond Street, yarning with D-list celebs, and Melvyn's near me all night, asking about Oz, asking if I'd take the job as his tour guide on a trip down there next year, wanting to know what activities and inside straights I could tee up for him, and I'm pouring out ideas for the trip, and we're upstairs at the club now, and we're so deep into talk he barely looks up when an ex-England-footballer comes over and says gidday, and then we're in a back room full of couches and cushions, and I realise it's just men in here until a door opens and a cheer goes up and twenty-odd birds wearing mint dental floss and rubber bands glide in and entwine their smiles and limbs with random blokes, and they introduce themselves as hostesses, but I suspect their hospitality goes beyond champers and canapés, and a guy across the room soon has his hands down two gyrating g-strings at once, and me and Melvyn all but ignore the girls 'cause he has me in stitches with a yarn about how he once worked as a purveyor of second-hand coffins, a grave-digger mate and him exhuming coffins the night after they'd been interred, removing the bodies, reburying the deceased *au naturale*, then flogging the coffins to a dodgy undertaker in Stockwell, and two of the girls are doing a 69 while three blokes paw them and toss themselves, and I can't wait to tell Nadia about this, but I better do it now on the phone so as to cut down on the suspicion factor, and Melvyn asks where I'm going, wonders why I'm leaving the room, and I tell him it's not my style, and he salutes that and lights me a big doobie, and Dessie still looks like the world's on his shoulders even though an eighteen-year-old stunner is sucking his surprisingly small cock, and Melvyn says we're off soon anyway, and holds another line under my nose, and I stand outside the club in the glorious cold and talk and laugh with my baby for a half hour, then head back in, the bouncers nodding at me politely as they open the rope for me, and I'm so high I have a bit of a boogie with a Brazilian couple I buy cocktails for downstairs, and Melvyn arrives and joins us, laughing that infectious boom and spanking the planks like he's ten years younger, and then I'm back in the car with the lads, and we're steaming down the A-40 towards home base with The Jam 'Going Underground' at full fucking tit.

Just the four of us now, in Melvyn's office. Scotch and cigars. Even Dessie's smiling a bit at the yarn I'm telling about this slapper Judy who used to work at the warehouse back in the old days.

'I used to fuck her now and then, along with about six others. Great fun in the sack. Anyway, she needed some coin for a trip to the Maldives, so she answered an ad in the personals looking for nude models. Good coin paid, tasteful shots only. Never done it before but down she goes, some dodgy little studio above a newsagent's in Wembley. Gets her kit off and the bloke snaps away for an hour or more. She ends up showing much more than she'd planned though; the dude must of had a good routine.'

Vernon: 'Oh, them nuddie-pic snappers? Forget about it! You could pop in to one of them cunts for a passport photo and end up over his couch holding your arse open.'

'Yeah, well that's about what happened to her. Anyway, she finished up and dressed, and he's told her he'll call her in a week and get her back down to see the shots and talk about which ones she's comfortable having him peddle. But a week goes by and she aint heard from the cat. So she calls him but can't get through. Same again the next day. So she decides he must be flat out and just to shoot down and see him. Arrives at 453 Wembley Road, and hello, no fucking studio any more! Just a Turkish bloke setting up a weaving loom and a landlord spitting chips 'cause he's owed four weeks' rent and the photographer was last seen in a minicab to Heathrow.'

Melvyn laughs louder than anyone, and for some reason we all clink glasses and drink to it.

Then it's a charging of glasses and a more solemn toast, to the work put in this last year, Melvyn assuring us of his deep appreciation.

He falls silent then but you can feel his excitement about something. It's contagious, and within a minute we're silent too, waiting for him to speak, anticipation roiling round in me.

He tells us that there's some *real* work round the corner now, that the three of us are gonna see just how well he rewards loyalty; and I'm doing sums in me head, adding them to what I've got saved up, and you can stick the Lucky Country up your arse, mate, 'cause I've fallen on me feet running here.

Then he tells us what he wants us to do . . .

. . . and it's like every drop of liquid in me gets sucked out in two seconds flat.

Melvyn, grinning camaraderie, slapping my shoulder: 'Whadaya say to that, Skippy? Eh? You'll be able to open your own surfboard fucking *factory* by the time we're done.'

Vernon's licking his lips. I throw my stare at Des, desperate for a buoy in this heaving sea.

And there's nothing in those big dark eyes for me but pity.

I feel my lips fluttering. 'Y . . . Y . . . You're fucking kidding me, Mel, right?'

'God no, son. This is a gigantic peach danglin two feet from the floor. You don't piss about when opportunity knocks like this.'

There's far too much to think about here; I'd need a super-computer eight storeys high to process it. Melvyn's starting to talk details, but I cut him off. 'I'm sorry, Mel, but you're gonna have to count me out of this. I'm not up for it.'

Bemused: 'You what?'

'I can't help you.'

Amused: 'Don't be bloody daft, course you can. Right, now Dessie—'

Me: 'How long have you been planning this?'

Smiling: 'Not long. Well, long enough to ave all bases covered, don't you worry bout that, my son. There's less risk to this than

319

there is of Camilla makin page three of *The Sun* sometime soon.'

'I'm sorry, but I can't help you.'

His smile only widens . . . enough for me to glimpse for the first time a chink in the mateship. 'Are you sayin no to me?'

Sand castles by tide lines. Wigwams in Tornado Alley. 'Wha . . . What do you need *me* for?'

'Nothin major. Just make sure one of the fork-lifts is fully charged before knock-off that night, then keep watch from the park round the back for us.'

'Mel, you don't know what you're saying, mate! They don't just load the best stock and leave them sitting by the outbound doors! You'd have to do it all yourself! It takes fucking *hours*, man, and leaves a paper trail a mile wide! And what about the cameras? And Security!' But I know these last two can be got around easily enough. With two guys, a lot of balls, and at least one firearm.

Melvyn leans forward, earnest, a father figure offering comfort. 'Listen to me. All that's sorted. You need to do nufin more than what I just said. Clear?'

I'm still picking myself off the floor, finding myself in an elephant stampede: it takes a while to click. 'You've already got someone on the inside. Jesus fucking Christ.'

Winking: 'That's on a need-to-know basis, for your own good. But it's *all* sorted. The only concern you'll ave is ow to spend ya twenty large. *Trust* me. Now, the first thing we need to do, lads, is star—'

'Oh yeah, like I trusted that you gave me work because you thought I'd make a good attendant?' *Did I say that out loud?*

Melvyn sighs. He unscrews the cap from the Dewar's bottle. Splashes some in his glass. Splashes some in mine. Reaches into the bar fridge beside him and gets some ice cubes out, clinking a couple into our glasses. Then he finally looks at me. He says nothing, swishing his drink around slowly. My mouth's filling up with saliva.

Tick follows tock follows tick follows . . .

'Listen to me, Ryan. I like you. I like you a lot. We all do.' He gestures to the others, Vernon nodding extravagantly, Dessie impassive.

Oh, Dessie, why didn't I listen to you, mate? He'd been trying to warn me. This is killing him, I can see it.

Melvyn: 'So let me make one fing crystal: if not for what I'd seen from you these last few monfs, you would *not* be being offered this. Now—'

'I can't do it. End of story. I'm sorry, but—'

Disappointed and defeated: 'All right. If that's the way you feel it's the way you feel.'

Not even trying to hide the relief tearing through me: 'Thanks, Mel. I really am sor—'

'You've left me in a very awkward position, though. Like I said, we *needed* you on this.' Sad shrug: 'And now you're a security risk n'all.'

Vernon stands up and takes his jacket off.

'But maybe I'm just too excited to look at the problem dispassionately. Cos there's always a solution, that's one-a my mottos. So me and Des'll just pop out for a minute and leave you and Vern alone, see if ya can't cook somethin up between the pair-a ya. Need anythin brought in, Vern?'

Vernon, rolling up a sleeve: 'Ahhh . . . yeah, might as well. Send us in a corkscrew, yeah? And . . . and that jar of chillis, them real hot fuckers on the top shelf.'

Ctrl+Alt+Del! Ctrl+Alt+Del! Ctrl+Alt+Del!

'All right, I'll do it!' In his fucking dreams I will, but getting out of this shit-hole intact is all that counts right now.

Melvyn: 'Diamond geezer!'

Vernon: 'Nice one, Ry. You'll be right, mate.'

Dessie's saying nothing, but there's something new in his stare, something that feels like a warm pocket in this cold black water sloshing around my nostrils.

He's gonna help me. All I have to do is get out of here.

It's all palsy walsy after that, a few more drinks, toasts, then I have to nod along eagerly as Melvyn lays his plan out. And it's so fucking smooth and viable that for a minute I almost forget how much I want out of here.

But nothing's worth this kind of risk, not to me. My lines feel wooden, though Melvyn seems to swallow them, and a firework of energy goes off as he dismisses us.

He calls me back as my hand touches the door knob. 'Not that I don't trust ya, Ryan. Standard procedure. Dessie?'

Des takes a clear plastic bag from out of his jacket. It *clunks* on the table.

Melvyn: 'Recognise this?'

And I feel like a man looking into his own coffin as I move closer to the bag.

The bag that has a gun in it.

A gun that looks familiar.

A gun that would *feel* familiar too, were I to handle it.

Again.

33

RYAN

Everyone else carries on like it's a normal day. Goes about their work. Gossiping. Tea and sandwiches. It's like watching a play.

Or watching a street while a car-bomb that only you know about ticks off the minutes.

The last two weeks have been pure hell. I've spent so much time on the toilet my anus starts bleeding at the first wipe now, the pain constant. Sleep, if any, has been a wasteland ruled by demons. Last night I was in prison. Like the night before. My arse was burning from something quite different from nerve-induced trots. My cellmates were from Scunthorpe and Grimsby. They'd punch me if I so much as spoke without raising my hand.

Waking up is even worse, the relief turning to poison as I re-remember the real nightmare.

I feel like flying to Burma and applying for political asylum.

Because I'm going to go through with it.

Another viable alternative simply hasn't arisen. Not even something semi-viable.

I'm just going to do what's been 'asked' of me.

I'm back from squirting my half-hourly dribble of arse acid. I know I've got to get through today without any odd behaviour drawing attention to me, but my mouth is so dry that simply speaking sounds suspicious. Alex, the big kahuna, is swanning around, lording it up, firing off orders. Gorging himself on the obsequiousness his position inspires, cracking jokes that the Alex I lifted from social purgatory wouldn't have uttered in his own fucking head. His eye catches mine as I cross the floor, but we glance away as one, not a word said, the way it's been since he arse-fucked Alonso.

There have been some tense moments in the house the few times I haven't been at Nadia's. But I've had the upper hand, because most of the others are dark on him too. He's moving out in a while. A swanky one-bedroom in Notting Hill. He's got a company car coming his way soon too. I heard he chose an Audi convertible. Gonna be a big summer for our former compatriot. Back-stage passes at Glasters. A berth on a yacht round Corfu.

Watching him now — his ebullience, his power, his prospects — occasions in me a belt of real hatred for the cunt.

Followed by a near-sob of self-pity.

The haven's gone now — *turncoat Kiwi prick* — so we've been reduced to eating in the canteen. I'd far rather spend the time alone but I can't be seen breaking from routine today, so I settle in at a table with some of the gang. Lisa's reading the review section of *The Independent*.

Greg: 'So, Lease, what might one's mind be enriched by courtesy of British free-to-air telly this evening?'

Lisa, pretending to read: 'Ammm . . . at seven we've got the "Fifty Best Fifty Best Ever Shows". Followed by "Who Dares Wins Eighteen", an account of the heroic exploits of the SAS through the foot- and-mouth crisis. That's followed by . . . "Immigrant Idol".'

Katie: 'What's "Immigrant Idol"?'

Lisa: 'Before a panel of celebrity judges and txt voting, fifteen budding immigrants compete for the prize of a fast-tracked right-to-remain visa. Categories include: How my skills can benefit *you*; Yes, I *am* happy to start wearing more than towels and curtains; Yes, I *have* been tortured by heartless experts and have the scars to prove it; Yes, all of my immediate family *have* been murdered by my president and so I *shan't* be attempting to have them join me; Yes, I *do* agree that the British colonialism which bankrupted my country and left a mad general in charge was a positive thing; and — everybody's favourite — Yes, I *can* learn to speak English with a regional UK accent in under thirty-five days.'

I make myself laugh along with the rest of them, but it feels more like retching.

I'm working a mouthful of sandwich around, trying to get it wet enough to swallow, worrying that it's not going to happen, that I'll have to spit the fucking thing out, when I realise everyone's staring straight at me.

'. . . Yes?'

Katie: 'Where the fuck were *you*, man?'

'Why?'

Greg: 'We just asked you if you were OK.'

Sharon: 'Three times.'

Me: '. . . Why wouldn't I be?'

Lisa: 'You look pale.'

Jim: 'And you've been really . . . remote for days.'

Katie: 'You look like a duck on a river.'

Ryan: 'What do you mean?'

'Calm on top, frantic underneath.'

I almost start to cry. Then, for a wild moment, I'm about to start gushing the story. '. . . Na, fuck off, I'm all right. Just been working nights a lot, pretty knackered, yeah?'

They don't seem to be buying it. Then Alex saves me, walking in with Tina, deep in managerial matters, lives moving and shaking to the beat of their words. They're both cradling big Styrofoam mugs of designer coffee that some temp was no doubt sent to buy for them from the Starbucks down the road. He stops beside us; waves to Tina that he'll join her in a minute. There are no free tables right now, so Tina casts about for a moment, then stops by where Ravi and some of the Sri Lankan crew are sitting. I don't hear what she says, but she does it with a smile. They vacate the table, but they're not smiling about it.

Alex: 'Hey guys.'

His hair's holding more gel than a high street salon, and he's had it styled again — a weekly occurrence. He looks to have got some highlights this time too.

Alex: 'Katie, about that bill . . .'

Katie's the house treasurer. Alex may be getting paid a lot more these days — more than any three of us together — but he's disputing how much she says he owes for last month's gas bill.

Katie: 'Not now, Alex, please.'

Alex: 'Why not now? I'm working late tonight.'

Lisa: 'Alex, why don't you just fucking pay it? You know the other bill's been lost somewhere and she can't prove on paper how much you owe, but you also know she's not a swindler. It's thirty fucking quid, man, it's not going to break you.'

Alex: 'I've got a lot of expenses coming up.'

I give Alex a look as I stand, making the most of coincidence. 'I'm off to the toilet.'

Three more hours till I leave. Three more hours until entering this place will forever feel like entering fucking Dachau. I barely get off the toilet in time to turn around and chunder my sandwich into it. Slump back down. Squeeze out some more arse vinegar. The first touch of the paper is fucking torture, and I can only make myself brush lightly with it. The localised agony is such an acute analogy of the place I could be headed for very soon, and I shudder at how much worse the pain of rape must feel. Spin around for another spew, and this is so fucked up I don't even feel ashamed at sitting doubled on the dunny for the next fifteen minutes, with a burning dirty arse, tears leaking through my fingers.

I was worried this would happen, that the tension would pile so high I wouldn't be able to function, to perform the last task that might still save me. So I came prepared, and now I cut and snort a half-gram of ching in a couple of minutes. Don't feel very high walking back out, more fuzzily disconnected, but it's an improvement, and my bowels feel more stable.

I spend the next few hours walking round talking to people, ostensibly about nothing, sniffing for the second insider.

It's getting quite late, the hustle of the place starting to drop, the sun long gone and the chill sinking in. My jaw's aching from teeth-grinding. My deputy dog act has yielded nothing, and I can't put it off any longer.

Time to become an accessory to armed robbery.

Goods In is nearly dead, the office dark and locked, just Greg on the floor with some check sheets. I've plugged the fork-lift into the charger on more occasions than I can count — about once a week drivers pass the buck and it doesn't get done, which is why I'm so invaluable now — but who would have thought that life could mutate so badly that tonight this chore feels like unlocking my own front door while Ted Bundy delivers newspapers.

'Hey, Greg!' It's Ravi, working late again, trundling a pallet across the Goods In floor. 'Verking hard or hardly verking?'

Greg: 'I'll be in the pub within thirty minutes, mate. You'll see me hard at work then. You coming?'

Dropping his pallet by the out door: 'Yes. One hour more. I see you there.' He heads back down the warehouse.

Ravi?!

There's no motherfucking way. But there's also no doubt in my mind as I walk through mud to the pallet Ravi brought down. It's all wrapped and ready to go. No paperwork. Boxes stacked as high as my navel. Console games. Playstation.

Unreleased titles. Brand fucking spankers. Forty thousand pounds' worth of plastic and programming.

Ravi?

I intercept Ravi in an aisle as he drags another pallet up. 'Hey, Rav. Hold up a minute.'

'Ryan! You come watch cricket next week? Sri Lanka versus—'

'What are you working on?'

'Just have some pallets to bring up, then pub. You come?'

'How many pallets?'

'Eighteen more.'

'Why is there no paperwork on them?'

'I do not know. I was told taken care of, to bring them, then knock off.'

'Who told you to do that?'

'Alex.'

No wind in me. I walk off. In the wrong direction. Stop. But what fucking direction? Sit on something. Ravi bringing the pallets up, the bassy roll of the wheels, full of weight and inertia, money and terror.

———

Alex is signing out when he sees Ryan coming. Alex expects him to stride right by; gets quite a surprise when Ryan stops. Then he gets an even one bigger one when he sees the look on Ryan's face, fearing for an instant that Ryan's about to snot him one.

Ryan: 'Come back inside for a minute.'

'What for?'

'*Come-back-inside-for-a-fucking-minute.*'

The tone is chilling. Better suited to a sentence like, *Hang up the phone and run: people are coming to kill you.*

He follows Ryan back in. Out on to the Goods In floor, Greg and Ravi long gone, twenty outbound pallets near the door. Ryan stops beside them.

Ryan: 'What are these?'

Ryan's staring at Alex so hard he feels he's in the dock somehow. 'They're called pallets, Ryan.'

'Where did they come from?'

'Why do you ask?'

Clenched: 'Wrong answer, Alex! On the strength of the times we had this last year, tell me about these fucking pallets!' His eyes are everywhere, but especially on the cameras.

'Dude, what's the matter? You look like the KGB are coming.'

'Just answer the fucking question! *Please!*'

'. . . Look, it's hush-hush. I was ordered to get the pallets prepared then transported up here last thing tonight.'

'Where's the paperwork?'

'There isn't any.'

'How did you know what stock was required?'

'I had a list dictated to me. I noted the titles and quantities, then looked up the locations myself.'

'Who ordered you to do this?'

'. . . I can't tell you.'

'Oh, fuck off!'

'I'm under orders to keep a tight lid on this. You seem like something serious is going on, so if you explain what it is maybe I'll tell—'

Ryan, trembling, shaking his head: 'You do *not* wanna know!

Trust me on that. And trust me also that I'm doing you the biggest favour right now that anyone has ever fucking done you . . . and you don't even deserve it.'

'How can I believe that if you won't back it up?'

Hissing: 'Answer *this* then, you stubborn little cunt! Is there any physical record proving that you were ordered to do this? Could you prove in court that you didn't do this off your own bat?'

'. . . The person who gave me the orders could confirm it easily.'

'And if he decided to lie through his teeth?'

'What would he wanna do that for? I'm his protégé, for god's sake.'

Bucket of water, and Ryan steps backwards. 'Fuck, it's *him*, isn't it? It's fucking *Julian*.'

'I didn't say that!'

'You didn't have to.'

'Please tell me what's going on!'

High with bitter irony: 'I can't! You've shown who your loyalties lie with now. You're beyond trust!'

Alex says nothing.

'All I will tell you is that if you don't get some proof that Julian told you to do this, and if he doesn't know you have that proof . . . you and I are both gonna get fucked harder than you can ever imagine.' A wild stare: 'Your call, hotshot. I've done nothing to lose *your* trust. Think about that.'

Ryan limps off towards the toilets. Alex calls after him. 'How am I supposed to get proof at this time of night?'

Ryan: 'That mobile they gave you. The NASA knock-off. I'm sure it's got a record function.'

———

Alex unlocks his office and sits down. Dottles absently on a pad. Ryan seems crazed, and Alex can't think of any reason for it.

He writes on the pad:

Ryan.

What could have worried him so much? He barely cares enough about this place any more to bother holding his job down. He's more likely to laugh than cry at an operational problem somewhere. Even if he had somehow been involved in the job in question — and Alex is certain he wasn't — and knew about a fuck-up, the worst that might happen to him is a dismissal.

Operational meltdown where?

Alex can imagine himself getting seriously worked up about the prospect of being fired, but Ryan?

He tries to think of other bad fates that could befall one at work . . . Nothing fits, nothing at all—

Sits up straighter.

Prosecution for theft.

And Alex knows Ryan's policy on five-finger discount.

On impulse Alex decides to call Julian.

Voice-mail.

He calls a second number of Julian's, one he hasn't used before, one reserved specifically for urgent business. So long as he's not on vacation or dying, Julian should answer this phone at any time. Alex is nervous and embarrassed at using it for something trivial, doesn't even have much cover to justify it with. But those particular nerves fade slowly, and then he's counting the rings. Ten. Twenty.

When neither Julian nor a voice-mail service has kicked in after thirty, Alex ends the call.

Sits perfectly still for a few minutes.

If a glitch in the chain was about to cause problems and Ryan knew about it, why would he keep it from Alex? He might do so out of spite if there was no risk to himself, but that clearly was not the case.

And what about Ryan's reaction after he heard of Julian's involvement?

Julian.

But Alex can't think of a single substantial link between Ryan and Julian. He doubts that Julian is aware of Ryan's existence.

His thoughts turn to the stock itself.

Unreleased titles, prime stock.

He had been told that getting the stock ready quickly and silently was crucial; that they were about to undercut a Belgian firm that had a share of the ASDA market. Winners want the ball on the big plays, and Alex had been thrilled that Julian had turned to him. Not entering so large a transfer into the system immediately — let alone for the whole weekend, as Julian had instructed Alex — was a major transgression of company policy. But shit, Julian practically *was* company policy.

Alex tries both numbers again. Voice-mail and no answer.

A while later — feeling disloyal and underhanded — he removes his own caller ID from his phone settings and calls both numbers again.

Voice-mail and no answer.

He crosses out one of his entries.

~~Operational meltdown where?~~

And having done it, having acknowledged that whatever Ryan was so worried about had nothing to do with work, Alex's mouth goes suddenly dry.

He calls Ryan. No answer.

Wracks his head for more potential factors, elements, additional dots to help define the picture.

Me.

34

If the lads back home could see me now.

Ryan had said this to himself plenty of times since leaving Australia. Smoking pot with a uniformed policeman in an Amsterdam alley. Naked in a Hilton jacuzzi with a Lufthansa stewardess and a beautician from Birmingham. Hitchhiking from Zagreb to London with five pounds seventy in his pocket.

He says it to himself again now, but the contrast in context could scarcely be starker.

Squatting in brambles by a fence near train tracks. Straining through another fire-water bowel movement, thighs screaming. Anxious not to shit on his jacket or his pants, shivering.

A set of binoculars at his eyes.

He has a good view of much of the warehouse from here, the rear length of it and the western side, quite bright under flood-lights. He can read the safety sign beside the in doors; can see Amy and Martin through the sign-in window, spying on night shift with CCTV.

He'd made his first call about an hour ago, at 12.50 a.m., when the final delivery left from Dispatch, right on time, the last truck due in or out until eight in the morning. There had been no voice at the number he'd been instructed to call, just silence as the call was taken. 'Halftime,' he had said, as instructed. No reply as the line closed.

Melvyn had ordered Ryan to make these calls with his own caller ID showing.

More leverage. More tonnes of rock.

He's too scared to lower the binoculars for long, struggles with one hand to rip toilet paper from the roll. Moves a metre or so from the stench of it when he's dressed, a peculiar reek that he knows will fill him with dread for the rest of his life should he ever encounter it again. Crouches down.

His mind is everywhere and nowhere, thoughts like leaves in a twister. All night, since before getting here, he's half expected a call telling him the job's off; half wanted that call, half dreaded it. Still suspects the call might yet come. Can't decide whether he should rejoice or despair if it does. His accosting of Alex had been a desperate stab in the dark, a barely thought-out act of panic. What he'd been hoping — what had felt cut and dried and wildly hopeful for about a minute — was that Julian would get cold feet when he heard Alex asking questions about the pallets, and call in a cancellation. But afterwards Ryan had looked at it from other angles and seen a frightening number of holes in the ploy. Gaping black holes.

He doesn't know what he wants out of this now. He wants to be to sweating his arse off in 45 degrees with flies buzzing around his head while he hauls a yabbie trap out of an outback dam . . . Nadia rubbing sunscreen on her legs, tossing him another cold one. He hasn't even been able to bring himself to answer Alex's calls. Wishes he'd told Alex nothing.

Wishes he'd told him more.

Inside the Security office, Martin pulls on his big blue jacket, nods at Amy, then disappears, reappearing outside five seconds later.

Ryan muttering: 'Oh Jesus, how the fuck did I get here?'

Martin stops by the first fire-exit doors, gives them a shake. Moves on. Turns the corner. Exigencies aside, he'll be five minutes checking things around the warehouse's far side, and Ryan will be able to see him for all of those.

He calls the number again. It barely gets through half a ring before it's taken. Ryan's voice catches in his throat . . . catches again . . .

Frozen vomit: 'Extra time.'

A minute later a truck slides into view like a cruising shark. And the sense of surrealism that has lain between Ryan and the real world for the last few days lifts as neatly as a curtain.

Thunderbirds are go . . . and I'm one of them.

All that can save him now is success. The immediate fear and cold are suddenly gone.

And then they're back mob handed. Ryan stands bolt upright with an incoherent yelp, almost dropping the binoculars.

Because a handful of bodies have appeared. From somewhere around the front. They're jogging towards the truck as it stops at the barrier arm.

———

Parked a hundred metres from the warehouse in a ten-tonne Scania, Des was quite looking forward to this. Hold-ups had been a semi-regular thing for him once upon a time. He had sworn by them. The hours were great and the wages fucking sensational. But he hadn't done one in years, and with the adrenaline building and bringing it all back, he realised how much he missed it. Nothing like the look on people's faces when hooded men burst into a room shouting and waving sawn-offs. Nothing like using the threat of extreme force to make off with what a lawyer couldn't have banked in half a decade. Doing jobs used to give him rock-hard erections.

And this one was going to be even more blinding because he knew how soft the target was. No dogs. No guns. No ex-SAS on thirty quid an hour. Just a couple of low-paid, soft, sleepy mugs — more than likely stoned n'all — conditioned to no more than feeling up Paki tea-leaves and playing with CCTV. Complacent as fuck, cos not only had this place never once been hit like this, it was doubtful management had ever seriously contemplated the possibility. The logistics behind getting enough of the right stock out to make a hostile raid worthwhile would have seemed insurmountable. Scams and out-bound smuggling were all their Security were paid and trained to deal with.

Vernon, in the passenger seat: 'Wakey fuckin wakey, Andromeda Security. It's about to get a little bit naughty.'

Des found that he couldn't fault the assertion.

No rigid time window. No police response for hours.

And best of all, this was Melvyn's swan song. He'd have his feet up in Spain two months from today.

Leaving Des a free man. With a juicy retirement to play with. He had his eye on a little pub in Folkstone.

He'd studied the photos of the warehouse, pored over the intell. He knew how lazy the little Security twat was; she wouldn't leave the office. If she even saw the truck, she'd wait for him to come to the window. Des planned on shoving the shooter under her chin, then hauling her out of the window by her hair, dragging her back in through the door. Nothing personal, but at times like that you had to act like you were capable of eating someone alive.

She *was* a bird, though, so she wouldn't be getting a tickle-up —
unless she misbehaved — but as for her sidekick . . . Once Des had
forced her to call him back to the office over the two-way, Des was
planning on clumping that lanky prick so hard he'd be shitting his
own teeth till Ash Wednesday.

His thumb was resting on the answer key of the mobile, and
he took Ryan's call almost instantly. Ryan sounded like he was
being strangled, and Des got a flash of worry. But then Ryan
croaked, 'Extra time.'

Des ended the call, fired the truck up, revved it, feeling a
different motor start to growl inside his chest.

Vernon: 'We on?'

'Aye.'

Vernon snapped the glove box open. Screwed a silencer on to
the barrel of a Beretta.

Des, shifting gears: 'That thing does *not* get fucking used,
Vern.'

Vernon, affronted: 'Yeah, *course*, Dessie, I know the score,
mate! We've only gone over it an undred times. Gotta look the part
though, int I?'

Vernon ducked down from sight as Des pulled past the big
EUE sign and into the driveway, stopping at the lowered barrier
arm. He could see the lights on in the security office about thirty
metres away. Des pulled his hard-hat down as low as it would go.
He bent down and took the sawn-off from under the seat, shoving
it into a long pocket sewn into the inside of his overcoat. A last
word to Vernon: 'Stay out of sight until the arm raises, then drive
in sharpish.'

Des turned to open his door.

There were five people standing below his window.

———

With twenty pallets of highly fenceable stock sitting by the outbound doors, all of it in systemic limbo and traceable only to him, with no answer from Julian or Ryan all night, Alex had decided to watch and wait.

There was only one way to get that much stock away from the warehouse: in a truck. And there was only one route in or out for trucks.

So Alex had opted to watch the driveway.

He couldn't see it from his office window, so he sat in Tina's, which was closer to the barrier arm than Security even, and right beside an emergency exit.

He wasn't really sure what he was waiting for, but he'd decided that if action was required he would be a fool to do it alone, so he sequestered four temps off the Labelling supervisor and set them up with some work in Tina's office. Two guys and two girls. He told them nothing of his fears. He wanted witnesses, not back-up.

Then he watched. He'd consulted the system for in- and out-bound vehicles much earlier, and he watched the last truck leave at 12.50 a.m. He was feeling very tired now, had been up since six. He was no less anxious, but his eyes were starting to droop. He wished he had some coke. He thought about phoning a guy he knew who did deliveries — he was usually more prompt than the pizza man —and was puzzling on how he might go about getting the coke bought and snorted while letting neither the driveway nor the temps out of his sight, when a lorry turned into the driveway.

It was so unexpected he did nothing but stand and goggle at it for a moment. Then he bolted for the door, yelling for the temps to follow him. He caught them by surprise, but his tone was so full of urgency they were hard on his heels in seconds.

Through the emergency exit, knowing it would sound an

alarm in the security office.

There was only one guy in the lorry, and he didn't notice Alex and the temps until they were right beside him. He looked big, but between the hard-hat and the scarf and the gloom Alex could discern little of his face. His eyes stretched wide though when they lit upon Alex, and though he'd only been moving gently beforehand, the way his body froze up fairly screamed.

Alex began talking nonsense into his mobile, motioning for the man to wind his window down.

Then a long, charged moment as Alex and the man stared at each other. A wave of vertigo; Alex could feel gears and wheels racing inside that petrified head . . .

The window came down a touch.

Alex: 'Are you the 1.45 from Manchester? Listen, we've had a security scare, you'll have to park up the road for a bit, no traffic allowed in or out till the cops have gone.'

The head just stared at Alex. Then it darted to twelve o'clock, and Alex saw Amy walking towards them. The head turned away, and Alex heard muffled voices, the words unintelligible but heavily tense.

Alex, loud, into the phone: 'D.C. Bennet? Where are you? Hogarth Lane? Yeah, you're nearly here, mate, just take the next left.'

The window shut and the truck ground into reverse.

Warm liquid raced through Alex. But then he saw some kind of commotion in the cab as it backed out, almost a physical struggle. Another head was briefly visible, and then the truck's headlights were in his eyes and he could see nothing. Ten seconds later the truck was gone.

Amy, stopping beside Alex: 'Who was that then?'

Realising he didn't even take the number plate down: 'I have absolutely no idea. Nor do I ever wish to have one.'

35

To the protests of four people of the ten in the lounge, Johan kills the Kaiser Chiefs mid-song and slaps on some Iggy Pop. The neighbours had complained about the volume earlier. Lisa turned it down a bit, but it's since crept up again. She hasn't partied with the gang in what feels like months, hadn't realised how much she missed it. Finishing her Red Square, she adds the bottle to the horde of empties in a corner and goes through to the kitchen for another one. There are six more people crammed in here, standing around, sitting on the benches.

Greg, for about the tenth time in three hours: 'Lisa! Nice of you to join us tonight. Which quadrant of this seedy city has been enjoying your radiance these last few weekends?'

Trent: 'More importantly, where's all your drugs? We're all out.'

Lisa: 'I'm all out myself. Looks to me like everyone here has had enough for one night anyway.'

Trent: 'What, are you not dealing any more?'

Lisa: 'I never *was* fucking dealing.'

Greg: 'She prefers the phrase "cherished public service".'

Lisa: 'Bullshit, I just used to help—'

Trent: 'Where are we gonna score from then? What's the time?'

Reuben, fresh off the plane from Sydney: 'Two forty-five.'

Katie: 'No one's gonna deliver this time of night. Ryan seemed knackered when he came in; doubt he'll get up and drive us anywhere.'

Trent, scoffing: 'Wouldn't take any help from that prick anyway.'

Lisa, cracking a fresh bottle: '*Fuck*, you can hold a grudge, Trent. Ryan hasn't slagged *you* off in months.'

'So? I didn't fuck *his* girlfriend under his nose. He was a mate of mine, for fuck's sake.'

Greg: 'I propose we steal Ryan's car.'

Murphy: 'We show up at sellers tis toime of night, in tis state, we're only gonna get told to fuck off anyway.'

Reuben: 'Fuck it, let's just do a ram-raid on a chemist then.'

Katie: 'How would we know what to take?'

Trent, yelling into the lounge: 'Alison! We're gonna do a ram-raid on a pharmacy! What should we grab once we're in?'

'. . . Anything ending in an i-n-e.'

'Hahahahaha!'

Alex unlocks the front door and walks into the kitchen, puts his bag on the table. Cold silence, but Alex seems too preoccupied to notice.

Greg: 'Working late, Alex?'

Alex: 'Yeah. Can I steal a beer off someone?'

Katie: 'Na, we're gonna need all of those.'

Alex just nods. 'Gonna shoot down and get a couple then.'

The Indian behind the counter in the twenty-four-hour Budgens sells them after-hours grog for a small backhander. Alex moves to pick up his bag, then changes his mind, pulling a handful of change from his pockets, counting it.

'Anyone want anything?'

Resounding: 'No.'

He opens the front door just as Jim arrives home, the pair swapping nods in passing, the door closing again. Jim walks into the kitchen.

Greg: 'Hey hey, here he is! How'd you get on, loverboy?'

Lisa: 'Where you been, Jimbo?'

Trent: 'Get this: he's only had a date with an *Argentinian synchronised swimmer*.'

Reuben: 'Bullshit!'

Jim: '*No* shit.'

Reuben: 'Fuck me! This place is a total snatch smorgasbord, isn't it?'

Greg: 'You got that right, bro. Welcome to Pussy Paradise.'

Katie: 'Or more to the point, Cock Camelot.'

Greg: 'So what happened, Jim?'

Jim: 'Oh, nothing too juicy. A few drinks and a bit of a boogie. She's a great laugh. Had some problems a while ago, but the doctors reckon she's fine now.'

Greg: 'Good personality?'

'. . . Three of them are.'

'Hahaha!'

Trent: 'Did you kiss her?'

'Bit of a peck.'

Lisa: 'On the lips or the cheek?'

'It was the first date, Lease: any kissing had to be *above* the waist.'

'Hahaha!'

Reuben: 'So you've got chicks from all over the world, most of them here for a good time not a long time. Good jobs everywhere.

342

World-wide flights for dirt cheap, first-rate drugs for cheaper. More pubs and clubs than you could check out in a decade, parties full of mad cunts like you lot going down at the drop of a hat. An awesome band or DJ somewhere nearby on any given night. Bugger-all street hassle . . . Why the fuck does anyone go home?'

Ryan comes down the stairs wearing just his boxers, and everyone shuts up. He looks sick, big bags under his eyes.

Lisa's shocked at the state of him. She hasn't seen an awful lot of any of them lately, been busy with Julian not only on weekends but for much of the week as well, absenteeism no longer an issue. 'Jesus, Ry, what've you been doing to yourself?'

Ryan: 'Who's in the toilet upstairs?'

Greg: 'Some Norwegian bird, she came here with Chico.'

Murphy: 'Tey were on the absinthe, she's been crashed out in tere for over two hours. Everyone's slashing out the back.'

Ryan disappears.

Lisa: 'What's *wrong* with him?'

Trent: 'Finally contracted AIDS, with any luck.'

Greg: 'Shut the fuck up, Trent.'

Katie: 'He changed for the better a couple of months ago. He was really bubbly for ages.'

Jim: 'Then two weeks ago he turned into a Stalingrad deserter.'

Murphy: 'I reckon it's the fucking charl—'

He shuts up as Ryan reappears, walking through them to the back door, bare legs under his jacket, mobile in one hand, toilet paper in the other. The door slams behind him.

Trent, crowing: 'And now he's shitting in the mud and the cold, the just deserts of dirty dogs from times fucking forgotten!' Walks through to the lounge: 'Turn that shit off, Shaz, I've got the new Michael Jackson album. Let's chuck that on.'

'I didn't know he had a new album out.'

'Well, it's not new material or anything, he's just gone and touched up a few of his old favourites.'

Murphy: 'So, Jimbo? Top lass, yeah? Could it be love at last, or what?'

Katie: '*Jim* in *love*? This is a guy who loiters outside abortion clinics scoping for loose women.'

'Hahahaha!'

Jim: 'Easy, girl. I understand love as fully as the next man. It's under L in the dictionary, somewhere between labia and lust.'

Reuben lights a big spliff. 'Fuck, I love this place. My mates were dubious, reckoned it'd be all drizzle and whingeing Poms.'

Greg: 'Well, you probably won't get the house and the retirement fund paid off in a hurry, bro, but if stress-free hedonism is your cocktail, welcome to the twenty-four-hour drive-thru.'

The front door bell rings, and Lisa goes through to the lounge to answer it. She's never seen the guy on the doorstep before. He seems too old to be connected to anyone here. Bald. Middling height. Overweight. 'Orr-wight, love. Is Ryan in?'

Something about his big, friendly smile, the casual tone, makes her say, 'Who wants to know?'

'Just a friend.'

'. . . Na, he's not home right now. Can I get him to call you if he shows up?'

Smiling wider: 'But that's 'is motor out front, init?'

'. . . Yeah, but he shot off with some others.'

Innocently curious: 'Ow long ago was that then?'

The guy's got a strong presence, the kind men step back from in pubs. Or fall in around.

'A few hours ago.'

The grin twists as if she's made a joke. 'If you say so, darlin. Ow bout Alex then?'

Glad she doesn't have to lie again: 'Na, he's not around either. Who are you?'

Greg: 'Who is it, Lease?' She feels him at her shoulder, hears surprise and sudden wariness. 'How can we help you, mate?'

'Lookin for Ryan or Alex, son.'

Lisa squeezes Greg's leg, but her stomach contracts as she sees the guy see her doing it.

Greg: '. . . Na, mate, they're both out—'

A glint of silver, a grunting yelp from Greg. Lisa tries to slam the door, but it cannons back into her, propelling her across the lounge.

As shouts fill the room, the man calmly enters it . . . and the shouting dies as eyes lock on him. Smile gone, not even looking at Greg as he steps around him. Greg struggling vainly to sit, blood leaking through the fingers clutching at his mouth. The party shrinks from the man, ten people crowding the room's back half, people from the kitchen rushing in, blinking, joining the pack.

The man faces them, a silver duster around the knuckles of one hand. Another man enters, fortyish, small and slight, curly hair. Then a third guy, much bigger, mournful eyes above a broken nose.

Bald guy: 'No one else gets urt tonight. We're ere for a word wiv Ryan or Alex, nufin more. Tell us where they are and get back to ya knees-up.'

Lisa feels her stomach filling with helium. Looks at the people pressed around her . . . Murphy, the big Irishman. Johan, Natal age-grade rugby rep. Toby, part-Maori, went toe to toe with a Nigerian bouncer a month ago, gave better than he got. Trent, never seemed scared of anyone. Jim, six foot three and ninety-eight kilos . . .

Nine guys all told.

She feels affronted suddenly. 'Who the fuck are you to break into our home, *punching* people?!'

Bald guy goes to speak, but Jim overrides him. 'Nine on three, pops. I suggest you fuck back off where you came from.'

Katie, shrill, picking up a lamp: '*Ten* on fucking three!'

Curly: 'Don't push it, kiddies. You're on strike two already.'

Toby: 'Strike *two*? Who the fuck do you think you are!' He strides boldly forward, more guys following him . . .

Curly darts in and catches Toby's arm, twists it . . .

The next few hours — seconds in real time — are ordered chaos, ordered only because of the thugs at the centre, moving as if this is choreographed. Lisa sees the bald guy square up with Jim, slap Jim's guard down, then drive the duster into his face. Curly grappling with Murphy, dwarfed by him, but doubling him up with a knee to the balls, driving the point of an elbow three times on Murphy's crown. The biggest thug, rock-like, getting hit and not noticing, dropping Johan with a punch that travels just inches. The numbers of the young guys seeming more hindrance than help, tripping over each other, cramping each other. Young Reuben, more sucked into it than anything, copping a head-butt that leaves his eye a jellied wreck. Bodies piling up in drifts. The girls screeching in a corner. Katie trying to crack the bald guy with the lamp, missing by a foot, him flinging her into the stereo . . .

Then it's over, those young guys still standing cowering into the girls.

No one has been allowed to leave the room.

Toby's still wailing. Curly, turning to him: 'Oh, shut up, you're gettin on my tits.' Lifts his foot, aims, drives his heel across Toby's jaw. Silence. Lifts . . . aims . . . kicks him again. Lifts . . .

Boss, not even puffing: 'Steady, Vern.'

Vern stops.

Boss: 'Take a butcher's.'

Vern goes up the stairs.

Lisa's mewling into Sharon's chest.

Boss: 'You.' He points at Trent, who had kept out of the fighting. Grabs a handful of his hair and drags him to the floor, kneeling beside him. 'Where's Alex?'

'. . . H-he's out.'

'Where's Ryan?'

'. . . He's out too.'

'Ever tried pickin up teeth wiv broken fingers? Where's Ryan?'

'. . . *P-p-p-please, man—*'

Pins Trent's head against the carpet . . . slams his forearm into his mouth.

Trent yelps, coughing teeth and blood.

'Where's Ryan?'

'I don't fucking know!'

Lisa: '*Let him go, you sick cunt*!'

Boss takes one of Trent's hands, grips his middle finger . . . wrenches it backwards. Holds a hand on Trent's mouth, muffling the scream.

Boss: 'Where's Ryan?'

Trent can't form words for a while, grunting and panting.

Boss: 'Where-is-Ryan?'

'*Fuck* you!'

Boss, sighing: 'You fucking mug.' He rises, bending over, clapping a palm over Trent's hand so that the fingers are splayed across the carpet. Raises the heel of his boot . . .

Stops when a mobile rings. The big guy answers it. 'Yeah?' Holds the phone out to his boss. 'It's for you.'

'Who is it?'

'It's Ryan.'

Boss, taking the phone, jolly even as his eyes dare someone to make a peep: 'Or-wight, Ry? . . . Hey, hey, geez, calm down. I know it weren't your fault . . . Is that right, son?' And then he changes: 'Don't be a fucking mug! You're goin down for longer'n anyone if you do that! . . . Look, everyone's in the clear, just gimme a chance to explain . . . *No*, stop blubberin and *think*. I can't tell you on the phone, it's not secure . . . I can be there in ten minutes . . . Good lad, just sit tight.' Ends the call. Turns to the big guy: 'E's sittin on the steps outside Acton nick.'

Vern comes out of the kitchen. 'Na, neither of em here. Found some ID and shit though. Tasty little cunt sat on the crapper too.'

Lisa sees he's holding Alex's bag.

Boss: 'Let's go.' Addressing the room as his flunkies walk out: 'Anyone grasses and I'll make it my life work to see you in a wheelchair, on my mum. This is for the damages.' He drops a few fifties on the floor. 'I'll be back shortly.' Closes the door quietly behind him.

Lisa turns and stumbles up the stairs.

———

From quite a long way up the road, Alex had seen them get out of a black sedan and approach the front door. He had no idea what he might have become enmeshed in, but after recent events, three strange men showing up here at three in the morning was not something he was willing to attribute to coincidence. So he vaulted over the stone fence of the property he was in front of and crouched down, sneaking looks up the road, plastic bag and three cans of Heineken forgotten beside him.

He could dimly hear the music, then it had stopped and he heard what might have been a scream. Which could just have easily been a drunken whoop . . . Surely . . .

He sinks lower into the cold concrete as the strangers reappear. Hears the car start, shuddering as it speeds past him.

But that shudder is nothing compared to the one that wracks him as he enters the house. The lounge looks like a squad of riot police have been through it, attacking anything male that moved. Broken bodies and blood, girls crouched over guys. And tension too, raw fear that dissolves into sighs as people stare at him. But in the next beat the relief in all those faces turns ugly.

Sharon: 'What did you *do*, Alex! What the *fuck* did you *do*?'

Katie pops up from where she was kneeling over Trent, charges at Alex, placing both hands on his chest, driving him backwards until the wall stops him. 'You fucking did this!' Waves a hand behind her: 'Are you happy? *You* fucking brought this on us!'

'What the hell happened?'

Jim, head tilted back, voice sawing through damaged sinuses: 'You better leave, Alex.'

Alex: '. . . You're kicking me out?'

Jim: 'No.'

Katie: '*Yes*.'

Greg, all vowels around split lips: 'They're uming ack.'

They're coming back.

Alex's bladder turns to a bag of ice. He doesn't want to meet these people.

Murphy looks and sounds on the wrong side of fifteen pints. 'We're all in danger so long as you're here. You most of all.'

The room holds its breath again when the back door slams . . . releases it when Ryan bustles in. He freezes.

Katie: 'What the *fuck* is going *on*, Ryan?'

Ryan, muted: 'I'm sorry. Really fucking sorry. Never dreamed it would come to this.'

Jim: 'Just tell us what's happening.'

'If I tell you that, they could end up back here with guns. And they won't be looking for me. Anyone still wanna know?'

Alex: 'I do.'

But nobody else does.

Greg, to Ryan: 'You etter eave too.'

Ryan: 'I couldn't agree more.'

He's heading for the stairs when Trent speaks up, sounding oddly serene considering his state. 'Thanks for the phone call, Ry.

You saved my arse.'

Ryan stops and frowns down at him. He can't talk for a moment, something contorting his face. '*I* saved *your* arse? I was watching through the window, Trent.'

Trent just shrugs. 'What are friends for?' He holds up a hand with a finger jutting out at a horrible angle, and Ryan gingerly shakes it. 'Least I've now got something bigger than two years of self-centred fucking about to define my time up here by. Maybe this was what I needed. Think I'll go home now.'

Reuben, muttering, flat on his back with Sharon swabbing his eye: 'Me too. I'm on the next plane back to Sydney.'

Lisa comes down the stairs, moving like a sleep-walker, a bulging pack on her back. She doesn't say anything, doesn't even look at anyone, floats towards the front door.

Ryan: 'Where you going, Lease?'

'Somewhere safe.'

Alex tries to call her back but if she's hears him she gives no sign, closing the door behind her. Katie runs outside after her.

Alex follows Ryan up the stairs and into Ryan's room.

'Who the hell *were* those guys?'

Ryan shuts the door before answering. 'Friends of your hero and mentor.'

'Friends of *Julian*? Bullshit!'

Hauling his backpack out, Ryan begins throwing clothes into it. 'Believe whatever you like.'

Alex feels like a claustrophobic in a tea chest. With someone about to push it off a wharf. Tries to pull Ryan around to face him. 'You *have* to fucking tell me! You got me into this—'

Ryan shrugs himself free, scooping papers and things out of a drawer, firing them into the pack. 'I didn't get you into shit. Your paragon pal Julian — the one you sold us all out for — he took care of that. I got my*self* into it, yes, but that's all.'

Anger rears up in Alex. It's far more welcome than fear. 'You fucking tell me, Ryan! My life's getting ripped apart here, and you know why . . . and you are gonna tell me what you know *right now* . . . or I'm gonna do something you and I will both regret!'

Ryan drops his pack and smiles savagely. 'Oh, is that right, mate? You've seen the things the people hunting me are capable of and you think you can stand here and physically threaten information out of me? Go fuck yourself.'

They stare off. Finally Alex's snarl implodes, and as he looks away his eyes fill with tears.

Ryan sighs, returns to his packing, taking a shoebox full of . . . *cash*, emptying it into the pack. 'Listen, I did some driving for some guys, turns out that they're low-level villains.' Alex's crying freezes. 'Then I've found out that they're planning to rob the warehouse. I knew the day but no details. I knew they'd need someone on the inside to pull it off. Then I found you setting up that off-system stock. You told me you were following Julian's orders, which was the first I knew of his involvement with these cunts. The rest you know.'

Alex sits down on the bed, blinking rapidly. '. . . So you think Julian set me up to take the fall?'

Sliding his passport into a pocket on the pack's side: 'Sure fucking looks that way.'

'How did they know my name and that I live with you?'

'I was talking with you on my mobile once and Des dropped me off right beside you. He must have remembered.'

'. . . Fuck it, let's just go to the cops.'

'With what? And if you think I'm turning Queen's against Melvyn you're very much mistaken.' Zipping his pack and swinging it on a shoulder. 'Good luck, anyway. We're both gonna need it.'

He turns to leave.

Alex, alarmed: 'Where are you going?'

'Somewhere safe.'

'Wait a minute, I'll just grab a few things. I'm coming with you.'

'No you're not.'

'*Why not*?'

'Because as long as we're both together, if they find you they find me too. I've risked more than enough for you already.'

Flabbergasted: 'What kind of a mate *are* you?'

'I could've asked you that twenty times in the last two months.' Shaking his head: 'I told you never to rely on me for anything again if you sacked Alonso, and you said fine. I fucking saved your arse yesterday, despite that — and could have got myself killed — but that's it. This is as far as you and me go.'

He leaves Alex standing there, gaping.

Then the fear comes charging back. He needs to get out of here. Alex decides he hasn't the time to pack, can easily buy anything he needs anyway. His mobile, passport and wallet are in his daybag downstairs. The others harangue him as he crosses the lounge, people wanting to know why he's still here, four or five of them now — Katie still the loudest — demanding that he leave. But his bag isn't where he left it. A quick look through the lounge . . .

No bag.

Then Trent tells him one of the thugs took it.

For a moment he's rooted to the spot. He's going to have to dash upstairs again, face the daunting prospect of foraging through his room for some photo ID, a Kiwi driver's licence he hasn't seen in nearly a year . . .

A car pulls up outside . . .

Katie, hysterical: '*Fucking get out of here, Alex!*'

. . . a car door slams . . .

And Alex is out the back door and over the fence in five and a half heartbeats.

36

LISA

I can still see the blood left on the big guy's forehead following his head-butt on Reuben. It's any one of about twenty snapshots from the attack that keep flashing back to me, the number growing as images I can't even remember attach themselves. The worst is the look on the boss's face as he snaps Trent's finger. No snarl, no anger at all really, just impatience. Like a kid forced to repeat a level on Playstation. Like he'd do this all day and expend no more emotion on it than a warehouse temp fixing price stickers to CDs.

Sitting in the black cab, shivering despite the heater the driver turns up at my request, I peer out at the streets, people on them even at this time, and wonder which ones are the sharks. No way of telling, of course, of beating the camouflage of human clothing.

I gave Katie the cab ID and licence plate before we set off, made sure the cabbie heard me do it too.

A place full of human carnivores, ready to burst into your life with no warning, no safety even when you're at 'home', surrounded by friends. A social pyramid of eight million people, compressed into an area smaller than the Pilanesberg National Park, sheer numbers guaranteeing a hefty percentage of thugs and rapists and pimps and extortionists and psychos and hit-men and every other toxic by-product of this dog fight masquerading as a city. Population density ensuring eventual contact with some of them.

For those further down the triangle, anyway. Those without the clout to insulate themselves.

I need to get as far as I can from waters infested by sharks like those I just watched feed. And that kind of distance, in this kind of place, isn't measured in units of length.

Less than twenty quid in my purse; I know I'll need more for the fare, that I should ask the cabbie to stop off at a cash point, but I can't face the streets right now. The thought of standing at an ATM for a few minutes at this time of morning, even with the cabbie waiting for me, turns my spine to ice. Because in a place like this, when someone is hauled down the rest of the herd think no more of it than thankfulness that they themselves have eluded the chase. He'd probably read a tabloid till they were done with me, then go through my pockets for his fare.

Remember something I need to do, and open my pack for the make-up bag I left near the top. It's not an easy job in a moving vehicle, but I'm grateful for the concentration the task requires. Grateful too for the cavernous space in the backs of these cars as I squeeze out of my worn jeans — not so grateful for the driver's four-eyed leer in the rear-view mirror — and into a short pleated skirt. Then I change my knickers too, slipping on a black thong with delicate chains woven into it. Finish off with a healthy wallop of the Chanel he bought for me.

Feel my spirits easing out of their clenched ball a little as we turn into shallower waters, spiked fences around the imposing houses, all solid brick, climb-proof paint, the names of rent-a-cop companies who guard them glowing from signs, a leafy private park centring the quiet square. A gust cuts through me as I step out, and my shivering is so disproportionately violent that it paralyses me for long seconds. Press the intercom for the dark third-floor flat.

I'm hoping he's not home; want nothing more than to fill a tumbler with cognac as the spa-bath fills with water and bubbles. I know the combinations for the two keypads which will get me inside, and I know where he keeps a clip full of 'change' for the taxi too. But when his voice comes through to me, the rush of warmth in my chest tells me I'd been kidding myself.

'It's me.'

'Lisa?' Something wrong with his tone. He sounds wide awake for a start. And he got to the intercom far too quickly to have been asleep. I'd expected surprise at my arrival. But he sounds agitated too. Scared even.

He's got another woman in there.

My face feels suddenly fat.

What the fuck am I going to do n—?

Julian: 'Lisa, come in, for Christ's sake! Since when did *you* have to knock?'

And the next breath feels like the first you take after diving too deep while swimming. 'Ammm . . . I need some cash for the cab.'

'I'll be right down. Is everything OK?'

'. . . It is now.'

————

ALEX

Not the best Sunday I've ever had. And it just keeps getting worse as each new piece of scenery on my journey up shit creek unfolds.

I'm bloody cold for a start. Dressed for nothing more than a quick dash down to the shop — a single layer of trackies, trainers and cotton socks, just a T-shirt under my jacket. The jacket's quite thick, thank Christ, good against this icy wind which happened to choose today to start blowing, but the dark cloud is pregnant with rain or worse — I can smell it above the smog and the trash of Edgware Road — and this fabric gets sodden real quick in the wet.

About ten quid to my name. Well, I've got a lot more than that to my *name*, I just don't have a name right now. Not with my wallet in the possession of a pack of violent animals who seem bent on erasing me in more than just the Kafkaesque sense they've so far achieved. No Barclays card or MasterCard is a big enough problem, but I don't have a single slice of ID on me, let alone one bearing a photo, the only ID that counts in these parts anyway. So even when the banks open tomorrow — shit, the next day, tomorrow's a Sunday . . . suddenly remembering that Monday is a public holiday too — the odds of them allowing me access to my cash are looking pretty fucking emaciated.

I jumped fence after fence in my flight from the house, flitting through people's yards, crossing roads as little as possible, got attacked by a bloody border collie at one point — the way this is shaping up I'm surprised it wasn't a pit bull — then finally went to ground on a dark cricket field, under the eaves of a pavilion. Fell asleep and woke up colder than I can ever remember being. So cold I'm surprised I woke up at all. Fought to get my limbs functioning, then staggered to a bus stop, hiding in bushes behind it, shivers travelling through me in brutal convulsions. A woman out walking her poodle in the grey dawn caught sight of me and crossed the road so quickly I could have been the antagonist in a Stephen King novel. Had an old travel card in my pocket, and, considering my financial state, intended bluffing my way on to the bus with it — Lisa tells me the drivers barely bother looking when you flash your ticket at them — but even in this extreme, when a bus appeared I realised I wouldn't be able to make myself do it, and fed a precious one pound twenty into the ticket machine.

The driver didn't even bother *barely* looking.

But the bus was warm and empty, the seats soft, and I couldn't care less where it took me.

Far too soon, it terminated at Paddington Station.

I just walked aimlessly then, trying to stay warm. Now find myself on Edgware Rd, a little after midday, a kind of little Arabia by the looks, hijabs and burkas, men crowded around hookahs in cafés, watching soccer and Aljazeera.

The smell of kebabs filling my head. Haven't eaten in an age either.

Stop and watch through a window. A clean-cut Arab boy with an earring and green eyes slices meat from a loaf with the flamboyance of a stage performer. Liquid fat glistening on the meat, trickling down, collecting in a silver gutter. Tomatoes, lettuce and chillis, please; hold the onions. Easy on the mayo, heavy on the garlic sauce.

The kid returns some change to the customer, then happens to look my way. I'm feeling so sorry for myself that I stare back sullenly for a moment. The kid says something to his colleague, then they're both looking at me and laughing, and I turn to flee so hurriedly I walk straight into a fresh flower display, upending buckets across the pavement. The big voice of a tiny woman flays my back with Arabic as I jog away.

Almost as bad as having no wallet is having no phone. And worse than having my wallet in the hands of thugs hunting me is having my phone in the hands of thugs hunting me. It means they've got access to the phone numbers — and in many cases the physical addresses — of practically everyone in my life. So not only can I not call anyone whose number I don't know by heart — which is barely any of them — I can't visit either. For their safety as much as mine. Look at the trouble people got into this morning just through knowing me.

Same reasons I can't go back to the house any time soon.

I guess that having my passport in those cunts' hands is the least dangerous of the three, but it somehow feels like the biggest violation of all.

Invested in a small bottle of water back at Paddington; it needs refilling. Feel like a shoplifter walking into a McDonald's and heading for the toilet without buying anything. A young staff member is cleaning vomit from the steps of the urinal, and the back of his shirt proclaims 'I'm lovin it'. A lurch as I catch sight of myself in the mirror. No wonder I'm getting short shrift in the eye-contact stakes. My hair's standing up in mad, gel-congealed clumps. My face is dirty from the cross-country running and sleeping, as are my clothes. Do as good a clean-up job as I can with the carbolic soap and tiny basin. Steal some toilet paper in case of running nose or guerrilla defecation. Actually feel a little better as I hit the street again.

I'm a long way from the house now, and this is a big old city, but chance meetings seem to take place with uncanny regularity here: I'm feeling far from safe in the open like this. Then I happen past an Oxfam shop and see the chance to cull a bird or two from the flock wheeling above me.

I may be five quid lighter by the time I come out, and minus the jacket that cost me sixty, but I've got a black beanie pulled down to my glasses, a grey scarf round my neck, and a long woollen trenchcoat that looks like it might have played a part in Napoleon's retreat from Moscow. Examine myself in a window, and yeah, I've certainly descended a rung or five in the presentation stakes, but even I barely recognise myself. Feeling warmer too, and less viscerally frightened of the rain that's starting to spit.

Invest in a punnet of chips and half loaf of bread, and eat on a bench outside an Argos. By the fourth chip butty my ordeal is starting to feel part adventure. I loved to hike and hunt back home, pit myself against the wilderness for a few days, and in some ways this isn't all that different. Guess the biggest difference is that at least here, surrounded by people — this landscape made wilderness only through lack of the correct tools — there's no chance of actually dying.

———

After he had eaten, Alex found his biggest enemy through the afternoon of that first day was boredom. He tried curing that with a fat sci-fi novel bought for twenty pence in a second-hand bookshop. But the characters were cardboard cut-outs, the prose less than voluptuous. With his mind slipping from the words, reading and rereading the same paragraph, discomfort began taking its toll. Given the rain, the choice of seating was seriously limited. He refused to sit on the ground like the homeless derelicts that dot the cityscape, and the angled seating in the bus shelters seemed ergonomically designed to inflict pain on anyone using it for a period longer than the average interval between buses.

With the sun long gone, tiredness seeped through his head and limbs, heavier and heavier. He caught himself a moment before he slid off the seat in a bus stop. This more than anything killed the sense of adventure and self-reliance that for a while had kept him buoyed.

The wind picked up, gusts flinging rain into his face, cutting through the overcoat. A display above a cinema — a group of friends laughing breathlessly as they dashed out of the rain — told him that the temperature was down to minus two. He tried to factor in the wind chill. Thought again of where he might possibly sleep tonight. Felt the temperature of his stomach plunge five degrees.

Then the rain changed to sleet, driven rattling by the wind across cosily lit windows.

Back against the wall of a Starbucks, the coffee smelling of distilled safety and health, he removed his glasses to wipe mist from them, and something big and wet struck him in the eye. It was too soft to hurt, and he soon blinked it out and got his glasses back on . . .

. . . and saw that the sleet had changed to snow.

Where the fuck am I gonna sleep?

Two pretty woman in furs came giggling out of the door beside him. They noticed him at the same time, and their laughter sliced off. Looked away too quickly, though they were careful not to let him out of sight completely as they took a wide berth around him, one of them flinging a last look over her shoulder as they linked arms.

He stumbled away, on to a road, leaping in terror as a squeal of brakes and a horn sounded right beside him, the bumper of the taxi stopping inches from his leg. A man with slicked hair and olive skin thrust his head through the window: 'You wanna get killed, you dozy cunt, you go and mess up some other mug's car!'

Alex: 'S-s-sorry, mate.'

'Just get outta my fucking way before I throw you out!'

Got off the road, clinging to a lamp post. The cabbie gave him a glare and a finger as he drove past.

Alex looked around. Saw a Hyatt down the road. Then, knowing he could walk into the place and be tucked up in bed within minutes if only for one of two pieces of plastic hidden from him somewhere in the city, his mouth curled into a bitter grimace. His stomach gave a long grumble. Looked at the dark windows in the hotel, rooms that would stand empty all night, rooms that, should he be granted use of one, could easily mean the difference between life and death tonight.

Rooms? Jesus, some kindly concierge would earn Alex's eternal gratitude just by letting him lie down in a *hallway* for a few hours.

. . . But that wasn't gonna happen. Alex realised like a physical blow that, in this corner of time and space, his life was worth less than a two-by-one metre area of carpet space. Of office space. Of the space in the boot of someone's car.

These people would rather see me die than run the risk of soiling the boots of their cars.

A doorman in tails and top hat bowed as he held the hotel door open for a stately older man and two women dressed for dinner and a show. Alex was surprised to find himself shadowing them as they passed.

'Awfully sorry to trouble you good people, but I'm in a real bind here. If you could spare me a pound or two towards a bed in a hostel it might well keep me from freezing to death tonight. I'd pay you back every penny plus interest, I swear it on my mother's soul.'

He might as well have been invisible. Only that's not correct: they knew he was there all right, their suddenly silent and fixed faces spoke very loudly of that.

'*Please.* I'm in a lot of trouble.'

No effect, and his footsteps slowly died as they hustled away.

He tried the same speech, with the same result, on another group coming the other way. Tried a lone man. Nothing.

Lowering the bar on the next party: 'Could you spare me some change, please?'

A man frowned, and said, 'Sorry, pal, I can't help you.' And just his deigning to reply gave Alex a spurt of gratitude.

'Can you spare any change, sir? . . . Spare change, ma'am? . . . Spare a few coins, please?'

I'm begging for about a minute before I fully understand what I'm doing. The shock is so bad the exhaustion and hunger slough off me. I sit down on the hotel steps, snow swirling around me.

A voice from behind: 'Clear off. You can't beg out here.'

It's the hotel doorman, coming towards me, a little guy with a big swagger.

'I'm not fucking begging any more, am I.'

Heard-it-all-before: 'Whatever. Just piss off. We don't need your sort round 'ere.'

Heating up and standing up. He's a couple of steps above me, leaving us nearly the same height. '*My* sort? Who do you think you are? Holding doors open and smiling for scraps makes you better than me, does it? You're as much a beggar as anyone, you're just on a better blag.'

His jaw sets. 'Don't fucking push it, loser. Piss off, sharpish.'

'Loser?' Sniggering at him: 'Listen to your accent. You're as working class as they come, mate. Worked your way up to fucking *doorman* and think you've cracked high society, do ya?'

It's so unexpected I don't realise what he's doing until the sole of his boot crashes against my chest. I reel back, keeping balance for the first pace, then slipping on the steps. A sickening swoop, time slowing almost peacefully . . . landing flush on my tail bone, pain like sheet lightning, knocking my head hard as I roll off the final step to the pavement.

He stands over me, saying things I can't hear through the agony; another explosion against my mouth, then he's gone.

Pain immobilises me for a long time. I should be terrified that I've broken something. I'm not. Finally I'm able to roll to my side. Wiggle my legs to check they're still working. They are. I don't stand up though. What's the fucking point? I'm just gonna lie here until the snow and the wind kill the pain in my spirit as well.

A new voice, close to my head; a reek of stale alcohol: 'C'mon, son, up ya get. That little cunt'll be calling the cops on ya, he's fucking notorious for it.'

Peering up. Framed by the snowy halo of a street light, some old guy is bending over me, long hair and beard matted with gunk. Burst capillaries, vivid crimson, underscoring his eyes. Some Santa Claus from a gothic parallel world. Feel his hands under my armpits; he grunts loudly as he hauls me up.

Me, dizzy with pain, disoriented, excess liquid from somewhere interfering with my tongue: 'Who are you?'

Gathering the battered satchel and the bin liner he'd dropped: 'I'm nobody. Same as you. Let's go.'

'. . . Go? Go where?'

'Someplace warm. Warmer than here anyway.'

He moves off quite quickly given the limp and the bow in his spine. Turning back briefly when I don't follow: 'Suit yourself.'

But the cold feels rooted in my genes now, and it takes me just a few seconds longer to admit that he's the best thing going. Walking is painful, but I soon catch him up.

Saint Hobo doesn't talk, doesn't even look at me for a few minutes; labours through the lights and the snow, people stepping around us without looking.

Spitting more liquid, realising it's blood, that the doorman must have punched me as well.

'Why did you help me?'

'You looked like you needed it.' Handing me a tissue: 'Swab your lip with this.'

Turn on to Oxford Street.

'What's your name?'

He frowns at me. '. . . Some folks call me Owen.'

'Did you see him kick me, Owen?'

'Saw the cab nearly kill you too.'

Startled: 'You were spying on me?'

'No. Just tend to notice other ghosts on my patch. Notice em more than the people.'

I'm too cold and tired and hungry and sore to question that. The opulence of the shops here taunts me in a silent roar. It's worse when we pass a KFC, old Colonel Sanders grinning at the riot his aroma incites in my stomach.

Owen: 'You hungry, lad?'

'Starving.'

'Oh no you're not. You've just walked further and quicker than a starving man can.'

'. . . Well, I'm not exactly stricken by indigestion either.'

He nods. 'How much money you got?'

Suddenly wary: 'Not much.'

'Figured that one all by my wee self. How much is not much?'

'. . . Couple of quid.'

'This one's on me then. You can get breakfast. Mind my gear.'

He drops his bags and disappears into a Tescos. I'm standing across from Marble Arch, at a corner of Hyde Park, millions of pounds' worth of metal and light negotiating the massive round-about. People are skating on an outdoor ice-rink as I spit blood. Traffic kills the sounds but I can feel merriment coming off the rink in waves. The lights and the arch dissolve into a blur . . . my head snaps back up.

Owen's beside me, holding a stripy Tesco's bag. 'C'mon, lad, not far now.'

He leads me into a pedestrian underpass. A large network of passages links the park and various points along the roads. We pass piles of blankets and cardboard among the graffiti and the urine puddles, humans identifiable beneath them only by the dirty fingers jutting out, holding the covers close. Bodies so still the blankets could be shrouds. Around a corner, a younger guy sitting up, legs in a bin bag, staring blankly at nothing. More bodies and their 'belongings'.

It's still freezing down here, but the wind and snow are no more. Part of me understands that this is where I'll be sleeping tonight, but I don't accept it, hold out in my head for Owen to be heading somewhere better, some abandoned cottage in the park, perhaps, with a fireplace and a lockable door. Until he drops his things halfway along an empty stretch of passageway.

Owen: 'Home sweet home.'

The muted roar of a truck overhead, shaking the place, causing the lights to flicker.

Owen's pulling newspapers out of his bin liner, spreading them by the wall. Producing blankets and a sleeping bag. He sits down. I stay standing.

Owen, rummaging in the Tesco's bag: 'I know it aint the Hilton, lad, but you'll find no better with two quid in your pocket and weather like this.'

Voices echoing, then a small group of thirty-somethings turns the corner, walks towards us. Heading home from a nice little Malaysian joint. They're talking too loudly — defence against the fear they feel down here — and I wait the half a minute it takes for them to pass us.

Then I sit down, something going out like a snuffed candle.

Owen insists I take the sleeping bag, and my teeth are chattering too strongly to voice much of an objection. He's wearing thermals under his old army-style jacket, says them and the blankets will serve him well enough. I'm able to bunch some folds of the sleeping bag under my arse to cushion the pain in my tailbone. With a plastic spoon I eat the tins of baked beans and tuna that he opens and hands me, chewing around my split lip.

More quiet surrender as I lie down properly, eyelids like

bricks. But they refuse to close, the setting lacerating all of my instincts. Knowing the answer: 'Is it safe here, Owen?'

'No, son. Better than it looks, but it's far from safe.' Reaching inside his jacket as he lies down beside me. 'But something like this tends to buy a fair bit of peace of mind.'

He hands me the last thing I expect to see. A knife. A hunting knife. Big and sharp, blood-gutters and serrations. Finger grips in the hilt feeling fashioned just for me. Something belonging on the hip of an SAS sergeant — lethal and brash and costly, so at odds with its owner. But my shock is drowned in gratitude.

Me: 'Thank you.' Pondering where best to keep the knife, weighing readiness versus safety . . . but the eyelids are happy to fall now.

———

Alex wakes up slowly. He sighs, seems very happy and relieved . . . then his eyes open properly, and bitter misery lands on him. Closes his eyes again for minutes. Finally sits up a bit, wincing and rubbing at his tailbone, gingerly touching his injured mouth. A heavy vehicle above shakes the tunnel.

Owen, awake beside Alex, sipping at a bottle of clear fluid: 'Didn't think to see you alive for a good while yet.'

'What's the time?'

'Goin on four, I reckon. Feelin any better?'

'No. Thought I'd dreamed it all for a second, was fucking *sure* I had.'

'I used to get that a lot. You should go back to sleep: it won't get more private sleeping rough. And we haven't a lot to do down here in the way of recreation.'

'My arse is killing me from where that cunt kicked me over. I'm gonna go back and do him tomorrow. The pain woke me up.'

Owen, offering the bottle: 'Few snorts on this'd take care of that.'

'What is it?'

'Vodka.'

Alex hesitates for a moment, then takes it. Wipes the mouth clean. Almost gags on the first sip. Takes a longer one, a grimace and shudder wracking him. Gets more down on the third. Raised voices echoing down the tunnel. Hands the bottle back as Owen lights the dirty stub of a cigarette.

Owen: 'Smoke?'

'No thanks.'

They say nothing for minutes, passing the bottle.

Alex: 'How long you been on the streets?'

'Lost count. Thirteen, fourteen years all told. Bout four on this last stretch.'

Alex, shaking his head in true shock: 'How do you keep facing the next day?'

'Because I'm too far gone to change. Because I prefer it to death.'

'. . . Why?'

'Well . . . I may be getting slaughtered in this race . . . but I'm doing fuckin blinding compared to the other three million sperm I beat on the race to the egg. Ask *them* fucks how they done.' He starts laughing, but it soon turns to wet, hacking coughs, the sound booming off the walls.

Alex: 'And that's reason enough to live?'

Owen, swigging again, relighting his cigarette: 'No. What is is that no matter how bad things get, something round the corner might still make you smile. Maybe we only get one go at this . . . and I just think I've got a few more smiles comin my way yet.'

Alex is quiet, absorbing this, then he nods and smiles a little himself.

Owen, big gaps in his grin: 'See? We just gave each other another one! Haha!'

Alex: 'Gimme that fucking thing.' Takes the bottle, wiping the mouth, swigging. 'You may've got a smile, but you'll have to get me a hell of a lot more pissed than this before you'll get a laugh.'

Owen, waving a hand: 'Ah, don't worry your head too much, kid. You won't be out here long. I've seen em all. You may be mislaid for the minute, but you're far from lost. How bout some grub?'

They spend the next few minutes making tinned corn-beef sandwiches. Settle back with the bottle.

37

There haven't been a lot of men in Julian's life to whom he's had to defer, especially over recent years. And he doubts that he's *ever* deferred to someone whose accent is somewhere between Bethnal Green and Bermondsey. To many the acoustics of the conversation would have sounded thoroughly unnatural: a Daimler yielding a parking spot to a dirty white van.

Julian: 'With all due respect, Melvyn, would you care to *repeat* your explanation? Your voice on the phone was somewhat garbled.' In fact Melvyn had been yelling into a second phone at the time, and hadn't really offered Julian much of an explanation at all.

Melvyn ignores him, bulling into the traffic along Buckingham Palace Road, forcing a motorbike to brake sharply. The rider waves a fist, screams obscenities. Melvyn, muttering: 'Next time let me in then, you prima donna wanker.'

The motorbike tailgates them aggressively, and with a set of lights up ahead, Julian find himself hoping that the rider won't pull alongside and make an issue of it. Though he has witnessed naked belligerence in Melvyn only once — and been utterly convinced it was going to be the death of him — he finds himself dreading another glimpse, no matter who it's directed at. Too much like a peek at tarot cards. For a moment it seems that the lights will favour them, but the Citroën in front of them brakes to a halt, forcing them to as well. Melvyn's tight sigh sounds like steam escaping. Its import is anything but.

Then Julian's wincing as the guy in the leathers on the big, throbbing road-bike is beside Melvyn's door, snapping up the visor of his helmet, screaming about attempted murder and learner drivers. Melvyn ignores him.

Biker, banging a gloved fist on Melvyn's window: 'Oi! I'm fucking talking to you!'

Melvyn winds his window down. He sounds quite chirpy. 'Talkin? Sounds more like yellin to me. I don't much care for being yelled at.'

'I couldn't care less, you liberty-taking cu—'

But the concussive 'c' is barely out before Melvyn's door, with his shoulder behind it, slams against the biker's leg, toppling the bike, pinning the rider beneath it.

Melvyn: 'Race ya to the next lights.' Shuts his door as he gets a green; takes off. Turns to Julian: 'What was that you were sayin?'

'Ahh . . . I just wondered if you'd mind explaining again why it is that you wish me to accompany you.'

Melvyn frowns. 'Whatchu mean?' But his tone is way too high. 'We've got a problem. Fings didn't run to plan. We've gotta club in and sort it.'

'I understand that it didn't work out, but I fail to see how I can help with . . . this end of things.'

'Oh, you can help *loads*, mate. Trust me on that.'

'Well . . . It would please me greatly to be of assistance, but . . .

it's just that . . . this wasn't really part of the arrangement, though, was it? I feel I've done all that was asked of me.'

'Course you ave, pal, course you ave. You played a blinder. Only we *all* done what were asked of us, and it still went Pete Tong. So this is what's known as above and beyond the call of, know what I mean?'

'Absolutely . . . Only . . . this kind of thing really isn't my field. I fear I'd be more hindrance than help.'

'You just sit back and let me be the judge-a that, mate. I won't be askin ya to do nufin I don't think you're capable of.'

Julian clears his throat. 'I appreciate that, Melvyn . . . but—'

Melvyn sits on the brakes suddenly, straining Julian against his seatbelt as they stop outside a cake shop. Turns to Julian fully, voice dropping several octaves, the phoney mateship miles behind.

'Now you fucking listen to me.' Julian tries not to shrink from him. 'Only two-a my lads know anythin about any-a this. *Any* of it. Less loose lips, less sunken ships. I like it that way. How bout you?'

'Christ yes!'

'Right. Now I've got them trackin down grass A right now. Which leaves me short of back-up. You're it. For ush-ush purposes, you would be even if you didn't ave oil on grass B. But you do. Now I wanna 'ear what you know.'

Julian manages to hold Melvyn's stare. 'I told you on the phone.'

'Refresh me.'

'I couldn't arrange the stock alone without denouncing myself. So I created a wicket-keeper. I promoted him in order that he have enough power and knowledge to have been able to orchestrate it himself. Then I quietly ordered him to set the stock up, and made sure there was no trail back to me.'

'No trail beyond 'is word?'

'Exactly. So as long as there was no link from me to you, it would be his word against mine.'

'And you're a pillar-a the community. Wiv impeccable breedin. Family cronies right fru the establishment. And a lawyer that could-a got Uncle Adolph a suspended sentence.'

'Precisely.'

Melvyn smiles. 'You cold son-of-a-bitch.'

Julian doesn't bother replying to that.

Melvyn: 'So why didn't you fill me in on this?'

'. . . Look . . . you knew I'd have to engineer something. What difference did it make if you knew the details or not?' Julian sees the drop from the tightrope he's walking crooning to him from within Melvyn's pupils. Then, the silence inspiring him: 'You didn't tell me *you* had a mole on the floor!' More silence, more inscrutable staring, and Julian blurts: 'How would it have helped anyway?'

A sneer: 'Ow much were spent on your education?'

'. . . Excuse me?'

'Ow do you think your patsy twigged?'

'I have no idea. You haven't told me exactly what went wrong.'

'What went wrong was that your lil fall-guy was waitin at the gate when the truck showed up, wiv five witnesses, in mid conversation wiv the fucking OB.'

Julian's stomach drops, but just for a moment. 'No. I told you. The police know nothing of this. Security haven't even logged an incident report. Alex must have been bluffing.

Finally Melvyn lets Julian's eye go. Sits back in his seat. 'Yeah. He must-a been.' A last sidelong look that dries Julian's mouth: 'Luckily for you, old son.'

Julian: 'So . . . how did Alex twig?'

Shifting the car into gear and pulling out: 'Lack-a communication. Turns out your patsy and my mole are only fucking buddies, int they.'

A bomb full of foolishness lands on Julian's head. Hundreds of hours of scheming and triple-checking, countless sleepless nights. To have the near-flawless plan undone for want of a quick conversation. That and fucking friendship. But then he feels the fog of ambiguity and danger that's blinded and tormented him since that first phone call at two in the morning starting to thin.

Julian: 'That's very unfortunate . . . but it could be worse, you know.'

'I know.'

'So what do we do?'

'You know Alex. Will e go to the cozzas?'

Julian mulls on this for almost a minute. 'I very much doubt it. He's got no evidence to speak of. What about your mole?'

'No chance. E knows what appens to grasses.'

Julian, barely daring to think it: 'So . . . we can just forget the whole thing?'

'Me, I *might*'ve been willin to walk away. Alex aint shit to me. And Ryan . . . well . . . at the end-a the day e's a good kid and I done wrong by im. And e showed real bottle elpin 'is pal out like that. So as long as e kept well off my radar, I could probably've lived wiv not draggin im back into it. But you? What's Alex like? Ow would you feel carryin on business as usual wiv an employee like im — even an ex-employee — knowing what e does about ya?'

The thought made Julian queasy again. 'I'd feel like a paperboy working Sniper Alley.'

'That's about what I figured. It's all hypothetical anyway.'

'Why?'

'Cos your ware'ouse is still a pair of nymphos knockin on my door legless at four in the a.m. The job's not blown.'

A distinct drawback to being in the clear, Julian now realises.

'But you're not willing to go through with it while . . . while the security breach remains active?'

'Not on your nelly.'

Thinking about what that entails: '. . . Is it really worth it?'

Melvyn's head swivels, and Julian's matches it against his volition. 'You come up wiv anuva way-a recompensing me for the murder-a my friend yet?'

'. . . No.'

'Well you better fucking *pray* it's worf it then, intcha.'

———

LISA

Something's changed in him. Or *with* him, at least. I can't for the life of me work out what. And I haven't found the nerve to ask yet. I noticed it from the first word over the intercom, when I leapt to the wrong assumption (though I couldn't keep from looking in the shower drain for alien hair in the morning). He took his time coming down to me; I saw him peep through the curtains and take a good look — at me, at the area around me, up and down the street. Then he came out, threw fifty to the cabbie — didn't even bother telling him to keep the change — and whisked me inside as if a lion pride had been reported in the vicinity.

And then he fucked me like a man released from ten years' solitary confinement.

Which isn't that big a departure: he's a great fuck ordinarily anyway. But last night's . . . Jesus. It surpassed even our first drunken, debauched rampage, and that one had earned itself a place in my top five by the second hour (of an eventual four).

But it was raw emotion last night, not much of the dirty or the playful. Reminded me a bit of a guy I went out with in uni. His mum died in a car crash. He held me and wept all day. Then he got shit faced and screwed me like I had the power to bring her back.

I had a speech prepared about why I was there — though it stopped some way short of telling him that I had effectively moved in — but I got through less than a sentence of it, him telling me I should shut up because he meant every word when he told me that this was my home whenever I wanted it to be. I loved him for that.

Liked him an awful lot, at least.

Went to sleep on Julian's chest, then woke up alone. Had been dreaming I was dressed all in white, sharp-nosed priests binding my hands, peasants building a bonfire. He was in the kitchen, on his mobile. I skulked in the hall and attempted an eavesdropping; couldn't make out the low words — he was doing most of the listening anyway — but they were bleeding stress and tension.

He wanted to take me out at around nine, a drive in the country, then lunch at a golf course his friend owns. I wanted more sleep. His eyes crinkled with faint annoyance at that (guess that's the first of my habits that'll cease being endearing) but he didn't complain, just lay beside me watching foreign films on Sky, sipping Johnny Blue, slipping out to talk on the phone now and then. I hinted that I was hungry at one, and when I next awoke it was to the sound of the door buzzer and a delivery from the local French restaurant.

Halfway through washing my hair when he slid the shower door open and had me standing up. Then I turned around and dropped to my knees, stared up at his eyes as I wanked him, tongue flicking his balls, soaping a finger and slipping it in his arse as he came on me.

Then he took another call and went silent and pale. Couldn't tell me when he'd be back. Held me for a long time, then walked out like a man served with conscription papers. He left on foot, trudging down the road with his head bowed.

———

RYAN

I never dreamed it would end like this. Of course, without a solid plan there was no predicting how it *would* end, but if forced to sit down and make fifty guesses at what the final phase of my time here would look like, not one of them would have borne much resemblance to this.

I suppose I should be feeling hard done by, not just for the obvious reasons — i.e. getting blackmailed into criminal enterprise by the world's biggest cunt, then having him wanting you dead — but for more prosaic ones as well. 'Cause I've seen countless Southerners wind up their time in London, and a lot of them had such a ball in those final weeks and days that it went down as one of the highlights of their whole era. Endless piss-ups and meals out, visits and phone calls, calloused palms and cracked ribs, pacts of eternal friendship and loyalty and plans for rendezvous. In some ways maybe that made getting on the plane even harder, but at least it could have been done with some sense of completion.

Instead of . . . what? Slinking out to Heathrow with not a handshake or clinked glass with any friend made in four-odd years. No gifts for the folks back home because shopping might as well be

Russian roulette. Cringing all the way to Passport Control.

Only none of that really matters. Because the end of my era is weighed down with something a lot more difficult and depressing than missing out on a farewell bash.

Nadia: 'You never told me you had no visa.'

You never asked? I thought I was sorted workwise and I didn't want to worry you? It wouldn't have made any difference: I can't stay now anyway?

'. . . I'm sorry.'

She nods after a while, lips twisting in a sad little smile I've never seen before. It says, 'Just when I think the world's on my side it turns around and slaps me again. But there are plenty who have it far worse than me, so I won't cry this time either.' And to see it, to know I'm the cause of it, turns my own heart against me.

'Look . . . I haven't said I'm leaving.'

'Yet. What else you gonna say? You want me to come live with you in Orkney Island? I can milk cows and you work for cash in fish warehouse?'

Closing my eyes: 'It's not as bad as that.'

But it is. It totally is.

She hugs me and my breath catches. 'Shut up, Ryan. Leave my last memories of you pure. You owe me that.'

'I owe you a lot more than that.'

Touches her nose to mine. Her eyes are dry. 'I am an Arab. Tragedy and pain are planted in my bones. We have a saying: "Do not ask me to draw rainbows: all of my ink is black". You don't have to worry about me.'

And that's just it: I'm as worried for myself as for her.

Shouldn't really have come to her. Even though we're both sure he won't look for me here. It was her idea that we deliberately foster in Melvyn the impression that Nadia would sooner walk the streets of Baghdad in a miniskirt on the arm of a GI than have the slightest social dealings with the likes of me. But there's always an outside chance that someone he knows has happened to see us out and about together. There were other places I could have hidden; when you love someone as much as I'm supposed to love her, you should move heaven and earth to shield them from even the most remote likelihood of danger.

But, with my London plans so radically rewritten, I soon realised that spending my last few days in the city, in the country — in the fucking hemisphere — anywhere where she was not would have been like spending them in a coffin.

She goes into the kitchen to cook dinner. Actually *cook* dinner, as opposed to slapping ready meals in the microwave. It's a big departure. She did the same with lunch — I lied well in praising her efforts — and I wonder what it means.

We open a bottle of bourbon after eating. It's her idea, and I'm not really that keen but don't once consider objecting out loud, and in an hour we're drunk and laughing and having such fun you'd never guess how finite the relationship has become. We made love in the morning and afternoon, and the experiences nearly wrenched my heart from its moorings, and the clothes are coming off again by the time we've killed the bottle, but no love's gonna get made this time, I can feel it. Saladin gets locked in the bedroom, and within a minute we're fucking like the damned.

It was tough letting her leave for uni this morning. Worried about letting her beyond my sight for safety reasons. Not wanting to waste any of the precious moments we've got left. But her mouth told me she hasn't missed a lecture in two years, and her eyes told me that she may be about to let me leave her with no love in her life but she's sure as hell not going to let me damage her future in any other way.

I can't be seen on the streets, so the only times I've left the house since arriving have been to take Sal running in the park at night. I needed *TNT*, so Nadia walked half an hour to the closest bin, then brought one back to me. Decent of her to go an hour out of her way considering all I want the magazine for is to shop for a flight home. Not that I had the bottle to tell her that. Though I'm sure she guessed.

I'm not supposed to, but she's not the only one I'm abandoning, so I share half my fry-up with Sal before hitting the travel pages. Counted me cash for the first time in two months a while ago; pleasantly surprised to find a fair bit more than I'd expected.

Twelve thousand sterling.

Crime might not pay but it sure gives good credit.

Find myself eyeing up some of the stop-over deals — Mexico City, Mombassa, Rio; picture myself nursing an elaborate cocktail from the safety of a beach chair, or jumping off a cliff into a spring in the hills of an Indonesian island. Then picture myself picturing her by a bus stop on a filthy London street as the grey fades to black at 4 p.m., buffeted by grim people in overcoats, people who aren't saying a word to her, an hour still to commute before arriving home to a dog and a Tesco's ready-meal.

Narrow my search to direct flights only. What a saint. Find some good deals, and call for availability on one, but the chick puts me on hold for so long that by the time she gets round to giving me the time of day I just hang up in her fucking ear. Call for another one, and the bloke wants my phone number so he can call me back when he can be arsed dealing with another possible tyre-kicker. When you're being hunted by organised criminals, giving your name and number out to strangers aint the slickest move in the world, so I give him short shrift as well.

Then I get to thinking about how I'm gonna get all this cash home. Don't fancy adding smuggling to my list of special skills, and so I start looking at money transferral options. But if the bloke with the bassy African accent who answers at the first place I ring thinks I'm entrusting any of my ill-gotten gains to him then he's been chewing *qaat* for way too long, because he sounds to me like a seasoned 419 scammer. You know, those emails from saintly sorts informing you that with a little of your help a hundred million US dollars can be liberated from the Swiss bank of some genocidal despot and delivered to its rightful inheritors. After your twenty-five percent has been skimmed off. They're called 419 scams after the subsection of the Nigerian penal code that criminalises the act of obtaining money by deception, and after I hang up on him this gets me thinking about the plethora of potential pitfalls in sending dirty money around the world, the jackals both legal and illegal, and I decide this needs a little more research and mulling before any steps can be taken.

Time to make some calls Down Under, to Dad or to some of the lads, let them know that the wanderer is returning, arrange a bed and shit. But I'm a few digits into it when I get to thinking about how long it is since I've been in contact, how hollow the excuses are going to ring, and how much easier the apologies will slide down over handshakes, yarns and schooners.

Nadia comes home at five. I've cooked a casserole and cleaned the whole gaff top to bottom, but she doesn't say much, spares me just a peck on the lips and a stare, while big Sal gets a five-minute massage. She lies down on the floor beside him afterwards, one arm around his neck, face buried in his coat, his chest the only thing moving. The picture is soon stingingly poignant. I wish she'd move or talk, but she doesn't. So I head into the kitchen and prepare the grub, going through the tasks robotically, my mind in some grey limbo world where the only thing senses are sure of is a clock ticking down.

Neither of them has moved by the time I bring the plates out — though Sal is wide awake and looks torn between not disturbing her and turning around to offer comfort. His eye tracks me with knowing recrimination. I can't think of a thing to say. Not a single word. I doubt Shakespeare could. In the end all I can think to do is lie down beside her.

Her body stays stiff against mine, and I sincerely wish for a car-sized comet to crash into the house.

I make myself hold her for the hour or more it takes her to stand again.

What a guy. What a rock.

———

—Where are you, Lease?

— . . . I'm at *his* house.

—Thought so. How long are you gonna stay for?

—I dunno.

—Are you coming to work tomorrow?

—I doubt it.

— . . . What are your plans?

— Plans are for architects and aldermen, Katie.

—I used to love that free and easy shit from you, but I'm not buying it any more. You can't bludge off Julian forev—

—What about you?

— . . . My visa's up in March.

—You still thinking about applying for another one? Highly skilled migrant?

—Not any more. Back to plan A.

—What? Working till summer, then trans-Siberian?

—Yeah. Angela's teaching English in a town outside Beijing, says I could get a job there in days.

—Would you be up for that?

—Not for long. I'm more into overlanding down through Tibet

and Bhutan while the summer lasts, head in home's general direction.

—Sounds cool.

— . . . Why don't you come with me?

— . . . I haven't got the cash for it. I've got enough to fly home with a stop or two, not much else.

— . . . I could spot you.

—Thanks, babe, but my conscience won't allow you such a high-risk investment.

— . . . How do you feel about going home, Lease?

—Terrified. You?

—I'm looking forward to seeing everyone, to living like an Aussie again, but I've got no idea what's gonna happen when that wears off. What about you?

— . . . I sometimes wish I'd never come here.

—Why?!

—Everyone back home's gotten on with their lives, Kate, you know? Career, social base, investments. They don't know any different, so they've got nothing to pine for. So not only will I be back at square one, but maybe no matter how well things work out for me down there, maybe it'll never be enough. Or maybe I'll give in and keep travelling, keep searching for something I'm not sure I'll recognise if I find it, and one day I'll wake up thirty-five with no kids, no money, no career and no idea where home is.

—Don't talk like that, babe. We're all in the same boat as you. If we stick together we can help each other through anything.

—Stick together. Right. That used to sound really soothing at three in the morning when we rolled in and sat round the lounge, still half wasted, the big city buzzing all around us. But we were kidding ourselves on borrowed time. When reality bites, we're all from different countries. And even those friends we made here from our own countries, most of them will end up settling in different towns from us: we'll see them once a year if we're lucky.

— . . . Yeah . . . but . . .

—When it comes down to it, the life of the traveller is the life of the lonely. Constant goodbyes to loved ones, to people you might never see again; returning to places you once knew to find that the water flowed on and stranded you upstream.

—Remember the golden rule, though, when the old traveller blues set in. All those at home, those who never made it out, deep down, they all wish they were us. You know you'd have felt like that if you hadn't of left.

— . . . Yeah . . . but you know what, Kate? What none of us who get on the plane stop to think about?

—What?

—One day we could just as easily be wishing we were *them*.

— . . . You can't really be regretting this! Seeing the world, meeting the people, tasting the cultures, face to face with the weird and the wonderful, the high times and the grim, discovering and challenging yourself. It's all a trade-off, babe! You go home and listen for a while to the attitudes and ignorance of the settled, and yeah, they might have their feet planted in ground they know, but you tell me then if you still wish you were one of them.

— . . . Yeah. But . . . I dunno. Sometimes it feels like I went travelling to find myself and just ended up more lost than when I started out.

—For fuck's sake, Lease, you're only twenty-five! You're grumbling away like a spinster of sixty!

— . . . Maybe you're right.

—Maybe schmaybe . . . Everyone's asking after you.

—What are they all doing?

—The house's empty. We're just gonna stop paying the rent and lose the bond, it's the same either way. It was a wake-up call for most of the old hands: they're making plans to move on. We're all scattered around now, dossing and shit. Some people wouldn't take us in when they heard what we were running from though.

—Any word from Ryan or Alex?

—Neither of them are answering their phones.

—I'm worried about them.

—You shouldn't be. They'll be fine.

—Fine? What happens when those cunts find them?

—They won't. And if they do, they made their own beds. Anyway, we're all gonna meet for a drink on Friday. You'll come, right?

—No fucking way.

—Those pricks won't find us, Lease.

—It's not just that. No offence, Kate, but I've had enough. I think I'm over the old tri-nations-traveller endless party thing.

—Oh right. Moved on to a better class altogether, have we?

—Don't be a bitch, it's not like that. I've been getting jaded with it all for a while now.

—If you say so. What about him, anyway?

—What *about* him?

—How are things between you two?

— . . . They're really good.

—Good enough to keep you in London longer?

— . . . Maybe. I like him a lot.

— . . . Jesus, you're not in *love* with him, are you?!

— . . . I'm not sure.

—Lisa! What's the fucking matter with you?!

—What do you mean?

—The man's a cunt! You used to *hate* him!

—I didn't even know him!

—Well, you knew what he stood for, and you hated *that*! Has that changed too?

—*No!* . . . I dunno. It's just . . . Look, I'm just starting to think

384

that part of getting older is realising that nothing's really as black and white as it once looked.

—Oh yeah? Well *I'm* starting to realise that nobody in history who betrayed their principles ever said to themselves, "Fuck it, I think I'll sell out now." They all rationalised and vindicated it in their heads as it happened.

—. . .Ouch.

—Where's the girl whose room I moved into two years ago? The one with Che and Nelson and Gandhi above her bed? The one who prised my eyelids open on a peace march, moshed round London with me, talking to the homeless and taking the piss out of Sloane Rangers? He's one of *them*, Lease.

— . . . There's a lot more to him than what we thought.

—Oh god, I shoulda said this to you weeks ago. I thought you were just having a bit of fun, infiltration of the enemy camp, seeing the other side of the city for a change. Score some nice pressies, shag him raw, then flip the finger and leave him panting.

—You don't underst—

—Yes I do. You were a challenge. And now you're a semi-exotic fuck. Young and pretty, irreverent and unpredictable. How long's *that* gonna be cute?

—But you haven't seen us together. We laugh and talk for *hours*.

—Of course you do, Lease: you're clever and quirky and he's snake-fascinating. But it'll wear off, and even if it doesn't, you know how appearance- and status-conscious these toffs are. He's never gonna take you home to meet Mummy.

—Mummy's dead.

—Whatever, you know what I meant. Just answer me this: have you met many of his friends yet?

—*Yes*. He wanted to take me today—

—Were they old friends, connected to the family?

— . . . I'm not sure.

—Yes you are. Look, it might feel lush but it's not your world, Lease. You weren't born into it, you didn't work your way into it, and he's sure as shit not going to escort you into it. It's your world until he's bored with you: best-case scenario.

—. . .What do you mean best-case scenario?

—I mean that love is blind. I'm not convinced he's not the calculating cunt we always thought he was. You might feel his teeth before you feel his elbow.

—I've gotta go.

38

RYAN

She sits on the floor with a laptop and a thick textbook, two thousand words to hand in before Thursday. I'm on the couch, flicking through channels. Some bird on *EastEnders* is moaning about an ex-boyfriend in her class who barely looks at her now, and my reflexive scorn keeps lodging in my brain before it can depress my thumb on the remote button. Then I feel my eyes watering.

Her name is Patricia.

Ads come, and I turn over to Russell 'the rumbler' Crowe in *Gladiator*, a film I've suffered through before, a film that should've gone straight to video instead of blitzing the Oscars. Maximus is behind bars, the public gawking at him. A kid talks to him, a kid who reminds him of his own lost son, and the conversation gives me goosebumps right down to the marrow.

Flick over again, and Rolf Harris is nursing a neglected old tom cat in *Animal Hospital*. I hate cats, and I hate Rolf slightly more, and as he strokes this one's toast-rack chest and its shudders turn slowly to purrs, I have to shut my eyes before a tear leaks out.

Look over at Nadia, and she hasn't noticed my mawkishness, absorbed in the textbook. Then I notice that she's on the same page she was on half an hour ago, and that the essay on the laptop screen has grown by less than two lines.

That hits me so hard the room seems to shrink.

With another person I'd suspect that her behaviour — the listlessness, the hollow eyes, the monosyllables — were partly overplayed for my benefit. God knows I've done as much myself in the past, if not for outright sympathy, then for attention or guilt-tripping. I'd probably do it now if I were in her shoes. But she doesn't have it in her. I'm sure of this. Life has woven too much steel and pride into her for that. In fact, what I'm seeing is probably just the dregs of a tide of depression that she's turning back at the borders.

I roll a cigarette, sense of touch anaesthetised to the textures of the tobacco and the paper, as my lungs are to the smoke that I drag down.

I've never felt this before. This brand of helplessness. This . . . *incapacitation*. The senselessness of how things are panning is stupefying. That I'm about to get on a plane alone and fly to a place ten thousand miles away *and not come back* seems monumentally absurd. A satanic murder-suicide pact. History's worst joke.

Sitting up suddenly: 'This is fucking *bull*shit.'

I surprise a flinch out of her. Revolving on her bum to face me: 'What is?'

Waving my arms: 'This!'

'What a*bout* this?'

'You know how I feel right now?'

There's a slight smile on her lips, the first with no pain in it for aeons. 'How do you feel?'

I need to make sure it's not the last for aeons. 'Like you and me are orange and the rest of the world is blue. Like . . . like you and me are in a play and we're the only ones who know our lines, but our parts are too small to salvage anything.'

She crawls to me and takes the fag, squats back on her haunches. Frowning hard: 'What are you saying?'

'. . . Let's go and live in the Orkneys.'

No response for seconds; and then a wide grin breaks her face, turning into a chuckle, a sound full of appreciation and love. But the pain's back too, with its dark, subtle shades.

She sits forward and puts her hands on my knees. 'That would be wonderful, *habibi*. Really, really wonderful . . . At first.'

'What do you mean?'

'I mean that love can conquer many things. In your West they claim love conquer anything. But even Superman get tired. Poverty, fear, loneliness, boredom, the missed opportunity, the isolation. Love changes, *habibi*, no matter who the couple. Those other things do not.'

'. . . I didn't mean the Orkneys specifically—'

'I know that. But it a good symbol. Cut off from most jobs because you have no visa. Cut off from most people because we scared who might hear of us. This would wear love away like sea on a rock.'

I know that she's right. But she hasn't heard me properly. 'I don't want us to live like that anyway.'

'Then what you saying?'

'I'm saying let's do whatever it takes.'

'Like what?'

I'm suddenly scared. Really, really scared. I guess she's been slowly stripping armour of one kind or another from me since the first night I met her, but now I find it *all* gone. Every last piece.

'Come home with me.'

Her head lowers, frown sharpening, tendrils of smoke curling around her face from an aborted puff. Not quite the reaction I'd hoped for. But then I wouldn't love her this much if I could predict her. 'Are you serious?'

'You bet your fucking arse I am.'

A gust of shock pushes her back. 'Fucking hell.' Turning away, staring into space. Tasting the word: '*Australia*.' I can see that's it never occurred to her that being with me could change her life this drastically, uproot her to a whole new continent, and my heart starts to sink as her face slowly tells me that it's too big a step. That I may mean a lot to her. But not *that* fucking much.

Then a couple of breathy giggles bubble up, right from her belly. 'Fuck, Ryan, life with you a real bloody roller coaster, you know that?' And I can see that, perhaps in spite of herself, the idea is crooning to her. She says it again, hope kicking in me: '*Au-straaaay-lia*.'

But then she turns back to me and sighs, and I can feel the veto that's occurred to her wrap itself around her like a blanket. 'But what would I do when fun stops? I need to work. I need to study. I have no work visa for Australia.'

But I know that. She's still not hearing me fully. And now there's no hope of finding a comfortable way down from this high branch I'm on. No recourse now but to leap, and the words have to fight their way through a blockage in my chest.

'. . . Then let's get marr—'

Three bangs on the door, and we jump like burglars. Great fucking timing, arsehole.

Then I become aware of Sal's big growl as he stands by the closed door into the tiny foyer. He growls when so much as the postman drops mail through the slot, but the sound now cleanly bursts the bubble of my irritation.

Leaving me in a whole different place.

She rises and crosses so calmly to the door that it eases my fear a bit (*real fear again, fear to tower over that you've just named, baseball-bats-on-skulls fear*) like she's expecting someone. Someone benign. But before she opens the first door, she tells me to come and hold back Sal, and the break from routine hollers at me.

I take him by the collar as she enters the foyer and puts her eye to the peephole.

Her voice is a mutter but it wraps my body in cold coils: 'It's him.'

Frozen to the spot.

'Go to the bedroom. I not let him in.'

I'm about to tell her how much choice I believe she's gonna have about that when the last voice I ever hoped to hear again reaches us from outside: 'I know ya there, Nadia; the light winked out when you looked fru the spy'ole.'

Me, dry as dust: 'No, stall him for a minute, then let him in.'

The foyer door closes on her and Sal, the sound of the locks beginning to open as I snatch up everything in the room that could give me away — wallet, mobile and jacket — and move down the hall as fast as I can quietly.

Leaving her to face him. To defend me. A thin wall of sand. A deluge it had no hand in making.

And I'm creeping back up the hall again without deciding to, my breath low whimpering, intent on the kitchen and its big butcher's knife.

Hear her snap some Arabic at Sal, slicing his growl off; the distinctive squeak of the hinges on the front door opening wide — no keeping the chain on then, she's gonna try for the Oscar. Holding my breath while I reach into the sink and slide the knife out from under a dirty pot.

Nadia, peeved: 'What the fuck *you* doing here, Melvyn? How you find where I live?'

'Good evening to you *too*, Sultana. Does e bite?'

'He *eats*. But only people he does not know who piss me off. How you find where I live?'

'Ryan told me once.'

'Don't fucking lie to me! They pick me up two streets from here, no driver ever comes closer than that!'

'Calm down, lo—'

'*Tell-me-how-you-find-me* or I closing this door and going back to studying.'

'. . . One of your friends who used the Euston gaff blabbed it out once.'

'And what give you the right to write it down?'

'I didn't.'

My plan changes with the poise of a blown fuse. Keep the knife but rush to the bedroom again. The coward in me, the coward, thief and scoundrel who will remain in no place without a bolt-hole, had been ready for this. The few items of mine lying around are in my pack and on my back in about five seconds flat.

The drop from the third floor — even giving on to the grass of the park like it does — is a killer, so it's a safe gamble that Melvyn hasn't left any flunkies watching it, and I'm soon out on the ledge. Take the time to ease the window down behind me for Nadia's sake (*you hero you*), and then my chest's pressed to the bricks, shuffling sideways along the ledge, far less wary of the fall than I should be. Past the neighbour's window and no one sees me. Past another, luck holding, then I'm snatching at the safety of a drain pipe and shimmying down into the park.

Resist the roar in me just to turn into the park and sprint into its depths; instead dropping the pack and crawling along the foot of the building. Straining for sounds from above, judging that at least a bark from Sal or a gunshot will have to ring out before any harm can come to her. Fully intending to run to the front door and do what I can if I hear either (*yeah, yeah*).

The park fence begins where the building ends, and I peer through its bars into the car park. Melvyn's brought the red Lexus. It's parked quite close to me. It looks empty, but I sit and watch, waiting for movement.

Which doesn't come.

Offering my soul to Satan, or my sex life to God, whichever of the two will make Melvyn appear first, make him wave her a sheepish goodbye as she watches from the lounge, make him slide behind the wheel of the car and fuck calmly off.

He doesn't come. Seconds marching through me like fire ants.

Think about phoning him again, the way I rescued Trent, but there's no way he'd buy that a second time; it'd just undermine any good she's doing. And as time goes by something in me becomes more certain that no news is good news, that this is something well within her capability. That in the food chains of Western society Melvyn may be a hyena, but in the ecosystem where this girl grew up — where the fucking *authorities* were tyrannosaurs — old Melvyn would be about the equivalent of a mild-mannered mongoose.

Then the inspiration of the terrified rocks me like a sonic boom.

An idea brimming with risk. And breaking from cover. Therefore a stupid idea. Not my style.

But an idea so beautiful and so brazen that with Nadia up there deflecting my hounds, if I don't do it then I *should* just fuck off into the park and hide properly. Slink from shadow to shadow, all the way to Heathrow.

I crawl back to my pack.

Because I've got a key for the Lexus.

39

Alex comes out of New Zealand House and on to Haymarket with a face like a thunderhead. He needs a crap. The staff hadn't let him take one inside. Crosses to a Burger King and into the toilets. Fills his pockets with tissues after he's finished, seething so loudly in his breathing that the people crowding the basins, people he barely sees, fall back from him. Then he sees them and despises them, a bitter resentment at watching the world turning, business as usual, utterly indifferent to his plight.

Washing his hands, shaking his head at the state of himself in the mirror. Three days without a shower, and grime and grease are dark on his stubbled cheeks. Gunk in the corners of his eyes behind the dirty, cracked lenses of his glasses. Nose an angry red from the vodka, from the cold, from a flu he's picked up, hardened snot collecting under his nostrils. Big, pussy scab on his lip. Debris from the street clinging to the beanie he dares not remove. Glad the mirror is small so that he doesn't have to deal with the full state of himself. Imagines how he must smell.

Sighs and shuts his eyes, the anger sluicing out.

Of course *they turned you away, you fucking clown; look at you.*

He'd been so excited and eager to get in there, not just for the help they would give him, but to share his plight with people he was sure would care. Fellow Kiwis. So sure of himself, of them, of the ways of his compatriots, that he hadn't even thought to make himself as presentable as he could. Hadn't even washed his fucking face.

He'd expected to be shown through to the High Commissioner, or at least an aide of, within a few minutes; to sit down to coffee as they goggled at Alex's misfortune and figured out a way for him to access his bank accounts.

He hadn't even been allowed to use the toilet. The receptionist's pretty nose had wrinkled at the sight of him — probably the smell as well — and when it became clear that he had no means of proving his name, let alone his nationality, it just kept wrinkling further. His voice had risen then, and other staff nearby who had been pointedly ignoring him began instead to stare. Then someone commented that his accent sounded a bit weird, and he saw the inference take root all around him: *You're just a bum on a blag, impersonating a Kiwi in your latest street-sly scam to get something for nothing.* He told them that was because of his wounded mouth, pointed at the swollen scab, but that just put them off further.

Then he'd got angry. And that was that. Security were suddenly there. Summary eviction. Barred from the harbour and sanctuary he'd felt sure would be his deliverance, the only prospect that had got him through the last three nights, like he'd been barred from everywhere else in the city.

Everywhere, that is, except the streets.

He knows they could have helped him. People on holiday must have their wallets and passports stolen all the time. But to come in there looking like a skid-row lessee, stinking of booze and bodily neglect, no luggage beyond a Tesco's bag . . . Then to start yelling and swearing instead of proving his story pragmatically. He should have just sung the national fucking anthem for a start.

Feels the anger building again, this time directed at himself. Gingerly washes the stinging scab on his lip as patrons move past him, keeping their distance. Starts to apply some of the antiseptic cream he shoplifted yesterday, the act of self-maintenance starting to dilute his frustration some. He needs to give it a day or two, then go back, but first he needs to get enough money together to buy some clothes and a night in a hostel, somewhere he can shower and shave.

But first he needs to eat.

A prissy voice from behind him: 'What do you think you are doing?'

Turns to the sight of a lanky Asian guy in Burger King uniform. An assistant manager's badge.

Alex: 'Just cleaning myself up a bit, mate. Be gone in a minute.'

Assistant Manager, knowing the answer but obliged to go through the tedious motions: 'Are you a customer of this restaurant?'

Alex considers for a moment. 'Yes.'

'May I see your receipt, please.'

'. . . I haven't bought anything yet. Gonna get a burger after I'm done here.'

A scoff, but just a small one, because people like Alex aren't normally worth even talking to: 'Sure you are. Unfortunately this is not the way it works in this restaurant. You must become a customer *before* utilising our facilities. Kindly do so and then return. Or kindly leave.'

Something like gladness starts to beat inside Alex, some warped strain of glee. 'Listen to me, you officious little fuck. Number one, this is *not* a restaurant, it's a vending machine, a cardiac-arrest factory. Number two, I'm gonna be all done here in under thirty seconds, then you're never gonna see me again.'

He turns back to the basin, watching in the mirror as shock prises Assistant Manager's eyes wide. But then the guy grabs Alex's arm. 'You will leave now!'

Alex turns slowly around. Stands eye to eye with him. Rips his arm free flamboyantly. 'Word to the wise, Gopta: don't you ever lay a fucking finger on me again.'

But if Assistant Manager is scared he gives no sign, seeming just to anger further, seizing Alex's arm again. 'You will fucking leave now or I will be calling the police!'

Alex knows he can have him. One punch, two at the most. But he knows it would be madness, so he rules it out. But then he starts thinking about an elbow. He's never used one in a fight before. Practised plenty of them on punching bags, but never in a fight. He's often thought about how effective an elbow might be when at close quarters: probably easier to land than a punch, maybe more destructive too . . .

So he slams his elbow across the side of the guy's face.

And yeah, it works really well. Assistant Manager's on his side in the urinal, gazing blankly around the room.

A burly forty-something Alex hadn't been aware of shrinks back from him with his hands held up, but Alex just picks up his plastic bag and floats out. His face feels all furry and fat as he descends the stairs and walks out on to the street, stepping on to a bus that stops in front of him, flashing an old ticket at the driver, climbing to the top deck, pleased to find the front seats empty.

And then he realises that eating's been relegated from the head of his 'to do' list now. He's going to get pissed again instead. Really, really shit faced.

———

ALEX

I find Owen where he said he would be, in Charing Cross Station, sitting against a wall, talking and drinking with a younger tramp, a few coins in an upturned beret in front of them.

Almost as depressing as blowing things in the embassy is realising I've become dependent on a man attached to life by a single strand of phlegm. A man so far below the bottom rung of life's ladder that the mud has almost drowned him. I sat with him and a few other tramps for about six hours yesterday, and the sheer listlessness of them was harrowing. Staring at the ground for hours, nothing to do and nowhere to go, nothing worth pondering, nothing around the corner. Chipped, empty glasses waiting to be smashed. It was almost a relief when they were arguing — drunken, brain-dead tirades that defied any sane understanding or resolution. A few of them came to blows at one point, and even their violence seemed listless and slack.

Owen's been good to me, though. I think he enjoys having someone to talk with who hasn't yet succumbed.

He looks startled to find me sitting suddenly beside him, sipping a can of Stella.

'Alex! What the fuck? Didn't think to see *you* again.'

'I told you I'd come back, if only to give you some money. I forgot to return your knife to you too.'

'It didn't work out then?'

I tell him what happened. The other guy's fallen silent, peering at me warily.

Owen: 'That's a right bastard that is. You need to get yourself cleaned up, then go back.'

'I know. I need to get my hands on some money first.'

The other guy speaks suddenly, a slurred brogue. 'Tirty

tousand years ago, mankoind worked a twenty-hour week to feed and house himself. And he enjoyed clayn water, clayn air, beautiful landscapes and stonning sunsets.'

I squint at him, waiting for the relevance punch-line.

Owen: 'Never mind Harry here. He doesn't often get his medication any more.'

I'm too scared to ask what Harry's medication's for. 'Any vodka, Owen?'

'You wanna watch how much of that shit you're throwing down your throat, son.' But he hands a flask over anyway. 'You don't belong out here, but there's not much that'll change that quicker than blasting holes in your brain with that shit every day.'

I get a long swallow down, convulsions rocking me. Feel the heat starting to spread immediately.

Harry: 'Six ways to get money on t' streets. Steal, scam, mug, beg, deal or fuck.'

Owen: 'Or busk.'

Me: 'I like the sound of the last one best.'

Harry: 'Fuck?'

'Busk.'

Harry: 'Used to boy sticks of liquorice, may. Cut em into small pieces, wrap em in tanfoil, then sell em to tourists as eighths of hash on Leicester Square.'

Owen, looking up the platform: 'Here it comes.'

Me: 'Here comes what?'

'The 12.20 from Edinburgh.'

An inter-city train slides into the station. There are people waiting to greet passengers as they disembark, lots of handshakes and smiles, kisses and hugs. Owen's chuckling softly at the scene. Two young children spy their mum, call out to her, then tear down the platform. The mother sweeps them up, one in each arm, tears and love glistening on her face. I turn to Owen and his cheeks are creased in deep smile lines as he watches, shaking his head in wonder.

Harry, loud: 'Tat overpopulation and poverty are laynked is a myth. India has a lower population dansity tan Holland.'

The people move off, leaving the platform empty and cold.

Owen: 'We should move to platform six soon.'

Me: 'What for?'

'The 12.52 from Cardiff.'

Harry: 'Not for may, Owen. Gotta go and meet Mort, so I do. Says he'll land me Ghost for t' day.'

Me: 'What's Ghost?'

Owen: 'Black Labrador, beautiful creature.'

'What do you want with a black lab, Harry?'

'Take out a whoite cane, sanglasses, then sit down with Ghost, outsoide St Mary's hospital in Paddington. Folks coming out of tere always wanna help a poor blindman down on his luck.'

I drop another hit of vodka, then another while I'm still grimacing from the first. Handing it back to Owen: 'I might leave you to it as well, Owen. I'll meet you in the spot tonight.'

'Where you gonna go?'

'Not sure. Might try and steal something I can sell. Camera maybe. Walkman or something.'

'You'll get collared. Tell ya what: you sing like a bloody troubadour, son, heard ya the other night. Why don't you do yourself a little busking?'

Harry: 'The quack of a duck does not echo. Science cannat explain whoi.'

Me: 'Busking? What, unaccompanied? It doesn't work like that, dude.'

'I know a girl who plays guitar. She busks of a Wednesday afternoon, just up the way. She's not a bad singer, but she hates it, she's always looking for a fill-in if they're up to snuff. We'll go see her in a bit.'

I've never done anything like that before . . . But how different can it be from Maori-oke? 'Sounds worth a lash. Better than sucking knob or dealing class A liquorice.' Attack my beer then, wincing, rubbing at my elbow.

Owen: 'What's wrong with your elbow, son?'

'I turned some twat over in the toilets in Burger King. Should-a seen it, it was fucking beautiful.'

He sits sharply up: 'You done *what*? What did you do *that* for?'

Surprised and defensive: 'He was trying to stop me from having a wash!'

'Jesus H. Christ! You stupid little bastard, give me the knife back!' I flinch when he yells, '*Now*!', and pass it to him.

Then he looms over me, staring at me, face shifting, glaring at me, squinting at me, his thoughts trying to squeeze through some kind of blockage. With this dirty great knife in his hand. There are people nearby and I'm glad when he puts the knife away before they can notice it.

Owen: 'We've gotta get you off the streets. You're gonna bloody kill someone. I've seen this before.' He labours to his feet and starts gathering his things.

Me: 'Get me off the streets? How the fuck does that work?'

'The girl I told you about. Maybe she can help. If she likes ya.'

Harry: 'A rumour tat doesn't go away is not a rumour.'

We find Jema up on Covent Garden. A tall, big-boned redhead, somewhere around her late twenties. She's not much to look at, bit on the androgynous side, shoulders wider than mine nearly, broad nose, big ears.

There are varying degrees of homelessness. The city gathers strays and makes waifs. Owen talked about it last night. At the farthest extreme you've got his sort, outdoors almost always, usually the older ones. Too tired and crushed to bother blagging and scamming much; too unattractive to get themselves invited anywhere or to make new friends. Reduced to begging and scavenging. At the other end you've got those on the dossing and squatting circuits, younger types, evicted or absconded, running from something or someone, mental and social problems, deep in debt, wanderers run out of money, between institutions, whatever, just unable or unwilling to pay rent any more. Prevailing on friends until a better offer comes or the welcome runs cold. Working a little — not easy without the trappings of the settled: national insurance number, bank account, proof of address, the same reasons most of the homeless are ineligible for the dole. Forever wheeling and dealing and conning in bids to stay not just fed and dry but stoned or high and clothed semi-decently, pride and hope and enterprise still alive in them. Living on the fringes among the dealers and the hookers, the thugs and the thieves, the border between order and chaos, some to find their feet eventually and start again, some to bubble further under, accruing the knocks, burning the hands around them until there's nobody left. Nobody but prison bars, coffin walls, or the other shambling, coughing drunks.

I guess Jema to be just a phase or three into the quagmire, the quicksand not much higher than her knees. Her clothes speak of that: the funky hippyish cut, cool and jaunty but worn. Her hair's done in dreads, a low-maintenance arrangement that hides the neglect quite well. A face with some lines it shouldn't have yet, a face that hasn't seen make-up in months. But she's far from beaten; has a vigour and verve about her that speak almost of contentment, of a lifestyle choice. A confidence and knowingness that's both magnetic and proof of her being no stranger to these straits. Her size helps, the near six feet of height the perfect vessel for her grin and her cocky hips, her big hands like a conductor's, a director of human traffic.

I know she's the one we're looking for from twenty metres away. She's standing by a guitar case, chatting with a skater, a backpacker and a man in a five-hundred-pound suit. And I like her before I've heard her say a word, before she notices Owen and forgets the others, stabbing a finger at him from the end of a long arm, grinning like a lantern in the gloom of this frigid London afternoon.

'Owen!' She takes four strides towards us, and then stops because any more would take her too far from her things, and this woman stopped making mistakes like that a long time ago. Owen's face is a relief map of smile lines again, head bobbing sheepishly. He tries to shake her hand, but she slaps it down with mock affront and hugs him instead, towering over him. She kisses his cheek in real reverence, holding him at arm's length. 'Where have you fucking been, mate? It's been weeks.' Her voice is as big as her frame and her presence, the accent unchartable Middle England. 'I thought you were dead, thought I'd seen the last of you!'

I'm invisible to them but glad for it, shivers running through me at the scene. Owen tries to wave her concern away, but you can see how touched he is, how much he loves her. Lifting a conspiratorial finger: 'Told you the last time: I may not have the will or the right to take part any more, but something inside me hasn't had its fill of peeping through the windows just yet.'

'Why haven't you been by the squat? It's still good, you know. Even got hot water on at the moment. This winter's too bitter to sleep rough all the time.'

He grimaces. 'Na. I'm past the shenanigans of you kids, past even getting in the way of them. Might pop round for a shower though.'

They catch up for a while, and the third-wheel syndrome is just starting to itch when she asks who I am.

'This is Alex. He's been keeping me company last couple of nights. He was wondering if he could sing with you some.'

She turns to me fully, grey eyes boring into mine. I don't extend my hand; I know it's not time yet. A quick glance up and down, then she's staring again, hard, as if I'm being weighed somehow . . . or as if there's something wrong with her. Sneak a look at Owen: he seems apprehensive, and the icy thought of Harry and his unmedicated condition stabs my mind. Then she holds her hand out, and something like relief warms me as we shake. She's got a grip like a man's.

'So you can sing, yeah?'

Embarrassed but level, because there's a time and a place for self-deprecation and this isn't one of them: 'Yeah.'

Tilting her head as she lets my hand go: 'You're a long way from home.'

'Sure are.'

'Kiwi or Aussie?'

For some reason it doesn't surprise me that she deduced it from just three words, maybe just from one. 'Kiwi.'

Mildly intrigued: 'Now how the fuck does a clever handsome Kiwi end up sleeping rough on the streets of London?'

Stunned by the compliments, and enormously flattered: 'Long, long story.'

Once out, the words feels like a rejection, and I'm scared she might take offence; but she just nods, has been here many times. 'All the good stories are, mate. See how we go, you might want to regale us later. Nothing like a good sing-song to loosen the tongue.'

'. . . I might like that.'

She beckons with her head and we cross to where her things are, me sitting on a knee-high bench while Owen sits on his bag a little way down from us. Jema cracks the guitar out — an acoustic that even my untrained eye can tell is worth a quid or two — then sits on the case. The strong, wide-legged posture should probably look crude, but she sure as hell doesn't care, even before the guitar fits into her lap like a block into a puzzle.

She seems really good as she tunes up, effortlessly adept, and the sounds the guitar makes, the movements of her hands, the rhythms rocking her, are like glamorous extensions of her personality.

She feels no fear. This is her place.

But seeing her talent and boldness, looking at the crowds flowing around us, a big belt of nerves hits me, some high-octane stage fright. Crack a beer and drop half the can in one. Owen offers me a wink.

At last Jema turns to face me, and that weighing look is back, maybe a bit of a dare too, certainly some scepticism. Strumming and picking softly, fingers never stopping: 'What say we get your application form filled in then?'

I can only nod.

'What do you know?'

'All sorts.' But it's just bluster really, and I'm suddenly wondering how I got into this, certain my knowledge of song lyrics is far short of her knowledge of the music, part of me *hoping* we can't find enough common ground.

'Stereophonics?'

You bitch. No doggy-paddling allowed. Swim or drown, 'cause that dude's got the voice from hell on him. I should just say no, try for something easier. 'What song?'

'Ammm . . .' Changing chords as she pretends to think. '"I Wouldn't Believe Your Radio"?'

Relief and fear doing battle because I know the song, I love the song, but Axl Rose could miss the big notes in that number. She sees my hesitation, and her head cocks a few degrees, eyebrows lifting a little, the scorn unmissable. Then she changes chord seamlessly, picking up the song's opening rhythm, and it hits buttons in me straight away, my foot tapping without asking, and it's now or never, so I nod, and her grin flashes, sharp as a blade, and her playing grows louder.

I'm not sure when to come in, and I try the first word, then stall, feel myself glowing bright crimson, but she just tells me to wait; then, a few riffs later, she's starts to sing it herself, nodding me in. I pick it up on the second line, hiding behind my eyelids, and her voice gives way almost instantly, leaving me to it. I've sung it a hundred times, the tune and the pitch are no problem, maybe not even the distinctive gravel. Open my eyes on the fourth line, and she's staring at me with new light, her foot tapping the beat harder. Smiles encouragement.

But we're just two lines off the big note now, and there's still a lot of doubt about her, though I feel her wanting me to succeed for the first time.

Telling her she can have it alllllll if she liiiiiiiikes. A few seconds of strumming that feel like minutes, and I'm shitting myself, but she's holding my eye, holding me in time with her, no smile now, just frank hope and support.

And she can have it *ALLLLLL* if she liiiiikes!

I hear her whoop before my eyes open, and she's banging her head and banging the strings, and we're grinning at each other, and my nerves are gone, and my chin's bopping away, and I sing the rest of the song holding nothing back, not even the facials, Jema singing harmony.

By the time we finish there's a few people around us and a few quid in the case, and Jema's clapping louder than anyone, leaning over to give me a hug, and right now I wouldn't trade places with any of those pricks in the suits in the towers up above us.

Owen: 'I told you, boy! A voice like a fucking bard, so you do! Give us another one!'

Jema, throwing me a tambourine: 'What else do you know?'

Wiping beer off my chin: 'All sorts.'

We're about eight songs into the set, and my soul's flying like my voice, the weight of people crowding around us warmer than a bonfire. Into the last section of Midnight Oil's 'US Forces' — a request from a group of Aussies loading up on their way to the Walkabout, the third request we've taken and one I wrongly doubted Jema would know. My admiration and envy of her has just grown, not only for the playing — she hasn't missed a bridge or a note, hasn't shirked a single solo — but also for her show-manship, her courting of the crowd. There's got to be at least fifty quid in the case.

More head-spinning applause, then the sound of a mobile ringing, and Jema's taking out a phone, looking at the screen, grinning at what she sees, then answering.

'Heeeey, dude! . . . Where are you? . . . Excellent! Man, have I got a surprise for *you*! . . . Have you got your amp in the boot again? . . . *Yeah*, fucking hell, bring it *over*! . . . Right where I was last time . . . Cool, see you soon.'

Me, my high popped a bit: 'Who was that?'

Jema, buzzing: 'A student I sell lessons to now and then. He's here, he's coming over. He's got an electric with an amp on him!'

'Is he good?'

'He's getting better.' A rapping chant, head wiggling: 'Good-enough-to-lay-down-some-power-chords-and-heavy-riffs-while-you-and-I-keep-on-kicking-these-people's-motherfucking-asssssssssses!'

Said people roar approval.

Jema waves for quiet. Suddenly sober: 'OK. Time for one more before our axe-man arrives. This is a wee ditty going out to my dear departed Dad who, if there's any justice in the universe, is right at this moment being sodomised by Satan with a white-hot baseball bat. Alex, you dark horse you, I'm not even gonna ask if you know it.'

And she was right in not bothering, her speech telling me what the song is even before she starts in with the haunting intro of Pearl Jam's 'Daughter'. And the venom in her introduction, the questions it raises in me, only intensified the energy I give to the words. A good thing too, because nobody should borrow Eddie Vedder's shoes with their guns half cocked, and not even the sight of an impossibly cool-looking guy in a leather jacket and slicked dark hair who joins the crowd halfway into the song, a face I can only half make out in the low light through the tears in my eyes, not even this can shake my commitment to the song by so much as a joule.

The crowd are cheering before we've faded the music and the words down completely, and the dude cooler than Fonzie must be Jema's student because he steps in to touch her, and a wide smile cracks her pain.

New guy: 'That was fucking brilliant, Jem! Where you find this guy?!' He turns to me with his hand outstretched, and given how drained and dizzy the song has left me, the sight of his grin at close range nearly slaps me off the bench I'm sitting on.

He keeps grinning, holding out his hand, frowning when I don't take it, the smile slipping. Then he leans further down, peering at me. His grin implodes totally. '*Alex*?!'

Sigh: 'Hey, Alonso.'

Gobsmacked: '*Jesus*, man! What the fuck *happened* to you? . . . And where you learn to sing like *that*?' He stares at me for a long time, and then he's laughing so suddenly I flinch. Turns to Jema: '*Full* of surprises *this* prick, huh?'

———

Jema, taken aback: 'Where do *you* two know each other from?'

Alonso gives his trademark grin, but it's sparkling like a scalpel. 'Tell her, dude.'

'. . . We used to work together.'

Alonso, merry: 'We sure *used* to, all right!'

Alex is floundering, the drink hardly helping. Alonso is a tangible chunk of the life he's somehow been written out of, the life he's longed to return to so desperately, the one he needs to get back or possibly perish. Alonso would probably lend him money if the terms were right.

But it occurs to Alex that he won't be asking him for any, and it has nothing to do with pride or fear of rejection. He won't be asking because he feels so terrible about sacking the guy. He tries to recapture some of the managerial ire and reasoning that had flushed through him as he carried out the act, just to ease his guilt a little. Can't find a single milligram.

This guy was my friend. And I sacked him. In the name of a faceless collection of rich people.

Anger licks him. *Sold him for a man who was making me a patsy.*

'Alonso?'

'Yeah, buddy?'

'I'm sorry.'

Too puzzled: 'What for, pal?'

'You know what for. I don't want a goddamn thing from you, on my mother, but if I can I'll make it up to you some day.'

Jema squints at them as Alonso waves off the words. 'No need, mate, forget it.' But there's something in his smile now that's like biting down on tinfoil. 'We all do what we got to do.'

Alex can only grimace.

Jema breaks the loaded silence. '*Well* . . . if you two are done with the tearful reunion . . . how 'bout we rip the roof off this joint?'

Alonso, grinning like a gun-fighter: 'I hear *that*.'

Alonso wheels a trundler forward, and Alex's breath catches at the sight of the guitar he uncracks from a case. A twelve-string Gibson, so black it glows. Jema and Alonso spend the next few minutes setting up the amplifier and talking shop, then they both plug in, Alex surprised to see that she has a pick-up on her acoustic.

Alonso: 'Shall I plug the mic in for him?'

Jema: 'No way, his voice is too strong. He'll drown us out through the same amp.'

Then they're flanking him, ready to play. *Rearing* to play.

Alonso, to Alex: 'What do you know?'

'All sorts.'

They stop two hours later because Alonso's finger is bleeding too badly to carry on.

A celebration had most definitely been called for, but there was no question of Alex or Owen gaining entry to a pub, so they found one with wooden tables outside, tables chained to the wall and rarely used between October and April. Alonso and Jema had gone in and come back out with armloads of pints.

Now the table's covered with glasses. The takings had come to a hundred and eighty-four pounds. Alonso doesn't want a penny of it.

The camaraderie that had woven the three of them together, the residue still strong even though the music stopped some time ago, is like nothing Alex has experienced. Even Owen's on a high, not saying much but chuckling and grinning uncontrollably. The nearest thing Alex can find to compare it with is the bond with team-mates after a good game of rugby. But this is different. Because there's something almost sorcerous about music and its effects on people, something unquantifiable and mystic. The very

410

reason that the best musicians attract such manic levels of worship.

Whatever it is, a minute after Alonso entered the equation the music had melted the ice between him and Alex with more fullness than a blow-torch. They're talking and laughing together more now than they ever have, even telling work and *après*-work anecdotes. Then Alonso wants to know how in the hell Alex ended up on the street, and Alex just tells him. Tells all of them.

He tells them everything, relief unknotting him still more. He talks for about five minutes, from Ryan's first terrified approach, to the truck at the warehouse, to the mayhem in the house, to the little Ryan deigned to share before abandoning him.

Stunned silence.

Alonso, wrapped in a calm that Alex finds somehow chilling: 'Where is Lisa?'

'I've got no idea. Dunno where Ryan is either.'

Alonso starts thumbing buttons on his phone.

Owen: 'We've gotta get you off the streets, son.'

Jema: '*Fuck* yeah! You've got villains angry and scared of you for coming between them and a job like *that* . . . and you just spent the last few hours *busking*?'

In truth, the fear of being hunted had begun to pale as the desperation of his circumstances had mounted. Alex can't recall even weighing the increase in exposure involved in busking. Muttering: 'Na, I'm all right. I don't exactly resemble my passport photo at the mo, and I think they're based miles away—'

Alonso gets a txt. Keeps thumbing buttons.

Owen: 'Not worth gambling your life on, son.'

Jema: '*God* no! You bump into people unexpectedly all the time in this city. Look at what just happened with you and Alonso. Where did you last see *him*?'

'. . . Miles away.'

Jema: 'Prosecution rests!'

Alonso starts speaking rapidly into his phone in Albanian.

Owen: 'Jema, can he go with you? I was hoping you'd take him in earlier.'

'Yeah, of course he can. I was going to ask him anyway. We'll take off now, and you're coming too, you stubborn old prick.'

Owen: 'No, lo—'

Alonso, looking up: 'Best if Alex comes with me.'

Alex, overwhelmed: 'No, man. I can't accept that. I meant what I said before.'

Alonso lowers the phone. 'I insist. I owe you.'

'You don't owe me shit after what I di—'

Alonso's stare is rock hard. 'What you did was drop. I owe you bucket.'

Owen: 'No offence, kid, but I think Jema's probably been round the block a few times more than you have—'

Jema: 'He's Albanian, Owen.'

Owen flinches. A big reappraisal is loud on his face.

Alonso: 'I can get him out of country if need be. I can make him disappear.'

Owen: 'I'm sure you can, son. I'm sure you bloody can at that.'

Alex finds the matter beyond his hands. Swallowing his pride, he thinks he's probably better off with Alonso anyway. Part of him is sad to miss the chance of getting to know Jema though, sad to be leaving Owen as well. And there's a tug of concern inside him somewhere. He can't place his finger firmly on it, but it's got a lot to do with the enigma that Alonso is to him, the silk-on-steel act, his transformation just now . . .

He hugs Jema as she makes him promise to call her once the heat's off. Then his eyes are stinging as he hugs Owen as unselfconsciously as he once did his grandfather, as he farewells the man who quite possibly saved his life. A man with his smile quota very nearly full. His voice catches as he swears to Owen he'll see him again soon, and that he'll pay him back tenfold.

But as he follows Alonso up the road, barely hearing the harsh sounds Alonso is snapping into his phone, Alex feels with heavy certainty that he'll never be given the chance.

40

Nadia, a fierce whisper: 'You did *what*?!'

Ryan had been second-guessing his move badly for the long minutes it took Melvyn to appear and drive off, and part of it was fear that Nadia would be gutted at him for an act that might unmask her.

But her reaction is the polar opposite: she's gleaming like a kid on a treasure hunt.

'I called myself from my spare phone, then hid the spare in his car seat cover with the line still open.'

Gazing rapture at the phone in his hand: 'Fucking hell. That is *brilliant*.'

She shuts Sal in the foyer, then hustles Ryan into the bathroom, the quietest place in the flat, closing the door carefully behind them.

They whisper as they listen to Melvyn driving in silence. She's sure Melvyn hadn't expected to find Ryan here. He'd partly been interested in anything she might have learned about him in their time together, but mostly interested in offering her money to play bait in luring Ryan out, to call and pretend to be in trouble, or to offer him sex. She'd refused to get involved — even when he threatened to terminate her employment — and he'd departed, annoyed but passive.

He tells her the phone's battery is full; that he emptied the address book, inbox, call register; emptied everything before planting it.

She has an arm wrapped around him as they perch on the bathtub, heads pressed together around the phone.

'Get outta the fast lane, you vine-swingin cunt.' They both jump. *'Or I'll pull you out at the lights and open you up, on my fucking mum.'*

Melvyn had merely been muttering to himself but his voice came through with surprising clarity, the irrational impulse that he was close by kicking fright through Ryan's stomach. Then a longer, slower dread at what he had done. Nadia, though, looks to be holding back giggles.

Then a loud fart rolls tinnily through, and she leaps into the corner, as far from the phone as she can, trying to muffle her laughter with a hand.

Ryan's surprised to find himself getting bored. A peephole into the doings of a man intent on killing him . . . and he's getting bored.

But he'd won two pieces of inside oil twenty minutes after starting.

—*Des. Anyone come back yet? . . . So the gaff's still empty? . . . Give it till three, then break in and look round . . . Na, I've still got im watchin for em at the ware'ouse, so you're it till I say so.*

But since then just an hour of near-silent driving, a couple of brief stops and exits, a Big Mac and two double cheeseburgers — *If I wanted fries I would have asked for fucking fries* — some unrelated phone calls, Melvyn's chummy nonchalance mirroring the voice-mail messages left on Ryan's phone lately, chilling against the corked anger, the ruthless purpose, in the conversation with Des.

It's going on eight, and Nadia brings Ryan a plate of toasted sandwiches that are burned around the edges and cold in the middle. She's whispering for him to go and unwind in the lounge for a minute while she does an eavesdropping shift, when:

—*Saddle up, I'm outside . . . Don't fucking give me that . . . Look, I'm gonna ask you once more, just the once.*

Nadia, enthralled: 'Who is it?'

Ryan shrugs.

A door opening and closing. No greeting, just a man sighing as the car begins to move.

—*I fail to see why you need me again.*

—*Your whinin is really gettin on my tits.*

—*Where are we going?*

—*Nowhere right now. I'm just drivin cos if I stop I think I'm gonna urt some cunt. Now get to work.*

—*With what?*

—*Call every person in that phone's inventory in the UK and get their physical address. It's gonna be a long night.*

—*You're asking me to call all of them?*

—*Nobody's asking you to do a fucking thing.*

—*A: I spoke to them all yesterday, as you well know, to no avail. B: I'm very much looking forward to learning why it is you believe me capable of inveigling home addresses out of perfect strangers. C: some of them are not perfect strangers. Of these, those who don't know me directly know of me, and given my current relationship with Alex, to be seen sniffing after his whereabouts would be epically foolhardy. Then D: to make matters infinitely worse, you wish then for you or me or both to visit these properties, and possibly announce our connection and complete the triangle, which will bring both of us significantly nearer to prosecution!*

—*Are you done?*

416

—*If your idea is pursued I could very well end up* done, *all right. Old Bailey style.*

—*You got any ova ideas for trackin em down?*

— *. . . There's really no other way?*

—*Look, I've got someone watchin the ouse and anuva bloke watchin the ware'ouse. So far no joy. I've sounded out every acquaintance of Ryan's that I know, and nobody's got a scooby doo. The only ova link we've got to either of em is that fucking phone. Now, if the key can't be found fru that some'ow, the only ova thing I can think of is to try and get our 'ands on someone close to one-a them, or even close to both-a them, but I dare not dream so igh. Now that involves snatchin somebody from somewhere. And* that, *my friend, ups our risk-factor a fuck of a lot 'igher than this way.*

— *. . . What if that someone didn't have to be snatched?*

—*What the fuck is that supposed to mean?*

— *. . . I may know of someone. And I may know where she is.*

Sounds of the car braking. Stopping.

—*You may* know?

— *. . . I do know.*

—*You better start talkin real fucking fast.*

— *. . . You know that if all went to plan it was going to end up Alex's word against mine as to who facilitated things.*

—*Yeah, so what?*

—*So I wanted to fabricate some additional motive for him, something beyond material gain.*

—*Somethin against you personally?*

— *. . . I seduced a girl he was infatuated with.*

— *. . . And?*

— *. . . And I know where she is.*

—*Where?*

— *. . . She's at my place.*

—*Right* now?

—Yes.

A roaring engine shatters Ryan's spell.

It's Lisa. It all adds up. The unexplained absences. The odd decrease in her stinginess and sponging just as her drug-dealing stopped. The new look, the new things . . .

———

Lisa replies to a txt from Alonso, assuring him she's fine. Pours more claret into her glass, then sits in front of the computer again. She ponders her cards. She needs one more spade for a flush. But going after it would mean breaking her pair of Kings. She's a hundred quid down already for this session. If it was her own account, her own money, she'd bet small and keep the Kings. But then if it was her own money she wouldn't have begun visiting *losvegas.com* in the first place. Giggles at that and ditches a King, going after the flush and throwing twenty into the ante.

Her card arrives and her heart's thumping as she moves the mouse to click on it. Jumps as her phone rings. Private number, so she presses 'silent' and ignores it.

Her card is the eight of spades and she grins ferally, bouncing in the chair. She'd folded two hands ago, leaving the pot to a guy claiming to be in Pretoria, and he'd then taunted her with chat, claiming to have been bluffing. She's going to raise by five hundred in the hope that he'll think she's bluffing back at him in revenge. Then when he matches her b—

She gets a txt.

```
Its Ryn callin. Ansa or
die, no shit.
```

Answer or die? What the fuck?

It has that mock-cavalier tone that he and she used to banter with, but it's out of place. And the 'no shit' affix is a total ringer.

She goes back to the game, a little miffed at Ryan for tarnishing the anticipation she feels by throwing five — no, *six* — hundred pounds into the pot. Takes the call when the phone rings.

'Ryan?'

'Lisa, get out of there! Right now!'

She could have just bet six million and those words in that tone would have knocked it from her mind. 'Fuck, Ryan, what's *wrong*?'

'You're in serious trouble! You've got five minutes to get out of there!'

'Is this a fucking joke?' She's suddenly sure it is. Wary: 'Get out of where?'

'Julian's house!'

The words slap her. Everyone must know. In a beat she feels naked and grubby. Groaning: 'Katie and her fucking mouth. Listen, I'm not leaving h—'

'Katie didn't tell me!' He's practically shouting, and frozen tentacles grope through Lisa's chest. 'Julian's in deep with Melvyn!'

'Ryan, calm down! Who the hell is Melvyn?'

'The guy from the house! The one who tortured Trent! He's coming for you!'

She leaps up, knocking the desk and spilling the wine across the keyboard. 'Ryan, this is *not — fucking — funny*!'

'It's not supposed to be! Four minutes, Lease. Either get out of there or lock all the doors and call the cops!'

She forces a laugh. 'Julian does *not know* that cunt! He'd never let anything happ—'

'Listen for yourself!' She hears some doors opening and closing . . . then some oddly toned voices, too faint at first, then much louder.

—*Ow did ya do it then?*

She'll remember that voice the rest of her life. She misses the chair, thumping hard against the carpet. But then she hears Julian, and the sound of his voice neutralises the terror.

—*They both barged into my office one day on some idiotic, self-important quest. I fully intended firing the pair of them. Then I realised Alex was my man: gullible, ambitious, naïve. Wearing his artlessness like a coat-of-arms, typical Kiwi. His desire for her was pathetically palpable, but it was a day or two before it occurred to me how I might use that as well. I watched the two of them through CCTV for a while, and yep, any fool could see that he was smitten.*

Flat on her back in the deep carpet, Lisa starts to feel like she's plummeting through clouds.

—*She wasn't a pushover. Had to concoct quite the façade. I spied on her more. Went through her locker after hours . . .*

She takes the phone from her ear and rolls to her side, pain like stomach cramps jacking her knees up. Vomits wine down her legs. Remembers Ryan and groans into the phone: 'How long ago did you record that?'

'I DIDN'T FUCKING RECORD IT! IT'S HAPPENING RIGHT NOW. JULIAN'S *BRINGING* HIM TO YOU!'

Part of her wants to lie down and rub her face against the carpet until they arrive. Part of her wants to sprint full noise for the door.

She starts scuttling across the floor on her hands and knees.

41

Melvyn and Julian have fallen silent, just the sounds of the car speeding through the streets.

Nadia: 'You have to go to her.'

'What difference can *I* make?!'

'Maybe nothing, maybe everything.'

'I'd just get myself killed!'

She squints at me. 'I thought you said she was your friend.'

She is. But the ratio between what I can do for her and the danger I'd be putting myself in just isn't compelling enough. I don't even know where the guy lives anyway. 'I don't even know where the guy lives anyway!'

'Just call again and *ask* her.'

'. . . I don't have a car to get there.'

'Take a fucking cab!'

'. . . Look, she'll be long gone by the time a cab can get there. I'll call her in a minute and check she's got away, then keep in contact and guide her back to here.'

'Stop looking for excuses! At least call the police!'

'What can the cops do? If I involve them now, sooner or later everything's gonna come out. We'll know from their phone or hers if they get her, and if that happens then we *will* call them.'

'Ryan, that is not good enough—'

She shuts up as Melvyn's ring tone sounds from inside the car.

—Yep? . . . Who? . . . Ave we met? . . . Murdoch Estate, when was that? . . . All right, yeah, I remember. Who gave you this number then? Kevin? . . . Right, well e should know a lot fucking bette—. . . You what? . . . Where is e? . . . Don't you fucking someplace safe me, you little cun—. . . All right, all right! . . . Whatchu want then? . . . Done! Be there in thirty minutes.

—Why are we turning around?

— . . . Or-wight, son. Meet me out front-a Murdoch Estate quick-style. We're on! . . . Just one of em . . . Na, not Kev, some Albanian fuck, 'mate' of Kev's . . . Just wants me to stay clear when im and 'is boys take the trade off Kev . . . Yeah, it's bound to appen soon anyway, the gaff gets more infested wiv the cunts by the day . . . E's given me a bargain and e don't even know it! . . . Good man, see ya there . . . Or-wight mate. Found one of em! . . . Tell ya later. Listen, I need ya to go to 32 Belgravia Lane. There's a bird inside flat three. Txt you the entry codes in a jif. Stay wiv er, don't let er leave, don't let anyone else in.'

—What's going on?

—'Ere, type out the codes for the doors into your gaff.

—What's going on?

—A friend of a colleague of mine just sold Alex to me.

—Who—

Three merry beeps announcing the expiry of the caller's credit, then nothing.

I'm almost glad for it.

Nadia, though, roars out some Arabic, glaring at the phone as if fighting not to smash it. My brain thrashing through mud.

Nadia, finally: 'What does all that mean?!'

First things first: 'It means that Lisa's safe for another half hour yet.'

'How you know that?'

'He sent either Des or Vernon to her, and they were both a long way away, at the house and the warehouse.'

Urgent: 'And what else? What does the rest mean?'

Looking slowly up at her: 'It means that Alex is fucked.'

Her fuming distress is so sharp you'd think he was her brother instead of some guy she's never even met. 'What you mean? There is time still! Who have him?'

Sure of it: 'Alonso. Must be Alonso. He lives on Murdoch. He's the only Albanian friend of Kevin's who knows Alex. And he's got a score to settle with him.'

Appalled: 'A *score*? He settle it like *this*?'

Grimacing: 'He's Albanian.'

'So fucking what?!'

'Those pricks have a whole different way of looking at things.' Shaking my head, ruefully justified: 'I warned Alex not to cross him.'

'OK, so it is Alonso. What your next move?'

'This isn't a game of chess, baby.'

'*Yes* it fucking *is*!'

Exasperated: 'I can't get involved!'

She takes a stunned step backwards. '*What*?'

I bustle through to the kitchen for a glass of water, and she's dogging my heels all the way. 'What you mean you cannot get involved? You *are* involved!'

'I mean that nothing I say to Alonso will change his mind if he's decided on this.'

'You have to *try* at least.'

'You don't get it. If I try, then he'll know that I know, and then it might make sense for him to shut me up for good.'

She frowns as if a stranger is standing in her kitchen. 'Jesus, man, how can Alonso find you if Melvyn cannot?'

'Alonso's a mate. He knows more about me than Melvyn does.'

And then she's backing off, face stretched in a shocked sneer that leaves me feeling made of straw and two feet tall.

I follow her into the lounge. 'Look, baby, believe me, there is *nothing* I can do.'

She sits in the corner of the couch, as far from me as space allows. 'Liar.' Unable to look at me now. 'Other men would find plenty to do.'

And then I'm beside her, angry and hurt, insulted and goaded. Grateful and resentful.

Thrusting the phone in her face I raise Alonso's number, and her mood shifts instantly. No room for applause or apology, just a committed comrade huddled close once again.

Alonso sounds pleased to hear from me, big grin vibrating through the phone. 'Ry! How the hell you doing? A *lot* of people wondering where you are, man!'

'Yeah, I'm OK, dude. Look, mate, have you heard from Alex?'

And the smile's gone so suddenly I feel it on my skin like cloud slicing sunlight off. 'Do not ask about him, Ryan. Believe me, you do *not* want to know. I am busy now.'

The line closes as if it's Alex's pulse.

I sag back into the couch. Feel it then. See him walking down the road to me that day, leaving the others behind. Feel it naked and factual, cutting through me like a northerly.

Nadia: 'OK, who to call now? Kevin?'

Hiding in my hands: 'No. Kevin's just a colleague. He'd deliver me to Melvyn without blinking.'

'OK, what?'

Meeting her eyes and feeling tears coming. Hoping she can see that; even now, with my friend being killed on a scummy estate, wanting the tears to come quicker so that she'll pity and not hate me. 'OK nothing. He's done for.'

Gritting her teeth: 'Bull*shit*! Call the cops!'

'It won't help.'

'Why *not*?'

'The cops don't go there after dark.'

Simple: 'Let us go and get him then.'

Pleading for reason: 'You don't know what you're saying! Between Melvyn, Alonso and Kevin, there's a whole fucking mob of them, all lethal and holding all the cards.'

Pleading for something quite different: 'You never know! We cannot just sit here and let it happen.'

Leaping up and hollering: 'You don't even fucking *know* him!' And that opens the gates, clogs my throat. 'Nadia, he turned his back on me!'

'So you let him die to prove your point?'

Scrubbing my vision clear: '*Let* him die? *No*. I can't control that! I'm just choosing not to die *with* him.'

She bounces up and steps into me as if she has some shouting to do herself. But then she swallows it and walks away, oddly purposeful considering, like there's an arsenal cached in the bedroom. But she stops at the hall and turns around, striding into the lounge's far corner. Freezes, then marches towards the kitchen. Freezes again at the doorway. Puts a hand on the wall and rests her head against her arm.

She stands like that for a long time, and I can't bring myself to move, hanging on her next act.

At last she blows a long, heavy sigh and straightens up, and when she crosses back to me I can see that my eyes aren't the only ones bleeding any more. She kisses my lips, then sits me down, kneeling in front of me. 'I need to say some things to you.'

Hating myself, hating this day, hating her: 'Nothing you say will change anythi—'

She shuts me up with one waved hand. Composes herself. Finally: 'Ryan, you got him into this.'

'*I did fucking not!*'

'Would he be where he is right now if not for you?'

'. . . No he wouldn't, he'd be in jail for a fucking long time!'

'Better that than dead. And you saved him from jail to save yourself from jail.'

My mouth tenses to retort . . . nothing comes out.

Nadia: 'I love you, Ryan, I really do.' I'm about to reciprocate when: 'Sometimes I wish I did not, but that changes nothing.'

'Thanks.'

'But I do not love you enough to bet everything I have on you.'

'Why not?'

'But I *want* to love you that much. Do you understand?'

'No.'

'You remember Dawoud?'

'Of course.'

'Back home, when we were in high school, my teacher find a leaflet for a banned group in my desk. An underground Islamist movement. I did not know how it get there, but my teacher phoned the *mukhabarat*, secret police, and they took me away. Do you know what this means?'

'. . . Big trouble.'

'The worst.'

'What happened?

'Dawoud handed himself in, told them leaflet was his. They let me go.'

'*Jesus. Was* it his?'

'No.'

'What happened to him?'

'They torture him for two days. But he know nothing and they saw that. His uncle was a somebody and he was released instead of shot.'

'Fucking hell.'

'Ryan, you have hidden from danger for three days now, hidden behind a woman. That is OK, it was the best course. You have brought danger down on me and then snuck from a window. Now you sit here crying while your friend's life ticks away.'

'. . . So you don't want me unless I prove myself some kind of superhero?'

'Not a superhero. Not even a hero. Just a man.'

'Suicide isn't a manhood criteria in these parts, Nadia! I'm not Iraqi.'

'Yes, *habibi*. But I am.'

I'm shaking now. I'm going to lose her.

Her: 'Answer me one question. If answer is "no" I will shut up and try hard to love you enough anyway. But if answer is "yes" and still you do nothing . . . then I will not be there to watch you die the slow death of having no love for yourself.'

'. . . Ask.'

'If he was here right now and you were there . . . would Alex come for you?'

I'd been waging a hard, quiet fight to keep that buried deep, and I don't have enough information to answer it definitively anyway — that's all I need to say to her, that's exactly what I'm *going* to say to her — but I know the answer instinctively, and the question is so unexpected and terminal that my eyes give me away before I can even come close to stopping them.

Silence and all its consequences.

And then I'm toppling into her.

'*Yes.*'

42

Melvyn's getting too old for this. Losing his edge. Losing his stomach for it. That much is plain to be read in the relief he's feeling as Alonso leads them through the estate. Problems like those he's faced in the last three days were never something he skated around in big technicolour circles. He's never been the fearless, felonious privateer, in it for the thrill as much as the freedom and money. No way. He's known guys who claimed to be that, but to him the ones who weren't lying were either nutters or mugs to a man. And bugger all of them put together a career of any longevity. No, Melvyn's way is to minimise risk, regulate control, then put firebreaks between himself and the worst-case scenarios.

Quite a simple formula really.

Murphy's law sometimes outdid him, though, swung him much nearer the occupational hazards than he was comfortable with, but you had to expect that at times. Then he'd have to trouble-shoot, and this seldom left room for exhaustive assessment. What was needed then was nimble calculation backed with commitment. And Melvyn was good at this too. Underneath the coolness an operator had to keep and the self-satisfaction of watching yourself excel under strain, underneath the façade that must always be presented to those around you, he may have hated every fucking minute of it, but that didn't change the fact that he was good at it. He had to be. If you picked enough fruit, you got good at brushing bugs off.

But he's been getting jaded with it for some time now. Worn down. What the younger man could shoulder the older starts to bend beneath. He'd known he was ready for a change — a big one — but he hadn't realised quite how strained he'd become until this last job — *the* last job, as fate would have it — sprang its leaks. In the past he'd gathered himself and dealt with worse and still had the stomach for more.

But the last three days have oppressed him like none other. He'd felt stress in the past when a clean-up was thrust on him — lorry loads of the shit — and he'd felt fear as well, sometimes even dread. But he'd never felt nearly naked before. A rung short of helpless.

And this had brought on mistakes. The worst had been taking the bait of Ryan's phone call, dashing off like a well-tweaked puppet when, he feels sure now, the pair of them had been within his grasp.

He suspects that part of it is superstition over this being his swan song, a nagging whisper that the luck he knows he's been blessed with had been bound to call its debts in sometime before he'd cashed out. Another part is sheer frustration at having his plans derailed by a couple of snot-nosed little prats thousands of miles from home when, in his time, he's undone opponents from divisions miles higher.

At the end of the day, though, the actual source of the worry is irrelevant. Because if he bottles now on a job this lush — his long-service reward, retirement payout and golden handshake in one — it's going to haunt him the rest of his fucking life.

And the luck he'd always detested relying on had come his way again. This time in the form of a grinning young pretty-boy whom first glances would suggest would be hard pressed knocking the top off an ice-cream sundae, let alone knocking a guy like Kevin and his crew out of the drug loop on an estate like this. Melvyn knows better, though. He has an eye for this sort of thing. The same eye that had told him that Ryan's chinning of Vernon in the club that night had been a one-off event, that Ryan's stones were no bigger than grass seeds when he wasn't trolleyed and grieving over something, that eye told Melvyn now that Alonso wandered alone around the grounds of this hell-hole and thought bugger all of it. And Melvyn didn't need to know Alonso's nationality to see that the kid was more than capable of selling someone to his death and then muscling turf off a gang of blacks.

He can feel the lines drawing up around him already as they pass through the concrete wasteland. Clumps of blacks in hoodies and caps, gathered round sound systems or tossing basketballs, still trying to look as if they own the place but mindful not to stray too far, the wagons not quite lashed together but definitely clustering. The Eastern Europeans, deceptively better dressed, eyes no longer fixed safely on the ground, talk and laughter booming where a year ago they would have muttered.

Melvyn shudders. It's a sign of the times to him. He's glad to be out of it.

Still, he's starting to feel much better now. Alex is as good as his, and quite likely Ryan as a consequence. And — another break he hasn't earned — Julian's handed him some girl who will give him another lead in Ryan's direction should Alex not be able to provide. Or should Alex not cooperate, something Melvyn seriously doubts. He hadn't fancied having Alex carried all the way to the car through a manor like this, so he'd arranged for Alonso to keep Alex in a place where he could be asked a few questions and then taken care of sharpish. Alonso was going to clean up afterwards n'all. Melvyn didn't care to know how, but he'd heard through Kevin that there were places on the estate, disused boiler-rooms and the like, deep down in the bowels, where the concrete slabs were a little loose and had more underneath them than dirt. Melvyn didn't doubt it. Which all meant that Melvyn's salvage had been downgraded from a hunt for two kernels of corn in a mountain of shit to a simple in-and-out assignment, and his agitation had dropped accordingly. As irate as he is at Julian for holding back about the bird — they haven't had that one out yet, and maybe won't have to — he's even got the space now to register a small amount of amusement from Julian's discomfort.

Melvyn chuckles silently. Discomfort is probably too mild a word. Julian might be just a mile or two from Belgravia as the bullet flew, but he was a fucking lot further from home than that, and he very clearly knew it. All three of them were anomalies in this place, fat neon signs to the locals opportunists, but the fear and softness in Julian's body language was like a limp on an antelope in Africa. They were walking fast too, sometimes forced down to single file, and just for fun Melvyn's made sure Julian is kept at the rear. He can almost hear the chords in his neck creaking as Julian's head swivels ceaselessly.

They are bunched up more now, walking across a frigid little courtyard, housing blocks looming above them like canyon walls, when a weedy black guy with a scraggly goatee breaks away from a knot of six of them and sidles up to Julian. The whites of his teeth and eyes glowing in a nasty, ingratiating smile. 'Hey, bruv.'

Julian tries his best to ignore him, but his head flashes wildly when the group begins dawdling in their direction too.

Keeping pace with Julian: 'You spare a man a couple-a quid?'

Melvyn almost scoffs out loud when Julian scoops a handful of change from his overcoat pocket and palms it to the guy. It disappears, and the group following speed up a bit.

'How bout a little more, bruv?'

Head checking the group: 'No.'

A touch piteous: 'C'mon, bruv. I could feed my kids for a year just on what your suits worf, init. Spare me a lil more.'

In the corner of his eye Melvyn watches Julian turning to him, expecting help. Melvyn ignores him. Julian then makes a total cock-up of trying to quietly remove a note from the wallet in his pocket. The black guy sees everything, could probably count the wallet's contents to the nearest tenner just from Julian's movements.

Julian hands over a fiver. It disappears, and the group behind speeds up again. Melvyn casts an eye over them too at this point and, as much as he is enjoying the wee cultural exchange, decides play time is over.

The black guy's routine shifts. 'Is that *it*? A fucking *fiver*? My son's reading's real bad cos his eyes is weak and I can't buy im no glasses, and you's givin me a *fiver*?'

Melvyn's about to speak when Alonso, turning his head a bit but not far enough to even see the guy, says, 'Fuck off.'

Melvyn hears the guy thinking about it. Then: 'What's it to you, man?'

Alonso turns around, walks back three steps and smashes the guy in the face so hard the sound echoes back at them. He has turned away and walked on again before the guy hits the ground.

The group loses interest immediately. Melvyn stays deadpan, despite wanting to laugh out loud at Julian's shock: the big toff rooted to the spot, then remembering himself so suddenly he flinches, nearly sprinting to catch up.

Melvyn, after a silent half minute: 'Shoulda got your money back off im, Julian.'

He and his flunky start to laugh at that, Alonso tossing a grin back too.

————

Ryan's really not that scared. Feels like he's been ripped into four by bulldozers, left in snow overnight, then riveted back together, but he's found a place beyond fear now. And it's not just that the danger he's about to put himself in is so extreme that even terror gets frozen solid. No, there's something else. Something that makes this feel almost inevitable.

Perhaps even pure.

Something like a young woman, small-framed and sickly, pregnant and with her waters broken.

Maybe it's just some fucked-up intoxication brought on by stress overload, or some trick his subconscious manufactured to keep him on the path, but Ryan's starting to see this as the manifestation of a crossroads that was always ahead of him.

But a second later he feels so dismayed and idiotic that he wants to tell the driver to let him out by the nearest tube stop.

And a minute after that the thought of just opening the door of the moving vehicle and rolling on to the road feels like a warm, downy blanket.

She'd wanted to come. That had surprised him, made him hate her less. Because it showed that she had never been asking him to do something she wasn't prepared to do herself. It showed that despite pushing him into a place where she might lose him, she was in fact terrified of losing him.

But she needed to respect her man as much as she respected herself.

Muttering: 'Fucking Easterners. What was I thinking getting involved with her?' But he can't make himself ignore the fact that his admiration of her has grown even deeper now. And that he knows exactly what he was thinking.

She's the manifestation of the unknown quantity that he'd come looking for. A future. A salvation. She makes him a better person.

And then the horror and surrealism hit him so hard again he feels like his arse is hovering an inch above the cracked vinyl of the minicab's back seat.

She hadn't been bothered by his argument that she would only get in the way, by his pleas that if it came to it he'd go to his death happier in the knowledge that she was safe. No, in the end all that could make her relent was simply his outright refusal to so much as leave the house if she was in tow. And only time ticking down had won him that final fight.

She'd given him a wild card, though. And for that he is inordinately grateful.

Sal sits up straight on the back seat, a hulking presence in the gloom. He seems less intrigued by the world outside the vehicle than he usually is. Not in a cowed way, though. Far from it.

Because, as only an animal can, Sal *knows*.

There's another wild card tied around Sal's chest: Alex's unwashed All Blacks jersey. Ryan had stopped off for it at the house.

Two more wild cards are in the daypack at his feet. A butcher's knife. And ten thousand pounds in used notes.

He knows you can often buy someone's death for less than that around here, sometimes for a lot less. Maybe you can buy someone's life too.

But as they get closer the wild cards start to feel like water pistols. He starts to hear nothing but distant surf. He finds it harder and harder to keep his eyes focused, his vision fixating on empty points.

434

He starts to see people in the car with him.

He sees Timothy in the passenger seat, new starter at Ryan's primary school, slow to make friends. Timmy's mum planned a big party for her son's birthday at McDonald's, had him invite near the whole class. They all accepted. Then Ryan made them see how funny it would be to all *not* go instead, and they'd laughed and laughed as they spied on Timmy and his mum in their party hats, sitting round the empty table as the clown brought the cake out.

Then Ryan sees that guy from the festival. He never learned his name. He was handsome and funny, had had Ryan's girlfriend in stitches. Ryan and some others followed him as he went into a Port-a-loo, wedged the door locked with a stick. Then they accompanied his screams with cheering and whooping as they tipped the toilet on its side, rolled it around, stood it on end . . . The small crowd had been laughing so hard by the time the guy was let out, *encased* in shit and toilet paper, that his moans and sobs were barely audible.

He sees Teresa Simpkins sitting beside him, giving Sal a pat. Shy and intelligent, pretty-ish but nerdy. She'd had a major crush on Ryan, and he'd taken a bet from an older mate at their high school: thirty bucks and a six-pack of VB said that he couldn't pop her cherry. So he invited her over one Friday evening when his dad was on night shift and won the bet. He'd been running late for a party by then, so he made his excuses and hustled her out. She had come on her ten-speed but she was too sore to mount it; gave up after two tries, started pushing it along the empty road instead. He'd watched her for a while, wishing he had the time to walk her home.

He sees others.

———

Julian's missing Lisa dearly.

He knows he's being laughed at, but he joins in obtusely.

They enter a block and walk down a corridor, rotting bin bags along the walls. A woman in a shawl with a bald patch exits a room in front of them, freezes, stares avidly as they pass.

He wonders how Lisa is. Wishes now he'd never met her as vehemently as he wishes he'd never met Melvyn. His bad luck charm. He somehow visited a house of mirrors and smashed every fucking one of them the day he wandered into Melvyn's club on impulse. He'd stopped drinking for weeks after That Night because to do such a thing to another person *and not remember how or why* was almost as terrifying as the occurrence itself. He'd been quite fond of the girl, enjoyed her post-coital company more than he had plenty of others, despite Loretta's being a hooker. Or maybe because of it. For weeks he'd tried to convince himself that her death stemmed from sexual misadventure, not malice.

Then he'd begun drinking more than ever.

He wonders what Loretta's first words were.

Alonso takes them on to a stairway reeking of urine. Up two flights, past two black boys smoking desperately through a tinfoil pipe.

The latest slice of Melvyn-related ill-fortune to strike Julian was his decision, delayed for as long as he thought he could, to hand Lisa over. Because just a minute or two later Alonso had phoned out of the blue and cracked the conundrum wide open. Julian felt he was in a dream at that point. A very bad one. Nothing new for him around Melvyn, but he had wrung his guts into a lather before betraying Lisa. (*Ha fucking ha, every word you ever gave her was a betrayal.*)

Julian had known himself for a bastard for a long time — since he'd decided that idealism was folly and greed was good. But bastards were common and greed even more so. Then, through

Melvyn and survival, he'd become a *fucking* bastard, fear redrawing his moral topography again. He'd tried to resist becoming a cunt, though (*tell that to Alex*); resisted that last step, the last sale of whatever sliver of principle and character that remained in him. But fear had won, and he'd sold it, and he'd felt it too, felt it like a plunge in raw sewage.

And for nothing.

Down another corridor, fewer functioning lights, rats stepping back from them, some of the doors to apartments missing or hanging on their hinges, the insides dark shells. Laughter booming out of one of them and startling Julian. Around a corner. A toddler on a tricycle. A door opening and a woman snatching him up and vanishing again, door slamming, the trike tipped on its side, one wheel spinning slowly.

Julian was gone at that point, with that decision acted upon. He was as empty of humanity as a Nuremberg Nazi just following orders, and he knew he could never go back. But Lisa was the opposite, and even if he couldn't save himself he could still save her. The furtive txt he had sent warning her as they sped to the estate did nothing to salve his scorched soul, was like CPR on a cadaver, but the image of her scurrying down the stairs brought a ghostly grin.

He wonders if that black guy who as good as mugged him is still alive. Alonso's fist had snapped his head back savagely, and Julian hadn't seen any movement after that.

Wonders whether Loretta had ever visited Paris. What kind of music she liked.

Loretta. Lisa. Sees a pattern. Wonders if he won't meet a Leanne soon. Then a Lana.

Out on to an open walkway that links blocks, wind whipping through the wire mesh enclosing it from banister to roof. A noisy crowd of blacks, both sexes, blocking it. Silencing at their approach. Alonso not missing a stride, and the group parting reluctantly, lining both sides. Julian feels the temperature drop as he enters the human tunnel, feels the hunger and the hate in the bodies just inches away. Too scared to meet any eyes, picturing them closing up behind him, blades set to perforate the cashmere of his coat, spots of skin on his back cringing and waiting, but fear not letting him turn.

Wondering where the chaos that is his life will spit him out next, but certain that stage at least will be an improvement on this one. He'd known these places existed, of course; the knowledge had resided somewhere inside him, somewhere near the knowledge of lightning strikes. But nothing he had experienced had prepared him for this, just as nothing could prepare him for what a lightning strike would feel like. Many old maps of the city had been colour coded. Blue, red, green and black. But the black areas had been just solid blotches, no streets or churches, schools or parks drawn inside them. Nothing. The reason was simple: the cartographers were too scared to venture there. And besides, the people for whom the maps were intended would surely never have business within the black zones. Not that the maps neglected all areas of disrepute, far from it. Because to the better half of London, the black zones were *not* areas of disrepute. They were areas of *no* repute. They were simply and literally other universes, swathes of space that were navigated around as instinctively as the river was crossed and not swum. Enclaves of anarchy and degradation.

Lesions on a plague victim.

This estate stood upon land that had been just such a zone. In many ways nothing has changed but the races. Julian and his kind never set foot here, avoiding these estates so tacitly — avoiding their very mention — that they barely exist to them. He couldn't wait until that order had reasserted itself. For him this place was nothing but a hulking monument to intimidation and fear. He had no right to be here. He was not equipped to deal with it, and the sooner he could leave this feral genus to its mystery purpose the better.

He was clear of the mob on the walkway; got some air into his chest.

So dead had Julian felt after selling Lisa that he'd suspected that one good thing to come of it was that his sense of fear had been scorched out of him as fully as his other emotions had, that he'd at last freed his life of it again. He hadn't been scared of Melvyn's backlash. But he'd been wrong. No more than a few footsteps into the estate had corrected him on that one.

And now he started to fear that fear might be the *only* emotion he could fully experience again. Was this the fate of all evil-doers? To hack at their hearts and pollute themselves until nothing remained but the fear that drove them in the first place? A self-sustaining cycle growing fouler and fouler?

The thought terrified him.

He hadn't been looking forward to seeing Alex. But now he thought it might not be so bad after all. Maybe he could disprove his theory.

. . . And even if he couldn't, maybe it'd be nice to watch someone else suffering for a change.

Up more stairs and across an empty walkway, much higher now, the estate spread out beneath him. The windows in the block above them were all dark, and as they moved inside and out of the wind, the building had the feel of a haunted house. A haunted prison anyway. Too quiet and too dark. Forsaken but not empty.

Occasional lights were still functioning along the corridor Alonso led them on, and the odd door was closed, a little noise coming through, but Julian could see that this floor was all but empty. On to another stairway, light filtering up from the floors below but nothing above except darkness. On the landing two flights up, the darkness so complete further travel was near impossible, Alonso finally stopped.

He addressed Melvyn. 'These levels abandoned, no power, no water, no people. You will not be disturbed. As you asked.'

Melvyn just nodded.

43

Alex is still drinking. He's not very drunk any more. For the first time in days he doesn't really want to be either. He's been sipping at his can for over an hour, carries on mostly for something to do. Getting plastered right now just feels like a bad idea.

He doesn't like the room for a start. There's not much to like about a derelict bedsit on the twelfth floor of a massive, monstrous housing estate. Gutted of carpet and fittings. Just a couple of dirty mattresses, a gas lamp in the corner, and a bucket half-full of shit and urine in the bath-less bathroom. Next to where he's spent the last couple of nights, Alex supposes he should be looking upon this place rather more favourably.

He's not.

The bars across the window haven't helped. He'd wondered what their function was, presuming that burglars seldom number abseiling among their vocational talents. Then he'd noticed the bars across all the windows of the apartments in the block facing him and realised what they were for.

Should life in the housing we provide prove untenable, the council shall not be party to your suicide.

In a way Alex feels even more lost and anxious than he had on the streets. At least what you saw was what you got out there; at least when you were reliant on only yourself nobody could let you down or push you over. But cooped up in here, this penthouse atop this three-dimensional labyrinth of poverty and desperation, naked but for the whim of a man Alex has wronged, a member of a faction notorious for its ruthlessness and retribution . . .

Alex is almost missing the Hyde Park underpass.

And he *is* missing Owen, no almost about that.

Something about Alonso too. On the drive from town the guy had been largely silent, speaking into his phone once or twice, but mostly just brooding. Alex hadn't been able to get him talking. There had been a smile or two, but they'd been too sudden and sharp, elicited by something a long way from the vehicle. Alonso had mustered some concern for Alex's condition, but not much. He'd brought him a family pack of KFC and a couple of burgers, but then, as Alonso marched him through the byways of the estate, ignoring the looks of loitering kids and young men that they passed, instead of a cosy cocoon with a shower and fresh clothes, Alonso had led him down paths and up stairs into a block that seemed largely abandoned.

And then into here.

Alex's pride had cracked then; he'd asked when he could wash and change, and Alonso had practically ignored him. He said he was leaving his friend, Gani, to keep an eye out for him, that for his own safety Alex should not leave the room. And then as he left Alonso rang Alex's alarm bells almost fully by throwing him the most troubling smile of the night, a grin almost obscene in the arcane glee it spoke of.

Then he'd locked the door behind him.

Gani's a swarthy Albanian kid — teenager — who doesn't speak much English. Just sits on a mattress, clutching a mobile.

Watching Alex intently.

Alex makes himself lie back on the corner of the mattress he's folded over for a pillow. His eyes won't close, though. There's something else about the room. It just tastes of . . . *wrongness*. The mattresses have planted a mantra in his head that he can't cut off. 'Go to the mattresses'. Old slang for a state of inter-family gang war in the US, so called because the houses of the gangsters involved were soft targets, so they'd drive around with mattresses in the boots of their cars and just sleep wherever until the killing was over. He can't tell in the weak light, but Alex is pretty sure the stains on the walls and floor in here are wine coloured. There's a rope in one corner, a car battery in another, and a cast-iron tub more than big enough to squeeze a head into. The window looks to be double glazed, expensive and almost soundproof. The door looks new, reinforced.

Then he sees a collection of circular burn marks in the wall beside his head. Like someone had brought a cigar up here and burnt holes into the wood. Someone bored. Or someone preparing themselves to do something. Alonso and Gani don't seem the type to buy big cigars for pleasure.

Across the small room Gani's eyes glow gently in the lamplight, riveted to Alex.

He fights down a shudder.

Gani, first word he's said to Alex unprompted: 'Cold?'

Startled: 'What?'

'You cold? You have my blanket if want. I un-cold.'

Footsteps in the corridor, the sound pulling Alex's stomach tight. Pulling it tighter as he identifies more than one pair of feet. Tighter as they draw nearer; and he knows he's being fanciful, that intuition is a commodity dealt in only by frauds and fools, but his stomach desperately wants them not to stop.

They stop, and he's on his feet, pushing his back into the wall behind him.

Wishing he could commit himself to another year on the streets in return for having Owen's knife on him right now . . .

From outside: 'Alex?'

A geyser of relief and elation erupts in him. Darting to the door. '*Ryan*?!'

Stress hissing out of Ryan like a puncture: 'Oh, thank *fuck*!' Then, lower and bewildering, but just as intense: '*Good boy*.' And an odd thumping sound.

Alex instinctively twists the door handle, finds it locked. Realises Gani is beside him.

'Who here?!'

Alex: 'It's my friend. Let him in!'

Absolute: '*No! No* friend! Alonso say friend no, body no!'

'Let him the fuck in!'

Ryan: 'Dude on his lonesome, Al?'

'Yeah.'

'Stand back.'

Alex stands back, and then the door crashes off its hinges, flattening Gani. Then Alex leaps back when a fucking *tiger* bounds in, realises it's a dog, then he's giggling joy at the sight of Ryan holding an All Blacks jersey and a butcher's knife. Alex snatches him in a bear hug.

The dog jumps on them, then Ryan's pushing them both away. 'Let's go.'

Alex, pleasure dropping to a grin as he watches Gani stirring under the door: 'You didn't have to do that. Alonso might be gutted.'

'Alonso's gonna be a lot more than gutted. Let's g— Jesus, *look* at you! What've you . . . Tell me later, we're gone!'

Alex: 'What's the rush?'

'Tell you later!'

But Alex is in happy shock, bent down and kneading the dog's head with two hands. 'How did you find me? Did Alonso tell you I was here?'

'Sal found your scent and led me here. Come on! . . . *Fucking MOVE, Alex, there's big shit coming our way!*'

The words straighten Alex like a lash from a whip, and then the three of them are running.

———

Alonso takes out a small torch, flicks it on, starts down the corridor.

At the rear of the party Julian, blackness at his feet and behind him, feels more vulnerable than ever, and he hustles forward until he's flanking the flunky, Alonso and Melvyn single file in front.

The place smells awful, a fetid stench of faeces and mildew. Between empty doorways the walls are dotted with gaping holes, cold air surging through smashed windows, debris strewn across the corridor. Julian trips on something and almost goes over. Melvyn laughs at him quietly.

Julian wonders if Melvyn had sex with Loretta.

If Alex had sex with Lisa.

If his mother had any sex at all in the five years before she shot herself, when she and his father had slept in separate rooms.

Alonso stumbles and drops the torch, arresting their progress. He mutters a sorry and bends down for it.

Julian wonders if Loretta had wanted to have childre—

A flash lights the scene like daylight, a hideous pressure pummelling Julian's eardrums, liquid hurled into his face. Another flash almost instantly, and through one eye Julian sees that the tableau has changed.

Melvyn is falling towards the floor, as stiff as a pine tree.

Half of his face is gone.

Alonso is crouching, turned back towards them, pointing . . .

Darkness.

Another flash, and Julian is roaring, tearing back the way he had come, towards the faint glow from the stairway, another flash helping him hurdle an obstacle, then it's dark again and his feet snag on something, sending him headlong, and he's up again instantly, but a body overtakes him, another flash as the flunky fires a gun blindly behind him, another flash and the flunky grunts and shudders, and Julian tries to pass him but can't, then they're at the stairway, slowing each other, and another flash from behind and the flunky yelps and Julian shoves him wildly and he disappears over the handrail, and Julian slips halfway down the first flight of stairs but barely notices, picking himself up at the switchback and plunging on, and he's halfway down the next flight when an almighty sodden *SLAPPPPPP* comes ripping up the stairwell.

Julian leaves the darkness behind and finds a reckless rhythm, three stairs per stride, three strides, then a great leap for the landing. Turn and repeat. He falls twice but cares only in that it breaks his tempo, bouncing up and plunging on like a man half his age. He meets people on the stairs but barely notices, either blows right by them or crashes into them, carries on . . .

. . . down and down . . .

. . . snarling and huffing.

He doesn't bother looking back or trying to hear if Alonso's following, but then he jumps to a landing, slips in something, stands up . . .

Freezes.

'Oh dear god!'

He'd forgotten about the flunky. There's a semblance of a corpse, but blood and gore are splashed and scattered as if the man

446

had been springloaded.

Julian feels his stomach rise . . . then fall again. A giggle grabs him. 'Hope your employer provided health cover!' Notices something black at his feet. It's the flunky's revolver. He bends down and picks it up. It seems to have survived the fall. Then he notices some faces nearby, gaping at him. They're between him and the door outside. He takes a step towards them, about to raise the pistol, but they scatter and bolt before he does. He giggles again, then bursts through the door, dashing down a walkway at random.

———

Ryan and Alex are sprinting, heedless of the attention they're attracting, Sal keeping pace beside them, people stopping to stare but stepping back at the sight of Sal and the knife Ryan's holding. Sal's growling at anyone who comes too close, but his tail shows how much fun he's having. Ryan starts to fear that he's got them lost, and panic, fed by their all-out flight, has eaten his sense of direction. Every courtyard and walkway, every new patch of dirty concrete, looks the same as the last. He's scared they're going round in circles.

Then he follows Sal around a corner, and he sees the fence and the road, a big red bus gliding past about a hundred metres away, and he booms out a violent, '*Yes!*' and they dig it in, Ryan realising that Sal had demoted him and taken the reins at some point.

He doesn't fancy being on the streets for long with Melvyn and Alonso prowling, and he's hoping like hell the driver waited for him as he'd paid him to, or that a black cab is cruising by, and then he grins ferally just for the joy and relief at having such matters to weigh when almost all of the person who had crept through the gate of the estate two centuries ago had been certain he wouldn't be leaving again.

He swaps a wild cackle with Alex, and then someone comes hurtling out of an intersecting walkway twenty metres in front of them, right under a light. Everyone skids to a halt.

The guy's dressed in a suit and overcoat that are filthy and torn. One of his shoes is missing, the white sock on his left foot stained red. But that stain is nothing next to the blood smudged across his face in awful finger streaks, matting his hair and eyebrows, soaked into his white shirt. His eyes are stretched wide and he's panting like a racehorse.

He looks like a berserker out sacking Milan.

Ryan sees the gun and recognises Julian at the same instant.

Sal's had enough, snarling and trotting forward, but Ryan yells, '*Ta-al!*' The dog flinches, then heels to his side . . . fixes his eyes on Julian again.

Alex, savagely jubilant: 'How's it going, you fucking old *cunt!*' Advancing: 'This finishes right now!' Ryan holds him back, and they struggle for a moment, then Julian half-raises the gun and Alex stills.

Julian, eerily reassuring: 'It's OK! It's over! We're all free to go!'

Ryan: 'What do you mean? Where's Melvyn and Alonso?'

Alex, roaring: 'You're free to go *no*where, you piece of *shit*! You and me are gonna have ourselves a performance evaluation!'

Julian, surreally beseeching behind the gun: 'I'm sorry, Alex. I really am. I had no choice. But we're all going to be OK now. We can all go back to normal. What do you want? Another promotion?' Mad grin: 'It's *yours*! You can have *my* fucking job. Just let me leave and I'll see to everything!'

Ryan tries to ask again where Melvyn and Alonso are, but Alex's rage drowns him out. 'Stick your job up your posh fucking arse, Julian. You're leaving this place in an ambulance!'

Ryan: 'Let him go, man! We've gotta bail!'

'Na, fuck him!' Spittle flying: 'I'm gonna *kick the living shit* out of this cocksucker!'

Julian's face freezes over, scaring Ryan deeply. 'Very well, Alex. But it's at your insistence. I'll end you both right here and nobody who matters will ever know.'

Alex, a fearless grin, spreading his arms wide: 'Off ya go, tough guy!' Thumping his chest. 'Right here if you got the balls!'

Julian's top lip lifts just a touch. His hand starts to rise . . .

Ryan drops the knife, throws his hands up, leaps back a pace, glaring at something past Julian's shoulder. A cringing roar: 'DON'T SHOOT, OFFICER!'

Julian whirls around, and Ryan says one word.

'*Ahajem.*'

Sal's off, driving himself across the concrete, accelerating . . .

Julian turns back, shrieking at what he sees . . . but cool enough to grip the gun in two hands, to take a second to aim carefully . . .

Nothing happens.

Then Sal's leaping at him, seizing an arm, tearing Julian off his feet, the shriek rising . . .

. . . Sal letting him go for an instant, shifting position, locking his jaws around Julian's face . . .

. . . shaking his head twice, shifting Julian's whole weight, the scream hitting a bloodcurdling climax.

Sal steps away almost daintily. Turn backs to Ryan, ears fawning back, guilty and anxious.

Alex is the first to speak, all the breath shocked out of him. 'Holy fucking shit, dude.'

They both approach slowly. Sal cringes, perks up at Ryan's distracted pat, licking his lips happily.

Julian's moving. One hand across his face. Wet hyperventilation.

Alex lifts Julian's arm gently, and they both recoil in horror.

'I was going to shoot him as well, but maybe now I not bother.'

Ryan whirls and jumps at the sight of Alonso standing beside him, eyes fixed on Julian, fascinated.

Ryan supposes he should attack, knows he's no match but sure the three of them are. But any violence he had in him is long since gone, and the next flash in his head asks him why Sal hasn't attacked already anyway, or even growled at Alonso. Then he hears the words properly.

'Ahhh . . . who else did you shoot, Alonso?'

Alonso, frowning at the obvious: 'Melvyn. And his soldier.'

In unison: 'Melvyn's *dead*?'

'Of course.' Looks back to Julian, then grins suddenly: 'You better hope Melvyn did not have AIDS, man!'

Ryan's head is spinning badly. 'That was your plan all along?'

'Yeah.'

'Why did you do it?'

Frowning at the obvious: 'You guys are my friends.'

Ryan and Alex gape at each other. Alonso squats down and grins at Sal, rubbing his ears as they sniff each other's noses.

Julian's trying to roll over but can't, moaning something too thick to make out.

Alex: 'What's he saying?'

Ryan: 'Dunno. "Low radar" or something.'

Alonso: 'You guys should leave.'

Ryan: 'My thoughts exactly.'

Alex: 'What about Julian?'

Alonso, shrugging: 'Shall I kill him? Will he talk to police?'

Ryan: 'They're the last people *he's* ever gonna talk to.'

Alonso: 'What do you want done with him, Alex?'

'. . . Let's call him an ambulance.'

44

It's getting towards five when Alex enters the restaurant. The scene stops his feet a few steps past the doorway. Through the long journey here he'd been acutely nervous about this moment, for reasons he couldn't easily name, the nerves hitting a climax a few seconds ago, but now he feels them fade almost completely, a grin taking over his face.

He just stands there, drinking the sight in.

He feels like he's come home. Ironic, considering.

Nobody notices him. Or maybe they just don't recognise him. He, on the other hand, would have to have been blind not to notice *them* — although it might have taken longer had he not been aware of today's occasion. Because most of the thirty-odd people sitting at a big central table, at least half of whom Alex knows, are in evening dress.

Ryan had grudgingly put the blue bow-tie back on for another round of photos; he takes it off again now, slipping it in the pocket of his dinner jacket, undoing his top buttons and leaning back.

He's squeezed between Greg and Jim, only half listening to Murphy's story about some girl he knows who walked out of Heathrow Arrivals wearing a rubber Bin Laden mask.

He can't take his eyes off Nadia for much more than a few seconds. She's sitting a long way down from him, laughing with Lisa and Katie. Nadia's wearing a big top hat stolen from Ryan, and she lifts it off and places it on Lisa's head, adjusting the angle slightly. Lisa strikes a pose, and they're all laughing again. It's the first time those three have met — the first time in fact any of his friends have met Nadia — and they all seem to have taken a real shine to each other. Nadia's shining with something else too — at least Ryan hopes she is — more vibrant, more relaxed than he's ever seen her in public. Anybody who had ever watched her dance would struggle to recognise her.

He supposes that if a line-up featuring all the girlfriends he's ever had was assembled, an impartial witness would not be naming Nadia among the prettiest, but Ryan knows that his own eyes would crown her queen in a second.

It's been a great day so far, with a huge night ahead, but as much as he's tried to duck acknowledging it parts of the day have left him feeling a little hollow. He wishes his father could have been here, along with a few friends from back home. But maybe because of how long it's been since he's seen any of them, or maybe because of what he went through six weeks ago, it's the absence of two other people that's contributed most to the day's incompleteness.

Alonso had said he would be here for all of it. But he was nowhere to be seen when they assembled at midday, his mobile switched off, as it remains now.

And Alex hasn't even sent a fucking txt. Not a word from the guy since Ryan emailed him the news three weeks ago.

Ryan's list of friendships made here that withered and died as soon as separate ways were went is by no means small. But for *Alex* to fall silent, especially at such a time, is beginning to feel like a serious betrayal. In fact he's starting to feel angry, is weighing up sending Alex a dirty txt, when someone taps his shoulder.

The guy with the backpack looks pretty cool; pretty tough too: head shaven number one, a bleached blond goatee, earring, blue eyes, deep suntan. But Ryan can't work out why he's grinning like an idiot . . .

Then Ryan's cackling and leaping up, hugging Alex, holding him at arm's length. 'What the fuck are *you* doing here?'

'Could hardly miss my best mate's wedding, could I?'

Others start to recognise him and crowd around.

———

—So how's things back home, dude?

—Familiar. Slow. Boring. Once I'd caught up with everyone completely and had my fill of the nature again, I couldn't get back here quick enough.

—Happens a lot.

—I just met your wife; seems like a hell of a lady.

—She is.

—How much does she know about . . . ?

—Everything.

—*Everything*?

—I've got no secrets from her, man. Who did *you* tell?

—Just an old friend. Did you tell anyone else?

—Des, one of Melvyn's boys, called me once. We both laid a couple of cards on the table. I'll fill you in later. He won't be making any trouble, though. He's happy taking early retirement.

—So what are your plans?

—I'm taking her home. We're just gonna get a car and drive for a few months, see where we wanna live.

—You're gonna settle down back there?

—At this point. I can get a British passport through Nadia in a while, so we might end up back here one day. See how it goes.

—When are you off?

—Two weeks. We checked Sal into quarantine yesterday.

—He's going with you?

—Fucking oath he is!

—Rat shit, I was gonna offer to look after him. How come Alonso's not here?

—Good question. He said he'd come but he hasn't shown. Phone's switched off too.

—You try Fernando or Claudian?

—Theirs are off too. It's pretty strange.

—I spoke to Alonso a few days ago.

—What about?

—Me, him and Jema are off busking around Europe next week.

—Really?! How long for?

—Don't know, don't care. Until we get discovered, I guess!

—How are you travelling?

—Alonso's got a van lined up. Reckons he's got it covered, doesn't want any cash towards it or anything.

—Good shit, mate! You guys'll have a ball.

—That's the plan. Top my glass up too, eh bro? . . . Cheers . . . Fuck that's nice, what is it?

—Dom Perignon, my friend. Nothing but the finest today.

—There's gotta be at least twenty bottles on the go! This must be costing you a fortune.

—It's not costing *me* a fucking cent.

———

At first Alex was angry with her.

'Lease, he did his level best to *seriously* fuck us both over! How can you stay with the cunt?'

'He was under huge pressure, Al. Melvyn had the power to see him jailed for life.'

'. . . How?'

She claims not to know, but Julian had told her, had broken down and wept about it in his hospital room. She'd thought about it for a day, then told him that if she ever saw another drink in his hand it'd be the last time he saw her. He hasn't touched a drop since, has taken up pot and opium instead. She keeps silent now, but she'd told Ryan about Loretta. A few days later Ryan had called to tell her that Melvyn's hold over Julian had been a fabrication — apparently a worker of Melvyn's had come clean to him about it.

Lisa is yet to inform Julian of this, though. His guilt makes him easier to control. And it's kind of fun watching him beat himself up about it.

Alex: 'That still doesn't excuse what he did.'

'No, but it explains it.'

'But I don't understand how you can love someone who—'

'Who said I fucking *love* the guy?'

'. . . I just assumed you must do to stay with him after all that.'

'Life's not always Mills and Boon, man. People stay together out of shit besides love.'

'What then? Sympathy?'

'. . . That's part of it.'

'How bad is his face?'

'Bad. He's gone reclusive, stays inside, won't see friends or family. He's got a lot of surgery ahead of him, and doctors say they can repair about eighty percent of it in time, but for now he needs a live-in PA basically. He didn't even go to his father's funeral last 'week.'

'He's not working?'

'He speculates online a bit, but no steady job. Not that he needs one, especially with his father unexpectedly leaving him half the family estate.'

'. . . I guess that means a significant pay rise for that PA you referred to.'

Oozing manners, feigning embarrassment, the maître d' quietly brings the current bill over to Lisa. Probably he was watching how much she was drinking, noted how young she was and worried that the cost might be getting beyond her means. She tells him that the credit card she gave him could cover her and her friends eating and drinking in here for the next year or two.

Alex sips his champagne quietly until the man leaves, then stares into space; and Lisa finds herself hanging on his next words.

He shakes his head abruptly, frowning at her. 'That's not right, Lease. You're degrading yourself. You're worth more than this.'

She feels herself flushing, and not just through anger. 'Spare me the fucking sanctimony, Alex! I haven't figured out what I want to do next, and this is the best stop-gap going.' She's leaning closer in to him, can't rein in the pleading she hears in her tone. 'I'm barely there half the time; I've got use of his car; he never questions where I go, even when I'm away for days! I can buy whatever I want; I'm sending money home by the fucking truckload. I'm doing some courses, photography and travel writing . . .'

Alex, implacable: 'It's still not right. It's beneath you.'

'No it fucking isn't!' Then, leaning back, harsh: 'I seem to remember someone else throwing in with Julian not so long ago, and at least I'm not shitting on my friends in the process.'

She sees that hit him like a knife in the guts. He looks away, grimacing, nodding to himself. 'You're dead right there.' Takes a long pull from his drink. Takes another, but his face has firmed by the time the glass comes down again. 'I've learned from it though.'

Putting a hand on his: 'I can see that, mate. We all can.'

A while later: 'So how do you reconcile this with your politics? Or should that read *former* politics?'

'Like fuck! I'm not working for Halliburton or marrying into the family!'

He murmurs something, looking both petulant and embarrassed.

Lisa: 'Pardon? I didn't hear you.'

'. . . Are you sleeping with him?'

'Why is *that* important to you?' She's careful to keep the disgust on her face until he looks away. 'Fucking *men*! Your heads really are that small when it comes down to it, aren't they.'

He says nothing.

On impulse, with no warning, Lisa pulls his head roughly towards her and kisses him. His mouth opens under hers, but it's a few shocked seconds before she feels his tongue responding. Then she pulls away just as suddenly.

He's staring at her as if she'd just rammed a finger up her arse.

Lisa: 'Feel better?'

Stares for a few seconds more . . . bursts into giggles. '*Yeah*! Yeah, I fucking *do*, actually.' He can't speak through laughter for a while, and she laughs with him. 'I wish you'd done that a year ago!'

'Oh no you fucking don't.'

'. . . So you're not faithful to him then?'

'Now why would I want to do a stupid thing like that?'

Down the table, they hear Katie swearing to herself as she puts her phone away. 'Where the hell *is* that guy?'

Lisa: 'Who, babe?'

'Alonso. I haven't seen him for weeks. I was sure he'd be here tonight.'

Greg: 'Why is it so important to you?'

Theatrical wail: 'Because I reckon he'd be the fuck of the century and I'm leaving the country in two bloody weeks!'

Everyone laughs, Katie as well.

Ryan comes around the table and pulls Alex and Lisa to their feet. 'Jim! Get your camera out again, I want a shot with me two old muckers here, just the three of us.' He pushes Lisa into the middle, and they all throw arms around each other.

Murphy's phone rings as the flash on the camera pops. He listens for a few seconds, then yells: 'You're fucking kidding me, man!' Then he turns away, murmuring intently before ending the call. He turns back but says nothing, frowning to himself.

Katie: 'What's up, Murph?'

Silence.

Greg: 'Come on, Paddy, what was all that about? Everything all right?'

Murphy: 'You know how I'm the only one here still working at EUE now tat all you lot are abandoning me?'

'Yeah?'

'And you know how I was told not to come in today?'

Jim: 'Burst water pipe, wasn't it?'

'Tat's what I was told tis mornin. But it wasn't tat at all.'

'What was it?'

'It was a fucking *robbery*, so it was! Three armed men in a truck made off with twenty-odd pallets at four o'clock tis mornin.'

The table erupts in furious chattering.

Except for Ryan and Alex.

Those two gape at each other over Lisa's head for a good ten seconds.

Ryan, at last, barely loud enough for Alex to hear him: 'No wonder he doesn't need any help towards that van, mate.'

Praise for *Stonedogs*:

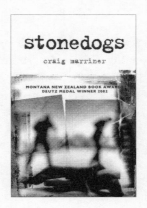

'It's the originality, the crackling energy, the subversiveness of *Stonedogs* which earns it a place in the Montana New Zealand Book Awards for 2002. There are not many books written in the comic tradition in New Zealand but *Stonedogs* is the authentic article, a book in the tradition of Ronald Hugh Morrieson's *Came a Hot Friday* . . . *Stonedogs* is a true New Zealand Original.'

— Judges' report, 2002 Montana New Zealand Book Awards

'It's a terrific read . . . the sheer force of the writing sweeps the reader along in a druggy-intoxicated Tarantino-comic-book version of trashy violence, pleasure, posturing and protest . . . Raw talent rules, okay?'

— *New Zealand Listener* 10 Best New Zealand Novelists Under 40

'One big novel worth the effort is *Stonedogs*, by Craig Marriner (Vintage). Part melodramatic crime novel, part splenetic socio-economic tract, part anthem on behalf of the slacker generation . . . *Stonedogs* spins a good yarn.'

— *New Zealand Listener* Best Reads of 2001

'Told in a brutal and scathing prose which keeps women in their place and multinational corporations cringing, *Stonedogs* is not for the easily offended. Marriner offers a chilling look at the seedy underbelly of New Zealand society, of blokes treading a fine line between idealism and anarchy, friendship and betrayal, misbehaviour and murder.'

— *Dunedin Star*

'It's all mouth and trousers, a tough-talking, hard-boiled portrayal of New Zealand's drug underworld . . . hold on and enjoy the adrenalin rush.'

— *North and South*

'It's superb to read a book littered with Lion Red cans, clapped out Holdens and rich boys from the North Shore. The language is spot on, the cadences and utterances utterly familiar to anyone who has been in a suburban pub, or to a rugby match, or indeed any small town in New Zealand . . . a tender and intelligently written novel.'

— *Evening Post*